PRAISE FOR LIZ TALLEY

"Talley packs her latest southern romantic drama with a satisfying plot and appealing characters . . . The prose is powerful in its understatedness, adding to the appeal of this alluring story."

—*Publishers Weekly*

"Relevant and moving . . . Talley does an excellent job of making her flawed characters vastly more gray than black and white . . . which creates a story of unrequited loves, redeemed."

—*Library Journal*

"Talley masters making the reader feel hopeful in this second-chance romance . . . You have to read this slow-burning, heart-twisting story yourself."

—*USA Today*

"This author blends the past and present effortlessly, while incorporating heartbreaking emotions guaranteed to make you ugly cry. Highly recommended."

—*Harlequin Junkie*

"Liz Talley has written a love story between a mother and daughter that captured me completely. By turns tender and astringent, sexy and funny, heart wrenching and uplifting, *Room to Breathe* is an escapist and winning story that will carry you away with an imperfect pair of protagonists who just might remind you of someone you know. A delight."

—Barbara O'Neal, author of *When We Believed in Mermaids*

"There is no pleasure more fulfilling than not being able to turn off the light until you've read one more page, one more chapter, one more large hunk of an addictive novel. Liz Talley delivers. Her dialogue is crisp and smart, her characters are vivid and real, her stories are unputdownable. I discovered her with the book *The Sweetest September* when, in the very first pages, I was asking myself, How's she going to get out of this one? And of course I was sleep deprived finding out. Her latest, *Come Home to Me*, which I was privileged to read in advance, is another triumph, a story of a woman's hard-won victory over a past trauma, of love, of forgiveness, of becoming whole. Laughter and tears spring from the pages—this book should be in every beach bag this summer."

—Robyn Carr, *New York Times* bestselling author

"Liz Talley's characters stay with the reader long after the last page is turned. Complex, emotional stories written in a warm, intelligent voice, her books will warm readers' hearts."

—Kristan Higgins, *New York Times* bestselling author

"Every book by Liz Talley promises heart, heat, and hope, plus a gloriously happy ever after—and she delivers."

—Mariah Stewart, *New York Times* and *USA Today* bestselling author

"Count on Liz Talley's smart, authentic storytelling to wrap you in southern comfort while she tugs at your heart."

—Jamie Beck, author of *If You Must Know*

Adulting

OTHER TITLES BY LIZ TALLEY

Bayou Bridge

Waters Run Deep

Under the Autumn Sky

The Road to Bayou Bridge

Oak Stand

Vegas Two-Step

The Way to Texas

A Little Texas

A Taste of Texas

A Touch of Scarlet

Novellas and Anthologies

The Nerd Who Loved Me

"Hotter in Atlanta" (a short story)

Cowboys for Christmas with Kim Law and Terri Osburn

A Wrong Bed Christmas with Kimberly Van Meter

Adulting

A Novel

Liz Talley

 Montlake

Text copyright © 2021 by Amy R. Talley
All rights reserved.

Published by Montlake, Seattle

www.apub.com

Amazon, the Amazon logo, and Montlake are trademarks of Amazon.com, Inc., or its affiliates.

ISBN-13: 9781542026031
ISBN-10: 1542026032

Cover design by David Drummond

Printed in the United States of America

This book is dedicated to the senior class of 2020, who missed so much in what should have been the time of their lives. Most especially, this book about growing up is dedicated to my own senior, Gabe, who will start adulting very soon, but pardon me if I hold on a bit longer to the little boy who curled up in my lap and wanted me to snuggle him (and scratch his back).
I love you, Beebs.

CHAPTER ONE

August

Chase London woke with a raging headache and no clothes. Never the best way to wake up, but at least she *was* awake. By rights, she could be dead. Which sometimes didn't seem so awful. The quiet darkness of death often sounded better than the color-soaked world of criticism and disappointment she normally inhabited.

Yeah, things suck when death looks like a better option.

She swallowed the acridness in her mouth because, well, what else was she going to do? Spit it out? She wasn't even sure where she was. She fluttered her eyelids and tried to bring the world into focus.

High ceiling above her. Bed beneath her.

But whose bed?

She moved her fingers against the fabric beneath her. Decent thread count, so there was that. She opened both eyes, blinked away the blurry, and turned her head slowly because she could hear heavy breathing beside her and had no clue who it might be.

The man lying next to her seemed to be naked underneath the tangled top sheet. His shaggy, violet-streaked hair looked spiky from sweat. He breathed through an open mouth, junkie purple shadowing his closed eyes, track marks dotting spread arms that lay palms up like an offering. A narrow chest, slim hips, and tattoos that wended their way around his body, disappearing beneath the shroud of the sheet only to appear again on a thigh, calf, or foot.

Oh God . . . what had she done?

Chase lifted her head and winced.

Jordan. She remembered him asking her over and over last night. *Say my name, babe. Come on. Say it.*

He'd had blow—a lot of it. His skin looked waxy, almost corpse-like. She watched him to ensure he was breathing.

His stomach rose and fell.

Thank God. She didn't want to deal with the police. Been there and done that before. Besides, she was supposed to be clean. She wriggled her foot, feeling the court-issued SCRAM on her ankle. The battery had died yesterday afternoon, and no one from the monitoring company had called by the end of the day. So she'd called her girls and said, "Let's go out before they change the batteries."

Which had been so stupid. But in her defense, she'd spent weeks doing nothing but eating takeout and watching *Real Housewives*. She wanted to move, to feel like a real person again. She wasn't going to drink much. Maybe one glass of wine. And she damn sure wasn't going to do drugs.

Chase carefully lowered her throbbing head back onto the mattress, telling herself she could figure this out.

Carefully, she rolled over. Empty champagne bottles dead soldiered the carpet, and her lacy thong lay like a surrender flag in the threshold of the large room. That's why her head hurt so bad. Champagne messed her up.

She pulled her hair from beneath the shoulder of the guy. Jordan's eyes fluttered, but he stayed asleep. Chase slid her own naked bottom toward the edge of the bed, which was flanked with swaths of linen. She winced as she sat up. The bright-white room tilted, so she grasped the edge of the mattress and stilled herself until the world stopped moving. Then she stood.

As soon as she reached for the bedside table to steady herself, the nausea from earlier made a curtain call. She headed toward the closed door, praying it was a bathroom. The door banged against the bedroom wall as Chase sank onto her knees and hugged the porcelain like it was a lifesaver tossed to her. She pleaded with her body to not heave forth the contents of her stomach.

"What the hell?"

Chase couldn't answer whoever was asking the question behind her. She was focusing on not throwing up.

A shadow fell across the toilet.

Jordan.

"Hey, you okay?" he asked, moving in her line of sight. He wore boxers. Thank goodness.

She didn't answer because she was too busy hugging a toilet and praying for the strength not to puke.

"Whoa, you feeling sick? Lemme get you something."

She was afraid opening her mouth to answer might be an invitation to her body, so she focused on the tiny blue writing on the lid and tried to fight down the nausea. Nothing so humbling as tossing your cookies into a stranger's toilet while naked. But she'd done it before. Halfway to a habit now.

God, she hated herself.

What in the hell was wrong with her? She should have called her parole officer and reported the dead battery. Brownie points could have been added to her file or banked for the next time she screwed up.

Something cold pressed against her neck. "This will help."

The shock of the cold sobered her, and she managed to push her blonde hair back as the nausea lessened.

Jordan sank down on the edge of the soaking tub. The bathroom was large, impersonal. Like a Vegas suite. Where were they? She couldn't remember anything after dancing at whatever club they'd gone to.

"Man, I can't believe I partied with Chase London. That's some crazy shit."

Chase took the cloth from the back of her neck and used it to wipe her face. She looked at the nearly naked guy sitting inches from her. "Yeah, crazy shit all right."

"I mean, I used to jerk off to you when I was little. That movie? The one with the cheerleader skirt? Hot as shit, and now I've had that ass."

Her stomach rolled over. "Yeah, happy to help you out with that fantasy. Could you hand me a robe or towel or something?"

"Nah." His gaze slid down her body, and Chase could see he was getting turned on because, yeah, he wore boxers and was really close to her. "You should never cover that body, baby. You're so smokin'. Come back to bed. We'll have some more fun."

"Are you joking? I feel like death. I'm not going back to bed with you."

Jordan made an exaggerated sad face.

"Where are we, by the way?" Chase pushed herself up. They weren't in a hotel, but the place was nice—she'd glimpsed the sand and surf out of the large sliding glass door in the bedroom, and the hand towel hanging by the sink was monogrammed with a scrolling letter she couldn't discern. "Are we still in Orange County? Please tell me we are."

Jordan looked at her like she was crazy. Then he laughed. "Relax, mama. We in Malibu."

Chase rose and went in search of her clothes and phone. As she shoved pillows out of the way, she tried to piece the night together. She remembered going with her friends to a new club. Maybe she'd popped a pill with the wine? No. Wait. She'd done a few lines in the bathroom. Once she did coke, she usually lost time. Still, how did she end up in Malibu, bombed out of her mind, with some guy she couldn't remember meeting?

Chase snagged her thong and wiggled into it, thankful to have something on.

"Aw, come on." Jordan stood by the bed, erection bobbing beneath the cotton fly of his boxers. "You look like you feel better."

Chase stalked over to the chaise lounge and grabbed her dress. The sequins would look ludicrous in the light of day, but she hadn't packed a bag, now had she? She slid it over her head, not bothering with her missing bra. Scanning the room for her shoes, her gaze landed on a syringe on the nightstand.

God.

Chase passed a hand over her eyes, squeezing them together as if she could erase what she saw. Erase the bad decisions she'd made. The ones she couldn't seem to stop making. Why did she keep doing this to herself?

She had no answer to that question. Her intentions were always good. Every time she went through rehab, went before a judge, got a second chance . . . or fifth . . . she swore she would get herself together and walk a straight line.

But she didn't.

Jordan had given up, flopping onto his stomach, burying his head under the pillows with a groan that jarred Chase into action.

Okay, first she needed to find her phone. Then she could Uber back to her place with no one the wiser. She could call her parole officer and tell her that the battery was dead. But wait. Social media. Someone had probably posted pictures of her last night. She was busted. No way around that.

Shit.

Leaving the bedroom, she made her way down the floating staircase, clinging to the iron handrail, focusing on where she placed her bare feet so she wouldn't take a tumble. She didn't want to end up in the hospital.

Because that meant dealing with her mother and her manager . . . who happened to be one and the same.

Lorna had drawn a line in the sand after the last screwup, and Chase really didn't want to deal with the fallout when she felt like warmed-up cat barf. If she could find her shoes and phone . . . wait, had she brought a purse?

Maybe that's where her phone was. What had she brought with her last night? The Fendi crossbody. Yes, the pink-and-brown one.

When Chase reached the bottom of the stairs, she noted five other people sprawled on the white linen couches, all in various states of undress. More liquor bottles and drug paraphernalia were scattered across the large stone coffee table. A wall of windows allowed the late-morning or early-afternoon California sunshine to flood the place, which now looked vaguely familiar.

Had she been here before?

Chase tiptoed over to the group of people, noting she didn't know any of them. Where were Margot and Jenni? They had promised they would make sure she only had a few drinks and went home safely. That was the deal when she'd handed over her credit card. They'd promised, pinkie sworn, made blood oaths—they would get Chase London home and keep her nose clean.

She raised a hand to a nose that felt raw and scratchy.

Well, that hadn't happened. Obviously.

"Looking for this?" someone said from the open area that led to what looked like a kitchen. Chase couldn't make out the features of the woman against the blinding light pouring into the airy space, but she knew the voice.

"Lorna?"

"That would be correct." The blobby shape holding her Fendi bag disappeared. "Come on into the kitchen."

Chase stared at the spot where her mother had stood, trying to make sense of what she'd just seen. Lorna? In this house? How had her mother found her? Probably Life360. But Chase had disabled that, hadn't she?

Maybe she was still asleep.

Or in an alternate reality.

"Chase," her mother called from the kitchen, her voice impatient. Chase heard a refrigerator door open, bottles clinking.

"How did you . . . I mean, what are you doing here?" Chase blinked against the brightness as she made her way past the huge stone dining table anchoring eight chairs. Outside the swath of windows, gulls screamed and dipped toward the surf pounding the California beach. The light still blinded her, so she shaded her eyes as she trudged to the kitchen island.

"First, breakfast." Lorna Steele London used a wooden spoon to stir the concoction in the skillet. The red Viking range had six burners and looked almost out of place in the sterile white-marbled kitchen. But her nipped-and-tucked mother looked even more out of place.

So many thoughts rushed through Chase's head. How had her mother found her? Why had Lorna showed up . . . *here*? Like she owned the joint. And how did her mother know where the pots and pans were?

Lorna whistled under her breath as she tended the eggs. Her mother wore a pair of Lycra leggings and a soft cashmere top that hit her midthigh. A silk scarf held sandy hair away from her smooth cheeks and perfectly made-up face. She looked like a modern version of Doris Day.

But much meaner. Definitely much meaner.

Lorna scooped steaming eggs onto a plate and set them on the bar at the end of the huge kitchen island. "Here. Sit."

Chase shuffled toward the bar, keeping an eye on her mother just in case she turned into a flesh-eating zombie. She eased herself onto a stool, her gaze still on Lorna.

The woman impersonating June Cleaver handed her a fork. "Eat."

Chase looked down at the scrambled eggs on the white plate. She'd known her mother had cooked once upon a time. Lorna had been raised in Georgia and bragged about her ability to make cheese grits and put a good scald on a pot of collard greens, whatever that was, but the woman had never made Chase breakfast before. Now, she *had* handed her a fruit cup or a protein shake on set, but to use actual fire to cook something? Never had Lorna ever.

Her mother leaned against the counter, picked up her cell phone, and started tapping.

Chase didn't eat. Instead she watched, waiting for her mother to rage at her for relapsing so soon after getting out of Northcross Rehab.

After a full minute, Lorna looked up, glanced pointedly at the plate, and arched a perfectly shaped eyebrow.

Chase scooped a bit of egg into her mouth, chewed, and tried not to gag.

Her mother gave a barely perceptible nod and walked past the island to the outside door. Opening it, she said, "Thank you for coming so quickly, Tom. They're in the living area and master suite. Please confiscate phones, delete any incriminating photos or videos, check their social media for pictures of Chase, delete accounts, and return the phones. If they refuse, call the police and have them arrested for trespassing."

"Yes, ma'am. I have Ubers lined up outside. No paparazzi at present." The older man clutched a handful of disposable-looking tops and bottoms.

Lorna nodded and moved back to the stove like she did this sort of thing every day. "Good. And, Tom, you don't have to call me *ma'am*."

"Yes, ma—" He bit off the last word and proceeded into the living area.

"What's happening here?" Chase managed to swallow the eggs without gagging and watched as the man disappeared.

Her mother turned away from her and scraped the skillet with the wooden spoon. "What do you think, Chase? Yet again, I'm having to save us from your bad decisions."

Us.

Chase studied her mother. Now she could see the anger present beneath the controlled words. Lorna set the spoon down, her blue eyes moving past Chase to the security guy, who escorted a woman wearing a T-shirt and a pair of the disposable bottoms by the elbow.

"What the hell, man?" the woman said, trying to jerk away. "I told you my password. Now give me my shit back."

"We have a car for you outside," Tom said, ignoring her words and struggles.

Lorna opened the door, and another uniformed man stepped forward. Tom clicked a few things on the phone and handed it to the other guy. "She's good."

One by one, the other occupants of the living room left the same way. Chase sat and watched, pushing the eggs around on her plate as her mother leaned against the counter and studied her phone with the intensity of a thousand suns.

Finally, Jordan was escorted into the kitchen. Chase looked down and studied her plate.

"Yo, we didn't do nothing wrong. We were invited here, so I don't know why you're busting our balls and shit." Jordan had put on clothes. Thank God.

"I understand, sweetheart," Lorna said, setting her phone on the counter. "But it's time for you to go home."

Jordan looked at Chase. "You invited us. Tell this bitch."

Chase opened her mouth and then closed it. She still wasn't sure where she was or what exactly had happened.

Or what was happening now.

So she shrugged and looked away.

"This is such bullshit," Jordan muttered, grabbing the phone from Tom. "And I want my shit back. It belongs to me."

Lorna gave her cat-with-a-feather-in-its-mouth smile. "Cocaine is illegal, sugar."

Oh no. Lorna had gone southern on poor Jordan.

Jordan looked at Chase's mother as if he knew a trap had been laid. A few seconds ticked by. "Yeah. So?"

"So that means we're gonna flush it down the toilet, sweetie. It's not good for you." Lorna made her refusal sound so caring. Chase knew it wasn't about caring. The woman wouldn't care if Jordan walked outside and got obliterated by a bus. This was about power.

Jordan made a face. "Yeah. I get that. But—"

"No, no. There are no *buts* in this, young man. If you want that co-caine back, you're going to have to call the po-lice. You don't want to call the po-lice, do you, su-gah?" Now Lorna had gone Deep South on Jordan.

Game over.

Jordan shrugged. "Whatever, man. This is bullshit."

"Be that as it may," Lorna said, picking up a mug and pouring herself a cup from the fancy silver carafe next to the Sub-Zero. She added a slug of cream and stirred. Everyone in the kitchen watched her.

As she intended.

Tom tugged Jordan's arm, and the defeated man went out the back door with the security guy, leaving Chase alone with her mother, and his co-caine to be flushed.

"You do that so well, you know," Chase said, setting her fork on the marble and looking at her mother.

"Do what?"

"Act."

Lorna studied Chase. "The apple doesn't fall far from the tree. You're a very good actress, Chase. You're just a stupid person."

The words hurt. They always did. Chase figured her mother didn't like her much. To Lorna, Chase was a tool, a way for her mother to make the money to pay for the cashmere, the plastic surgery, and her house in Beverly Hills. Lorna needed Chase. She just didn't want her.

"Where are we, by the way?" Chase looked around the kitchen and dining room.

Her mother sucked in a measured breath, then released it through her mouth. "We're at the beach house, the one we bought three years ago. It's on the market now, of course, because you can't get work and we still have bills."

Chase looked around. "*This* is the Malibu beach house? I knew it looked familiar."

Weird. She'd seen the place years ago when she'd bought it. Back then, it had been filled with modern pop art, black leather furniture, and bad lighting. Her mother had hired a decorator, but Chase had been on location in Brazil for a horror movie and had missed the beach rehab edition of *LOLA* magazine that featured a spread of the house. Then she'd gone to Cannes for the film fest, back to rehab, five days in county for the DUI, a stint of community service, and then a hazy period of partying and a month in Paris. She'd planned to come live at the beach, do yoga, meditation, eat healthy crap, but for some reason she hadn't made it. But she'd had the keypad entry code on her phone. She now remembered finding it last night while the Uber driver waited to make sure she could get inside.

"Yes, I hate to sell it, but we can't keep it and stay afloat. I'm sure you're wondering how I knew you were here? No, the monitoring company didn't call me. I'm guessing you figured something out with your ankle monitor." Her mother's eyes moved down to the heavy black monitor on her right ankle.

"The battery died. I took the tracking app off my phone, so I'm guessing someone called you?"

"We have a doorbell camera, not to mention other security cameras. A few of your friends put on quite a show, I must say. But no matter. We're done with this sort of behavior. Marshall called, and they can't get you insured. Conrad Santos still wants you for the part, but if you can't get insured, you can't work. Do you see what I'm saying here, Chase?"

11

"That you don't want to drive a used Honda?" Chase drawled, borrowing her mother's sweet-as-sugar Georgia accent. But in an ironic way. In a smart-ass, ironic way.

Lorna's mouth went flat. "*This* is your problem. You trudge around like the walking wounded, and you have no cause to be. You had everything at your fingertips, and you tossed it just to hurt me. You think I don't know you think I'm a shitty mother?"

"You *are* a shitty mother. You're a good manager, but a shitty mother." Chase shoved the plate away. "I'm going home. I'm not dealing with this right now."

"You're *not* going home."

Of course. Lorna was making her go back to rehab, and Chase didn't want to go to stupid rehab. None of the various ones she'd visited had worked anyway. Neither did therapy or angry judges threatening her with jail time. For some reason, she couldn't seem to stop her behavior. Stop wanting to erase who she was. "Well, last time I looked, Lorna, I'm an adult. I can do whatever the fu—"

Lorna looked past Chase at someone who'd emerged from the living room, causing Chase to stop talking and turn. Her parole officer stood in the doorway of the kitchen.

"Okay, Tonya. Go ahead and arrest her," Lorna said, before sliding her phone in her tunic pocket and walking out the door.

CHAPTER TWO

Olivia Han nuked her coffee in the microwave for the third time and walked across the tasteful waiting room toward her private office, which was situated steps away from the canals of Long Beach. She'd allowed the Blue Mountain blend she imported from Jamaica to grow cold while she tackled a towering to-do list that kept growing by the minute. Olivia hated wasting anything, but most especially good coffee.

"Miss Han, you have a call on line four," Marina said, peeking out from behind the computer in the reception area where she rat-a-tatted memos and worked magic on the client database.

Olivia nearly stumbled. "Line *four*?"

Marina's eyes were big as she shrugged one shoulder.

Line four was for personal calls only. Olivia rarely got personal calls. No, that wasn't true. She got a personal call twice a month. Usually when the money ran out.

Olivia shut the office door and sipped the hot coffee. Not as good as fresh but better than lukewarm. She girded herself for talking to her sister, Neve, who would no doubt want to discuss the cabin and the bequest from their paternal grandfather. Olivia slid open the desk drawer and stared at the key. The key chain was a braided one she'd made for Grammy Rose at day camp one summer. Tender memories crowded her resolve. Once upon a time they'd all been happy there.

Be strong, Olivia. Be strong.

She closed the drawer and angled her ergonomic desk chair toward the window. Outside was the serenity garden she'd installed as a place to meet with clients when the confines of the office were too much. Lush hibiscus crowded the bluestone paths, prickly bougainvillea climbed the stone walls, and a large obsidian water feature provided the background for sleek outdoor furniture. The red glass hummingbird feeder had guests. She could have moved her office, but she'd started her career in social work in Long Beach and had a fondness for the ocean air and lush greenery.

For a moment she closed her eyes and focused on her breathing.

Stay strong.

She reached for the phone. "Good afternoon. This is Olivia Han."

Normally, she wouldn't greet her sister so formally, but putting distance between them at the outset of the conversation would be the best practice. Neve had always been manipulative, excuse at the ready for everything she did or didn't do.

"Livy, it's been too long," the voice on the other end drawled.

For a moment, her heart stopped.

"Conrad?"

"Of course it's Con. Who else calls you Livy?"

"Uh, only you. I didn't know you had this number."

Conrad chuckled. "I managed to squeeze it out of your sister. You don't seem to be returning my calls on your cell phone, so . . ."

Probably because she had been afraid to open a can of worms that would make her feel icky. Every time she saw a message from him, her heart skipped a beat and she remembered. It was easier to pretend her feelings for Conrad and the drama from her past away. "Sorry. I've been so busy."

"Understandable." He didn't sound offended. Very matter-of-fact. That made her wonder why he'd been calling her. "How have you been? Besides busy."

Olivia pressed a hand against her chest, fingering the pearl buttons at her throat. "I'm well. Very well. Thank you."

"I bought your book and gave it to everyone I know. Well, almost everyone. Some people are hopeless." His bark of laughter caused a frisson of the feeling she'd buried to skitter across her heart. She loved his big, blooming laugh of total abandon. Her mind tripped to him throwing back his head and clutching his stomach when they watched *American Pie*, sneaking it from the video store because it was rated R and her dad would freak if he knew they watched it. This was why she'd been avoiding talking to him. He made her feel weak, made her remember all she'd lost.

"That was kind of you. To buy the book."

"You know I'm not kind, Livy." Amusement nattered the edges of the affected growl he'd used to make the joke. Conrad Santos had erected a veneer of nonchalance long ago, something pretty much required when one grew up in West Rancho Dominguez, but beneath the laissez-faire facade was a person who'd given his last bit of hamburger to a stray cat and hung out with a nerdy girl at an ice cream parlor.

"If that's what you want me to think, but I know the truth."

"Using your shrink speak on me, huh?" Con said.

"I'm not a shrink. I'm a life coach and author. Didn't you read the bio?" She watched as two hummingbirds took exception to each other. The birds were notoriously aggressive, but she understood fighting for what one needed. Sometimes one had to swoop and dive. And sometimes one had to retreat in order to fight another day. She'd learned to recognize the need for both.

"I read it. How could I not? I'm so proud of you, Livy." The sincerity in his voice knocked loose several bricks in her wall of defense, the one she'd erected when he'd broken her heart. He always wriggled in. Always.

"So, is there something I can help you with?" Olivia asked, trying to steel herself against her emotions and figure out why Conrad had gone to such lengths to reach her.

"Actually, there is. I need a favor, and you're the only person for the job."

"You want a favor?" So this wasn't about her or Marley or some therapeutic action to absolve himself from the guilt. This was, indeed, business.

"You've heard of Chase London, right?"

Chase London had been the toast of Hollywood as an eleven-year-old ingenue. She'd starred in a Stefano Nash film, playing a lost waif in a postapocalyptic world, the sole survivor who discovers a new species and brings life back to a devastated world. She'd been nominated for an Oscar and won the Golden Globe for best actress. But after the initial buzz, she'd settled down into starring in typical teen dramas and Disneyesque productions that were more about her bouncy blondeness than her acting chops.

When Chase hit puberty, she'd embraced the Hollywood lifestyle with both arms and—as the gossip rags liked to imply—both legs. Multiple DUI arrests and a brief stay in a county facility should have been wake-up calls but, if *National Inquisitor* could be believed, hadn't even come close. Chase London was a train wreck. A has-been. A sad case of Hollywood squeezing everything out of a talented actor and then kicking her to the curb.

"Please tell me you aren't casting Chase London in your next film." Olivia picked up the paperweight her youngest sister had given her years ago. Marley had painted a butterfly on the rounded stone she'd found when their father had taken them to the beach one spring day. Marley had been about eight, golden curls, eyes the color of the ocean, giggles and wiggles. She'd wrapped it up and given it to Olivia for her eleventh birthday, a little ball of wrapping paper and ribbon.

Olivia pressed the stone to her lips and closed her eyes before setting it back on the desk.

"She's perfect for this particular role. She just needs help. That's where you come in." Con's words held something more.

"You're not sleeping with her, are you?"

"No, of course not. Chase is an infant."

"She's in her twenties. You're thirty-six. That's a Hollywood power couple," Olivia said. She wasn't normally sarcastic, but she wasn't a big fan of the entertainment industry even as she knew she'd made her career on Hollywood by-products. Catch-22 for her. She needed what she despised. Like dentists and hard candy.

"No. I want her for this film. The script's a dream, we've got solid backing, and casting is holding off because we're waiting on Tom Reynard to wrap his latest film, which is a month behind on production as is. If I can get Chase insured . . ."

"But you're not her agent. Why are *you* calling me?"

"I'm aware I'm not her agent. But I'm producing and directing this one, and I really feel like she's the perfect actress for this role."

But he didn't have to say it. She knew. Conrad Santos could never undo what had been done to Marley, and thus his penance would never be paid. He'd turned away from her sister when she'd needed him most, and he couldn't get that monkey off his back. It was the same monkey she carried, so she knew. Like Conrad, she, too, did her best to save others. Because she had also failed to help Marley in her eleventh hour.

And then there had been no more hours.

"Come on, Con. I know what you're doing. Actresses are a dime a dozen. Even good ones." She said the words but knew her old friend had already committed himself. Conrad Santos—the king of third chances. Maybe even fourth chances.

But not with Olivia.

"True, but you know how I am when I sink my teeth into something. I feel this in my bones. It's a pivotal role in this film. I have to get this one right. This might be the one. The script is fantastic and . . ." He trailed off. "I need you to help her, Livy."

His words were plaintive . . . sincere . . . something hard for her to say no to.

Olivia picked up her planner. Everything in the world was digital, but try to pry her planner from her cold, dead hands. "My team's booked solid for the next few months, Con. I can recommend someone else who may—"

"I don't want someone on your team. I want you."

How she'd longed to hear those words from his lips, but she'd never been the one he wanted. Not truly.

"Sorry. I'm just not available, Con."

Olivia no longer worked directly with clients. Square One had taken on a life of its own after she'd successfully graduated multiple high-profile clients from her unique life-coaching service. A book deal and talk shows followed, along with a business model that had turned into a highly in-demand lifestyle consulting business with twenty-three life coaches, sobriety coaches, and adulting lecturers on her staff. Olivia Han was the captain, and she wasn't about to let a junkie like Chase London sink her ship. The last actor she'd worked with had nearly wrecked her, and only a good publicist who was a spin doctor had been able to divert a disastrous lawsuit.

"You mean you don't want to get your hands dirty," Con said, disappointment evident in his voice.

That small censure plucked at her. Because it was Con, and she'd never been able to tell him no. "No, I don't."

"Because of the Linden thing?"

She wasn't going to admit how much the false allegations against her by Allie Linden had shaken her faith in herself and made her feel like her own father when he'd been accused of wrongdoing. "No, I have a conference in New York next week, and then I have to work on the next book. The draft is due by the end of October."

"She's in rehab at present, so the New York thing is fine, and you can work on the book while you work with her."

"Con, I don't want to work with Chase London. Frankly, I'm not sure I can help her." Chase seemed to have the exact same problems Allie had. Olivia's ego had led her astray with Allie. She wasn't shoving herself off that cliff again.

A pause on the phone made her wonder if he'd hung up. Con had a temper and, as a highly creative person, wasn't beyond a snit. Finally, he sighed. "You owe me, Livy."

"Yeah, I do. But not with taking on a ten-car pileup like Chase London. She's . . . she's not . . . what I'm saying is that I don't work this way. I help those who are ready to be helped. The first step in my program is not convincing someone to change their life. They have to already be there. *You* are calling me. Not her. Not even her mother or agent. And that tells me a lot."

"Please, Livy. Chase is lost, and we lose too many like her. She's worth saving. If you can't do it for me, do it for Marley. Do it for the girls who never had a chance."

Her heart cracked, but she ignored it. "Chase has had multiple chances. She wasted them."

"The same way Marley did?"

He might as well have punched her in the face. Olivia closed her eyes tight, screwing up her face at her sister's name on Conrad's lips. Damn him. "I can't. Don't use Marley against me. That's not fair."

"Life ain't fair. We know that, right?"

Another lengthy silence. Olivia stared at her planner, wishing she had more on it to prevent her from even considering Conrad's request. But she'd cleared her schedule because of the book. Her publisher wanted a follow-up to *Two Steps Backward: How to Unlearn Your Past*, and she'd promised to have *Two Steps Forward: Adulting for a New*

Generation in before the end of the year. So she'd blocked out a big chunk of time over the next few months.

But she'd also been itchy lately, dissatisfied, complacent even. Still, this sort of challenge felt like too much, especially since it not only involved an unknown entity in Chase London, but it would include Conrad, and he always made her feel . . . too many things. That's why she'd steered clear of him beyond Christmas cards or birthday wishes.

Still, a voice inside her whispered what she didn't want to admit. *You've been running from him and from your past for too long.*

And beneath that voice was another one, faint but still present. *You can be near him again. Maybe . . . just maybe . . . you could take back a piece of what you once had.*

"If I do this, it's going to cost more than the normal fee," she said.

"Fine. Done."

"Damn it."

His laugh made something squirm inside her. The power this man still had over her. One night was all it had taken to stitch the thought of a soul mate into her heart. He hadn't had to mention Marley. All he had to do was need her. She could be that honest with herself.

"Chase has been at Cedar Point for a week. I talked to the judge and her attorney. The rehab wants her to stay for the next eighteen days, and then they will release her to you. Her mother will be calling you once I tell her you've accepted. Lorna is grateful. She loves her daughter but is at her wit's end."

"She may not be grateful when I'm done, and I want Chase to have at least a week with one of my staff members to continue the sobriety coaching. I not only want her clean, but I want her feeling healthy, rested, and open to the next step in the process," Olivia said, leaning her head back against the chair, her gaze on the two hummingbirds going at one another. No retreat left.

"I have faith in you. You're Chase London's last chance to come back."

Olivia picked up the pen Vashad Jackson had sent her after he'd won his first Super Bowl and wrote Chase London's name on the second Thursday of September. "Okay, you've got me. Let's see what we can do to get Chase London back. Consider the favor repaid."

"Thank you, Livy."

"I'm only doing this because you're the one asking."

"And because you love me," he joked.

But that was the problem, wasn't it? Olivia had always loved Conrad Santos.

And he would always be in love with her dead sister.

CHAPTER THREE

Chase schlepped down the hall, her slippers scuffing the linoleum floor. She'd been a client at Cedar Point Rehab before and knew how to punch all the buttons of the staff, which for some crazy reason made her feel better. Yeah, it was a dick move, but she had been detoxing, and one took pleasure where one could.

She plopped her coffee mug down on the counter, sloshing the liquid onto it.

The woman sitting behind the L-shaped station frowned. "Really?"

"My coffee is cold. Again." Chase arched an eyebrow, knowing she probably looked like Lorna and hating that about herself. But not enough to relent or apologize. This was what people expected from her. Bad behavior. So she gave it to them.

"There's a microwave in the common area. You know how to use a microwave, don't you, princess?" The woman plopped a stack of napkins onto the counter and turned back to her computer screen. She had red hair that looked like it came out of a box, wore a cotton tunic top that was too tight and showed her back rolls, and displayed a bitchy attitude. Chase stared daggers at her, wishing she had enough nerve to toss the coffee on the woman. She couldn't quite go there.

So instead she left the coffee without wiping up the spill and started back to her room.

"Hey," the woman called at her retreating back, "come back and clean this up."

"That's what you're paid for."

"You little . . ."

Chase smiled as she headed to the private room they'd shoved her into almost three weeks ago. And then left her to detox (which sucked) and gave her ugly sweats to wear. When she complained, they shook their heads and said, "You know the drill."

Yeah, she did.

And she hated everyone at Cedar Point, but even more than the well-intentioned counselors, she hated her mother.

Lorna had actually called her PO and reported her for being in violation of her parole. What kind of mother called the police on her own kid?

Officer Tonya Gilbert had taken Chase's "tattletale" ankle bracelet off, muttering about stupid batteries, and put her in cuffs. She'd spent a whole twenty-one hours in a jail cell after she was processed. Thankfully, it had been a holding cell, and she'd gone before the judge the next day. Her attorney had gotten her community service. Again. And court-ordered rehab. Again. So yeah, she knew the drill.

She entered her room and looked at the breakfast she'd ordered. Totally sucked. Most of the patients went to the café for breakfast, but Chase wanted to spend as little time as possible with the other residents. Last time she'd gotten a hanger-on who had somehow gotten her phone number from a staff member. The woman had texted Chase emojis and GIFs for the remainder of the rehab period, which at first had been kind of fun, but then the lunatic didn't stop. Chase had to get a new number and a restraining order after the woman had turned up at her house one day.

So Chase kept her distance, sharing minimally during group therapy and avoiding everyone's curious glances. People loved to watch someone like her fall down. They didn't extend a hand. Instead they whipped out their phones and filmed the flailing. So she wasn't going to give anyone the chance to be a lookie-loo. Or a stalker.

Chase took the tray and sat it outside her door. The room was okay. More hotel room than hospital room. That was because Cedar Point was *exclusive*, its clientele *discerning*, and its staff *discreet*. Or at least that was what the brochures said. She'd picked up some in the lobby when she'd gone outside for a pretend smoke because she didn't smoke cigarettes. Then she'd brought a stack back to circle the buzzwords and write how the claims were bullshit. How did the picture of her in group therapy, sans makeup, end up in the *Hollywood Spotlight* magazine last time, huh? The patients couldn't use their phones anywhere but their rooms, so *they* couldn't snap her picture, could they? Discreet staff, her ass.

She planned to put the brochures back with the truthful information in place so people would know that Cedar Point's claims were total crap.

Kicking off her slippers, she opened the drawer of the cheap dresser and looked for a clean pair of socks. When she'd first arrived in her sequined dress, which in hindsight was better than the orange prison jumpsuit, her mother had gone to Target and bought her new socks and underwear. Lorna had bought cheap cotton panties and ugly socks with fluorescent doughnuts on them. Ludicrous. But at least she'd agreed to go by Chase's apartment a few days later to grab toiletries, her new Nike trainers, and Chase's facial cleansing products, an exclusive line she'd bought when she was in Paris. She glanced at herself in the mirror. Her hair needed highlighting, her skin a good exfoliation, and her nails an emery board. She'd go to a spa as soon as they released her from this horrible place.

The upside was she was sober.

There was that.

Chase had just pulled on her shoes when a tiny bird landed on the windowsill and looked at her as if it had a pressing message.

"Weird," Chase said to herself after the bird actually tapped on the window.

She rose, laces dragging, and walked cautiously toward where the sunlight streamed into her room. The little bird didn't fly away. Instead it sat there, unafraid of her approach.

Chase didn't know anything about birds, but she'd seen a lot of prison movies where inmates found and kept a pet bird. Maybe that was what this was. This tiny sparrow was her prison bird, a symbol of freedom sitting right outside her window. Maybe she should let the little fellow inside. She could keep it in her pocket, squirreling away crumbs to feed it. Maybe she'd name it Tweety. Kind of basic, but it was *her* prison bird. No one was going to judge her for giving it a lame name. It would be her best friend. Her only friend.

Chase reached toward the window, and when she touched the glass, the bird took off.

"Yeah, I'd fly away, too. You don't want none of this, Tweety." She stroked the sun-warmed glass, staring at the spot where the bird had sat.

The message wasn't lost on her.

A knock sounded on her door. Like another omen.

Chase glanced at her watch. Gone was the Apple watch—no communication with the outside world—so she had been left with the Breguet, a jeweled affair one of her past lovers had gifted her. The diamonds and sapphires rocked on the red carpet, but next to the cheap cotton sweats, the flash looked wrong. Why her mother hadn't just bought a cheapo at Target was lost on Chase. The price of this watch could pay her rehab bill. She wondered if the billing department would be up for a tradesy.

Chase shook her head, walked to the door, and opened it.

"Hello, Chase," the woman standing on the threshold said as if she'd known Chase for years.

Not totally unexpected. Sometimes Chase saw the glint of confusion in people's eyes when they couldn't quite figure out how they knew her. She could see them flipping through the Rolodex in their heads, scratching out *high school classmate* or *mom from my kid's playgroup* before realizing they knew her from the big screen or supermarket tabloids. But this woman's manner wasn't one Chase often encountered in fans. No, this woman had a purpose.

Chase arched an eyebrow and said nothing.

"Do you mind if I come inside?" the woman asked.

Chase didn't move backward. Instead she studied the woman in front of her. Glossy brown hair likely flat ironed within an inch of its life, oval face, light-handed makeup, compact body created in a gym, tasteful clothes, and small earrings winking between the layered strands around her face. She wore glasses that made her look smart.

Total therapist.

Chase crossed her arms. "I don't think so."

The woman tilted her head about five degrees, so slight, so knowing. An imperceptible lift of the corner of her lips made Chase frown. Amused, was she?

"I'm Olivia Han."

She said her name like it should mean something.

"And . . . ?"

Irritation flitted over Olivia Han's face. "The facility will be releasing you today, and I'm here—"

"I thought I had another month," Chase interrupted, a myriad of emotions flooding her. Elation at the thought of leaving, but maybe a tinge of apprehension at the world beyond the door. Deep down, she knew her sobriety was eggshell thin, liable to spider crack under the slightest pressure. But she needed out so she could get insured and get back to work. As much as she resented her mother and the thought of being manipulated into a role, she knew it was her best shot to reenter credible acting. And she was good at pretending to be someone else, so she might as well make bank off the skill.

"We'll be completing your sobriety treatment at a private location," the woman said, stepping closer to Chase.

Her closeness made Chase step back, surrendering her defensive position. Olivia stepped inside and eyed the sterile room with a curious once-over. Some patients made their rooms cozy with a plant or even a few pictures. Lorna had brought a quilt from her house and folded it at the foot of Chase's bed, her only concession to giving Chase any comfort. Chase hadn't bothered with anything more. When flowers arrived from her so-called friends, she set them back outside the door. Someone must have taken them, because within hours the elaborate bouquets were gone.

"You said 'we.' Why would I go anywhere with you? I don't know you," Chase said, her hand still on the doorknob. She wanted this woman to leave. Getting out of here sounded great, but something felt wrong about this. Like an outta-the-frying-pan sort of thing.

"You're right. You don't know me." Olivia turned around and studied her.

Chase ran a hand through her hair before she could stop herself. "Okay, enough of this cryptic bullshit. Tell me what you really want."

"That's an odd choice of words. You think I want something from you." Olivia sank onto the edge of the armchair under the window where the little bird had perched. She folded her legs beneath her, relaxing her posture into one Chase was familiar with. Nonthreatening. Therapists liked that pose. They thought it made them approachable. Chase thought of it as a trick. She hated how designed everything was for shrinks. They said the same shit, tried the same techniques. So laughable.

Olivia Han waited for a response, like a good little therapist. Chase wasn't going to give her one.

Finally, the woman folded her hands and said, "Conrad Santos hired me."

This. Now *this* surprised Chase. She'd worked with Con Santos on her second film. She'd been twelve, still innocent, still rearing to tackle the film industry with her immense talent. Con had been an assistant director, working under the legendary Milos Bergman. In his midtwenties, he'd been dazzling, driven, brilliant. And surprisingly patient with an annoying twelve-year-old who had just started getting too big for her britches. When she got lippy or tried to grandstand, instead of ignoring her, he sat with her and talked about odd things, like how snakes shed their skin or how earthquakes happened. Stupid stuff, really, but hardly anyone actually sat and talked with her while she ate a "healthy salad and fruit cup" in order to avoid becoming too plump for good roles.

Con had risen in the directing ranks like a comet—he was hardworking and had a great feel for what worked in shots. Last year he'd been nominated for an Academy Award for Best Director for *Mission: Forever*. Rumor had it he'd grabbed a screenplay about a beleaguered Victorian police inspector who hides his homosexuality (and murdered wife's body) as he navigates political turmoil. Dark and supposedly brilliant, the script had been on all the studios' radars. Santos had won the rights to produce it, and investors had lined up. He'd called her agent about the role of the neighbor's niece, a heroin-addicted dancer who becomes suspicious of the inspector. She assumed he wanted her to draw upon her experience as a drug addict. Her plié wasn't bad, either.

"Conrad Santos? *He* hired you?" Chase crossed her arms, knowing it looked defensive but doing it anyway because she felt defensive. Like this woman could dig in the cracks she'd carefully plastered over.

Olivia glanced down at her hands. Her fingernails were painted a neutral color, and she wore a single ring but not on her left hand. "That's correct. It seems Mr. Santos cares about you."

"No, he doesn't. Conrad Santos doesn't even know me. He needs me to play a junkie in his next film. Bring some real experience to the role. My agent already told me."

Olivia's tongue darted out to dampen her upper lip, and she paused for a few seconds before lifting a shoulder. "Maybe you're right. But there are many actresses who can play an addict authentically. He's not the kind of man to ask for a favor. Maybe you can connect the dots. Or not. Either way, I'm willing to work with you."

"I don't want you to 'work' with me." Chase crooked her fingers in quotation marks.

This made Olivia frown. Chase found she liked making Olivia frown. She looked less robotic, less composed. More real. A few seconds ticked by before Olivia stood and said, "Okay, then. Hope all goes well here."

The woman started for the door.

"That's it? You're giving up?"

Olivia paused and turned toward where Chase stood beside her unmade bed. "*I* didn't give up. Conrad believes everyone can get better, everyone can turn their lives into something good. He's such a romantic that way."

That wasn't even an answer. "What kind of therapist are you?"

"The kind who has learned not to waste her time with people who don't want to change." She turned and opened the door.

"Wait," Chase said, wondering why she wanted this woman to give her more time. Something in the therapist's eyes, the way she so easily accepted Chase's answer, the way she didn't seem to give a damn one way or another. Her easy acceptance bothered Chase. Conrad had hired this woman to do a job, and she walked after the first bump in the road? Chase had never met a therapist who accepted the first thing a person said. Therapists knew people needed, uh, therapy. Their job was to convince them to stop doing destructive things, to get on board, to stop snorting coke and sleeping with strangers. That kind of stuff.

Olivia didn't turn around, but she paused, hand on the doorknob. "Yes?"

"That's it?"

"What's it?" she asked, turning toward Chase, her expression steady, her eyes . . . something. Disappointed?

Why would Chase give two figs about disappointing a stranger, someone hired to save her from herself? Lord. But oddly enough, the way the woman had surrendered had . . . intrigued her? It was probably some trick. That's how sneaky these people were. But still, maybe wherever this woman wanted to take her would be better than these four walls and doing group therapy with the guy that scratched his privates incessantly and the pathetic sixteen-year-old who sobbed before she could say two words. Chase did feel a little sorry for the girl, but the kid needed to dry up and deal at some point. "Where would we be going, um, if I were to do this therapy thing with you?"

"Your mother has approved us staying in the house you own in Malibu. You'll spend another week or so there, completing your sobriety therapy."

The waves, the sand, and the soft bed sounded amazing. Plus, she wouldn't have to listen to the losers in her group therapy. Okay, maybe she was being harsh. She knew these people had problems and needed help.

The way you do, dumbass. You're a loser, too.

"And then?" Chase asked.

"Then we start the process of discovering who you really are, Chase. You need to unlearn your current coping strategies and learn effective methods that work for productive, healthy adults." Olivia looked like she believed what she said. Like she would be giving Chase a gift, unwrapping secret wisdom that only she was privy to.

Whatever. Bunch of mumbo jumbo crap. How many therapists, life coaches, agents, directors, and friends had promised her something she knew she wasn't going to get? She didn't have enough fingers and toes to count those on.

Still, if she could get out of here, why not?

At that moment, she heard a tapping. Turning, she saw the little bird from earlier sitting on the sill. It tapped a few more times and looked at her expectantly.

Opportunity knocking?

Or a bird merely seeing its reflection?

Either way, she could fly the coop if she told this uptight, squeaked-when-she-walked woman that she was cool doing this therapy crap. A week or so at the beach house, some outpatient therapy with this chick, and she'd be done. Ready to work. And this time she would truly keep her nose clean. She'd actually paid attention to some of the exercises in the workbook she'd been forced to do. For some reason, this time she got honest with herself about some things and was sure she could come out on the other side of addiction and stay there.

Chase looked back at Olivia. "You're not going to use shrink tricks on me. I hate that bullshit."

Olivia studied her again. "You may be the most mistrustful person I've ever met."

Chase stared right back at her. "I'm sure you'll fix me right up."

"You'll have to sign the agreement before you're released from Cedar Point."

A niggle of something squirmed inside her brain, but then Dr. Gary Watkins, Dr. Caterpillar himself, stuck his head inside the door, looking impatient. "We're waiting for you, Miss London. Again."

"Keep waiting. I'm busting out."

Dr. Watkins raised his creepy bushy eyebrows nearly to his receding hairline; then he looked over at Olivia, who stood framed against the door. For a moment he stared, maybe because Olivia was totally out of his league. She wasn't hot, but she was confident and elegant. "What's going on here?"

Olivia extended her hand. "Hello."

He took her hand, squinting his eyes like he was trying to figure out exactly who she was and why Chase was getting out. His caterpillar brows wriggled.

"I'm Olivia Han, and I'll be—"

"Olivia Han?" he interrupted.

"I've been hired to work with Miss London. You should have gotten a call from her mother and the court at the beginning of the week?"

"I didn't." He dropped her hand, looking confused. "I know exactly who you are. You know, we both attended a workshop on accelerated resolution therapy at Berkeley a few summers back."

Olivia donned an impersonal smile, folding her hands in front of her. "A very different approach for PTSD therapy." An awkward pause ensued before Olivia said, "I don't want to hold you up. I know your patients need you."

Dr. Watkins still looked weirded out. "Yeah. I should go."

But he didn't look like he wanted to. His earlier irritation had fled to be replaced by intense interest in Olivia. Maybe she was a big deal in the world of shrinks.

Her new therapist glanced back at Chase. "Pack your things, and call reception when you're done. My assistant will have you sign the paperwork and then take you to my car. Dr. Watkins, I'll walk with you to group therapy, if you don't mind. I have a few questions."

Dr. Watkins looked back at Chase, a calculating gleam in his eye. "And I have plenty of answers."

Olivia shut the door, and their voices faded away.

As Chase stared at the closed door, a realization bloomed in her brain—the staff knew she was being released, and both doctors were distracted.

Which meant she had the perfect opportunity to slip out unnoticed.

Chase could be like the little bird on the windowsill—free from the webbing that pinned her against a world she often despised. Sometimes she daydreamed about dyeing her hair, changing her name to something more common, and living a different life. Then she wouldn't need the booze or the drugs to help her get through the day. She wouldn't have to deal with her mother, her agent, or the incessant pressure to get a bigger and better role in the next movie. She would be regular ol' Katie—that was the name she'd give herself—answering phones at an office, lunching with the girls, talking about who slept with the delivery guy last week.

Olivia Han was merely another web spun her way, binding Chase to who she had always been. She'd be trading one prison for another, even if it had a great view with no lookie-loos.

So Chase grabbed a plastic grocery bag and stuffed her granny panties and ugly socks inside. Then she tied her sneaker laces. She wondered who she could call to help her. She needed money, hair dye, a new life.

Maybe this time she could truly erase herself.

Time to run.

CHAPTER FOUR

Olivia knew she shouldn't have agreed to take on Chase London. Her tender feelings for Conrad had moved her to do something asinine. She didn't need to get her hands dirty. She'd spent many years working intimately with clients, wiping off the mud, filth, and crap they shook off them in order to emerge clean and ready to face life again. Why had she let herself be convinced that she was the only person who could help Chase?

Because she needed . . . to undo the things she'd done. Because if she could save Chase, a beautiful blonde actress with an addiction problem, it would be like saving Marley. Olivia was as stupid as Conrad and his ego-stroking words.

And she liked the words Conrad had said, words about how he needed her, how she was the only person who could make a difference. Damn her pride. Damn her heart. Doing this favor for Con wasn't going to change the past. She'd always love him, and being close to him in any way only reminded her that she would never have him. Olivia wasn't going to play second fiddle to someone who was dead, scrapping up the crumbs, telling herself that she'd be satisfied with only a little.

So Olivia got what she deserved . . . which was driving around the busy area surrounding the exclusive treatment center, looking for her new client who had bolted.

The phone rang.

Olivia pressed a button on the steering wheel. "Any word from Cedar Point?"

Jamie sighed. "The director said the attendant looked at the paperwork, gave Miss London her personal effects, and buzzed her out. She said she was carrying a plastic grocery bag that looked to have clothes in it. Oh, and that Miss London thanked them for their care and seemed very excited about working with Olivia Han."

Sarcasm wasn't her normal, but her sobriety program manager was a master of fitting herself to any circumstance. Olivia affectionately called her "Play-Doh" because Jamie could be whatever or whoever was needed in any situation, from bulldog to mother hen. The older woman was her right hand for good reason.

"So maybe she just went to get us coffees?" Olivia turned left at the next light, keeping her eyes peeled for a blonde in sweatpants carrying a grocery sack.

"Yeah, that's what she's doing. For her new bestie therapist," Jamie drawled, adding a clipped laugh. "Call me and let me know when to send Rick over to Malibu. He has her files from rehab. From the last three rehabs, to be specific."

"I'll call when I find her. *If* I find her," Olivia said, turning into the strip mall sporting a Clipper Cuts and dry cleaner's. She pressed the button on the steering wheel and scoured the parking lot and business fronts. She should call Conrad and tell him she'd be returning the initial deposit he'd sent on Chase's behalf. Olivia wasn't going to play games with this spoiled junkie no matter how much she got paid. She'd left those days of cajoling, pleading, and throwing bones behind years ago.

Then again, she had to rectify the situation before she withdrew from the predicament that she'd allowed herself to get tangled in. She was responsible because she'd let her guard down and had allowed Chase's about-face to lull her into false confidence.

Idiocy.

"This is totally on me," she breathed as the wheel slid through her fingers. She stopped as a car went past and then turned toward the offshoot of a strip mall tucked off the main road.

"Bingo."

Chase stood outside a run-down diner, tapping on her phone. Even wearing sweats and with her hair in a tangle, the actress looked out of place against the gritty and garish backdrop. That was part of Chase's problem—she had the little-girl-lost vibe, the kind that crippled men, the kind that made women want to offer her their last dollar bill.

But Olivia knew how facades worked. She was an effin' pro at seeing past the bullshit. Well, at least she had been. Needed to knock the rust off.

Olivia's tires squealed when she pulled into the parking spot right in front of her runaway actress. Chase jerked her head up, her blue eyes widening with panic as she stepped back toward the smudged glass.

The moment felt very much like one in a movie. The title for this one would be *Runaway Junkie.*

Rolling down the window, Olivia gave Chase her best authoritarian glare. "Get in. Now."

"Fuck you," Chase said, looking right and then left, almost on cue.

"Not interested. We are client and therapist. I don't cross those lines."

The space between Chase's baby blues formed a V. "What the hell are you talking about?"

Olivia inhaled and exhaled, trying for calm. "You said—"

"Look, I'm not . . . what I meant was I'm not coming with you. I don't know you. I don't trust you. I don't like you. I'm getting out of here."

"No, you aren't. You're going either to a room at Cedar Point or a jail cell."

Chase narrowed her eyes and said nothing.

Olivia schooled her features into something half-sympathetic and half-irritated. "If you don't get in this car, I'll call your parole officer, and you'll be in violation of your probation. You'll have to take those attractive sweats off and trade them for an orange jumpsuit. They won't put you in holding this time. You'll go straight to county lockup. Then you can yell the same obscenity at your new roommate, see how that goes. I'm sure they get prison cred for showing soft blonde actresses how it's done on the inside. Of course, I've only watched *Orange Is the New Black*. I've not actually had the experience."

"Fuck you."

Olivia sighed. "You need to work on more expressive vocabulary."

Chase glared at her before looking down at her phone, lips pressed into a tight line, nostrils flaring. If irritation had a stance, hers would have won an Academy Award. Fitting for a talented actress, even one as messed up as Chase London.

"So what will it be? You want to get in the car? Or you want me to call the police?"

A woman exited the diner, carrying a takeout box and a toddler on her hip. She glanced first at Olivia's car, her eyes sliding appreciatively over the glossy new Volvo, before looking over at Chase. The woman must have had a gift for reading body language, because her face creased with concern. "Everything okay here?"

Most Californians didn't stick their noses in situations that didn't concern them, but this woman had a thick midwestern accent. And in Olivia's experience, many midwesterners considered everyone a friend and thus were often helpful even when the situation didn't call for it.

"Everything's fine, ma'am," Olivia said, keeping her voice level and moderate in tone.

"No, it's *not* fine." Chase jabbed a finger at Olivia. "She's trying to make me get in the car with her."

"You signed the paperwork, Chase," Olivia said, glancing in the rearview mirror at movement behind her. Someone approached. More well-intentioned people coming to the rescue of the "helpless" young blonde.

"Oh my God, are you joking me?" The nosy woman's mouth fell open in shock. Olivia put the car into park. This wasn't going to be easy. She had a sneaking suspicion that nothing was easy when it came to Chase.

"Finally," Chase said to the man walking toward her.

"Sorry, Ladybug. You know how traffic is out here," he said as he leaped gracefully over the concrete parking bumper and pulled Chase into a hug.

"Oh my God. That's Spencer Rome, Sadie," the midwesterner said to the toddler in her arms as if the tiny girl could understand. "He's the Hammer. The Hammer!"

The man turned, and damned if Olivia didn't feel something squiggly in her tummy at the sheer prettiness of the man staring at the woman and toddler with a quizzical look on his face.

Olivia recognized him from the billboard years ago that had made him famous, the one featuring him sprawled in a rumpled bed wearing nothing but a fancy watch, his skin golden and rippling with sleek muscle. The come-hither look paired with the sheer perfection of his body had caused three wrecks within a week's time. She'd heard the advertising agency responsible for the ad had won a Clio for the sexy billboard that had appeared in Times Square and downtown LA simultaneously. After that, everyone had wanted to know who the watch guy was. He became a sensation, one that even a girl like Olivia had looked at multiple times.

"What's going on?" Spencer asked, looking from Olivia to the midwestern mommy, who now seemed to be in danger of drooling as much as her teething toddler. "You said it was an emergency."

"It so is," Chase said, stepping from the curb, seemingly heading toward Spencer's vehicle.

"Stop, Chase," Olivia said to the woman's back, opening the car door and stepping out. She glanced over at Spencer. "She can't go with you."

Spencer looked even more confused. "Wait, who are you?"

"She's nobody. Let's go," Chase called back over her shoulder.

"If Chase gets into your car, I'm calling the police, and you'll be part of this."

"Whoa, whoa, whoa," Spencer said, holding up a hand. He wore black athletic shorts, white sneakers, and a T-shirt, which somehow looked about as sexy as that past billboard. Almost.

The woman with the toddler had pulled out her phone.

Crap on a cracker. This was about to be an issue.

"Ma'am, can you please put your phone away?" Olivia said, turning to the woman, ignoring Spencer.

"I don't have to. I know who she is. I see it now. Chase London," she said, lifting the phone in Chase's direction. "They pay for this stuff."

Spencer stepped toward the woman. "Hey, what's your little girl's name? She's a cutie."

He had to have employed his notoriously charming smile, because the woman lowered the phone, and the expression on her face made Olivia think about rolling her eyes. Instead she turned and followed a determined Chase, who had her hand on the door of a low-slung sports car that was thankfully locked.

"Chase, please. This situation is getting out of control. Come with me, and I'll take you back to Cedar Point. Or I can call the police. And it's going to blow up if the police come. Any chance you have to recover and resurrect your career will be gone."

Chase jerked on the handle, frustration on her face. "What if I don't want to be in that movie? What if I want everyone to stop telling me how to live my life, to stop telling me what to do, how to live . . . what if I want to quit?"

Olivia took a mental screenshot of that info to file away for later exploration.

"No one says you have to be an actress."

Chase paused. "I thought Con hired you to get me insurable so I can do his film?"

"He did, but my job is to help you get better and become more productive. What you do once we're through is up to you."

She stilled. "Would you really call the cops?"

"I would have to. You are now my client and signed out of a court-ordered rehab center. My protocol is the same as the center's. I don't think you belong behind bars, but I follow the rules."

Chase looked over at where Spencer stood with the woman. He held the baby in his arms, cajoling the struggling toddler while her mother tried to take a picture of the two of them. Then she looked back at Olivia. "Fine. Okay."

Olivia nodded and then started walking back to her still-running car, grateful for Spencer distracting the mom with the phone. She felt Chase following her, thank goodness.

Spencer saw them out of the corner of his eye and handed the now-crying toddler back to her mother. The woman couldn't hold the kid, her food, and her phone, so she slid the phone back in her pocket.

"Oh my gosh, I can't believe that I got Sheridan's picture with *the* Spencer Rome. Me and my husband watch *The Hammer* every week. Can you tell me if he and Marcy English are going to hook up? I mean, I think she's perfect for the Hammer. Not Chastity. I hope they don't put you with her. She's—"

"Yeah, you know I can't reveal anything. I have a gag order in my contract, and they're serious about that stuff. But just so you know, I'm team Marcy. Don't tell anyone that, but it's true. Hey, the writers don't listen to me," he said, with an *oh well* shrug followed by a blinding smile. "Gotta run. Bye, Sheridan."

He jogged over and opened the door for Chase, giving her a pointed look. Then he opened the back door of Olivia's car and climbed inside. Leaning up between the two front seats, he looked at Olivia. "Let's roll."

She hadn't been prepared for Spencer Rome to climb into her back seat, so she hesitated.

"Um, like now, lady. She's quick with that phone," he said, sounding not so charming and way more demanding than she'd expected from a man who wore a silver unitard and made wisecracks laced with sexual innuendo on television.

Olivia hopped in and shifted into reverse, pulling smoothly out of the spot and speeding off without breaking the posted speed limit in the parking lot.

"Jesus, Chase, what the hell is going on? You call me and land me in this?" Spencer asked, leaning up between the seats, startling her.

"Uh, could you both please fasten your seat belts?" Olivia asked, clicking her belt into place and putting on her turn signal.

She felt the eye roll from the passenger beside her.

"I called you because I don't have my car. And besides, you're the kind of person I can count on," Chase said, pulling the seat belt across her torso. Spencer didn't follow her directive. He stayed put, and she could smell the scent of clean laundry and expensive cologne wafting from him. She wondered briefly who did his laundry. A girlfriend? A housekeeper? Or did he do it himself?

A car horn jolted her from her weird reverie. Olivia realized she'd been sitting at a green light. "Where am I going? Because your car is back there." She met his eyes in the rearview mirror. A flush crept up the back of her neck before she jerked her gaze back to the busy street.

Keep focused.

"I don't know. Pull in a parking lot or something. We just couldn't stay there with that lady wanting to film this whole . . . whatever this is," he said, gesturing with one hand.

Olivia spied a parking lot in front of a coffee shop and pulled into the lot where only a few empty cars were parked. She shifted into park and then shut the engine off.

Chase stared resolutely ahead, saying nothing, so Olivia turned in her seat and shook her head, trying to figure out what to do.

Spencer regarded her with suspicious eyes. He arched one eyebrow. "So? What next?"

Olivia extended her hand. "First, I should introduce myself. I'm Olivia Han, and I am currently responsible for Chase as of"—she glanced at her watch—"thirty-three minutes ago."

"Responsible how? And why did she call me if she had you?"

Exactly. Olivia knew she looked incompetent for letting Chase out of her sight. Her worst nightmare, even in front of someone who likely didn't know her or her reputation.

Chase glanced over the seat. "She's my new therapist who checked me out of Cedar Point. I'm sober already, so I decided to leave on my own. I don't need any more 'help.' I'm good."

Spencer studied Chase for a few seconds. "You sure? 'Cause someone who is running away from court-ordered rehab may not be good. You knew you'd get into trouble, so why did you do that?"

"Because," Chase said, turning her gaze outside the window.

"Because why? She just said that you'd go to jail if you didn't go with her, so why would you drag me into this?" The boyish *aw, shucks* was gone. Spencer sounded annoyed, as he should have been.

"You weren't going to get in trouble," Chase scoffed, flipping down the visor and sliding open the mirror. She frowned at her reflection. "And why do you think I left? No one wants to be in rehab. I had to get out of there."

Spencer's eyes met Olivia's in the rearview mirror. She could see aggravation in those baby blues. Goodness, his eyes were pretty. Robin's-egg blue. Or maybe California-sky blue. Just . . . whoa.

Olivia cleared her throat. "Okay, so I'm going to drop you back at your vehicle, and then I'll drive Chase back to the rehab center, get her checked in, and this will be a blip on all of our radars. Something to forget about."

Chase flipped the mirror up. "Wait, I thought I was going with you."

"After this stunt? No. I can't trust you not to bolt again, and frankly, I did this as a favor to Conrad, and I'm about all out of favors. You can go back to Cedar Point and forget you ever met me." Olivia meant it. She didn't want to deal with theatrics, search and rescue, or whatever else this drama mama intended to bring her way. She had too much else to attend to in her life—namely, a book breathing down her neck—to take on this kind of trouble.

Chase looked at her and then back at Spencer. "I don't want to go back to Cedar Point. I won't leave until I finish your program. I promise."

"Yeah, well, you already broke the agreement you signed," Olivia said, putting the car into reverse.

"No, I didn't sign it. I looked at it and pretended to sign it, shoved it in the folder, and handed it back to that dragon at the front desk. See? Technically, I didn't violate your agreement."

Olivia shook her head. She wasn't even responsible for this bit of baggage? Made it a ton easier to drop Chase at Cedar Point and then get back to her own life. "Good. That makes everything easier when I take you back."

Spencer pressed a hand between them. "Let's all calm down. How about I go inside and get us a few coffees? While I'm gone, you two sit and think about what will be best for Chase. I'm assuming you're a therapist, and they always want what is best for their patients, even their 'almost' patients. A round of lattes will help us all feel better. I know it will help me, because I had just gotten up when Chase called. I'm caffeine deficient at present."

Olivia glanced at the dashboard clock: 12:47 p.m.

What adult got up that late?

"Fine. Make mine nonfat, no whip, soy milk if they have it," Chase said, picking at her fingernails. Bright-pink flecks clung to her nails where Chase had likely picked off the rest of the polish over the last few weeks.

"Just black coffee for me," said Olivia. She'd toss Spencer a bone and let him think she could be swayed.

"Got it," he said, hopping out and starting toward the coffee shop. Halfway there, he pivoted and came back, tapping on the window.

Olivia rolled it down.

"Uh, I don't have any money. My wallet's in my truck."

"Oh, for heaven's sake," Olivia said, pushing Chase's leg aside and grabbing her purse. She found a twenty-dollar bill and handed it to Spencer. "That should cover it. If not, just use your dimples."

He showed those pretty things to her. "Thanks, Mom."

It was a joke. She knew that. Still, something ugly pricked at her. So she was responsible, dressed conservatively, and drove a Volvo. And had no social life. And two cats. Whatever. She was not a stereotype. She was a successful woman who had chosen to live her life the way she wished. She wanted to shout that little nugget at the too-pretty actor who slept until noon and made his living leaping around in a cape and leotard, but instead she hit the button to roll up her window.

For a few seconds, neither she nor Chase said anything.

They watched as Spencer walked across the parking lot and opened the door for someone coming out balancing a holder with four coffees. Thankfully, the woman didn't actually glance at who was holding the door. The Hammer didn't even bother to put on mirrored sunglasses like all the other celebrities around town and was easily recognizable.

"So . . . are you going to let me sign the papers and go with you to the beach house or not?" Chase asked, staring at the air-conditioning vent.

"I don't think it's going to work. I understand you're frustrated with your situation, but I don't work with people who are still running from their problems."

"Look, don't be offended. I needed to get out of there. I couldn't breathe."

"You *were* getting out. I was giving you an opportunity—"

"People are always giving me opportunities, lady. But they always want something in return. You're no different. You're getting paid— probably a lot—to get me to a workable state. People don't help other people without something in return. I'm sure you'll want me to vouch for your stupid life coaching or whatever this thing is. You'll want to put me on a pamphlet saying 'Olivia helped me see where I went wrong, and now I'm completely happy in my life. I'm living my best life now. Woo-hoo.'"

"Yeah . . . um, no. I don't have pamphlets or testimonials. So relax." Olivia inhaled deeply and held it for five seconds before releasing the breath slowly, trying to center herself and control the irritation uncoiling inside of her. "But you're right—I'm getting paid. And paying back a favor to an old friend. Honestly, I didn't want to work with you, but Conrad reminded me everyone is redeemable."

Chase snorted.

"I know. Practical people like you and me understand that some people don't want to be better. They don't want to be happy. They like punishing themselves and the people around them."

"You're implying I'm hopeless?"

"No. I don't know you well enough to make that decision. Really, my 'life coaching' isn't about fixing people. It's about knocking down ruins and building from a new place. You have to own those ruins, though. You have to recognize who you once were and why you became that way before you can build a new life."

Olivia paused and realized she was likely wasting her breath. "But I don't have to sell myself to you. I'm taking you back to Cedar Point. You can resume your treatment, get out, promise yourself that you will stay clean and healthy, and go right back in a few months. Or to jail. Depends on if you kill anyone in your next car accident." She punched the volume on the stereo, and Michael Bublé crooning about something sappy surrounded them.

She could feel Chase's anger, but she ignored it. Instead she tapped her fingernails on the steering wheel and studied the glass door Spencer had disappeared through, willing him to come back and let her end this stupid debacle. She wanted to go home, make a pot of tea, and watch, well, not *The Hammer*. She had recorded the television series but hadn't watched it yet.

She felt Chase studying her.

"What?" Olivia asked, not liking the perusal. She had lines in her forehead that likely needed Botox. She'd get it if she weren't so afraid of needles. And she couldn't remember if she'd tweezed her eyebrows that morning.

"I already know why I'm the way I am. When I was thirteen, my dad let one of his friends have sex with me."

CHAPTER FIVE

Chase knew she had said those words too casually, probably because to say them the way they felt inside her would reveal too much. Telling someone you had sex with a forty-year-old man when you were barely a teenager was akin to lifting one's shirt and showing that you were wired with explosives.

Made the mouth dry, and the soul tremble.

Chase had never uttered those words out loud before. Not ever. Not to her mother. Not to any of her dozens of therapists. Not even to a close friend. That moldering rot had stayed inside her, locked down, her own "precious" that had turned her into a feverish Gollum hiding her wound from the world. She'd kept what had happened all to herself because her father had told her that if she told what had happened, everyone would think she was a whore, that she'd asked for it. Logically, she knew that wasn't true, but the haunted place deep inside her didn't recognize logic. Instead it bowed to fear and loathing.

Olivia jerked her head toward Chase, her expression horrified before she masked it with her noncommittal therapist stare. Chase felt a slight flutter of victory at breaking through Olivia's control.

"What? You were . . . what?" Olivia stammered.

Chase shrugged and then turned toward the window and stared out at the sign for the coffee shop. Common Grounds. Very California sounding. But the font didn't match the business name. They'd used an Old English font.

"Chase, look at me," Olivia said, touching her forearm gently. "What do you mean you were *thirteen*?"

Chase brushed Olivia's hand away. "Forget I said anything about it. Guess I thought you should know that I am self-aware. I've read a lot of books on childhood sexual abuse. I know why I keep fucking up, so that work is already done."

Silence sat like a fat slug between them—just icky and bloated. Chase was cool with not talking because, truthfully, she was still grappling with the fact that she'd admitted to losing her virginity to Peter Rinduso, a bit character actor. And that she'd done so to a therapist she hardly knew made it all the worse.

Yeah, Chase needed a moment's respite as the inappropriate thrill of shocking Olivia faded, leaving her with a shit ton of ugliness flooding her soul. She hated thinking about stupid Peter . . . about the way he'd tasted like cigarettes and Beefeater. How he'd tried to flirt with a thirteen-year-old. How he'd jabbed his fingers inside her, telling her she'd like it if she just relaxed. Sometimes she had nightmares about that night. The scenes that ripped through her head were tinged with blood and always ended with brains splattered on a wall. Freud would have said that reflected her sanity being broken apart by effing Peter Rinduso throwing his used condom at her after she'd screamed for her father to help her.

Her father hadn't come to her rescue like a normal dad would have. In fact, when she'd finally emerged from the guest room, tears staining her face, her daddy had winked at her like it was their little secret, and then he'd made her a drink with real alcohol in it. She'd drunk it all down because she wanted to erase Peter's grunts in her ear and the way he'd bruised her hips with his fingers.

She guessed the only silver lining was that Peter had used a condom and she hadn't gotten pregnant or syphilis.

"Chase, that's not a conversational comment. That's a nuclear bomb you just tossed at me."

"No shit," Chase said, trying to sound breezy, like she didn't care that she'd just revealed something she'd planned to never, ever, in a million years tell someone. She'd have the nightmares tonight. She just knew it.

"That's your response? To shrug it off?" Olivia sounded almost angry, like now she was knee-deep in Chase's psychological bullshit and didn't have a surefire way to get out.

"Who's shrugging, Olivia?" Chase refused to look at the woman who she'd poked with a really sharp stick. She knew she hadn't pulled herself together enough to surrender her current position. If she looked at Olivia, the woman might see the regret. Might see the pain she crumpled up and swallowed so no one else could read it.

The glass door opened, drawing Chase's attention, and Spencer emerged, balancing a cardboard container. He hadn't gotten her what she'd asked for, because he knew what she really wanted. They'd worked on *High School High*, *Bring It Back*, and *Prom Queen Switch* together back in the day. They'd remained friends, even though he had, admittedly, distanced himself from the disaster that was her life. Still, she knew she could count on Spence when she really needed him, which is why she'd called him and not one of her sycophants. They shared that bond—one of growing up under the microscope in the paper-thin Hollywood world, a tenuous place that could collapse with just one punch.

Spencer waved farewell to a group of boys accompanied by a mom who was already tapping on her phone as she tried to wrangle them into her minivan. No doubt the Hammer had taken a few pictures with his fans. She had to admit that Spencer was really good at being a movie star. He took selfies with fans, signed body parts, and looked like he actually enjoyed interacting with the people who always wanted something from him.

Olivia looked annoyed that Spencer was about to interrupt their nonconversation.

Spencer slung open the back door. "Hope you two have settled down, because I got double espresso shots." He handed the cardboard container to Chase so he could fold his frame into the back seat.

She spotted the whipped cream confection she'd always requested on set. He'd even gotten her sprinkles. Something warm curled inside her, crowding out the blackness that ebbed and flowed. Spencer was a good friend.

"Doesn't matter now. Olivia's taking me back to rehab."

Olivia stared straight ahead, her knuckles white against the wood grain steering wheel.

Spencer closed the door. "Doodlebug, I think you should stay with Olivia. She's the right person to help you get back on your feet. She came after you, didn't she?"

"What do you know?" Chase said, rolling her eyes. "Do you think she's going to do anything that any other therapist hasn't already tried? I know why I do what I do. I just can't seem to stop saying *To hell with it* and chucking all my good intentions. I think that's the definition of *hopeless*. Is that it, Ms. Han? That hopeless part?"

Olivia's hands merely tightened.

"Here's your coffee, Shrink," Chase said, pulling the cup from the holder and waggling it in the air near Olivia's face. "Spencer, I'm assuming this tea is yours. God, you're such an old lady."

"No, I'm not. Dudes like tea," he said, plucking the cup with the dangling tea tag from the container. "Don't hate 'cause I'm confident in my masculinity. Wearing tights every day does that to a guy."

The smile popped up on Chase's face before she could stop it. She loved Spence. He could charm the bloomers off a maiden aunt. Total bee's knees of a guy. Strange that she'd never been interested in him romantically. They'd been friends, almost family for a time, but she'd never seen him in a romantic light. Couldn't imagine even kissing his sexy lips for more than a friendly peck. If that.

Olivia still hadn't taken her coffee, so Chase set it in the cupholder and took a sip of her frothy confection.

Total heaven.

Spencer clicked himself into the back seat. "Um, so are we just gonna sit here? I have to meet my trainer in an hour, so . . ."

Without a word, Olivia shifted the car into reverse and backed out.

For the next few minutes, while Chase slurped her decadent coffee whip and Olivia maneuvered around the busy street, no one said a word.

Chase didn't want to go back to Cedar Point, but she wasn't sure she wanted to go with Olivia. For one thing, she didn't like the woman. She'd never cared for people like Olivia—people who thought they could fix other people. She'd learned that if she looked closely enough at the "fixers'" lives, they were even more screwed up than her own. If she were a betting woman—and let's face it, she was—she'd put down a couple hundred that Olivia Han was as emotionally wrecked as she was. But the most important reason she wasn't sure she should go with Olivia, if she were offering, was how easily she'd allowed her secret to spill out.

"Which car is yours?" Olivia asked, lifting her eyes to the rearview mirror so she could see Spencer. Chase caught the faint flush on Olivia's high cheekbones. So the ice princess wasn't unaware of the Hammer's obvious charms. Interesting.

Or not. Everyone thought Spencer was the cat's meow.

"Right there. The navy Bronco." Spencer pointed out a vintage jacked-up dinosaur that looked like something a farm boy might drive, splashing through rutted roads and pastures. So apropos for Spencer.

No wonder she hadn't been able to open the gleaming Mercedes coupe she'd tried to climb into earlier. Trust Spencer to be ironic with his driving choice.

"That's your, uh, truck?" Olivia asked, making a confused face.

"She's a beaut, isn't she? Got her last year. She's got a new custom engine, and I had her reupholstered with the softest gray leather. Feels like you're ass deep in a cloud. I thought about dumping the bench seat up front, but that didn't seem fair to a piece of history like that. Plus, I might want a California cutie to snuggle up next to me."

"Lord," Chase breathed, rolling her eyes again.

"So?" Spencer asked as Olivia put the car into park. Chase watched him in the mirror. "You going to take Chase and patch her up? She could use a friend. You look like you could be a good friend, since you came after her and didn't call the police."

Olivia flinched. "I'm not a friend. I'm a life coach and therapist."

Spencer's pretty blue eyes narrowed. "Oh, I see. Total professional. Yeah, I get that. So maybe Chase is right—you won't be able to help her."

"Why do you say that?" Olivia jerked her chin up and glared at Spencer in the mirror.

"Well, I can tell a lot about how a person responds to particular statements."

That seemed to flabbergast Olivia. Chase nearly laughed, because Spencer was an enigma, one of those guys who seemed like one thing on the surface but whose layers played havoc with those who had expectations. Often people didn't know how to take him, uncertain whether what he said was a joke or what he truly believed.

"What was wrong with my response?" Olivia demanded.

"I'll leave you to figure that out. Catch you later, June bug," Spencer said, leaning up and brushing Chase's cheek with a kiss. "Take care, okay?"

"Thanks for coming for me. You're a real hero."

Spencer snorted and then climbed out, leaving a whiff of cologne and an emptiness that couldn't be explained. He felt like her only friend, and he was bailing. "Best wishes, Olivia. You need me to send you the money for the coffees? Happy to reimburse."

"Oh, that's not necessary," Olivia said.

"Cool," Spencer said, slamming the door shut.

They watched as Spencer jogged loose limbed toward the Bronco, fishing his keys out of his pocket so he could manually unlock the vehicle.

Olivia's gaze remained on him as he climbed in.

"So are we going, or what?" Chase asked, licking the whipped cream off the lid. Damn, that stuff was good.

"Oh, so he doesn't think I'm the right person," Olivia said under her breath as she put the car into gear. "What does he know? What does anyone know?"

"You know you're talking out loud, right?"

Olivia made a frowny face and buttoned her lips.

Gone was the calm therapist with the placid demeanor, and in her place was a perturbed woman. Chase had to admit this Olivia was much more interesting.

"Can we go through the In-N-Out before you take me back to Cedar Point? The food at rehab blows."

Olivia jerked her attention to Chase. "Do you have any money?"

She hadn't thought about that. "Uh, maybe you can loan me ten bucks?"

"That's not how life works. You don't just get things because you want them. You can't depend on others to rescue you because you're a celebrity."

Okay, so Olivia had gone back to being a bitch. "Is that one of your tenets for—what's your program called?"

Olivia clenched her jaw. "It's called Square One for many reasons, and you are correct that learning to rely on yourself instead of others is a basic principle. In fact, that's pretty basic to being a decent person."

"Huh, I never knew," Chase drawled, aiming the vent away from her. The air-conditioning blew like an arctic storm, making goose pimples blanket her legs. Ice princess indeed. "So I'm guessing that's a no on the burger and fries?"

"You catch on quick."

Chase shrugged and turned her attention toward the buildings rushing by them. Wasn't a total loss of a morning. She'd gotten to see Spencer, a guy who had always made her feel somewhat normal, and she'd gotten a coffee latte whip with sprinkles. Plus, she'd missed group therapy.

Several minutes later, Cedar Point appeared, a glass-and-wood monstrosity that repimpled her legs with goose bumps. Olivia pulled through the horseshoe drive to the covered entrance and put her car into park. The security guard grabbed a clipboard from his office, which opened to the drive, and started their way.

"Well, it's been interesting," Chase said, unbuckling her seat belt.

"Is that what you call it?" Olivia muttered, rolling down her window.

Chase grinned, opening the door and standing. "Sure. You got to meet the Hammer and spend time with *moi*. I'm always a good time. Ask anyone."

"Including your dad's friend?"

It was as if a wrecking ball came out of nowhere and slammed into Chase. The seat belt buckle flew from her hand, snapping back into place. She'd just stepped onto a slight incline leading to the front door and lost her balance, crashing into the side of the car, her back striking so hard her breath whooshed from her body. She slid back into the car seat, unable to breathe.

For a moment she knew how falling through ice into a winter pond felt. Her head went under, her body froze, and her mouth gaped. She'd felt this way once when she'd fallen off the monkey bars. Wind knocked out of her.

Blinking rapidly, she turned and clutched the dashboard, trying to suck in air but failing.

"Chase?" Olivia asked.

She couldn't answer.

"Chase?" Olivia asked again, her voice rising an octave.

Chase looked at Olivia and tried to remember how to breathe. She couldn't do it. The air wouldn't go in.

Olivia grabbed her arm and pulled her back fully into the seat. Then she set her hand on Chase's back, and with the other, she bent Chase forward until her chest brushed her knees. "It's okay, Chase. Let your body work. Draw in air. Breathe through your nose."

Finally, Chase was able to fill her lungs with air. "Oh God."

Olivia rubbed her back, which made Chase want to punch her. Olivia was the one who'd done this to her, and now she wanted to act like she gave a shit? Chase pulled air into her lungs and huffed it out. "Stop it. Don't touch me."

Olivia stopped patting her like a damned dog. "I shouldn't have said that. That wasn't well done of me."

"Everything okay here, ma'am?" The security guard leaned toward the car, tucking his clipboard to his side. Chase knew he was staring at her trying to breathe. Tears stung her eyes.

"Yeah, we're fine," Olivia said, trying to smile at "Lenny," who now looked super concerned.

"She don't look fine."

"Her coffee went down the wrong pipe. She's good now," Olivia said, looking back at Chase. "Right?"

Chase didn't say anything at Olivia's lie. She didn't trust herself to say anything. What Olivia had done had been mean. So effing mean. Even if she'd apologized.

"Okay, so how can I help you ladies?" Lenny asked, not looking wholly convinced that Chase was okay.

"Actually, we were looking for an In-N-Out Burger," Olivia said, giving him a sheepish look. "My navigation led us here. Stupid thing is always messing up."

"You have to download updates," Lenny said, finally settling into a less alarmed demeanor. "But if you turn around and go back about a half mile, you'll see Sunnyvale Drive. There's one right on the corner. Eat there all the time myself."

"Thank you so much. You're so kind." Olivia rolled up the window and put the car into gear.

"What the hell are you doing?" Chase asked.

Olivia looked over at her. "Close the door. Buckle up."

"No way."

"Shut the door," Olivia commanded.

Chase reached out and shut the door, unsure that she should, but Olivia was already pulling away. "What are you doing?"

"Getting you an In-N-Out burger and fries," Olivia said, turning out of the rehab center's parking lot, heading toward the direction Lenny had pointed. "And then I'm taking you to Malibu."

"But—"

"You signed the contract. You're now a client of Square One."

"I didn't sign it."

"You will."

Chase grabbed the buckle for the seat belt and slowly pulled it across her lap, trying to figure out if she wanted to go with Olivia or not. The woman played dirty, but then again, so had Chase when she'd told her about her dad's friend Peter. She was mad at Olivia for what she'd done, but at the same time, she thought given the same circumstances, Chase might have done the same thing. It had caused a reaction, that was for damned sure.

Olivia stopped at a red light and turned to Chase. "You've never told anyone about being raped, have you?"

Rape sounded like the wrong word. So hard. So ugly. Chase hadn't really thought about it as rape because her father had essentially given Peter permission. But it had been rape. She'd been a child, and it didn't matter that she'd matured early and looked more like a woman than a girl. Peter had raped her, and her father had let it happen.

Chase stared at Olivia. "Why do you think that I've never told anyone?"

"Have you?"

Chase turned back, directing her attention to the light that had just turned green. A horn sounded behind them.

Olivia didn't move.

"It's green. Go."

"Chase?" Olivia said, her voice soft.

"Fine. No. I never told anyone. Jesus." Chase folded her arms and clenched her jaw. "Just take me back to Cedar Point. I didn't sign that contract. I told you that."

"You'll sign it," Olivia said again, pulling forward after the car whipped around her, the driver giving her the finger.

"Why?"

"Because."

"That's not a reason."

"Well, you seem to think so," Olivia said, turning the radio on and heading toward Malibu. "We're doing this thing. You made sure of that."

CHAPTER SIX

Two weeks later

Olivia bent and eased her sandals from her feet, checking that the area around her was free of glass or sharp shells. The sand on this stretch of the beach usually lacked sharp objects that would send her to the emergency room. That's what one got with private-access beachfront. Still, she'd seen enough social media shares of simple cuts going from benign redness around a wound to death within twenty-four hours. She wasn't quite ready to die yet. Especially from flesh-eating bacteria.

Not when she had such a Herculean task in front of her.

She straightened and searched the beach for Chase. Today was the last day of the actress's sobriety treatment, and Chase had received a stamp from Rick, her company's top sobriety counselor, indicating that she was physically and mentally ready to move to the next phase of the Square One program, where Chase would hopefully construct solid ground on which to build her overall recovery. Achieving sobriety and returning to a healthy physical regimen was necessary before they could begin the process of unearthing destructive behavior and learning why, how, and when triggers diverted a person's intentions. Olivia knew that

Chase's choices to date were a result of something deeper and that she'd glimpsed what had damaged the actress while they'd been parked in the driveway of the rehab center.

Over the past couple of weeks, Olivia had become more determined to dig beneath the brittle armor Chase had carefully put back in place after she signed the contract and settled into the Malibu house. Olivia was fairly certain she could help the actress sort through the betrayal from her father, the sexual trauma, and the escape she sought through addiction, but she'd given Chase a reprieve while Rick focused on Chase getting physically healthy. Olivia would have time to help Chase grieve the past, come into conflict with what had happened to her, and then rewrite a new story.

Yes, Olivia was prepared to help Chase because she understood too well all the emotions that battered the actress.

If only she had had a plan years ago when Marley had suffered through addiction. But she hadn't. Olivia had been in college, only a junior when Marley had started casually smoking weed and drinking too much. Olivia had chalked it up to being a young adult, but Marley had moved on to other drugs—pills and heroin.

Olivia had started college thinking she'd follow in her father's footsteps, molding young minds in the classroom, but decided after Marley's first near overdose that she could be better used helping others examine their lives, acknowledge their pasts, and then build, change, and grow. Marley had set her on the path she was on, and yeah, she had her own issues she liked to avoid. Her career had become the center of her life, taking precedence over her personal life. Her mistakes defined her like any other person, and likewise, she avoided the things that hurt, the people who reminded her of what she could have changed.

Here lately Olivia flirted with . . . not really depression, but bouts of discontent. She wondered if she'd let her own ugly wounds go unattended for too long. Maybe that's why she'd pulled away from Cedar Point with Chase next to her.

She shielded her eyes and scanned the beach for Chase, wishing she'd grabbed her sunglasses.

"Hey," said a voice behind her.

She'd heard that voice in her dreams, but it had been so long since she'd heard it in reality.

Olivia couldn't recall how long it had been since she'd seen Conrad, but turning to see him standing there in the flesh caused her stomach to wobble and her pulse to speed up. She would rather have had time to prepare herself for seeing him again.

"Con," she said, stilling her nerves and giving him a soft smile. "You startled me."

Conrad flashed those almost too white teeth. "Sorry. The waves are noisy."

An awkward pause hung between them, the only sound the crashing waves and the occasional screech of a seagull. Olivia felt an itch between her shoulders, that old familiar guilt, longing, sadness that had sat between them for too long.

"What brings you all the way out here?" she asked, suppressing the urge to smooth her hair and lick her lips. Conrad hadn't always made her nervous, but the man standing in front of her didn't look like the boy she'd hung out with in high school.

That Conrad Santos had also exuded energy, as evident in his constant motion, but he'd been unpolished and so rough around the edges one would likely get a splinter. Their teachers used to say it was fidgeting, but Olivia knew it was the result of his synapses constantly firing with absolute brilliance. The guy had too many genius ideas, too much to learn and do, too much of the world to conquer. All that drive had to have an outlet, so even when still, Conrad always tapped, ran his hands through his inky hair, his gaze fixed on the distance with a study of determination on his handsome face.

This Conrad standing beside her, one foot on the boardwalk, no longer fidgeted. He had a bit more polish than the energetic boy who'd not known which fork to use, who had looked beneath worn cushions for enough change to eat lunch each day, who had rummaged through thrift shops for jeans without stains.

"I had to come out this way for a meeting. Thought I would drop in and see how things are progressing." He squinted against the sun, shading his eyes with one hand. "Where's Chase?"

"I sent you a report a few days ago." She didn't like being checked up on.

At that, he looked at her, a knowing grin appearing. "That was a few days ago."

Olivia ripped her gaze from his lean, tanned body clad in cream linen trousers and a crimson shirt that most guys wouldn't touch but that seemed right on Con. No pinstripe or business blue for this guy. Classy and creative, Conrad Santos was a man everyone wanted a piece of. "She's out here somewhere, taking a walk."

"By herself?"

Once Olivia had gotten Chase to the Malibu house, she'd called Conrad to let him know the situation so he was aware Chase had bailed shortly after meeting Olivia. "She's completed the sobriety portion of the program, and though she's still not really sharing much with me, we've come to an understanding. Mostly, that I will call the police to come haul her away if she pulls any more shenanigans, so she always comes back."

Con raised his eyebrows. "You're trusting her?"

"Well, I can't handcuff her to me. I mean, I could, but showering would get awkward."

Conrad smiled at that, and she was reminded of the first time she'd met him.

It had been her freshman year of high school when she'd moved to a struggling school her educator parents had been recruited to help turn around. Her father had insisted his children attend the schools in the neighborhood where he'd be working as a principal. Not only that, but they would be selling their comfortable house in Bixby Knolls in Long Beach to move to Gardena, which bled into Compton, a place so different from all she'd known. Her father's concession to the family's complaining was to purchase a security system, a handgun, and two beanbags, which seemed to satisfy Marley, who'd cried for three days when she found out she was moving away from her best friend. Olivia hadn't been nearly as dramatic, or satisfied by something as stupid as beanbags for her room, but neither had she wanted to leave behind the window seat where she cuddled on the plush cushions, read her mother's stash of Georgette Heyer books, and sketched birds and flowers.

Suffice it to say, regardless of what the children wished, the Hancock family moved, and on a blistering morning in late September, Olivia set her old school uniform aside to squeeze into last year's jeans and walked begrudgingly through the doors of Elm Park High. She was well aware that it was a school with such poor scoring, high truancy, and increasing student arrests that the state had placed it on a list of proposed closures.

To say that an awkward, plump white girl was a fish out of water in that particular school would be the understatement of the decade—no, the century. Olivia stood out like a tampon in an elevator, because everyone looked at her, but no one was going to acknowledge her unexpected presence. Not even the teachers, whose eyes widened when she entered the room, pulling the class's attention her way. In the teachers' defense, they had their hands full. Her schedule, done at the last minute, had placed her in general classes rather than the advanced courses she was normally accustomed to, which meant she felt even more out of place among raucous students who didn't seem as concerned with academics as her former classmates.

Finally, in seventh period, a very frazzled-looking woman with three pencils shoved in her bun and glasses askew appeared at the door asking for Olivia to gather her things and come with her. Olivia had risen, and the woman had taken her by the elbow and steered her outside to the temporary buildings clumped into a circle.

"I know it doesn't look like much, but this is the brain trust," the woman who had introduced herself as Margaret Thomas said, gesturing at the sad little clustering. "Well, not officially, but that's what we teachers nicknamed it. The state was supposed to release funds for a new math-and-science building, but those disappeared—poof!—as they're wont to do. So we're left with this, but we don't have many qualifying students for AP courses, so here we are making do until we get the funding. *If* we get the funding."

Olivia had never seen advanced students shoved into temporary buildings. In most schools, they coddled the brightest with fancy science and computer labs. Her world had indeed been turned upside down.

"Okay, so this is your last period class," Ms. Thomas said, licking her fingers in that disgusting teacher manner and thumbing through papers that stuck up in disarray from her binder, "and here is your schedule. The highlighted classes are in the main building. That would be your foreign language—no honors or AP for Spanish—and your PE class, which is, of course, in the gymnasium. Oh, and film studies. That's also in the main building in the auditorium. Okay, then. Go ahead. Mr. Littman and biology await you."

She turned Olivia toward the weathered metal door, knocked, and shoved her forward. "A new one for you, John. Have fun."

The room smelled like sulfur and formaldehyde, and the diminutive man wearing an odd polka-dot shirt and weathered jeans looked only a few years older than her sister Neve, who was in her freshman year at USC.

"Oh, well then." The teacher adjusted his wire-rimmed glasses and gave a soft smile. "We're honored."

And of course, Olivia turned three shades of magenta.

Then as she stood there, nudged forward by Ms. Thomas's knee while everyone in the classroom stared at her, a boy wearing high-top

Converse tennis shoes, holding an old-fashioned camera, rose and buzzed around her.

Olivia had never been the kind of person who liked attention. In fact, she stood in the back for family pictures, dressed in the most discreet colors, and used a book as a shield. People didn't talk to kids who had their noses deep in books. That everyone was staring and some weird guy was filming her made panic rise inside her. Her cheeks burned, and tears flirted at the periphery of her vision.

The door shut behind her.

"Conrad, please stop circling our new victim, um, I meant student." Mr. Littman gave a goofy laugh, and the guy buzzing around her pressed a button and pulled the camera away. The student's face was lean, and he looked so intense that Olivia stepped back.

"The best capture is a natural one," the kid said, not looking at the teacher but keeping his brown eyes trained on Olivia. She shifted her gaze back from the goofy teacher to the creature watching her like a police detective interrogating a suspect.

"Con," Mr. Littman cajoled.

The boy shrugged one shoulder. "'If art is to nourish the roots of our culture, society must set the artist free to follow his vision wherever it takes him.' Or at least that's what Bobby Kennedy said. And if you want to ignore *him* . . . well . . ." Then the guy with the camera plopped into an open desk and crossed his long legs.

Good Lord. What kind of class was this?

"Sorry about that, Miss . . . I'm assuming Hancock? I read about your father in the last district newsletter. Sorry about Conrad. He's our resident director and has the camera attached at his hip. Or his hand, if we're being anatomically accurate."

Olivia didn't move. She didn't know what to say and wished she'd just stayed in the class where the teacher was crying in the corner while the students sat on the desks, listened to music with a lot of bad words in it, and screamed with laughter at the jokes one dude was telling. At least no one really paid attention to her in that class.

This class filmed her.

"Okay," she managed to say, bending and sliding into one of the nearby empty desks. She hoped she fit in it. The thing looked tiny. Like a leftover from an elementary school. "And it was John Kennedy who said that. Not Robert."

Why she'd added that she wasn't sure, but the weird boy who'd filmed her laughed and said, "That was a test to see who knew I was wrong. The new girl wins."

The rest of the class groaned as if this boy constantly tested them with just this sort of thing. There were only seven others in the class, a motley crew consisting of two other girls and five boys. All looked about as different from one another as possible—like the cast of a TV show. Olivia's mother didn't let them watch much cable, but Olivia had seen a few sitcoms at a friend's house. This class looked like one of those, replete with a few nerdy-looking kids, one tough guy who slumped and looked bored, a girl who was plucking her eyebrow in a compact mirror, and that intense know-it-all, Conrad.

"Okay, then," young Mr. Littman said, clapping his hands, "let's get back to the study guide, since the test will be Friday. I think a team approach would be good. Those who need to study the anatomy of the worm, well, Master Diego Wormfood is right over there in all his annelid glory."

"Or is that annelidical glory?" one of the guys said.

Mr. Littman actually giggled.

Olivia glanced over to the lab area and noted a foam tray with pins poking out. Something brown lay split upon it.

Gross.

The students pulled out notebooks, and Con leaned over to her. "What's your name, new girl?"

She turned and cast a worried glance at the teacher, who had started writing with chalk on the board, before looking back at the odd boy who wore torn jeans and a bleach-splashed T-shirt. She rarely talked to boys, so she still felt nervous, but his eyes were intelligent . . . warm . . . interested in her.

"Olivia."

"Okay, Livy. Be my partner."

And even though she'd been put off by his brashness, his assuming nature, his hunger to get exactly what he wanted, she had been his partner for the test on the worm. And they had remained the best of friends for all four years of high school. She'd gone to USC, like Neve, and Conrad had gone to a film school in NYC before deciding he liked sunshine and only the *idea* of wearing a parka. He'd come back to LA in the middle of his sophomore year, no longer thin and boyish. He'd grown into a man, and Olivia had fallen even harder for him. Not that he ever really knew it until that one weekend.

The weekend that had changed everything.

Now he stood, looking expectantly at her, a man who wore the success he'd earned like a crown set upon his brown curls. Beside them, waves rolled onto the beach, the whooshing ebb and flow a reminder of her own life . . . perhaps even Con's life, too. The sea giveth and it taketh away, the way it had the day she'd found her sister dead.

Conrad's stare jolted her back to the beach. What had he asked her? She couldn't remember, but he was staring at her expectantly. "What were we talking about?"

"Chase?"

Olivia ripped her gaze from Conrad and searched the beach. "Well, she's barefoot and has no phone, so she can't get too far."

"Maybe you wish she would. Then you could get on with writing your book and wouldn't have to see me."

Hurt tinged his voice, flooding her with guilt. She'd been avoiding seeing him. Surely he knew why. Or maybe he didn't. Conrad had wonderful traits, but he wasn't beyond being oblivious. After all, he'd never realized she'd been in love with him for most of her life. "The first part of that isn't totally untrue, but the fact is, I drove away from Cedar Point with Chase sitting next to me. It wasn't because she was some kind of challenge. I've passed up plenty of hard cases that would test my ability to pull a person from the darkness and give her the possibility of a new life."

"So why did you agree, beyond my asking you to? You had a good reason to scrap this when she ran away."

"Maybe it was because she didn't seem to care whether she went back to Cedar Point or came with me. That acceptance scared me. It was something I sometimes glimpsed in Marley's eyes. So I brought Chase here. And book or no, I'm stuck with her, and I'll finish the job."

"And the second part? Why do you avoid me all the time? We said we'd always be friends."

"What do you want me to say? You know why it's hard for me." Olivia fixed her gaze on the horizon. A boat jetted by, kicking up ocean, oblivious to the hurt that oozed from her. She didn't want to talk about why she ignored his calls. Why she'd never given him her private number at the office.

Conrad's sigh was deep enough for her to hear. "I miss you."

She couldn't help herself. She raised a hand to her chest as if she could hold in the pain. "Don't, Con. It's in the past."

"I know. Still."

She had to get back on track. Chase. That was what they had between them now. "Chase is physically healthy. Completely sober and detoxed. So the next phase addresses her spiritual and mental health. Time for me to get to work."

"To do what, exactly?"

The sea breeze whipped her hair into her face, and she wished she'd slept better the night before and worn mascara. She felt too vulnerable on every level. "Tear away her walls, mend her heart, and teach her how to be the best version of herself."

At that moment, she saw Chase out of the corner of her eye. Thank God. She did not want to continue the conversation with Conrad regarding their odd relationship.

The actress walked slowly toward them, too far away for her to see Chase's expression but close enough to read her body language. Reminded her of her younger sister so much.

Conrad, too, turned and watched as Chase approached. Though her demeanor still seemed belligerent, she looked much healthier than she had days ago. Her skin glowed from the daily walks on the beach, and her face seemed more relaxed and less tense. She wore her hair in a ponytail and no makeup, which made her look much younger than the pictures displayed in tabloids. Olivia had gone back and looked at Chase's life in news clippings, and the trail of excess in the photos showed a young woman nearing a hard crash. Maybe Olivia had gotten to her in time.

Or maybe not.

Chase stopped a few feet away from them and held up a shell. "Last one for my collection. Rick said I'm sober and healthy, so when do you want me to start, Con?"

"Actually, you're not done," Olivia said.

Chase snapped her head toward Olivia. "Uh, yeah, I am. I'm sober. I've done this a lot, ya know."

"Yeah, I read through your records, Chase. And correct me if I'm wrong, but every time you completed treatment, you found yourself back a few months later. This time you're doing it my way, and sobriety is only half of the equation to getting healthy."

"I answered all your stupid questions in the workbook. Aren't we going to do, like, outpatient therapy?"

"My kind of therapy is not outpatient, Chase."

Chase rolled her eyes. "You mean I have to stay here with you? How long?"

"Until I've determined you're ready to face the real world again."

Chase turned and hurled the shell toward the water, looking as much like a toddler as, well, a toddler.

Conrad watched all this with veiled amusement and perhaps a bit of alarm. But really, the man had to be used to tantrums and grandstanding. She'd seen the women he dated, and while she would never judge a book by its cover, she wasn't blind. His taste ran to young, complicated, and a little spoiled.

Which meant he had a large dating pool in Tinseltown.

"This is total bullshit. Con has a movie to make. When does it start? Next week? End of the month?" Chase advanced on Conrad, moving close to him as if that would put him on her side.

He took a step back, holding up a hand. "Hold on, Chase. There's been some delay on the shooting schedule, so just focus on getting yourself—"

"I'm fine. Can't you see that? Look at me. I've been doing yoga and eating stupid vegetables. I mean, that's what all this is for, right? I need to get back to my life. I need to get back to work. My mother's breathing down my neck, and we need to sell this place before we have to file bankruptcy. So please, for the love of God, let me move forward."

Olivia almost gave her a slow clap for her performance. If she'd sunk down on her knees, clasping the sand and proclaiming "God as my witness, I shall never be drunk again," Olivia might have. But her relationship with Chase was tenuous at best.

"You *will* move forward," Conrad said, slinging an arm around Chase in a brotherly fashion. "Come on, Chase, Livy is the best."

Chase gave her a withering look. "At what? Sucking the fun out of everything?"

That made Conrad laugh.

So that's what he thought of her? Of course he did. He'd always been the one who reached too close to the sun. And she'd been the one standing behind him holding the sunscreen.

"Olivia's fun. Sometimes," Conrad said, giving Olivia a wink.

Olivia gave him a flat look. "My job is not to be fun. My job is to help you change. To do that, we have to start at square one."

Chase snorted.

Olivia ignored her. "You're healthy. That's good. Because now we have to work on the other part. So pack your bags. We'll grab toiletries and necessities when we get to the cabin, but you'll need at least two weeks' worth of clothing. Oh, and bring a jacket."

Chase's hands fell to her side. "Wait, what do you mean pack? Why can't we stay here?"

"It's time for phase two. We pull out at one p.m." Olivia picked up the sandals she'd set aside, turned away from the beach, and started back toward the house.

"Wait a second!" Chase called behind her.

Olivia kept walking. She felt movement at her side, and Conrad fell into step beside her. "That was a dirty trick."

"It's not a trick. It's a necessity. Chase signed the contract. You paid the money. I'm going to deliver an insurable actress."

"Do you really have to leave LA to help her throat-punch her demons? Lorna isn't really on board with Chase going off into the wild," Conrad said.

Olivia glanced at him. "Lorna is not my concern. Chase is. And I have to take her from here so she can see what the real world is like, so she can see who she really is. She can't do that here, in a plastic world where nothing is real. Do you know that she's twenty-five years old and twenty-five percent of her body is not her own? And this . . . it's all so far beyond what a normal person experiences." She waved at the huge glass-and-concrete beach house worth millions, then spun around to include the Hollywood Hills.

"So where are you going to show her the real world? You going to take her back to our old hood? Lots of real there."

"No, I'm taking her to the cabin I just inherited from my grandparents. In Cotter's Creek."

"I forgot about that place. You loved your summers there. You always said that it was the place you knew yourself best."

Olivia smiled. "Which is why I'm taking Chase there."

CHAPTER SEVEN

Chase threw her Louis Vuitton duffel bag into Olivia's stupid grandma mobile and climbed into the front seat. "This is so ridiculous."

Olivia adjusted the air-conditioning vent, totally unfazed by Chase's irritation. "I'm sure you think so, but in truth, it's very much part of the Square One process. In your case, it's important to remove you from the world you know. Think of it as research for acting. Many actors do just this sort of thing in preparation for a role, but instead of trying to create a character, I want you to focus on digging beneath the one you've created for yourself to the very essence of who you are. It's time to strip away facades, learned behaviors, and experiences that crippled you, to see who you are at your very core. If you don't like who that person is, we'll work from there. It's a process."

"Sounds awesome," Chase drawled as Olivia shifted the car into reverse and backed out of the driveway. The rolling ocean and hazy horizon beyond the beach house disappeared as the agave and rock in front of the house took its place. The FOR SALE sign swayed in the sea breeze, and for a moment, Chase felt something she'd not felt in a long time—a sense of regret. Or perhaps it was more a longing to stay in this place.

Chase had never wanted to go to the beach house much before because her tony apartment was in the middle of the action, but she'd found she enjoyed being in Malibu more than she'd expected. When Olivia had first brought her there, the space felt unfamiliar, overshadowed by the memory of the night she'd gotten trashed and slept with that guy. She was blinded to the beauty of the exclusive beach house in one of the most sought-after communities. Only the huge asking price Lorna refused to budge on had kept the house on the market. But at that moment, pulling away from the house, Chase didn't want to sell this place where she'd found a slice of peace, even though the money from the sale would give her reprieve. Or rather give Lorna reprieve from the creditors. Her mother had made most of the financial decisions. Chase still didn't know how much money she did or didn't have. That was another mistake she'd made.

At first, Chase had disliked staying in the house with Olivia and Rick, mostly because they were insistent on a routine, and Chase didn't do schedules. Olivia liked to pull out that damn contract Chase had signed and wave it every time Chase argued with the "sobriety itinerary" and tried to toss the covers over her head or skip dinner. Chase's days started bright and early with yoga and a healthy breakfast, which Chase complained about, but then after a few days didn't really mind so much. Olivia led the yoga, and though Chase still didn't like the woman, she could admit she was good at the practice.

Over the past days, Chase had begun to appreciate not only the aesthetic beauty of the house but the healing power of the waves and warm sand. Since she was still without her phone, she spent several hours each afternoon walking the beach, reading books the decorator had placed on the shelves, and practicing the meditation she'd learned from a yogi several years before. The healthy foods Rick prepared, paired with the first good sleep she'd had in ages, had given her skin a glow and her eyes a less haunted look. She was sober, but also more in tune with her health than she'd been in years.

"So where are we going to find the real me?" Chase finally asked.

Olivia lowered the volume of the radio. The woman listened to classical music all the time. Did she actually like Chopin and Beethoven, or was it an affectation? Chase wasn't sure, because though she'd spent mind-numbing time with Olivia, they had only talked about Chase and her problems. And that was always so fun.

"My grandparents lived in a small town called Cotter's Creek. It's about eight hours north of here near Mount Larsen. It's fairly remote, but a lovely little town nestled in the foothills about eighty or so miles to the Oregon border."

"We're going to your *grandparents'* house?" Chase was so not down with that. She didn't like old people. Or Oregon.

Olivia's mouth twitched before she assumed her normal in-control look. "My grandfather passed away six months ago, and the property belongs to me now. He owned a logging business and has a house on the edge of Cotter's Creek."

Chase had overheard Olivia say "cabin" to Conrad, but if her relative had owned a logging company, the place was likely similar to the lodge she'd stayed at in Jackson Hole a few years back. She'd loved the rustic vibe and the hot tub. Mostly because she'd been in it a lot with Tucker Vance, lead guitarist for Suede. Tucker was so hot and such a bad boy, which was the attraction, of course. As a person he was a bit of a douche. She missed the hot tub more than she missed him.

Still, Cotter's Creek sounded like Hicksville. Foothills? Small town? What in the hell were they going to do there? Couldn't she find her true self in Malibu? She liked her bedroom with its clean lines and good sheets, and the impersonal bathroom now felt like it belonged to her, which of course it did. But with the bath salts and good conditioner that made her hair silky sitting in the shower, it felt like a home. She didn't need to go to Cotter's Creek to learn whatever it was Olivia thought she was going to teach her. Which was probably a bunch of made-up life coach crap.

"I'm hungry. Are we going to stop for lunch?" Chase asked, changing the subject since Olivia didn't seem to care what she wanted regarding their location for this Square One bullshit.

This is your fault, moron.

She shouldn't have signed the contract that Olivia had printed off as soon as they'd arrived at the beach house. Chase could have stayed at Cedar Point if she'd insisted. Olivia couldn't kidnap her. If she'd just toughed it out at Cedar Point for a few more weeks, she would have been back at her apartment, moving on with her life.

But what life would that be?

Ugh, she hated the voice that popped up at the absolute worst time. Miss Voice of Reality should have made an appearance before she snorted that line off the glass-top coffee table and then had sex with Jordan "Say my name" Cokehead. She could have also used it that day in Olivia's car when she blurted out that nugget about her father and Peter Rinduso. But no, reason never showed up when it should.

"There's this little gas station that sells the best burgers. I don't usually indulge in red meat, but it's really hard for me to turn down a Foghat burger." Olivia actually looked to be in a good mood. Maybe burgers did that for her.

"I thought you were a vegetarian or something."

"No; I do, however, try to stick to a plant-based diet. Good health is important to me," Olivia said, turning the radio back up.

"Can we listen to something that doesn't feature a cello?"

"You don't like classical music?" Olivia asked.

"Um, sure, but I like other kinds of music, too. We've been listening to this for, like, thirty minutes." Chase tried to sound agreeable.

"How about you have the next thirty minutes to listen to what you want," Olivia said, gesturing to the radio.

Feeling victorious, Chase turned the dial. "Wait. You don't have satellite radio?"

"No."

Weirdo.

"Well, do you have Bluetooth or something? Like on your phone?"

Olivia narrowed her eyes suspiciously but used her thumb to open the home screen and handed her cell phone over to Chase.

Chase downloaded the Spotify app, entered her own account info, and synced to the radio. Since she doubted Olivia would care much for the metal or rap she preferred, she very nicely put on her eighties rock playlist. Journey came on crooning about "open arms," and Chase settled back, tugging on Chanel sunglasses and cracking the window so a breeze came through.

Olivia may have frowned at the window going down, but Chase didn't acknowledge her grinchy look. The air felt nice on her skin.

After a few hours of napping and then staring out the window, Chase turned to Olivia. "Okay, so since I have to go to your pawpaw's house and Rick is no longer here to talk about *Dancing with the Stars* and Adam . . . I mean, how much did we really need to know about Adam Levine? God, he wouldn't shut up."

Olivia actually smiled. "He seems to be a big fan."

"Like a stalker or something. So anyway, let's play twenty questions."

"Like the game twenty questions?"

Chase had never gone on family trips, but she'd once played in a movie where they had to pretend to go camping. The scene called for the two kids to play twenty questions in order to get their respective parents who hated each other to actually talk to one another. It was a stupid movie, but she remembered liking the idea of a road trip. "Yeah, like I ask you questions and you have to either answer them truthfully or I can dare you to do something crazy."

"That's not twenty questions. That's truth or dare," Olivia said, turning onto another highway that was steadily taking them north. They'd left the city behind, and the air felt cleaner. To Chase, it felt like a different world, one she knew existed but had hardly ever ventured out to experience.

"So truth or dare, then. Whatever," Chase said.

"I don't think I want to play that game with you." Olivia eyed the navigation screen and clicked something on her dash.

"Oh, come on. We still have a few hours, right? This is my first real girls' trip. Or rather first girls' trip with someone I'm not paying to fly with me to Paris or something."

"This isn't a girls' trip."

Boom. Something in Olivia's quick refusal of that term hurt. Felt like rejection. Okay, yeah, she knew she and Olivia weren't friends, but did the woman have to be such a bitch about everything? "Right. I know. Just pretending for a few minutes that we're normal people."

At that, Olivia glanced at her, and Chase knew that Olivia knew how she'd sounded. "Fine. As long as your dares are not dangerous. I'm not doing something dangerous."

"Fair enough." Chase turned up the radio. "Girls Just Want to Have Fun" had just come on. Maybe Olivia would get the hint and lighten up. "I go first. Truth or dare?"

Olivia sighed. "Truth."

"You're scared of my dares, aren't you?"

"That would be correct."

Chase laughed. "Okay, have you ever faked an orgasm?"

Olivia made a face. "Seriously?"

"You have to tell the truth."

Olivia rolled her eyes. "Fine. I have faked an orgasm."

"I knew it," Chase said, folding her arms and settling back. She didn't know why this pleased her. She supposed she wanted Olivia to be, like, an actual human.

"Okay, my turn." Olivia glanced over at her, and something in her perusal caused a flicker of alarm. "Have *you* ever faked an orgasm?"

"Um, yeah, like, every time."

Olivia pressed her lips together and then said, "Really. Huh."

"What do you mean by that? Don't most women fake orgasms?"

"Some do. I guess both you and I have, but it's interesting you said *every* time. Have you not had an orgasm before?" Olivia looked at her with something akin to concern. Which made Chase want to climb from the car. While it was moving.

"Um, it's not your turn." Chase knew where this was going, and she wasn't hitching a ride on that bus. Olivia was a therapist, which meant she liked to dig beneath surfaces. That's what therapists were—emotional archaeologists, digging around, looking for the truths, searching through old hurts and poking at them with a sharp instrument. Saying things like *You can't heal if we don't get the yucky stuff out.* Well, maybe some things are better left unexplored. "Truth or dare?"

"Dare."

Chase hadn't expected that. She figured Olivia would want to stay within the questions. "Awesome. So when we stop for a burger, you have to go up to a random guy and throw your arms around him and say, 'Oh my God, I can't believe it's you. I've been wanting you to meet your son for years.' You know, like he's the father of your child."

"No. Absolutely not."

"You *have* to do it. It's a dare, and those are the rules."

Olivia shook her head. "No, because that could be dangerous."

Chase sighed. "No it's not. It's funny."

"First, germs. Second, that's emotional abuse. It's not amusing to make a guy think he has a child as a joke. Why would you think that it was?"

Because guys were mostly jerks who took little responsibility for their actions. And it would be funny. Sort of. Okay, maybe not.

"Fine. When we get to the burger place, you have to do the Meg Ryan orgasm thing while you're eating your burger."

"You sure are obsessed with orgasms." Olivia gave her a flat look.

"Only because I now know you're good at faking them," Chase said, laughing.

And, lord of lords, Olivia actually laughed. "Okay, so what's this Meg Ryan orgasm thing?"

"You've never seen *When Harry Met Sally . . .* ?" Chase stared at Olivia like she was an alien. Lame music, faking orgasms, and hadn't seen the romantic classic?

"Nope. I guess I missed that one."

"*Sleepless in Seattle?*"

Olivia shook her head.

"*While You Were Sleeping?*"

Olivia made a face. "Nope."

"You're *so* weird." Chase was only twenty-five years old, but even she'd seen the romantic classics of the last few decades. "I hope your pawpaw's house has a DVD player or Netflix. No wonder you have to fake orgasms. You've failed to watch only the most romantic movies ever."

Olivia shrugged. "I've been busy. My turn. Truth or dare?"

Chase didn't want to tell another truth. She hadn't meant to let the one about orgasms slide. She'd had orgasms before, but only when she was by herself and didn't have to feel someone touching her. She knew she was damaged and probably needed help, but since she'd never admitted to another therapist that she'd been raped when she was young, she'd never brought up her sexual dysfunctions. She'd had plenty of sex with plenty of people, which was shameful when she thought about it. She knew it wasn't cool to shame women for having lots of sex these days, but she still felt like much of her sexual experience had been done trying to erase herself. So shame and censure were tangled up in her conceptions of sex. "Dare."

Olivia grinned, and in her smile Chase saw someone she might not mind so much. Maybe Olivia wasn't such a loser. If they had to spend the next few weeks together doing only God knows what, maybe they could at least find something in common . . . besides faking orgasms.

"Oh wait. Here we are," Olivia said, slowing the car and putting on her blinker. "God, it's been years, but it hasn't changed a bit. Still has the old soda machine on the porch."

To their left was a general store similar to ones she'd seen on movie sets. The front porch had an old-fashioned soda machine, the kind where you turned the lever and a glass-bottled soda rolled out, along with rocking chairs and a table that no doubt held a checkers board. Lettering scrawled across the window advertising FISH AND CHIPS and THE BEST BURGERS IN THE STATE. Only a few cars and trucks surrounded the older wooden building, which boded well since people still recognized her if they read dumb grocery checkout magazines.

Olivia pulled into an empty parking spot and shut off the engine. "I used to come here when I was younger. Every summer we drove up here to spend a month or so with my grandparents. My sisters and I piled into the back of the minivan, fighting over books and the iPod shuffle, while my parents yelled things like 'Settle down back there.' One thing we always agreed on was stopping at Foghat's. They have the best onion rings."

"You eat onion rings?"

Olivia smiled. "Almost never. But we can split an order so you can try them . . . and I'll worry about the calories later. If they're as good as they once were, it will be worth every one of them."

"How many sisters do you have?" Chase asked, noting the wistfulness in Olivia's voice. Chase's parents divorced when she was three years old, and thus she'd never truly had a sibling. Her father had remarried a twentysomething nubile dancer who'd given him two kids before her father drove his car into the canyon, drunk as a skunk. She knew their names were Meryn and Willa. They lived in Vegas, and she'd met them only once at his funeral, so she had no nostalgia for two kids she barely knew, but it was obvious that her new therapist had good memories of her siblings.

"I had two. Now just one." Olivia unclicked her seat belt, her expression shuttering. The woman didn't want to talk about her sisters. That much was certain.

"What happened to the other one? Is she dead?" Chase persisted.

Olivia made a face as she opened the car door. "Yeah. She's dead."

Chase didn't make a move to climb from the car. Olivia turned. "Are you coming?"

Something in Olivia's face before she retreated behind her normal, placid mask of control intrigued Chase. Lots to unpack in that look, but mostly, Chase had glimpsed immense sadness.

People often didn't understand that the best actors were empaths who could decipher in small reactions the truth of a person. On the outside, Olivia presented herself as a very knowledgeable, confident therapist, but Chase was almost certain that beneath her carefully culti-vated professional demeanor was a woman who wasn't so far away from who Chase was. "How did she die?"

Olivia sighed. "Chase, I don't want to talk about my sisters."

"I do."

"You don't get to make those kinds of demands. That's my personal life, and it's not accessible to you."

"But mine is? You want me to trust that you have my best interests at heart. You want me to tell you why I can't get off when I'm with a guy. You want me to vomit out the crap that happened to me when I was a child, shit that would make a stone-cold gangster cry, but you won't give me anything? It's a fact, isn't it?"

Olivia narrowed her eyes. "What is?"

"How your sister died. That's a fact. Not an emotion."

Olivia slammed the car door and started walking toward the restaurant.

Her response felt like a slap in Chase's face. God, she was trying to connect here, and Olivia was being a total bitch. Okay, so maybe what-ever happened to her sister was upsetting. She understood traumatic death—didn't her own father have to have a closed casket because he'd essentially smashed himself to pieces? But that didn't mean Olivia had to be so effing rude.

Chase unclicked her seat belt and climbed from the car. "What's your problem?"

Olivia turned, held up the key fob, and pressed LOCK. The car beeped behind Chase. "Let's just eat, okay?"

"Why can't you be a regular person for a few minutes? You want me to share shit with you"—Chase stomped behind her, still peeved that the woman was such an effing robot—"but you shut down when I ask a simple question. How can I trust you if you can't trust me with a fact?"

Olivia stopped and turned to Chase.

"Trust you? You're a flight risk, an unwilling participant in—" She waved her hand. "In all this. Why would I tell you any intimate detail of my life? You aren't committed to anything we've been doing. You stonewall me at every turn, refuse to even try. Everyone in your life wants you to get better . . . but you. If you can't at least pick up the reins, you'll go nowhere, and to date, you're still sitting on your horse refusing to move."

"No, I'm here with you, and since that day I ran, I've done what was required of me."

"Begrudgingly."

"Yeah, begrudgingly. I don't know you. That's what the truth-or-dare bullshit was about. We have to spend time together, and I thought we could converse like real people and not like I'm required to do with you as part of 'Square One.'" She hooked her fingers dramatically in the air. "I asked you a question. Yeah, it was personal, but not really."

Olivia moved toward her, stepping into Chase's comfort zone, staring her right in the eye. Olivia's brown eyes were resolute, her mouth a tight line. "My sister died from a drug overdose. I found her in a motel room. Happy now?"

Chase blinked but managed to recover from that punch in the gut. She'd expected her sister had died in a car accident or a weird childhood disease. Not from addiction. And Olivia had been the one to find her sister dead? Perhaps this explained why Olivia did what she did. "I'm sorry."

Olivia swallowed. Hard. "Me too."

Chase nodded and brushed past Olivia, heading toward the restaurant steps. A couple had just emerged and carried a Styrofoam container. They looked at Chase curiously before stopping to study a sign advertising a concert. On the other side of the porch, a trio of motorcycles roared up. Sensing that Olivia was not behind her, Chase turned around. "Are you coming?"

Olivia nodded but didn't move.

"Come on. I'll share the onion rings with you, and I'll even let you off on the whole fake orgasm thing. I bet you couldn't do it right anyway."

Olivia shouldered her purse and walked up the steps. "I can. I'm good at faking."

And that made Chase smile. Because the two of them were nothing alike, but they had that in common.

They were both good at faking.

CHAPTER EIGHT

Her grandparents' place was not the cozy, large cabin Olivia remembered. Of course, nothing is ever as one remembers from childhood. Her memories of the rustic two-story cabin nestled at the base of Mount Larsen a few hundred feet from Cotter's Creek would always be tinged by the scent of spruce, smudged with woodsmoke, and framed by inky skies full of stars scattered like celestial confetti. Those memories were wrapped in Band-Aids, sticky marshmallow, and ghost stories told while tucked tight beneath a quilt in the lofted beds she shared with her sisters. If she listened close enough to the ghosts of her past, she could catch hold of her sisters' giggles, her mother singing Aerosmith in the kitchen, and her grandfather listening to NPR on the old entertainment console radio.

But now the house seemed so small, so worn.

Perhaps she should have visited before her grandfather died. No, she *knew* she should have. The last time she'd seen the man who'd taught her to whistle had been in the hospital when he'd had a stroke. Before that was at her grandmother's funeral, and even then she hadn't been able to come to the cabin because the hurt had been too raw, the upheaval in their family too great. Her grandfather had passed when she was on a speaking tour in Europe. She hadn't known about his death until the morning of the funeral, and by then it was too late to fly back to the States. When she'd received the package from the attorney's office with the key to the cabin, she'd finally shed the tears she'd held in for too long.

Chase stirred when the car came to a halt. She'd fallen asleep through much of the drive through the mountains, missing the best part. Olivia had always savored the winding roads and the gorgeous vistas, fields dotted with cows, but she'd let the actress sleep because she'd needed some time to work through saying the words "My sister overdosed."

Because she'd rarely said them out loud. And she'd said them to a person she didn't trust as far as she could throw her. And considering Olivia's arm strength was likely subpar, that wouldn't be far. Those who knew her well enough knew how Marley had died. Those who didn't know her well didn't have to know. None of their business. Olivia had legally changed her last name, shortening it to the first three letters after the debacle with her father, and nothing about her family or personal life was ever included in her bio. In some ways she'd erased that part of her life, but if someone looked carefully, they could see the marks and indentations her past had made on her life. Chase seemed pretty good at seeing those kinds of things.

Chase sat up and blinked, working a kink from her neck. "Oh wait. *This* is it? I thought you said it was a nice house?"

In the fading light, she could see that the cabin had a missing shutter, and the flower beds her granny had once meticulously tended had gone to seed. The grass had been freshly mowed thanks to a call to a lawn service, but the general sense of abandon hung over the place.

"Yep. Home sweet home for the next two or three weeks."

"You're joking, right? This is . . . a dump." Chase rubbed her face as she blinked at the house. "No. We have to get a hotel or something.

This looks like a place where we get hacked to death by the resident serial killer."

Right as she spoke those words, someone tapped on the driver's window.

They both screamed.

Olivia clutched a hand to her chest and turned to see someone standing outside the car holding an ax. She couldn't make this stuff up.

Cautiously, she cracked the window.

The guy, wearing a buffalo plaid flannel shirt, worn jeans, and cowboy boots that had seen better days, leaned down. His eyes narrowed suspiciously, but he didn't look like he was about to hack them to death. "You Olivia?"

"Yes?" she said, swallowing and praying Chase hadn't just summoned a killer. One who knew her name. Good Lord.

"Hey, I'm Zeke," he said.

Zeke? Was she supposed to know who that was? She searched her memory.

"I used to hang out with your sister Marley back when y'all stayed with your grandparents . . ."

This guy was the roly-poly kid who lived down the creek with his grandmother? She remembered him much, much differently. She'd teased Marley mercilessly about her "boyfriend," which always made Marley screech and throw things at her. "You're that Zeke?"

"Yeah. I guess it's been a while since you've seen me. Dave Pope told me you were coming, and since I live next door, I've been looking out for your arrival."

"Who's this guy?" Chase asked, leaning toward her, trying to peek through the window at the torso of their neighbor who had gone from doughy to a solid, bearded hunk with dimples. Yeah, he had green eyes and dimples.

"This is our neighbor," Olivia said, unclicking her seat belt and shutting off the engine.

"Not mine, because I'm not staying here. Look at this place." Chase jabbed a finger toward the house.

Zeke stepped back as Olivia climbed from the car. He glanced at the house and then back to her. "Yeah, the place needs a little work. You may want to call someone to, I don't know, clean up a little? No one has lived out here since your grandfather went into the home. I kept the yard up and checked on the place when I could, but I didn't have a key. I can find some contractor names for you."

Olivia hadn't thought about how the property had been unattended. In her mind it was the same as it had always been. She'd been naive to not think about how the place would have changed.

"No, we'll take care of cleanup."

She heard Chase make a noise of disgust. Then the door opened and Chase climbed out. "I'll take the names, uh, did I hear you say 'Zeke'?"

Zeke stared at Chase, and Olivia knew he recognized her as a celebrity, but he quickly blinked and looked back at Olivia. "Sure, I can make a list of some guys who might work."

"We'll be fine," Olivia said, closing the car door and walking around to the back of the small SUV. She lifted the back hatch and pulled out her rolling suitcase. "Grab your bag, Chase."

"Let me give you a hand," Zeke said, walking toward the back of the car.

"Chase will get her own bag, and while we're at it, we should address the elephant in the room. Yes, this is Chase London, the actress. I'm her therapist, and we'll be staying into October or perhaps longer. It's a small community, but we're hoping to keep a low profile, maybe even have Chase not viewed as a celebrity, because for the time being, she's giving up who she is. I would appreciate some discretion."

Zeke looked over at Chase, who was no doubt rolling her eyes. Olivia had a sixth sense when it came to such displays of disgust. "I'm not the kind of guy who spreads rumors or makes judgments, but I *am* the kind of guy who helps a lady with her bags." He took the handle of Olivia's suitcase and opened the back door, snagging Chase's bag with two fingers.

Then he headed toward the cabin.

Okay, maybe she shouldn't have led with a warning, but she could see he recognized the actress . . . and that he appreciated her assets.

Chase studied Zeke's retreating form, a bit of appreciation in her own eyes. "Yo, Zeke, I'm not really a lady."

He turned and lifted an eyebrow. "You want to carry your own bag?"

Chase showed her own dimples. "Looks like you have it under control."

Zeke said nothing and instead climbed the five steps to the wide-planked porch. He pointed out a loose board on the third step. "Watch your step, *ladies*. That one's rotted."

Chase skirted it, shooting Olivia another glance. "I hope that's the only one that's rotten. I don't want to break a leg. That would defeat the whole purpose of this therapy stuff."

The swing that had taken up the end of the once-happy porch now hung drunkenly by rusted chains. The rocking chairs, where her granny had snapped beans and told stories of her own grandfather, who was a mining camp preacher, bore splintered spokes and blistered paint. The poor things were about as inviting as a rectal exam. Okay, maybe a bit more inviting than that, but they promised the same result—definite discomfort for the ol' gluteus maximus.

Chase turned to her. "I'm game for whatever weirdo therapy you have in mind, but this place . . . come on. Tell me this is some kind of test and that Sasquatch here is in on the whole thing."

Zeke's eyes widened. "Sasquatch? I'm not that hairy, am I?"

Chase glanced over at him. "No, you're totally cute. I was being dramatic."

Zeke actually looked pleased at the "cute" comment. "Kinda your job description, right?"

Chase's mouth twitched. "This guy so gets me. Anyway, Olivia Han, this place doesn't look safe. And I know how you like safety."

Olivia shoved her irritation at Chase's dig down and focused on what she needed to do at present. "It's fine. Just needs to be swept and dusted."

Please let those words be true.

She should have done a better job at picking a place to do the boot camp. Most of her therapists tailored their therapies to each client on a case-by-case basis. It was never a requirement to leave the client's world, but Olivia had felt strongly that Chase needed to be away from her normal in order to breach the defenses she'd erected and raze the fortress of her emotions to ground level. In order to handle the world Chase wanted to climb back into, she needed to meet herself and learn to be a person first, celebrity second. Since Olivia needed to visit the place and attend to any issues before she and her sister made the decision on whether to put the place on the market or not, Cotter's Creek seemed the right place for Chase to do the adulting boot camp.

Olivia was beginning to doubt her judgment.

Chase gave an overdramatic sigh when Olivia pulled the screen door free from its frame with a terrifying squeal. She fit the key into the dead bolt and opened the door to the dank mustiness within.

"Oh my God, what's that smell?" Chase asked, poking her head around Olivia.

The smell wasn't good.

Zeke pushed past them. "Mildew. Definite leak somewhere."

Olivia refused to look at Chase because she didn't want the woman to see the disappointment in her eyes. She'd known the cabin was rustic, but she'd not expected it to be so dilapidated. Perhaps she should have sent someone other than the lawn care service out to get the place in livable condition, but that would have meant getting her sister to sign off on it. And she didn't want to deal with Neve, who had immediately wanted to list the cabin for sale unseen when the bequest came. Besides, Olivia had been determined that Chase's first task in learning to adult would be getting the cabin up to date. At present, that task seemed Herculean.

Olivia held the door while Chase lifted her shirt over her nose and moved inside. The screen door slammed against the frame like an omen, making her feel trapped in a situation of her own making.

Zeke walked to a lamp and turned the switch.

Nothing.

"Did you have the utilities turned on?" he asked.

Olivia inhaled. "Of course I did."

She riffled in her bag for her planner and looked back at the last several days. The decision to come north to the cabin had been made a week ago. A quick scan showed that she'd made a note for Marina to call and turn on utilities. Had she sent that memo to her administrative assistant? She couldn't remember. Damn it. She had no patience for herself when it came to incompetence. "Let me call the office and get my assistant to look into it. Until then, let's pull the dustcovers off and open the windows to let in some fresh air. That should help the smell."

"I hope so," Chase said, muffled beneath her slouchy long-sleeve T-shirt.

Olivia dialed the office, switching on her Bluetooth as she ignored the horrid odor, and ripped back the heavy drapes, exposing the glass-paned windows that were original to the house. Golden light streamed in, catching dust motes in the beams, highlighting the worn wood floors and hand-hooked oval rug she'd once played Barbie dolls upon. Zeke had begun the process of pulling off the sheets and exposing the olive-green tweed couches beneath. The squat coffee table held several outdated copies of *Reader's Digest* and *National Geographic* along with some pottery ashtrays her granny had made.

Chase stood and watched. Of course.

"Chase, can you open the windows in the kitchen?" Olivia said before diverting her attention to the call. "Marina, I need you to call the Shasta County Water Department and California Electric on the following property. Do you have a pen?"

Chase finally moved into the dining area, stepping as if mines were hidden beneath the floorboards.

"Yes, ma'am. I'll call them now and get back to you, but it's after hours. If you want me to call a hotel for you and Miss London, let me know," Marina said before hanging up. Olivia clicked her phone off right as Chase screamed.

Zeke leaped into action, bolting into the kitchen and moving a terrified Chase back into the dining area.

"Oh my God, oh my God, oh my God," Chase screeched, pointing to the open cabinet. "It ran in there. It ran in there."

"What? What ran where?" Zeke asked, his head bobbing between the freaked-out actress and the kitchen.

"I don't know. Some kind of furry animal. I couldn't see because there aren't any effing lights!" Chase moved back into the dining room, wrapping her arms around her torso. She tossed a glare toward Olivia— who'd moved to take a look into the still-dim kitchen—as if it were her fault that there was some creature roaming the house.

Zeke moved toward the back door, twisting the plastic blinds over the small window, letting in just enough evening light to showcase how run-down the kitchen looked. The space no longer radiated cheer and laughter. Instead it masqueraded as a horror film set with chipped Formica and worn flooring. When he pulled back the drapes on the window next to the old-fashioned dinette set, a missing pane explained the unknown critter's presence.

"Well, this would be how whatever it is got inside. You're going to need to call a glass company, but I can fetch something to cover it tonight. It's already getting cool. Wonder if there's a flashlight around here? With actual working batteries?" Zeke glanced around the space, which looked fairly bare of counter appliances.

"Here," Olivia said, clicking on her cell phone flashlight app and handing it to Zeke.

"Thanks," he said, taking it from her and stooping to shine the light within the cabinet. Two glowing eyes caught the beams before they illuminated a hissing cat. "Well, the good news is it's only a cat. The bad news is that it's really pissed off."

They could hear the low, feral growl coming from the collection of pots and pans in the cabinet. The kitty was indeed spitting mad.

"What do we do?" Olivia asked.

Zeke stood and shut the cabinet. "I know what I'm not going to do, and that's reach my hand into that cabinet."

Chase poked her head in. "Maybe we can call a rescue or something? I had to do community service for one in Beverly Hills. They have traps and stuff."

Zeke made a chuffing sound. "Yeah, uh, this ain't Rodeo Drive, and that's not a pet, so right now, I think we better leave it be."

Olivia's phone rang. She tapped her Bluetooth. "What did you find out, Marina?"

"They turned the service on and said it must be an issue on your end. I called an electric service company close to your location, but their only available tech is on another job at present. The soonest they can send someone out is tomorrow. And that's only if, uh, Raymond doesn't get hurt again this year. I don't know what that means, but it has something to do with a rodeo in town?"

"A rodeo?"

"Yeah, and another piece of bad news—there are no hotels or motels available in a twenty-mile radius. You can drive into Redmond and I can get you a room at the Motel 7, but that's the only hotel available."

"You mean Motel 6?"

"No, it's definitely Motel 7. It has a one-and-a-half-star rating, so I didn't bother getting a room. The last review said something about a pest infestation?"

"Fine. Just set the appointment for the morning if Raymond isn't injured. We'll be okay for one night." She clicked off the call, so perturbed she could spit nails. Which would actually be helpful considering the paneling in the kitchen looked loose in several areas.

Chase drew in a deep breath. "We don't have to stay here tonight, right? There's no heat, it smells like death, and there's a rabid cat trapped in the cabinets. That's a deal breaker, Olivia."

"You guys can come stay at my place," Zeke offered. "I have an extra bedroom and a pull-out couch. Sometimes I snore, but I've been told it's sort of adorable. Besides, I made a big pot of chili earlier, and though I have to be up at the ass crack of dawn and can't offer you breakfast in bed, I think you'll be more comfortable with heat and hot water."

"Perfect," Chase said, spinning on her heel and heading toward the bag she'd placed on the dining room table. "Let's go."

"Not so fast," Olivia said, setting her hand on the top of Chase's bag. "We're not going to Zeke's. We're staying here."

"Are you insane?" Chase said, pulling her bag from Olivia's grasp. "You can stay here. I'm going with Big Sexy to his place. He has chili. And heat."

Olivia crossed her arms. "You owe me a dare. So, Chase, I dare you to stay with me in this cabin overnight."

Chase narrowed her eyes. "We're not playing that game anymore."

"Who said? If I remember correctly, you said 'Dare,' and I got distracted by our arrival at Foghat's, but if you remember, *I* did my dare."

"And scarred half the restaurant. That poor man tried to do the Heimlich on you. Not to mention, you're really bad at faking orgasms."

Olivia frowned. "Well, maybe so, but I did it. Are you chickening out, Miss London?"

"You can't do this." Chase tugged on her bag again. "You're not being fair. Staying in this place is dangerous, and you said dares couldn't be dangerous."

"It's not dangerous. Maybe uncomfortable, but not dangerous. Besides, it's unlikely you'll have someone assault you the way I did at Foghat's. That man nearly cracked my rib."

Chase blew out an aggravated breath. "You should have sold your orgasm better if you didn't want people to think you were having a seizure or something. That's on you."

Behind them Zeke muttered, "What kind of therapy *is* this?"

Olivia ignored him and leveled a look at Chase. "Well. Are you in or out? Because if you forfeit, I win."

Olivia knew her words were the right ones. Chase narrowed her eyes and twisted her mouth to the side and then glanced around at the dimming light in the living area. Then she glanced back at the kitchen, at the closed cabinet harboring the thankfully no longer hissing feline. "Fine. I'm not scared to stay here."

Then Chase put her bag back on the table and turned to Zeke. "Rain check on the chili, handsome?"

"I can do better than that. I'll bring over some wood for the fireplace and enough chili for you both and won't even ask about what you two did at Foghat's."

"Our hero," Chase said.

"Nah, just a guy." Zeke flushed, and that's when Olivia realized she might have a problem with these two.

CHAPTER NINE

The absolute quiet of the cabin paired with springs that poked Chase every time she shifted her position on the musty couch had kept her from falling back asleep after she first woke. So when enough milky light streamed into the living room for her to see exactly how ugly the place was, Chase uncurled from the warmth of the sleeping bag and foggily headed toward the kitchen to see if there was a coffeepot.

Because she needed coffee like an addict needed—wait, scratch that—she just needed something to clear her head and chase away the chill. Coffee would do the trick.

Not that she actually knew how to make coffee. Well, unless it was Keurig. And she'd lay down a hundo that there wasn't a Keurig in this joint.

Besides, if she banged around in the kitchen long enough, Olivia would probably wake up and make coffee for her. She squinted toward Olivia, who lay perfectly still, on her back, arms crossed like she was a waxed figure in a museum.

Come to think of it, that's what the woman reminded Chase of—a perfect mannequin maneuvered into positions that were supposed to mimic a real person but didn't quite succeed.

Chase tiptoed out of the living room in the fuzzy socks she'd tossed into her bag at the last minute only because Olivia had said to bring a jacket. Now she knew why. *Brrr!* The fire had long died in the grate, and the chilly morning air caused prickles to skate on her skin as she moved toward the kitchen.

The weak morning light revealed a tired-looking kitchen that had been modern maybe in the 1980s. Yellow Formica countertops, white appliances, and a linoleum floor that bore rust marks from long-ago chairs were the good things about the kitchen. Stained window treatments and strange wall art shaped like owls reminded her of something from a Hitchcock film. And then Chase noticed the open cabinet door, which meant . . .

She looked frantically around only to find the beast sitting above her head on top of the refrigerator.

"Holy shit," she squeaked, moving back from the fridge, keeping her gaze on the cat studying her unblinkingly from its perch, its tail curled around its feet. Chase wasn't sure if it was merely observing her or if a ferocious attack was nigh. Cats didn't show their hands. Or was that paws? Too bad they didn't have opposable thumbs, because they'd kick ass in a poker game. No tells from this creepy cat.

Still, the thing didn't look quite as scary in the light of day.

"Uh, hey, beast," she said, leaning way back and feeling a bit ridiculous for (1) being afraid of something that probably didn't weigh as much as her boots and (2) talking to an animal as if it were a person.

The cat's only response to her query was a few flicks of its tail at the tip.

It wasn't a pretty cat. The black-and-brown fur matted into terrible tangles, and the tufts surrounding its face stuck out at odd angles. Alabaster whiskers stood out against the dark fur. An urn of white covered its chest, disappearing into the underbelly only to reemerge on the tips of the two forefeet.

She spied a coffeepot on the counter just as she realized that they had no groceries. No coffee.

Duh.

Really, this whole Square One bullshit was the absolute worst. How had she let herself end up with this crazy-ass therapist freezing her butt off in the middle of nowhere? Maybe the drugs and booze had damaged her brain? Okay, that was probably a scientific given, but that didn't explain why she had agreed to work with Olivia, the total weirdo who could *not* fake an orgasm, by the way. The woman sucked at acting.

Zeke probably had coffee—good, stout coffee that made hair grow on one's chest. One of her former directors had once said that, which she guessed meant the coffee was up to standard.

Zeke had been a bright spot in a dark hole. He wasn't the sort of guy she was attracted to—a rough-around-the-edges sort with calloused hands and jeans that were worn from actual labor rather than distressing from the hand of a fashion designer. Solid with a dark beard and shaggy hair, he'd showed back up last night with cold bottles of iced tea and a Tupperware full of delicious chili made of venison. He'd built a roaring fire, set an air freshener on the table, and brought them sleeping bags. When she'd later snuggled into the depths of the flannel-lined bag, she'd imagined it smelled of him—woodsmoke, Breath Savers, and something homey and foreign. Not that she was into him or anything. He was just . . . nice.

"What are you doing?" Olivia asked from behind her.

"Staring at this cat."

"Why?"

"Because I stumbled in here thinking about coffee, and then I realized we don't have coffee. Or anything else for that matter. And he was up there plotting our demise, so I thought I should keep an eye on him." She turned to look at Olivia, who looked . . . like she hadn't spent the night on the couch in a sleeping bag. Every hair was in place, her skin was dewy, and her eyes weren't remotely puffy. "How do you even look like that?"

Olivia tilted her head and blinked. Like a doll. Like a weird robot doll. "Like what?"

"My hair's snarled, and I look like the walking dead." She pulled at the bun she'd twisted her hair into the night before. Half of it was hanging around her face. She may or may not have drooled, and the constant waking during the night ensured the skin beneath her eyes was shadowed.

"You don't look like the walking dead. Maybe the walking wounded."

"Thank you, therapist," Chase drawled, noting it was the exact description her mother had used weeks earlier. Chase had never thought about herself in that way.

Olivia looked at the cat. "Doesn't look so mean, does he?"

"I think that's his ploy."

Sure enough, when Olivia moved into the kitchen past Chase, the cat arched his back and issued a panther growl. "Yeah, so let's open the back door and shoo him out."

"Uh, you can do that. I'll watch from back here," Chase said, stepping back, rubbing her upper arms.

Olivia looked at the door and then the cat, who had settled back down into a sitting position. The thing looked calm, but his tail told a different story. It lashed back and forth in an age-old warning to back the eff off. "You know, why don't we make ourselves presentable and go into Redmond to get our supplies? I'll leave the window cracked. Hopefully by the time we return, we'll have electricity, hot water, and no cat."

"That sounds better than fighting this cat, because I think he would win." Chase left the kitchen doorway, grabbed her bag, and riffled through to find her heaviest shirt. She'd slept in her jeans because they were the warmest thing she had. She grabbed a flannel shirt and tugged it on as a jacket. Then grabbed her jacket and pulled it on, too. She combed out her hair with her fingers because she'd forgotten a brush and took her toothbrush to the half bath. Minutes later she emerged looking not much more than presentable. Which might be good since they were going to be around people. Maybe no one would recognize her dressed in modern bag woman chic.

Olivia walked out of a room in the back of the house looking ready to model the latest in activewear. She sported a pair of leggings, an athletic long-sleeve shirt, and a headband. Trainers graced her feet, and she held a jacket over her arm. She looked very together. Maybe she was an alien.

Ten minutes later, they were in the blessedly warm car heading east toward Redmond.

"Why didn't we go to Redmond in the first place?" Chase asked.

Olivia glanced over at her, offering a protein bar. "I had my reasons."

Chase shook her head at the offering. "Which were . . ."

"Not any of your concern." Olivia opened the protein bar and took a bite before turning the radio to the damn orchestra crap.

"Right. So then do you care to explain to me this whole deal? Like why we're, like, here? 'Cause I'm not sure how this is supposed to help me get my life on track. It's totally weird."

"It's part of the process."

"Which is code for *Shut up and don't ask questions?*" Chase asked, watching the vivid green world pass by outside the window. She'd not even known there were so many shades of nature. Cobalt mountains hunkered on the horizon, crouching low in the stretch of valley and meadow below. *Toto, I've a feeling we're not in Kansas anymore.*

"That's not what it's code for." Olivia turned down the radio with a sigh. "Before I started my own business, I worked in Long Beach at a clinic that serviced emotionally and physically abused children, most of them from low-income areas. Every now and then, social services sent us a client who hailed from a privileged background. One time I got assigned a kid who had been a child actor."

"Who was it? Lori Shiffen? 'Cause she was fuuuuucked up."

Olivia's eyes flashed with irritation. "I'm not telling you who it was. That information is confidential. But anyway, I mistakenly thought working with her would be easy, but I soon realized she had similarities to my clients who lived in poverty. She just wore a prettier dress."

Chase made a face. "So you're saying someone like me is like a poor person? 'Cause that's not true. And I don't get what that has to do with being in whatever the name of that town is."

"On some levels you aren't close to being similar to someone who has not had their basic needs met. But on many levels you are. You grew up in a world that's not the norm. I don't know everything about you, Chase, but I know a lot of people let you down, and though you may have had your physical needs—like food and shelter—met with great satisfaction, your emotional needs were ignored in favor of promoting your career. Or at least that's what I have learned with actors, athletes, and virtuosos who spent their childhoods striving to elevate themselves above the normal. They circumvented important stages of development in favor of success. And there are penalties to pay when one does that."

"Okay, so I wasn't raised like a lot of kids."

"You weren't raised like a kid at all. Where did you go to preschool?"

Chase shook her head. "I didn't. I was homeschooled. Lots of kids are homeschooled."

"Of course they are." Olivia maneuvered the car off the two-lane curving road onto a highway. The sun peeked out from behind a cloud, and Chase pushed her sunglasses from atop her head onto her nose.

"Who were your friends when you were a child? Say, when you were around six or seven years old? Name them."

Chase didn't have an answer. She remembered playing with one little girl who lived near her before she started doing commercials. They'd played in a nearby park. She could still remember the way the metal slide burned the backs of her thighs and the time she fell and chipped her front tooth while jumping rope. Her mother had been furious, and Lorna had refused to let her go back to the playground. When Chase had made it onto feature films, they'd had an on-set tutor for any children in the production. In between worksheets, she learned to play poker and *Grand Theft Auto* with some of the older kids. "I didn't have any."

"Did you learn to ride a bike?"

"No." Like Lorna would have let her do something that would skin up her knees or break her face.

"Have birthday parties—"

"Of course I had birthday parties," Chase interrupted.

Olivia glanced over at her. "That other children attended?"

Chase made a face. Her parties were usually attended by her mother's friends. Or people on the set. Her cakes were always elaborate for the publicity photos, and she was allowed only one small piece.

"Did you learn to swim, take family vacations, go roller-skating, own a pet, have a sleepover, play with Barbies, go camping, write letters, do chores, go on a date, attend prom, graduate with a tassel and confetti?" Olivia spat those out like a tommy gun.

Okay, now Chase was effing depressed and pissed. "You know the answer to most of those, but what in the hell does that have to do with this stupid Square One bullshit? You want me to have a sleepover? Dress up like a princess? If you say I have to wear a fucking diaper, I'm so out on this."

Olivia actually laughed. "No diapers."

"So, what? What's the deal?"

"Adulting."

"Adulting? Like how to figure a checkbook or make a meat loaf?" Chase made a face, irritation at the thought of something so asinine clawing with impatience at her insides.

"That's sort of the idea."

"How in the hell is that going to work? Makes no sense. Please tell me you have something more than me learning to fold a fitted sheet in mind. 'Cause, dude, that's what housekeepers are for." Even as she said those words, she knew how she sounded. Self-absorbed. Entitled. Like a not-so-nice person.

Well, wasn't everyone a little not so nice?

"Listen to you," Olivia said with a smile.

"What? I mean, I know I don't know how to do some stuff. Lots of people don't know how to do lots of things. Whatever."

"It's the whatever I'm after, Chase. I know you think it's silly, but you need to know yourself better in the real world, with real people, doing real things that matter."

"Making movies doesn't matter? Because it does."

"Of course it does. I'm not saying that what you do is easy. I'm saying that your career—pretending to be someone else and then living a life among chauffeurs, personal shoppers, and sycophants—skews your perception of who you are and what your purpose in life is."

Chase folded her arms, and even though she felt super defensive about the things Olivia was saying, she knew there was truth within the words. She still didn't know how learning how to do "adult" things was going to help her fight her demons. That seemed like throwing a handful of sand on a forest fire. Or some other euphemism she couldn't quite grasp at the moment. Maybe that was another thing she didn't know how to do—make comparisons that made sense.

So for the next half hour, Chase watched the trees, sky, and an occasional logging truck or car pass by. Eventually she started seeing houses, a gas station, and cell phone repair shops. Which reminded her . . .

"When will I get my phone back?" Chase asked.

"When you can pay the bill."

"I do pay the bill."

Olivia pulled into the parking lot of a small grocery store that looked sort of low rent and turned to her. "Do you?"

Chase wasn't sure. Her mother had given her the phone. She'd not set any kind of plan up or ever seen a bill. Any bill. Lorna took care of the money. But she wasn't going to admit that to Miss High and Mighty.

Olivia's lips may have twitched into a knowing smile, but she didn't say anything more. Instead she turned the engine off and pulled a piece of paper from her big, accordion-like bag. "Here you go."

Chase took the offered paper. "What's this? A list?"

"I need to purchase bedding, a new shower curtain, and some things to do general repairs at the cabin, so I'm dropping you at the grocery store and heading over to a few other stores. While I'm doing that, you can start adulting by getting the groceries on the list. I'll be back in exactly one hour to pick you up."

"By myself? You're trusting me to do this alone? Aren't I a flight risk?"

Olivia looked hard at her. "Are you a flight risk?"

Maybe she was. But probably not. Who would she call? She didn't know anyone in this area outside of their new neighbor, and she didn't know his number anyway. "No. But I don't . . . I don't have a phone. That's dangerous. And what if people recognize me?" She didn't want to admit that she was nervous doing this by herself. Usually she had people around her, other people to help her figure out how to do things.

Olivia stilled, her gaze fixing on a magpie hopping around a flattened fast-food bag. "That's a fair point. Here's your phone. Data is turned off." She reached into her bag of tricks and pulled out Chase's bejeweled pink cell phone.

"You had it all along. It's ridiculous that I can't have my phone. You're such a Nazi."

"Do you actually know any Nazis?" Olivia asked, sounding serious.

Chase didn't want another lecture, so she opened her car door and climbed out. "Fine. I can do this. See you in an hour."

She shut the door but then remembered that she didn't have any money. Or her purse. She raised her hand to knock on the window, but Olivia had already started lowering it.

"Here." Olivia handed her a stack of reusable grocery bags and an ugly crossbody purse that looked to be black plastic. "Your ID is inside, along with a prepaid credit card. I loaded two hundred and fifty dollars on the credit card, so you'll have to keep your total bill with tax under two fifty. Think you can manage that?"

"Of course I can. Regardless of what you think, I know how to use a credit card."

Olivia's mouth twitched. "I don't doubt that."

Chase would have told her where she could stick her stupid prepaid card, but Olivia rolled up the window and pulled away, leaving her holding an ugly crossbody purse and several cloth bags in the middle of the Sav-A-Bunch parking lot. A homeless-looking man walked by and glanced at her. Chase clutched the purse tighter and moved toward the entrance, where several wounded grocery carts tilted drunkenly.

Olivia wanted her to adult?

Fine.

Time to prove Chase London could handle her own damn life.

CHAPTER TEN

Olivia turned out of the Sav-a-Bunch parking lot and pointed the car toward Bed Bath & Beyond. She'd examined the cabin bedding the previous night, using the flashlight on her phone to determine if the stacks of linen in the upstairs closet would work or not. Her grandmother's numerous handmade quilts looked to be in decent shape and once laundered would be perfectly cozy, but some of the sheets were moth eaten. She'd added towels and a new shower curtain to the list, too. Once she got the needed bedding, she'd go to Home Depot to get the cleaning products, light bulbs, and other supplies. She'd intentionally waited to make her list until after they'd arrived at the property so they would know what they needed. No sense in buying things they couldn't or wouldn't use . . . or having to go back to the city any sooner than they had to. Of course, she had expected to have electricity so list making would be easier. Guess the lack of heat and a hot shower had at least given Chase a decent first challenge for the adulting boot camp.

She had to give the actress credit—Chase hadn't complained much once they'd devoured Zeke's chili and saltines and settled onto the couch. In fact, Chase had zipped herself inside the sleeping bag and dropped off to sleep while Olivia prowled the cabin full of memories, making her lists and trying not to let the wisps of giggles and camp songs haunt her. Three little girls in footie pajamas playing pick-up sticks and dancing to old records seemed to appear as she went from room to room.

Poor naive little girls.

They couldn't have known their family would come so unraveled.

Olivia struck the thoughts that pulled her into the past from her mind and focused on the list she'd pulled from her bag. Surely Chase could handle the groceries. Going shopping with limited funds would be a challenge for someone who was accustomed to having credit cards without limits. Then again, maybe Chase had limits now. Olivia wasn't certain what the actress's financial situation was. When she'd met briefly with Lorna a few weeks ago, the woman had been tight lipped on the financial situation. What Olivia *was* certain about was that Chase needed Square One, and the actress needed what was about to happen in this adulting boot camp.

Of course, most wouldn't think putting damaged actors and athletes under such pressure would be the way to rewire their thinking. Olivia had spent years researching adults who were deemed phenoms—small stars who were thrust early into an adult arena while still mentally and physically children. Olivia had discovered a commonality—a missing skill subset. Which made many of the formerly shiny but now-unpredictable wash-ups unable to cope or communicate their emotional needs. Those skills had been skipped over on their road to success. Most didn't have solid friends their age, basic life skills, or a stable foundation that allowed them to weather defeat. She'd seen many who were one step away from a death spiral.

Oddly enough, she'd hatched the idea of Square One while working on her thesis, which drew parallels between marginalized children and übersuccessful prodigies. One afternoon after sifting through mountains of data, she sat down to a cold lunch and a half hour of television, which allowed her brain respite from the data. A rerun of *Little House on the Prairie* appeared on the screen. In that particular episode, Pa Ingalls had taken on some rather badly behaving children and worked them so hard on his farm that they were too tired to cause trouble. The episode was a pseudolecture on indulgent parenting and the need for boundaries. The next day, she couldn't get the episode off her mind, as she often recognized that out-of-control, repercussions-be-damned behavior in her own clients. It led to her exploring the idea of challenges as a way to reimprint and reengage a person. Unable to shake the idea, she'd logged in to a database and searched for statistics of at-risk youth who entered the military as a way to change their course.

All the while, her mind beat the drum with the *what if* question.

What if instead of military boot camp, she could create a life skills boot camp. Instead of obstacle courses and runs, her clients would navigate the obstacles that life threw at them—flat tires, cranky committee members, lack of money in their accounts. Could she break them down like a drill sergeant and then build them back up with successes that empowered them?

Through cognitive psychotherapy, she knew she could help them address their past mistakes and deal with their emotions, but without real, tangible skills, how would they claim their futures? If she could challenge them on responsibility, communication, boundaries—all the things capable adults must master in order to survive—could she foster self-worth, compassion, and commitment in these entitled child stars? In other words, could she take a person standing two feet from the edge of the cliff and Pa Ingalls them into stepping away, about-facing, and rebuilding a new life from their crumbling one?

It sounded absurd, but there was a kernel of something there.

So she talked the parent of a really out-of-control, self-absorbed tennis star who'd rampaged her way through the pro circuit popping Adderall and giving blow jobs to European royalty into admitting her to a three-week adulting boot camp after she completed sobriety treatment.

Olivia was shocked by the results. The first week sucked. Her baby tennis star had been an absolute terror, throwing tantrums, but once Olivia shifted away from vacuuming and budgeting and placed her client on a committee for a pet adoption event, she saw a change. By the end of the trial period, her tennis star had not only learned to balance a checkbook and use a Weed Eater, but she'd signed on to be the spokesperson for the Florida Humane Society and had even recruited other tennis stars to help with adoption events around the country. Miss Wimbledon Champ also learned to make killer cupcakes that she took great pleasure in sharing with the press. Currently, that former queen of the net coached youth tennis while balancing a young family. She still sent Olivia cupcakes and a handwritten thank-you note every year.

Square One had been born.

Olivia parked the car, grabbed a cart, and went in search of linens. She'd already loaded up some clearance towels and a few new kitchen utensils when her phone rang.

Conrad's number appeared on the screen.

"You're making this quite a habit," she said in lieu of a greeting. She eyed a shower curtain with birds on it. Not the right vibe.

"It would be if you hadn't spent so much time avoiding me."

Something weird fluttered in her stomach. Those words. "Chase is doing fine."

"Maybe I wasn't calling about Chase. Maybe I wanted to talk to you."

"Con, what's going on?"

"What do you mean?"

"This . . . whatever you're doing. Saying things like that."

"What? You're my friend, someone I care about. Look, I gave you space because I needed it, too, but that didn't mean I didn't miss having you in my life. And then when that stuff happened with your dad, I tried to help, be there for you. But you are still running from me."

"I don't run from you." Not really. But she kind of did. It was easier that way because when she talked to him, she remembered what she'd missed out on. And then there was the fact that his voice brought back too many memories of her sister. "Look, you have to understand that it's easier on me to not see you, Con. That's the honest-to-God truth. It hurts to remember."

Silence sat on the phone.

"But I miss you, Livy."

Olivia clutched her chest and closed her eyes because his words were like a knife cutting through the bindings she'd tied around herself. She didn't want to feel this way, like a fledgling fallen from the nest, naked and eyeing the hawks circling. Because that's the way she felt when she thought about Conrad and how they never had a damn chance.

After that weekend, one so bittersweet and tinged with laughter and sobbing, she and Conrad had decided that too much stood between them to continue with what they'd started. They'd had one momentous, affirming night, and that was all they would have. Conrad had agreed that being friends was best, breaking her even more than she thought she could handle. So why was he saying things that gave her twinges of hope, things that made her wonder, *What if?*

"I don't even know what to say to that."

Silence sat on the other end of the line for so long that she thought they'd been disconnected. Finally, Con said, "I've been thinking about you, about that night."

Her fingers started trembling. "Yeah?"

"Maybe we're different now."

"I'm not different. Same Olivia. But maybe you're the one who's different. You're growing older, and maybe you're just tired of . . . I don't know . . . trying to replace grieving with nubile starlets." She wrapped her hand around the handle of the cart to still the trembling.

"Damn. You don't hold back. Maybe that's what I missed—someone who doesn't take shit off me. But I don't want you to be my therapist, Livy. I got those."

"I'm making an observation, not saying that's your issue. We made a decision long ago, and that was hard on me. I—I wanted to be more, but I agreed that it was impossible. Look, we will always be friends because we're . . . we're . . ."

"Family?" he finished for her.

"Yeah, to a degree," she said, pulling her cart back so another woman could grab shower curtain rings.

Olivia was a firm believer that families didn't have to be blood relations. She and Conrad had grown up together, sharing lazy afternoons, dreams, and the occasional milkshake. Conrad hailed from a large family, crammed in a small house, so he liked being anywhere but there. Most people, even in the toughest of LA neighborhoods, didn't mess with kids, especially not a quirky Hispanic boy who wore vintage clothes before they were cool and a plump white girl with glasses pedaling their used ten-speeds past pawnshops and gas stations. Their favorite hangout was a pastry and ice cream shop on the edge of their neighborhood where they scraped pennies together to buy chocolate shakes. Mr. Cortana begrudgingly let them hang out at one of the corner tables and watch telenovelas—which is how Olivia had learned to speak Spanish. She and Con had sneaked into rated-R movies, played video games at a run-down arcade, and curled into the beanbags Marley abandoned in Olivia's bedroom, and listened to old music like the Kinks and Led Zeppelin.

As they grew older, the way she felt for him changed. She started to notice the way his too-skinny face broadened and his smile became more mysterious than goofy. One day when they were at the pool and bumped heads, coming up sputtering, she had an inclination to kiss him. Which was so odd, but the way the water caught in the long lashes above his brown eyes and the way his white teeth flashed against his tanned skin as he smiled at her did something funny to her. She'd read enough Sweet Valley High books to understand that something had changed . . . at least on her end.

Conrad didn't notice her in that same way. Not that she'd given him much cause. Olivia had been a late bloomer, clinging to her baby fat a bit too long. Her parents couldn't be talked into contacts because they were too expensive and something about infections of the eye. Olivia experimented with makeup but always felt her heavy-handed eye shadow made her look more Marilyn Manson and less Marilyn Monroe.

Then their senior year, the year she finally dropped some weight and saved her money from working at a childcare center to get contacts, a fifteen-year-old Marley had gone from skinny nuisance to curvy, blonde goddess.

Let's just say Conrad had noticed Marley.

"Are you still there?" Conrad asked, jarring her from thinking about the night when Marley came home from spending the summer with their grandparents while Olivia worked. Her baby sister hadn't looked so babyish. Instead Marley had turned into a tanned, confident woman-child who wore her newfound sexual awakening like she wore her Revlon lipstick. Obvious.

"I'm still here."

"I'm not asking anything of you, Olivia. I just miss you. I didn't realize how much until I saw you. Guess I'm being vulnerable here, and you know how hard that is for me."

Conrad was a master of hiding his emotions. Growing up in poverty, hungry for what he didn't have, different from all the other kids in his neighborhood, Conrad learned how to beguile and maneuver. And cover his feelings with false bravado.

"I know. I just don't know what you're asking for, and I'm being vulnerable when I say that I don't know what I can give you. We had a chance, and that—"

"Was taken from us." He sounded aggravated. She wasn't falling into line with what he wanted. Classic Conrad.

"By the person you were in love with, Con. Marley's death was a bomb, but even if she hadn't died, we still would have had a huge hurdle to clear. We weren't going to work even if she hadn't died. So why resurrect this?"

"Because I need . . ." His words fell away, and a few seconds passed. "You know what? How about I come up to the cabin in a few weeks? I'm dealing with some stuff here and need a change of scenery. I'll bring an updated script for Chase, and maybe you and I can have some time together . . . to catch up."

"Catch up?"

"We used to be close, and when I was out on the beach with you, I felt more myself than I had in a long time." He paused, and she heard the sound of a car door opening and closing. "Besides, you looked beautiful."

Her heart skipped a beat, and something scary and wonderful bloomed in her stomach. *Beautiful.* A simple word used for so much. *Your baby's beautiful. That painting is beautiful. You scored tickets for the game? Beautiful.*

But she hadn't ever remembered someone saying she was beautiful. Pretty? Yeah. Attractive? Sure. But beautiful? No one had ever said it about her that she could remember. Not even her own mother. So that word coming from Con's lips seemed . . . wrong.

A few seconds ticked by because she didn't know what to say. How to feel. If she could open herself up to the hurt that would surely come. She loved Conrad, and in his own way, he loved her. But the past was a chasm between them, and she could see no way to bridge it. Marley, even dead, would always be between them.

"Livy?"

"Sorry." She searched her mind for how to respond and settled on what she always said when she wasn't sure what to say. "Let me check my calendar and get back to you."

"Okay."

He didn't try to persuade her. Was that what she wanted? For Conrad to want to see her so badly he would force his way to her mountain cabin? How did one cope with the sudden appearance of a man she'd always loved, had believed could be hers for just one night, and then had watched slip into a deep pool of grief and guilt, leaving her to blindly grope her way around her own loss. Their brief love affair had been a mistake. He'd said those exact words. *Mistake.* She'd echoed the same back in agreement. What could change any of that?

Still, hope crouched like a small goblin inside her heart, holding tight to a secret longing she refused to expose to the light. He'd hurt her, but nothing had been worse than the pain of losing Marley. Olivia had blocked out much of what had happened that spring weekend—it was the only way she could move forward. Every time a memory of what had happened flitted into her consciousness, she sent it packing. She didn't want to feel that loss again, didn't want to remember how a piece of her had shattered and scattered to the winds that next day, a day that had begun with breakfast and laughter and ended with Olivia deciding which dress to put on Marley for her viewing at the funeral parlor.

For someone who urged her clients to wade into emotion and live in their feelings, it all seemed a bit hypocritical. Nothing like being the epitome of *Do as I say and not as I do.*

"Livy?" Conrad asked, his voice now worried.

"I need to go, Con."

"Okay. So talk to you soon?"

"Sure." Olivia hung up and stared blankly at the shower curtains, reeling with the things Conrad had revealed. She'd accepted her life without him in it, so why was this happening now?

She suspected whatever "stuff" Conrad was dealing with required distraction, demanded someone he could lean on. She had a sixth sense about discord, and she would lay down a bet that Conrad was looking for something or someone to give him comfort. It likely had nothing to do with her being beautiful. But Conrad wouldn't use her love for him to make himself feel better. Conrad was a lot of things, but at his essence, he would never hurt her. Not intentionally anyway.

Glancing at her watch, she realized that she had only thirty-five minutes to check out and run by Home Depot for the things she needed there. She'd given Chase an hour, and she needed to keep to that time limit herself.

She rolled her shopping cart to the checkout, wondering how her cheerleader prom queen actress was doing at the grocery store. The list had too many items, some not specified by brand or number, and so it would require discernment and attention to price.

How would Chase do at one of the most basic skills an adult performed on a weekly basis?

CHAPTER ELEVEN

The doors of the grocery store slid open to bright fluorescent light and the beeping of cashiers scanning grocery items with brisk proficiency. The scent of fresh-baked bread embraced Chase like an old friend, making her stomach growl in a reminder that she hadn't had breakfast. She should have taken that stupid protein bar Olivia had offered.

Chase had been grocery shopping before but never with a list. More like picking up beer or a few snacks. She glanced at the list in her hand. The thing was, like, long and full of unfamiliar items.

"Ma'am? You need a basket or cart?" someone asked her. Probably because she stood in the entrance, keeping the doors from closing.

"Oh, yeah, I have a long list here," she said, turning to the guy who wore a red apron and had a lazy eye. She averted her gaze because she was never sure where to look and didn't want to hurt his feelings. She looked back down at the list instead.

"Over there," he said, pointing to rows of metal shopping carts.

"Thanks," she said, tugging on a cart . . . that didn't move.

"Here," he said, pulling two carts apart with a grunt. He used a wipe to swipe the handle and pushed it toward her.

"Thanks," she said again, putting her purse in the basket part and setting the list on top like she'd seen other people in stores do before. She pushed into the store and glanced at what Olivia had listed. Hmm. Most looked to be ingredients for cooking. Wouldn't it have been easier to order some meals they could put in the micro . . . Wait, was there a microwave in that dump?

Chase didn't remember seeing one in the morning light, but then again, she'd been eyeing that feral beast, so maybe she'd missed it.

She decided to start in produce.

Apples.

She knew what those were, of course. But as she scanned the section, she realized she didn't know what kind Olivia wanted. So she found a little paper bag below the fruit bins and got one of each variety. Done.

Leeks.

What in the hell was a leek? She'd seen it mentioned in soups on a menu before but couldn't for the life of her remember what they looked like.

"Excuse me," she said to an older lady who maneuvered a motorized cart around a freestanding bin of tomatoes. "Can you point me to the leeks?"

The woman lifted her head and looked at Chase like she'd asked her to clean a toilet or something. "I don't work here."

"I realize, but I thought you might know what a leek is?" Chase tried to smile, like she'd done when she played Laurie Jingle, a sweet southern debutante, in *Bringing Down the House.*

Annnnd, that didn't work, because the woman gave her a disgusted look and rolled away without a word.

O-kay.

Chase headed over to the vegetable section, reading the signs above, like she should have done in the first place. That whole depending on the kindness of strangers obviously wasn't for people in Redmond.

Finally, she found something that sort of looked like celery but the sign indicated was a leek. She shrugged and plopped it into the cart. Maybe one was enough?

Next . . . onions.

Not hard. She got a yellow, white, and red to make sure she covered her bases.

Slowly, she worked her way through the produce aisle, keeping an eye out for the mean woman on the motorized cart just in case.

Before Chase left produce and headed into the bowels of the store, she pulled out her cell phone to check the time. She'd managed to get all the fruits and vegetables on the list in under ten minutes.

"Not bad," she said to herself.

Then she checked to see if she could get service on her phone. Nope. Damn Olivia.

She *could* make a phone call, she supposed, but to who? Lorna?

No way. She was still angry AF at her mother for turning her in. What kind of mother did that? But she knew. Lorna had to make sure Chase got her shit together so she could get a job to afford her mother the life to which she'd grown accustomed. A few months ago, she'd discovered her mother selling off some of Chase's clothes and shoes on some resale app. Lorna hadn't even asked if it was okay to do that. So call Lorna? The woman could make her scrambled eggs every morning served to her on a tray with fresh flowers for the rest of her life, and Chase still wouldn't call her mother on purpose.

She clicked the text app and saw none of her friends had messaged her. Except for Spencer.

Checking on my boo. Hope that cute therapist worked out. You got this, Golden Girl.

Aww! The dude had used correct grammar and everything. Like Chase was worth spelling things out and using commas. That made her smile.

And he'd called Olivia cute? Hmm.

She texted back. I'm cool. Just in Bumfuck, California. Come rescue me. You can distract the "cute" prison guard while I escape. ♥ ⚘

Five minutes had gone by while she piddled on her phone. She wasn't going to get this list accomplished in the allotted time if she didn't get her ass in gear. Pushing the cart toward Aisle 2, Chase nearly jumped out of her skin when someone standing near the endcap asked, "Care to sample a pizza bite?"

"What?" Chase asked, halting her cart.

An older woman wearing a hairnet and apron held out a paper cup containing a piece of bread with something weird atop. "It's Pizza Pronto's newest offering—nacho pizza bites. And here's a coupon, too."

"Oh." Chase didn't want to take it.

The woman shoved it her way again. "Go ahead. Try a sample."

Chase hadn't had anything to eat and *was* kind of hungry, but should people mix pizza with nachos? Seemed like a bad idea, but she took the little cup anyway. "Uh, thanks."

The woman raised her eyebrows, waiting on Chase to taste the concoction.

Chase popped the sample into her mouth and after one chew wished she hadn't. But she nodded and said, "Mm-hmm, very interesting."

"Take a coupon," the woman said, shoving that at her as well. "You can find them in the frozen foods aisle."

Chase wanted to spit the horrid appetizer back into the cup, but she didn't want to hurt the lady's feelings. The woman really seemed sincere about her product.

Instead Chase swallowed the bite and sharply turned the cart, clipping a potato chip display. A few bags fell onto the floor, causing a man perusing cans of tomatoes to frown at her. Then he squinted his eyes. Like he knew her.

Oh. Crap. She figured with the ratty clothes, no makeup, and unstyled hair, people wouldn't recognize her as a used-to-be-famous actress.

"Hey, aren't you . . . that blonde girl in all those campus movies. Drew . . . someone? No, maybe it's Reese something? I know I've seen you in something."

"Um, nope. Sorry. But you know, people tell me that all the time," she said, stooping to grab the bags and jam them back into the cardboard display.

"Well, you're a dead ringer for one of those actresses."

"Yeah, so they say," she said, scooting by him, hoping that she didn't have to get canned tomatoes. She looked at the list. Damn it. She did.

Chase stopped a few feet from him and stared at the offerings on the shelf. How many kinds of canned tomatoes were there? Stewed, diced, petite diced, whole. And then some cans had herbs and seasonings with the tomatoes. She grabbed the diced ones and hoped like hell it was right. On to spices.

Thirty minutes later after a really hard time finding yeast and evaporated milk (which was *not* in the refrigerated milk section), she rolled her loaded-down cart to the checkout line. She had only five minutes to spare, but considering that she'd had to figure out what a rump roast was, she thought she'd done pretty good. *Take that, adulting.*

Then she looked over and saw her face on the cover of the *National Tattler*.

Spencer Rome Orders Chase London to Therapy. "Get sober or get out!"

What the hell?

What was she supposed to get out of? Before a few weeks ago, she hadn't seen Spencer in months. They meet up once in a parking lot, and suddenly they're in a relationship? With him having enough authority to issue an ultimatum to her? Where did the *Tattler* get this crap?

"Ma'am?"

"Huh?" Chase ripped her gaze from the gossip rag.

The cashier looked at her, penciled-on eyebrows raised in question. She tapped the moving conveyor belt. "Your groceries?"

"Oh, sorry," Chase said, unloading her cart. The cashier grunted and started scanning, little beeps making Chase feel satisfied at mastering grocery shopping, even if she was annoyed by the stupid headline on the stupid magazine. Why wouldn't they leave her alone?

"Do you have any coupons?" the cashier asked.

"Oh, one. For the pizza bites," Chase said, handing it over, not sure why she got the pizza bites when she hadn't liked the nacho ones. Probably because she'd had that coupon and felt obligated.

The cashier scanned it and said, "Okay, that will be two eighty-three seventy-nine."

Chase pulled out the prepaid card Olivia had given her and then paused, glancing back at the total on the register screen. "Will you check this card to see how much is on it?"

The cashier rolled her eyes but took the card. Three seconds later, she said, "Two hundred and fifty dollars."

Glancing at the line behind her, Chase bit her lip. "Um, so what do I do?"

The man in line behind her gave an elaborate sigh and muttered, "Oh brother."

"Well, you either have to pay the remainder with cash or another card, or you have to put some of your groceries back," the cashier said. None too politely, either.

Chase pulled out the list. Okay, she'd sneaked in some extra items. "Um, so let's put back the ice cream, the OREOs, the pizza bites, the popcorn, and, um, maybe some of those onions? What onion is the most basic? The list says 'onion' but not what kind."

The man moved his cart up. "Is this chick for real?"

The cashier whose name tag read Lisa shrugged.

Now the man looked at Chase. "I'm in a hurry. I have to be somewhere, and you're preventing that because you obviously don't know how to live within your means."

Chase looked at him, trying to figure out what he wanted her to do or say.

"Are you retarded or something?" he asked after she didn't respond.

Chase felt tears spring to her eyes. Why did this guy have to be such an asshole? She was trying to figure out the situation. "You know, it's not nice to use that word, sir."

"It's also not nice to waste people's time, blondie." He raked her with a glance, taking in her wrinkled clothes. "I guess I shouldn't expect people like you to know how to add."

"Fuck you. I'm trying to buy the things on this list, asshole," Chase said, waving the list in the air. Tears were definitely present. Usually she could control them, but she was embarrassed that she didn't understand how all this stupid checking out stuff worked. She'd never not had enough money before. She just gave them a card and they swiped it. Presto chango.

"Okay, ma'am, calm down," Lisa said, looking nervously at the front, where a man with a thick mustache craned his head toward them.

"Calm down? Look, I've never done this before, okay?" Chase said, looking at Lisa, who had started taking the items she'd indicated from the bags and rescanning them as returns.

"You need to watch your mouth, young lady. We don't tolerate cursing around here," the stupid man behind her said.

"But you can use hurtful words? I'm pretty sure 'fuck' never hurt or belittled anyone before, but what you used does. Maybe you should watch *your* mouth." Chase turned around to Lisa and looked at the screen. The total was still too high.

Chase went to the bags and took out some seasonings that were higher priced along with the coffee creamer that had not been on the list. "Take these off."

The guy with the mustache moseyed over. "Do we have a problem over here?"

Lisa shook her head. "It's cool, Tony."

The asshole behind her said, "We have a shopper who doesn't know how to add."

"And an asshole who insults people," Chase responded.

"Ma'am, calm down," said Tony, whose badge revealed he was the assistant manager.

"I don't need to *calm down*. I need to not be insulted by people like this jackass. I made a mistake. It's my first time shopping on my own, which obviously I can't do." As she said the words, she realized they were true. She hadn't been able to do a simple task like get items on a list and check out.

Lisa didn't look quite so grumpy anymore. Something softer appeared in the cashier's rheumy brown eyes. Her pity made Chase even more upset. She didn't need these idiots' sympathy or censure.

"Oh, and to make matters worse"—Chase reached over and grabbed the *National Tattler*—"Spencer has given me an ultimatum! And I'm not even dating him, so how could he give me an ultimatum, I ask you. Any clue?"

The three strangers stared at her, looking absolutely puzzled.

"You know what? I'm out of here! So done." She slapped the magazine on the conveyor belt, grabbed her prepaid card from Lisa's hand, and shoved the empty cart out of her way. She flipped off Tony with his passive-aggressive male chauvinism bullshit and walked out the sliding doors, where the guy who'd helped her earlier gathered up the stray carts.

The tears that had threatened spilled down her cheeks. Angrily, she brushed them away while she looked for a place to sit and wait on Olivia, who would no doubt give her another lecture and be oh so disappointed that Chase couldn't do one simple adulting task.

God, she wanted a drink. The need to erase everything with the sting of vodka clawed inside her. *Make it go away.*

She found a plastic bench advertising nail salons and insurance companies and wondered if there was a package liquor store in walking distance. Nothing made her forget to feel like vodka did. Except maybe cocaine. She doubted if the cart boy could score her some blow.

"Hey," she called to the cart guy. "Is there a package liquor store around here?"

The guy shrugged his shoulders.

Yeah. Of course.

Didn't matter because Olivia's Volvo appeared like a menace, smoothly gliding into the trash-strewn parking lot. Olivia caught sight of her. Chase bent over and started reciting the serenity prayer in an effort to stave off the craving for booze and drugs. She'd started through the second stanza when Olivia's pristine running shoes appeared in her line of sight.

Olivia's hand lightly brushed her back. "Are you okay?"

Chase nodded.

"Good."

Olivia didn't say anything else for a few seconds. Just stood beside her, which was weird but also comforting.

"I couldn't finish checking out. Here's the card."

Olivia took the proffered plastic. "Was there a problem?"

"No. I just suck and can't adult. I'm going to the car. The stuff is at register five. I got everything on the list." Chase rose and started toward the Volvo.

Olivia grabbed her arm. "Let's go back in together."

"I don't want to go back in there. They're assholes. They called me names."

"Who did?"

"Never mind. Just get the groceries, and let's go back to Bumfuck."

Olivia shook her head. "No. Pretend you're a mother who has to feed her two children. Do you walk away empty-handed? Or do you humble yourself and get what you need to take care of your family?"

Chase rolled her eyes. "I don't have any kids."

"You're an actress. Pretend." Olivia walked toward the entrance, stopped, and waited on her. "Come on. We're going to figure this out."

Chase didn't want to go back inside, but she also didn't want to look like a quitter. "Fine."

They walked in together, and Olivia headed toward the register where Chase's cart sat to the side. She looked like a soccer mom about to go at a referee. The nasty man who'd called her a slur stood laughing with the manager, who sacked the guy's groceries.

Their laughter faded as Olivia stopped beside Tony and stuck out her hand. "Hello. I'm Olivia Han. Chase tells me there was a problem. That she was disrespected in your store."

The manager looked over at Chase and then looked at the magazine that still sat at the end of the checkout counter. "Is that really her?"

Olivia narrowed her eyes. "That isn't relevant. What is at this moment is why she left without procuring the groceries we need and why you as a manager allowed a woman patronizing your store to leave without"—Olivia glanced up at the motto on the store's front wall—"satisfaction."

The asshole guy snickered.

Olivia turned toward him like a weapon repositioning on a target. "Do you have something to say?"

The dude shrugged. "Just that whoever that girl is, she has a dirty mouth and can't seem to do basic math. But what do you expect from a drug addict?"

His words were tiny stinging darts, and Chase felt the tears prick at her eyes again. Why did she care what that loser thought of her? He wore a Hawaiian shirt, saggy shorts, and sandals that revealed yellowing toenails. Probably hadn't been laid since Bush was president. So gross. Yet his censure battered her ego.

Olivia pulled out her phone and snapped a picture of the manager. Then of the man standing at the checkout.

"What are you doing?" Tony asked, alarmed. "Hey, you can't take our pictures like that."

"I can if there has been harassment of a customer. I only have a little over two hundred thousand followers on Twitter, but they may want to hear how this store allows other customers to behave disrespectfully to women, and how the store manager—I'm assuming you're the store manager, Tony—doesn't care about how his shoppers are treated. How many followers do you have, Chase?"

"Uh, maybe almost a million?"

"I'll share this picture with you. We'll come up with a clever hashtag about how Tony lets people be verbally assaulted in his store. What do you think? Something that goes with Sav-A-Bunch . . ."

"Now wait a minute," Tony said, holding up a beefy hand. "That's not true. We didn't allow anything to happen. She got mad and walked out."

Olivia hooked her eyebrow, looking cold as shit. "What recourse does a woman have when she is being bullied?"

Something warm bloomed inside Chase. For a moment she envisioned her and Olivia as Thelma and Louise. They weren't going to take shit off anyone. Or maybe Olivia wasn't. Chase had sort of allowed Tony, Lisa, and the asshole extraordinaire to chase her from the store. But Olivia had her back. That felt good.

Needless to say, five minutes later, she and Olivia loaded the groceries into the car. Tony had even thrown in the pizza rolls as a gesture of good faith.

As Chase set a bag of groceries in the Volvo, she turned to Olivia. "That was pretty badass."

Olivia set the last bag in the trunk and closed it with a soft whoosh. She smiled at Chase. "No, Chase. *That* was being an adult."

CHAPTER TWELVE

Olivia wiped the kitchen counter clean and leaned over to catch Chase in the living room poking ineffectively at the fire she'd made in the fireplace.

"Try some kindling," she called.

"What is kindling, exactly? Like the weird nest-looking stuff?"

Olivia set the cleaner under the sink and surveyed the kitchen. Still dated but decidedly cleaner. And cat-free. Leaving the window open had worked, and their feline squatter had found better digs. Once the glass was repaired, they could be assured they'd have no more rogue cats crawling inside. So far the board Zeke had put over the small square of window had worked to keep the night air out, too.

She walked into the living room, thankful for the warmth coming from the dying fire. The day had been plenty warm, but the house had stayed drafty. They'd put away the groceries and cleaned the mildewed carpet where the air conditioner had leaked, which, after the grocery store fiasco, had been easier than she'd thought. Maybe because they both agreed that the smell had to improve. Cleaning had also given Chase some space.

She'd learned that after a defeat, most people needed time before diving into what missteps had been made.

Olivia went to the small box her grandfather had always kept filled with kindling and fire starter and picked up a few sticks. "See these smaller pieces of wood? They're dry and catch fire easier. The small tumbleweeds of wooden wool are used in place of starter fluid. Our fire is—well, sort of already going." She bent and placed several sticks of kindling at the base of the larger logs that were no longer actively burning. The flames sprang up.

Chase sat the poker back on the stand. "When will the electrician get here?"

"By the end of the day. The company he works for said he survived the rodeo unscathed. Thank God."

Chase gave a heavy sigh and sank onto the sofa.

"You want to help me clean upstairs while there's still light?" Olivia asked.

"Tell me again why we can't call someone to clean this dump?"

"Because we're adults with two hands and able bodies. And I bought a duster and cleaning products," Olivia said, starting back toward the kitchen, intent on using the time they had to get the place in a somewhat decent state.

"Then can I take a shower? I feel so gross."

"We have water, but without electricity, we don't have *hot* water. Do you like cold showers?" she called back, pulling out the duster, lemon furniture polish, and bathroom cleaner she'd bought earlier. She set them in a plastic tub, adding paper towels and a few sponges.

When she returned to the living area, Chase sat on the rug in front of the fire, staring into the flames. Her too-pretty face looked so tragic that Olivia's heart caught.

Which was a rare occurrence, because Olivia always kept her distance with clients. Her observations of their moods were clinical in nature. But sometimes the way the light caught Chase's face—the expressions, even the way she smiled—delivered a throat punch of emotion. She looked like Marley. That's what Conrad had seen. That's what Olivia saw each day.

Olivia set the tub of cleaning products on the dining room table and walked toward the hearth. Sinking down on the brick near Chase, she said, "You ready to talk about this afternoon?"

"No."

Olivia didn't say anything. She waited.

Chase kept her gaze on the fire. "I mean, I'm fine. I could have gotten the groceries. You saw that I had gotten everything you told me to."

Olivia nodded her head. "You got everything on the list. And pizza rolls. But I wasn't talking about the actual groceries."

Chase pressed her lips together hard before sucking in a breath. "I know."

"So tell me what you felt."

"I don't want to talk about it right now."

"Okay. Can I tell you what I think you felt?" Olivia waited because she wanted to ensure that Chase was open to hearing truths.

The actress gave a quick lift of her shoulder. "Yeah. Sure. Tell me. I've been dying to know what I felt."

Olivia chuckled.

Chase glanced at her flatly and refocused her attention back toward the flames now licking at the logs.

The warmth had grown in intensity, almost too hot against Olivia's back. "You felt shame. You felt judged. You felt less than."

"I didn't feel less than. Around *those* people? Did you see them?" Chase tossed her head, another defense mechanism clicking into place. Her anger and judgment of the people who hurt her was a deflection from her own pain.

"Even people who mean very little to us have the power to hurt us. The people who mean very much to us have even more power to wound. But this isn't qualitative. Hurt is hurt. Shame is shame."

"That man didn't *hurt* me. He's a dumbass. A nasty person who likes to belittle others. I shouldn't have run from them. I should have stayed and fought, ignoring them, conquering my list." Chase twisted her fingers against her shins, her expression darkening even as the light flickered over her face.

"But you didn't stay, and that's okay. You're not perfect."

"That's what therapists always say. *You're not perfect. You're human.* I thought you were going to be different. I thought you were going to tell me the truth," Chase said, looking up at Olivia, her blue eyes crackling like the fire before her.

"I am telling you the truth. We have two responses to situations such as that one—fight or flight. What might have happened had you stayed?"

Chase pressed her fingers to her eyes and groaned. "I don't want to talk about this."

"Okay, we don't have to." Olivia rose from the hearth. "Let's go upstairs and get our rooms in order."

Chase glanced up at her. "You're not going to make me tell you, like, what I should have done?"

"No. I showed you what to do. You have to advocate for yourself, and you are strong enough to do that. You have agency." Olivia went to the dining room table, picked up the tub, and started up the stairs. No way was she going to push Chase to unearth her emotions. Of course, she knew walking away would make Chase examine what she should have done even more closely. The woman's mind would natter away, turning each situation this way and that, trying to decide what had indeed been the best course of action to handle the shame and censure she'd felt at the grocery store.

And that was a good thing. Chase had spent a lot of her life not thinking. Either she compulsively acted or others decided for her.

The upstairs of the cabin opened to a large in-between loft space lined with bookshelves holding old novels and board games she remembered playing as a child. Ratty boxes of puzzles sat stacked beneath a mountain landscape her grandmother had painted one summer when she'd taken an oil class. A large window seat overlooked the sloping yard that ran toward the creek. The leaves on the deciduous trees—the names of which escaped her—had started turning golden, tired of summer, ready for a respite and a soft landing in a month or so. In the background loomed misty, violet mountains framed against a fading sky. For a few seconds, she paused and looked at the familiar view, one she'd taken for granted as a child but that now summoned such nostalgia.

Why had she waited so long to come back to this place? Those lazy summers and the careworn hands of people who loved her had shaped her, had taught her lessons, had given her memories that she shouldn't have let fade into the shadows. So why had she let what had happened with her father rob her of the joy she'd experienced in this place?

Of course, she knew. Just like with Conrad, she had avoided hurt. Her father's arrest and ensuing incarceration had brought mistrust and discord to their family. The one time she'd come to the cabin after the feud began with her father, she'd felt like the cabin had taunted her with the good memories. Memories that were all a lie. So Olivia had taken the jumbled boxes packed with pain, shame, and weighty things sitting in the middle of her soul and pulled a blanket over them. Pretty dumb for someone in her profession, but at the time she'd needed to move, to survive, to direct her energy to her burgeoning business. Eventually it got easier to step around the blanketed emotions and not see them. Coming to this place had pulled the edges of that blanket back.

Chicks always come home to roost. Or so they say.

Olivia shook off her thoughts, remembering that both she and Chase needed to get settled so they could truly start making progress.

Upstairs there were three rooms. One her grandparents had used, the other, her parents or her father's siblings had stayed in. The last room held bunk beds and air mattresses for the children of the family.

She needed to choose one to use as her own while she and Chase completed the adulting boot camp and the sneaky therapy she would slip in while Chase learned to use a lawn mower and bake a cake.

She chose her grandparents' room, which was smaller than the one used by the rest of the family. Olivia had always liked the coziness, the rocking chair in the corner, and the wedding ring quilt her grandmother had made the first year she'd been married to Papa Joe, the year after he'd brought her from Maine to California for a new start.

She'd just flung open the old drapes to let sunlight in when she heard a knock at the door. Had to be the electrician. Thank goodness. She needed a shower, too.

Olivia set her cleaning products on the bedside table and jogged down the stairs, pausing when she saw who stood on the threshold.

Not the electrician.

Neve.

Her older sister stood framed in the open door. Chase stood, hand still on the doorknob, a guarded look on her face.

Olivia blinked a few times. "What are you doing here?"

Neve looked older than her forty years. Life had done that to her. She'd once been trim, with gold-streaked chestnut hair, clear brown eyes, and glowing skin. She'd taught herself to play the guitar, had a passable voice, and planned to be a music teacher. That was before Scott.

Neve had dropped out of USC to marry a guy she'd only known for a month. Turned out Neve was good at bad decisions. The guy she'd met at the bar, who'd romanced her and used her student loans that semester to finance his bodybuilding career, turned out to be an asshole who couldn't hold a job or win any competitions. He took his failures out on Neve, verbal abuse that started several weeks after they'd run off to Vegas together. Of course, Neve never let on what was happening behind closed doors. Olivia's sister made excuses for her husband's drinking and joblessness, and it had ripped a hole in their relationship, especially when Olivia had tried to help. Neve hadn't appreciated her successful sister pointing out Scott's issues. She never appreciated much about anything Olivia tried to do.

Neve held up a key. "I could ask you the same thing. You know Papa Joe's lawyer sent me a key, too."

"Well, you can't stay. I'm using the property for work."

Neve's face darkened. "Who said you get to call dibs, Liv?"

Olivia ignored the irritation in Neve's voice. They hadn't gotten along well in years. "Where's Mom?"

Chase's head bounced back and forth as she watched Olivia and Neve's tense exchange.

"She's with her friends. They're doing a 'girls' weekend' over in Calosa, so I drove them there and came here to see what needed to be done to the place. I was thinking maybe we could make it a Vrbo or something since you won't sell it."

"I never said we weren't selling it," Olivia said, walking down the stairs, alarm pricking at Neve mentioning dropping her mother off with her friends. They had a deal about their mother and gambling. Calosa had the One Horse Casino. "But we're not leasing out the cabin. No strangers in here tramping around and tearing things up."

Neve looked around. "Well, no shit. No one would rent a dump like this."

Chase arched a brow. "That's exactly what I said. It's practically unlivable. We don't even have electricity."

Neve looked over at Chase. "Who are you?"

Chase made a face. Olivia wasn't sure if it was because Neve didn't recognize her or if it was because Neve was so abrupt.

"She's none of your concern. I'm sorry you drove all this way, but you can't stay at this time. I'm using the cabin for Chase's therapy." Olivia crossed her arms, the way she always did when it came to dealing with her difficult sister. Neve had always been confrontational, argumentative, and plain exasperating. If you told her something was yellow, she would say it was orange. That was her way, and she'd gotten worse since her divorce.

Neve shook her head. "Nope. There are three rooms. I'm staying in one of them tonight. Maybe tomorrow night, too. I'm picking Mom up on Saturday afternoon. Besides, you're not the only one who gets to decide what happens with this cabin, and really, you should have made sure it was okay with me before you rolled up here and parked your ass in something I'm half owner of."

"I'll write you a check for your half right now. I had it appraised right after Papa Joe passed away and the cabin came into our possession. I'll give you half of the appraisal amount." Olivia was not dealing with Neve for two nights.

But she'd overplayed her hand. Neve smiled. "I don't think so."

Damn it. Olivia should have offered to buy the cabin months ago when Neve needed money for the car she wanted to buy. Now Neve knew Olivia wanted the cabin. Of course, Olivia didn't know if she wanted to keep the place. This afternoon as she'd cleaned out the kitchen, sorting through worn flour sack towels, old wooden spoons, and her grandfather's prized cast-iron skillets, she'd thought about keeping it as a getaway. The memories had wafted out like bacon on those long-ago mornings, and Olivia wondered if she could part with the one piece of her past that meant something to her. Deep in her marrow, she knew this cabin could be the perfect place to retreat from the hardness of the world, but she would have to settle things with Neve.

It was as if she'd summoned the devil with that thought.

And now she'd tipped Neve off. If anything, her older sister knew how to read a room and would use that knowledge to her advantage. Olivia would have to wait her out.

"Fine. You can sleep in the bunk room. Chase and I already have our rooms selected, and that's the only one left." No sense in standing there arguing with Neve. Her sister had dug in her heels.

Neve looked over at Chase. "Wait. I know who you are. I just saw you on the cover of the *Tattler*. Spencer Rome? You really tapping that? 'Cause damn, girl."

Chase made a face reminiscent of the day Olivia first met her. Total disdain and mistrust.

Nonplussed, Neve continued. "Think you can get me his autograph?"

Chase closed the door behind Neve and shot Olivia an annoyed look. The actress bypassed Neve and started toward the staircase without a word.

Olivia had just turned to follow her upstairs when another knock sounded. She closed her eyes and released a breath. Thank God. Finally.

Chase stomped back over to the door and opened it.

Zeke.

Not who she wanted.

But another guy stood on the porch behind him.

"Afternoon, ladies," Zeke said, his gaze finding Chase, his smile widening a little. "Found this guy out on the main road, looking for your place."

The man wore jeans and a shirt labeling him as the guy they'd been waiting for all day. He tipped his ball cap. "Afternoon. Sorry I'm late. Had the rodeo last night and a job to finish over in Burney. Boss says the service has been restored, so it's likely a problem here at the house. Some of these older electrical boxes need to be replaced, but we'll see."

Randy the electrician glanced back at Zeke. "Thanks, man. I'm going to call you about that trip. Been wanting to get my hook in some bigger fish."

Zeke extended his hand. "I'll set you on some."

Randy turned and went out to his van, leaving Zeke with them.

Neve narrowed her eyes. "You look familiar."

Zeke arched an eyebrow. "You do, too."

Her sister took him in from the top of his ball cap to the toes of his beat-up running shoes. Olivia had to admit the lean man with the beard and green eyes was handsome in a rough-around-the-edges way. Her sister extended her hand. "I'm Neve. My grandparents used to live her."

"Zeke Kittridge. Mine lived up the road."

"Oh my Lord. You're the chubby little kid that was Marley's first boyfriend? No way."

Chase seemed to take offense at Neve's words, because she stepped past her, walked out onto the porch with Zeke, and closed the door in their faces.

"What the hell's wrong with her?" Neve said, turning to Olivia.

"She's protective of Zeke because he brought us chili last night." Olivia gestured toward the living room area. "Why don't you come in the living room while we wait on the electrician. Tell me how Mom is doing."

Neve looked suspicious. "Why are you being nice all of a sudden?"

Olivia fought back irritation at her sister. What was wrong with being polite? Why did her sister have to ascribe a motive to everything? "I'm not, Neve. I wouldn't dare be nice to you."

Her sister rolled her eyes but slid past her into the living room. "This place looks the same."

Olivia followed her sister. "Weird, huh?"

Neve pushed her hair back from her face. "Yeah, weird."

Olivia hadn't seen her sister since their mother's birthday in June. They spoke as briefly on the phone as possible, mostly on routine matters like their mother's medications or the leak that required a plumber. Too much had sat between them for many years, but once upon a time they'd been sisters. The kind that dressed in their grandmother's old dresses and climbed trees. Two girls relishing their secret society, squabbling over who got to marry which crush, and getting up early to watch *Tom and Jerry* before school. They'd dreamed under a blanket of stars glowing bright on the ceiling of their shared bedroom. They'd worn matching Christmas pajamas, fought over the cereal prizes, and held hands when they jumped in the lake. Sisters the same as any other.

But somehow they'd gotten sideways after all the trouble with their father and never found their way back. Neve resented Olivia's success. Olivia resented Neve's lack of motivation. They each stood on the other side of the fence when it came to their parents. Neve enabled their mother's gambling and unhealthy lifestyle and went weekly to visit their father, who had served his sentence and worked for a waste disposal company outside San Diego. Olivia did neither.

Neve picked up a *National Geographic*, a smile flitting across her lips. "Remember when we used to look at the naked pictures?"

Olivia nodded. "And Dad caught us and punished us? Ridiculous to put a stop to our curiosity, which was natural, but I suppose we now understand that he knew little of what was natural."

Neve's mouth twisted. "Please, Olivia. Don't."

Admonished, Olivia shrugged a shoulder. "Of course."

Why would they talk about the thing that had ripped them apart? Their father's actions had torn their family, smashing their illusions, making what had happened to Marley even more devastating. And Neve overlooked it.

Their dad, of course, never admitted to his crimes. Both Neve and her mother believed that he'd been falsely accused of lewd conduct and sexual relations with a minor, that his affectionate nature had been misread. They'd stood beside him, even as her parents divorced from the emotional strain. Olivia and her father had butted heads during the trial, and he'd accused her of choosing sniveling liberals over family loyalty. Olivia wasn't sure her father had done as claimed, but she'd lost all respect for him. They'd had a huge dustup, and now they no longer spoke to one another.

"I thought Mom had stopped gambling. I'm assuming that's where you took her?" As soon as Olivia said the words, she knew she shouldn't have, because that was another point of contention between the two sisters. Their mother had visited casinos off and on for years, and her "sometimes" addiction had nearly caused her and Neve to lose the house their family had once owned free and clear; not to mention, credit card debt had crippled them both for many years. Olivia had eventually stepped in and helped them script a plan to keep the house and hold the creditors at bay, but it was a monthly struggle that usually resulted in Olivia giving them money to stay afloat. Olivia did so with the understanding that her mother stay away from casinos.

"I know what you're going to say. Look, Shirley paid for the room, and Mom said she wasn't going to gamble—just hang with her friends. I took the credit cards. She has only fifty dollars to spend on food."

Olivia wanted to rail against her sister for even letting their mother consider a trip to the casino but bit her tongue. She'd talked to Neve about setting boundaries for their mother, and her sister had at the very least done that when she took away the credit card. Both she and Neve had agreed that their mother had to make her own decisions and own her own mistakes but that neither of them would be at financial risk again. "Well, that was a good move at least."

"I know you're against it, but those are her friends, and it's hard to sit on her 24-7. It's not my job to be her jailer."

"No, it's not your job. I appreciate you limiting her as much as you could. We'll hope that she can stay away, though I find that unlikely."

Olivia sank onto the couch and watched Chase through the hazy glass. The actress stood on the porch, listening to Zeke tell her something. He used big motions with his hands, and Chase looked intrigued. Her earlier defensive action was both alarming and productive. Chase had actually showed empathy by closing the door on Neve's hurtful comment, but Olivia was worried about her client's potential attraction to Zeke. She'd seen that spark of interest in Chase's eyes. Distractions like their hunky neighbor could be counterproductive for someone who needed to self-examine and enact change in her life.

Olivia looked back at her sister. Neve had sunk down in the harvest-gold tweed lounger with a little poof of dust, released into the late-afternoon sunlight streaming into the cabin.

Olivia decided to try again. "So are you still seeing the ER nurse? Um, Daniel, right?"

Neve shrugged. "We hang out every now and then."

"What about Scott?"

"He's been leaving me alone. I heard he's moving down to San Diego with some chick. God help her." Neve passed a hand over her face.

"Good. So I thought Daniel was exactly the kind of guy you were looking for? He has a stable job, a nice place, and treats you with respect. You said that's what you wanted. Deal breaker without those qualities."

Neve shot her an annoyed look. "Thank you, Dr. Phil. You know, you don't choose someone to love based on checking off all the right boxes. I guess you never learned that. But then again, you don't date, do you?"

Of course, Neve knew exactly what wound to poke to cause Olivia the greatest discomfort. She hadn't actively dated in the last few years because she'd been too busy . . . and still thinking about Conrad, which was unfair to the guys she'd tried to enter relationships with. "We're not talking about me, Neve."

"We never do. You give out all this great advice for other people, but you don't ever turn the finger you're pointing back at yourself. Why is that, I wonder?"

"I don't point fingers."

"Feels like it. You judged me about Scott, but you don't understand what it's like to take a chance, to hope beyond all hope that someone has changed. You refuse to live in a glass house because you're afraid of the stones that would be hurled back at you. You're like a hobbit living under the ground, safe and snug . . . and dead inside."

Olivia gripped the arm of the couch. "What a nice comparison. Thanks, Neve. So you know, I'm not protecting myself. I've just been busy."

Liar.

That word might as well have been shouted in the space between them. Olivia could see as much in her sister's eyes. Neve knew she was lying. Olivia knew as well. But thankfully her sister remained silent for a few seconds, giving Olivia an out. A generous move for a woman who wasn't always generous.

"So what do you want to do with this place?" Neve asked after a full minute had ticked by.

"Not rent it. It's actually a great place for the type of therapy I do, so I had been thinking we should keep it."

"So you can work with spoiled rich kids? What are you going to do? Teach them how hard life is by making them scrub the floor or chop wood?"

Olivia's lips twitched because her sister had totally simplified her therapy down to the bare bones of truth. Yet take the activity of chopping wood—one utilized the physical self, completed a task from start to end, used the resulting product for practical purpose. Overall, learning how hard work benefited a person was one of the building blocks of Square One. "Eh, maybe. A little."

"Are you serious? Your therapy involves getting free labor? You're way smarter than I thought you were."

"No, it's not about free labor. Learning how to contribute, be part of a team, and appreciate the simplicity of starting and finishing a job is part of the process. I'm not exactly Mr. Miyagi, but there's truth to what he taught—we learn how to deal with issues through practice."

"Lord." Neve shook her head. "You get paid a lot of money for a lot of bullshit. I should have stayed in school and graduated in counseling. We could have paired up and both sold this hooey to everyone."

Olivia tamped down the anger at her sister's winnowing her research and proven track record down to selling snake oil. "What I do, Neve, is not something fictional dreamed up to part rich people with their money. My program has had success helping certain types of people heal, unlearn destructive behavior, and thrive. The principles might seem atypical or unusual, but they work. So I don't appreciate you belittling what I do and making it sound like something it's not."

"Jeez, don't get your panties in a wad. What's that old saying? If you have to defend something so hard, it's partly true."

"It's not true. My methods work."

Neve shrugged a shoulder. "So what about Miss Bitch Kitty out there? She seems to like Zeke, and I hear she's the kind who likes lots of fun. You might want to lock that shit down, you know."

Olivia had been thinking the same thing, but she wasn't going to admit that to Neve. "While we're waiting on the electrician to restore our power, let's get Chase and make the upstairs habitable. We were in the process of tackling that when you arrived."

Neve rose and glanced around again. "You sure you want to keep this place? It needs new furniture, carpet, and probably appliances. That's a big expense when we can sell it and be done with the headache."

"Sell me your half and your headache is over."

Neve looked at her, her brown eyes calculating. "I don't think so. Not yet. Perhaps I'll consider selling if you do something for me. Like maybe listen to what Dad has to say about what happened with those girls."

Neve might as well have thrown a bucket of water in Olivia's face. "I'm not interested in anything he has to say."

"Don't you think our family has suffered enough? Those were false accusations. Both those girls had parents who were angry at Dad and trying to bring him down. It was a witch hunt. Do you really think Dad would do something so heinous?"

Olivia's stomach twisted, and she squeezed the armrest, trying to center herself and not let her emotions ricochet out of control. "Don't do this today. I mean it, Neve."

"Why are you doing this to us? You teach people to forgive themselves, but you withhold forgiveness from our father just because he said some crap about therapists. I just don't understand you."

How could Olivia relay how her father made her feel? How he always made her feel—not good enough. Charming and smart, her father had navigated the education system like a professional gambler, knowing when to hold the cards and when to show them. He'd been almost untouchable until he'd been arrested.

Charged for lewd and lascivious acts with a minor, her father had proclaimed he'd been misunderstood, that his overaffectionate, hands-on methodology of providing a loving environment in the school had been misconstrued. At first Olivia and her mother and sister had believed him, but while her father was awaiting trial, Olivia had counseled some children who'd been abused by their babysitter and had begun to suspect their father's insistence that he was being railroaded might be off. When she'd confronted him, he'd belittled her profession and accused her of siding with the alleged victims because she wanted to advance her career. The blowup around her father's case led to their falling-out and necessitated a name change. She'd never known if he was guilty or innocent, but after seeing her father's true colors, she hadn't cared.

"Fine. Let's go clean *our* cabin. Since it belongs to both of us, I'm assuming I can loan it out to friends? We can make a schedule or something. Maybe a few months where it belongs to me, and others that belong to you. Ground rules would be good, and, of course, if you're making money using it for clients, we'll have to talk about my percentage. How much is this chick paying you?"

Olivia gritted her teeth because she knew exactly what Neve was doing. "I get it. You're going to try to hold me hostage with this cabin. Why are you helping Dad? He destroyed our family, Neve."

"Don't believe your own bullshit, Liv. You're the one keeping our family apart. Dad served time for something he didn't do just to make things easier on us. You built an enormous wall just because he called out your profession. Just because he disagreed with you. Your ego is the issue."

Fury erupted inside her. "What happened was between me and Dad. It has nothing to do with you and Mom. Plus, you don't know the truth, do you? You only know his side. I talked to the girls. Everything about what happened was inappropriate. So don't believe *your* own bullshit."

Olivia stood and walked out, done with Neve. She didn't need the stupid cabin for her business. She could buy another ten times nicer than this one. Sure, they'd just arrived, but Chase would probably love to pack their bags and head back to Malibu.

Olivia jerked open the front door.

Chase and Zeke were leaning against a suspect rail and stopped midconversation at the abrupt interruption.

"Get your things, Chase. We're leaving."

Chase's eyes widened. "Why? The electricity can't be fixed?"

"It's not that. I've decided this cabin is not the right place for your therapy."

Chase shook her head. "But we're already here, and I told Zeke I'd go fishing with him tomorrow. He's a guide, and he's going to teach me how to fly-fish. I've always wanted to try fishing."

Zeke watched Olivia with a cautious expression. Olivia felt the world closing in, pressing her. She didn't want to stay here with Neve. The earlier memories that had been so comforting now felt as if they were tightening a vise around her body, squeezing her too hard. She'd been stupid to bring Chase here, insane to drag herself into her own past. With Neve showing up, the sense of reckoning had become even stronger, drowning out who she normally was. She needed to get control of the situation, and she couldn't do that here.

"You said you didn't want to stay," Olivia said.

"I don't. Or I didn't. But where are we going if we leave?"

Good question. She truly didn't want to take Chase back to LA. She'd thought Chase needed a reprieve from the world that had face-planted her into addiction, but maybe going back to LA would work to Chase's advantage. Olivia could stay with Chase for a few weeks, helping her to navigate the world the actress would eventually live in. She'd planned on staying with Chase a week after the adulting boot camp as a sort of reentry anyway. Chase would do fine in LA. Besides, obviously this run-down cabin next door to a male distraction was a bad idea.

For the first time in a long time, Olivia didn't know what to do. Which was intolerable because Olivia Han always had a plan. But at present, she felt upside down. And why in the devil after complaining nonstop about the cabin would Chase want to stay to go . . . fishing?

Fishing.

"I thought we could go back to the Malibu house. I'm very surprised you *want* to stay here." Olivia spread her hands out to encompass the house and land.

Chase shrugged. "Well, it's not so bad once we cleaned that mildew up. Besides, so far I've learned how to grocery shop, dress down a manager, and start a fire. And tomorrow Zeke's going to teach me how to fish. That's a good start to this adulting thing, and once we get electricity, we can get the cabin in better shape. Is this sudden about-face about your sister? You want to leave because of her?"

Yes.

"Not necessarily. I can deal with Neve. I just thought you wanted to go." Olivia didn't meet Chase's gaze.

"And since when did what I want matter?" Chase asked.

"With the chaos and the cabin's condition, I thought it might be better to cut our losses."

"We're already here, and besides, we have pizza rolls." Chase gave Zeke a saucy grin.

Olivia not only felt upside down but inside out. Chase wanted to stay, Neve wanted to stay, and it looked like Zeke wanted at least one of them to stay. Which was a problem.

"We'll stay for the time being," Olivia said, spinning on her heel, confused, angry, and slightly bolstered by Chase's response. At least the actress's attitude had improved. She knew that had to do with Zeke, but she would address that later. At present, Olivia needed to get herself together and stop letting Neve get to her. She also had to stamp out the stupid memories, the things she'd already shut the door on.

Accepting the things you cannot change was a motto she'd learned was true long ago.

But that was easier said than done.

CHAPTER THIRTEEN

The meadow was filled with scraggly yellow-tipped flowers and small purple ones, which made it look almost like a movie set Chase had once worked on in Montana. That movie involved a group of killer grizzly bears and unsuspecting college students. Stupid movie. Everyone knew bears were solitary creatures. Still, the scenery on location had made Chase feel alive. She wished she knew the names of the flowers swishing against her calves. Growing flowers was something her mother used to do, letting Chase help her plant happy pansies or luscious impatiens in the window box of their small apartment.

That had been before Chase got her first commercial. Before she had a real agent. Before her mother focused on Chase's career and forgot that her first role was being a mother.

"Careful," Zeke said, motioning her around a rough patch of brambles and steering her toward the woods that looked like a dusky ruffle at the hem of Mount Larsen's gown.

Chase had no clue why she was so excited about going to the river and trying her hand at fishing. She'd never thought much about fishing before, other than seeing it on TV or passing some old guys sitting on buckets lining the piers on the California beaches. The smell from their bait had made her nauseated, but for some reason, tromping through Northern California with Grizzly Adams was appealing. Yes, she knew who Grizzly Adams was because her father had acted on a few shows with the guy who played him in a television series. She couldn't remember his name, but he'd been an animal trainer who had turned actor. Her father had showed her the programs one time, and Chase had marveled at the bear and man living such a dangerous yet somehow desirable existence. Little did she realize that the mean streets of Beverly Hills would be more unforgiving with just as many rattlesnakes.

"So you said it's unlikely I'll catch a fish. I thought you were a guide. Don't you get paid to help people catch fish?" she asked.

"Are you paying me?" He stopped and lifted a shaggy brow. He so needed to wax those things.

"If you get lucky," she drawled, stepping around him.

"Don't play with fire, actress."

"You're good at the clichéd lines, huh?" she joked. Flirting with Zeke had proven entertaining. Almost as fun as aggravating Olivia. Of course, now she didn't have to worry about that. The therapist's sister was starring in that role. Chase had become the understudy.

"You can say that again," Zeke quipped.

Chase laughed and looked up at the sun in the sky, then back at the pasture beneath the rays. Seemed to her as if Mother Earth had taken a deep breath and exhaled the world she wished—strewn with bright blossoms, dotted with buzzing flies, and wrapped in vivid colors of azure, smoke, and straw. She liked being in this beauty with Zeke. She felt like almost a different person, someone who belonged, if only for a moment, to this world.

They reached the edge of the woods, and Zeke pointed out a path to her right. Dressing that morning, she'd pulled on tennis shoes, but when she'd emerged with them on her feet, Zeke had shaken his head and pulled out a pair of waterproof boots that were about as stylish as a garbage bag. Of course, she'd once gone to a show in Paris where the designer had dressed his models in actual Hefty garbage bags. Supposedly, it was a message on the nonrenewable earth. Chase suspected the guy had missed the point since he had actually *used* plastic in the collection.

The earth beneath her ugly boots seemed to shift as they picked their way toward the rushing waters below. Zeke occasionally took her elbow, which made her feel safe, something that warmed her from the inside out.

Every now and then she peeked through her eyelashes at the man, who wagged his head left and right keeping an eye out for cougars, which he said came down from the mountain sometimes. A decent haircut would do wonders for the man, not to mention a good trimming of his beard. Still, the mussed-up, carefree traveler look worked for Zeke. His shoulders were wide enough to withstand trouble, his rangy body alert. Those emerald eyes reminded her of fresh clover (the shade of eye shadow she used, not the actual plants), and his lips were full, a sort of Brad Pitt thing. Zeke mostly stayed quiet, his gaze attentive and intentional, but when he spoke, it was with animation and passion. She could hardly look away from him.

Yesterday on the porch, while Olivia engaged in a struggle with her sibling, Zeke had explained he was a fishing guide who owned his own business. He also made jigs that he sometimes sold online. She'd had no clue what a jig was, but he'd explained how he used bits of hair or feathers bound to a hook that looked enough like an insect to seduce a fish. Zeke had only been doing the guide service for a few years. Before that, he'd worked in NYC. She'd tried to find out why he'd ended up back in Cotter's Creek, but he'd shrugged off her questions. Like Olivia, he seemed fine avoiding his own past. And that was something Chase understood well.

Finally, they reached the banks of the Upper Sacramento River, a forty-mile stretch of wildness and rushing waters at the base of a mountain. Zeke sat the rod cases he carried against a large boulder and peered out at the water, which had sounded more powerful than it looked, as if he were inspecting the river. The stream still rushed all in a hurry around rocks, forming brackish pools. Leaves skated on the surface, small flies hovered, and overhead birds called to one another. Sunlight fell onto the murky waters in patches, and in one pool she could see shapes moving.

"Are those fish?" She stopped on the rocky bank, the water kissing her boots, and pointed to the shadows in a nearby pool.

"Probably," Zeke said, doing something with the rods and a case he carried, but she didn't bother watching him prepare to fish. She couldn't seem to pull her gaze from the beauty before her.

They were completely alone, buried in the evergreen dabbed with brilliant gold and persimmon along the stream. She stooped and felt the water. Not as warm as she'd expected. Cool nights and mornings had lowered the temperature.

"The water's down, but that's not a bad thing," Zeke said.

She rose and glanced over at him, where he tied a feathered bit with a hook on the end of a line. So that's what a jig looked like. It was really small. She'd seen fishing supplies in a store once and the baits were much larger. "When is the best time to fish?"

"Every day," he said, looking up with a grin that made her stomach flutter.

And why in the world would that happen? If anything, Chase was experienced around guys. Too experienced, some would say. But Zeke made her feel different. Maybe it was because he seemed unfazed by her fame. Maybe it was because he wasn't so careful with her. Treated her like any other person. Made her think about all those times she thought about getting in her car, driving, cutting and dyeing her hair, and starting over as Katie. So many days she wanted to be that girl. Someone normal who came home, made a cup of soup, and took her dog for a walk. A girl who bought her clothes at Target, sang in the church choir, and volunteered to read books to old people at senior citizen centers. Just boring ol' Katie. Not train-wrecked Chase.

Yesterday, when she'd jokingly told Zeke she wanted to go fishing, he'd nodded and said, "How about tomorrow? I had a cancellation."

She hadn't been serious when she'd said she wanted to go, but when he'd offered, it became imperative that she experience fishing. Olivia's questions about her lack of a childhood had banged around her brain. She'd not realized how many things she'd missed out on—roller-skating, the circus, road trips, a first date where she was so nervous she nearly puked. But going fly-fishing with Zeke could fill one of those holes in her life. At the very least, Olivia's weird brand of therapy had made Chase determined to get a shovel and attempt to fill a few.

Then Olivia had tried to hijack her outing with the whole dramatic "let's blow this joint" routine she'd done on the porch yesterday. Obviously, Olivia didn't like wrinkles. Neve was like a tsunami of wrinkles plopped into Olivia's world. If, you know, there could be an actual tsunami of wrinkles. After making sure they could stay at least long enough for Chase to try her hand at fishing, Chase had given Zeke a salute and followed her combination therapist, drill sergeant, and pain in her ass back inside the house.

Zeke took his leave, promising to pick her up the next day after lunch. Chase tempered the excitement of doing something totally out of her comfort zone with the thought that she had to spend an awkward evening with Olivia and Neve.

When Chase had walked back inside the cabin, she noted that Neve looked smug.

For some reason that bothered Chase. She'd known women like Neve—shit stirrers who took pleasure in causing others discord. But she didn't say anything to either woman. Just looked at them with bored eyes before Olivia handed her a broom and started up the stairs.

Chase found her bag in the larger of the bedrooms. The room had a westward-facing window that allowed warm sunlight to slant inside, making the room less dreary than the others. She pulled the blankets off the queen-size bed so they could be laundered. New sheets sat in a package on the writing desk beneath the window next to a folded quilt.

"Olivia, this package says I should wash the sheets before using them," she called out the open doorway.

Olivia appeared in the doorway, looking perturbed. "We don't have electricity."

Chase pointed to the instruction again. "You told me to read the instructions. Just following orders."

Olivia seemed to repress a sigh of irritation. She opened her mouth to say something, and the lights came on.

"Oh, thank God," she said instead, closing her eyes in what Chase guessed was gratitude. "Look, for now, dust the room, sweep, and make a note of anything that needs addressing."

Chase made a face and then handed the package to Olivia. "Fine. Here are the sheets."

Olivia looked at the package, and her mouth went flat as a toad's. "The washing machine is downstairs. You can toss them in now that we have power."

"But I don't know how."

"Figure it out. There are instructions on the washing powder. Once you're done with laundering your sheets, we'll start supper." Olivia set a duster, a bottle of cleaner, and a broom inside the door and turned to leave.

The whole idea of figuring this stupid stuff out made Chase itchy. After all, she'd failed at actually checking out groceries. How in the world was she supposed to figure out a washing machine? She sent her clothes out to be cleaned, or her housekeeper, Tracie, did the washing once a week, folding the clothes neatly in her dresser. God, she missed Tracie.

"We?" Chase repeated.

"Yes, we. This is an adulting boot camp where all the adults present pull their weight." Olivia looked resolute. Her gaze swept the room. "You should be able to tidy this room in thirty minutes."

Then she left.

"So fly-fishing takes practice," Zeke said, jarring her out of her contemplation of how she was terrible at dusting. How could one be bad at wiping off dust? Meet Chase London, failed duster.

"Seems a lot in life takes practice," she said, tired of hearing those words, even though she knew they were true.

"Sure. But worthy things come from practice, and there's something pure in practicing. You come at whatever the thing is with intent and focus, expecting to fail, but also expecting to move toward a goal. Personally, I never minded practicing. Come here and let me show you some basics, starting with some terminology."

Zeke sitting against that boulder, the river moving swiftly beside him, the dappled sunlight falling through the canopy to speckle his khaki hiking pants and chamois vest restored something to her soul. The craving inside her for normalcy, for simplicity, for peace, was allayed by the beauty, by his words, by the fact he'd taken the time to bring her to this gorgeous place and teach her something as old as time.

For the next hour, she did not worry about catching anything. She merely practiced the technique, the rhythmic dance of the line swirling overhead, the staying low, the quick retrieval. All the while, Zeke stood beside her, encouraging and sharing his love for catching brookies up the mountain or the way browns got territorial and thus a black or orange fly mimicked another fish and often netted more strikes. He talked about his flies—what a wet or nymph fly looked like as opposed to a dry one, like the one she was using. He taught her about caddis hatches and mayflies and which rivers yielded the best results in the fall.

Chase didn't understand most of it, and her arm ached from the motion needed to successfully cast the line, but she enjoyed the way he told stories, reveled in his tales of funny guiding trips, and tried very hard to perform the cast and retrieval.

So it was fairly amazing when upon a good cast (finally), something grabbed her fly.

"Oh! Oh!" she shrieked. "Something's got it."

Zeke snapped to attention. "Seriously?"

She might have been offended by the surprise in his voice, but she was too busy pulling the line and tugging against the jerking of the rod. "Oh, it's a big one. Help me!"

Zeke stood behind her, wrapping his arms around her and supporting the pole. He guided her right hand to the line, showing her how to retrieve it. "It's okay to take your time. Enjoy the weight of the fish on your line. Steady now. Step out here. Mind your footing."

He supported her elbow, moving her forward. In the back of her mind, she reveled in the feel of him against her. He smelled like wet canvas and earthiness, not unpleasant in the least.

Moving forward, stepping into the moving stream, she focused on not falling on her ass and keeping the fish on the end of the line. Faithfully, she pulled the line, wedging her borrowed boots into the streambed, adjusting her feet to shoulders' width for better leverage. Zeke moved from behind her to beside her, clasping a net he must have nabbed at some point. When the fish got close enough, he reached out and grabbed the line, lifting the writhing fish into the sunlight.

Her catch wasn't very big, but it was lovely, with pink and salmon striping catching iridescent in the sunlight.

"Oh, I did it," she crowed, punching a fist into the air, nearly falling into the gurgling waters at her feet. She steadied herself and beamed at Zeke, who had untangled the fish from the net. "Zeke, I caught a fish."

Zeke cradled the slender fish in his paw and grinned up at her. "A nice one, too. This is a rainbow trout. You want to touch it?" Zeke removed the jig from the fish's lip but kept the fellow in the water.

Chase bent down, holding the rod aloft so she didn't accidently dunk it. Reaching out a finger, she touched the fish. Didn't really feel slimy. "Cool."

Zeke smiled. "I'm letting him go now."

"We're letting him go? We're not going to eat him?"

Zeke chuckled. "Not unless you want to clean it."

"No. I want to set him free."

At her words, Zeke released the fish, and it flipped away, brown tail waving a goodbye.

"I can't believe you caught that trout." Zeke rose, a somewhat bemused look on his face.

"I can. I have a good guide." She handed him the fly rod and shaded her eyes, looking in the direction in which her fish had disappeared. "I hope my fish has a good life, and when he thinks back on getting caught, he will know that I had nothing but goodwill for him."

Zeke laughed. "You're an actress, all right."

Chase smiled at him. "You know, I needed that small victory because last night in my Adulting in the Kitchen 101 class, I had multiple failures."

"Adulting?"

She followed him to the bank, stepping carefully in the moving water. "That's what Olivia calls her program. Well, technically it's Square One, but essentially it's learning how to do shit you don't know how to do because no one ever taught you how to do it."

Zeke made a confused face. "So like what?"

"Like chopping onions and not cutting off your finger," she said, holding up her bandaged pinkie. "Or knowing what kind of soap to use in a dishwasher."

"Oh no. You didn't," he said, looking absolutely delighted.

"I did. We had to mop for over an hour."

Zeke started laughing, and the sound made her tummy all floppy. Kind of like that fish. "You used dish soap?"

"I didn't know you couldn't use the dishwashing liquid in the dishwasher. I mean, they do the same job. I just grabbed it. Of course, Olivia pointed out that had I read the directions, I might have seen it expressly stated on the back label that it wasn't for use in dishwashers."

Zeke shook his head. "Did the dishes get clean?"

Chase shrugged. "I don't know. Olivia was so put out with me that after we finally cleaned up the suds all over the place, she sent me up to my room to do some homework."

"Homework?" Zeke had started disassembling the rod she'd used. The sun had started sinking lower, and the light had gone more golden as the day made plans to take its leave. The hike back to Zeke's jeep was at least thirty minutes. Time to leave peace behind.

"Like worksheets on emotions and crap. Things that make you think about the bad stuff that happened to you or the reasons you snorted coke in the bathrooms of clubs or went down on guys you don't even know."

That was probably too much information, because Zeke's brow lowered, and he glanced away from her. She knew he was too nice to ask the question, *Did you do those things?*

And she was glad he didn't ask, because she didn't want to have to answer it.

Because her behavior embarrassed her. It wasn't the first time she'd felt ashamed of the life she'd led, and it wouldn't be the last. She couldn't change her poor choices in the past. That was what the homework emphasized. She'd begun the book in rehab, one that was similar to all the others she'd done. Before, she'd answered with what she thought the therapists were looking for, but this time, after she'd thankfully bailed out of Cedar Point, she'd continued doing the workbook even though she was no longer in group therapy. A teeny part of her missed group therapy because most of those people had been as effed up as she was. Misery loves company, right?

"You probably haven't had much bad stuff in your life, have you?" she asked, stepping out of the stream and holding her rod case out to Zeke.

He took it, his expression darkening a little. Then he lifted his head, staring out across the river at the signs of fall coloring the opposite bank. "You know, I'm like anyone else. Life hasn't been a continuous picnic. I guess that's why I came back here. It's easier to think in this world, to live intentionally, like Thoreau suggested."

"Who?"

Zeke pulled a book from the top of the case he carried. "*Walden.* Henry David Thoreau was a transcendentalist who lived back in the early 1800s. He advocated living simply, returning to nature, to marching to the beat of your own drum. I keep a copy and pull it out to read sometimes when the fish are being disagreeable. His observations remind me why I came back home. Why I make my living in this world and not on Wall Street. I'm sucking the marrow from life."

Again, Zeke's words were impassioned, a man who believed in the decision he'd made. Chase wanted that certainty about her life, but she wasn't to that point yet. Olivia had mentioned that Chase could quit acting, but that life was the only one she'd ever known. When she'd been younger, she'd been very good at her job—she could shift from loathsome cheerleader bully to lost ingenue in seconds. Her Golden Globe sat on her mantel, a reminder that she'd once been a serious actor, one who hadn't necessarily mastered her craft but had an opportunity to grow into a Meryl Streep. Instead she'd gone the way of too many child actors—totally off the rails. Why hadn't she been able to control herself? To control her thoughts and emotions?

"Sucking the marrow from life sounds like serious business," she said, trying to shift back to the lightness they'd shared moments before when she'd been struggling against a fish and not massive doubt.

"It's more of a necessity for me. I need to know what I do is good, not just for me but for the world around me. Because my last job wasn't, and I was good at that job. It's hard to reconcile being so good at ruining people. So I don't do that anymore. I get up every morning and live with intention and honesty as best I can."

This dude was too good for her. "That's . . . pretty cool, Zeke."

"You want to borrow the book? We can talk about it next time." He held out the ratty, dog-eared copy. Chase took the book, almost appalled at the shape it was in. When the man read a book, he read it.

"Next time?"

Zeke's smile felt gentle. "You've proven you're definitely a decent fly fisherman. Or fisherperson? I guess that's more correct these days. Gender neutrality in fishing."

Chase wasn't sure that Olivia wouldn't be waiting back at the cabin with her car running, ready to flee from Neve and whatever else haunted her. Her empathetic radar had raised its antennae, making Chase almost certain that coming back to her old childhood home had set Olivia on a path she'd not reckoned. Therapist or no, Olivia had issues. Perhaps, if they'd not come to this place, Chase may have never seen the cracks. But those puppies were widening by the day. "I guess I wouldn't mind going fishing again. Maybe this time *you* can catch a fish."

Zeke snorted. "You catch one piddly trout and you're taunting me now?"

His words were laced with laughter and were balm to her soul. She needed someone like Zeke.

He handed her one of the bags he carried, reaching up to brush something from her hair. Chase swayed toward him, her eyes on his lips, marveling at how the bottom one curved generously and how that bee-stung upper lip seemed to be asking to be pressed against hers. She lifted her gaze to his.

Hunger sat in those green depths.

"I really want to kiss you, Zeke," she said, stepping back, "but I know I can't do that right now. I'm too messed up for you."

"No, you're not," he said, holding his ground.

"Yeah, I am, but I would really like to have a friend. I don't have too many of those, to be honest." She'd been vulnerable many times in her life, but she'd never felt quite so vulnerable as she did presently, standing in an unfamiliar world with a guy like none she'd ever known, asking him to be her friend.

Zeke's mouth curved. "I think you can count me as one."

She swallowed, not realizing how much those words meant to her. So many of her other "friends" had been so because they could name-drop, go clubbing with her, meet celebrities, use her credit card. Truth was, she wouldn't mind being more than friends with Zeke. The old Chase would have stepped into that kiss. The old Chase would have straddled him on the rock before they ever made a cast. She wasn't the old Chase anymore. "Thank you, Zeke."

Starting back up the path, he looked back over his shoulder at her as she picked up her ugly boots and followed him. "But maybe when you get your shit together, we can revisit that kiss thing. I'm not opposed to kissing my friends. Well, some friends."

His eyes were all twinkly, emerald, and flirty. He even winked at her before redirecting his attention to the path ahead.

"I bet you're not," she mumbled with a chuckle, scrabbling a little as she lost her footing, looking up at the steep hill in front of her. A harbinger of things to come. Even so, she was ready to climb to a new place in her life.

And now she had a friend.

A friend who was utterly kissable.

Someday.

CHAPTER FOURTEEN

Olivia wanted to strangle her sister but wasn't sure that she wanted to live out the rest of her life in a small jail cell. Neve was counting the Fostoria glassware and talking about how she could sell it online "for a lot of money."

Ignoring her sister had been the plan when she'd woken that morning. After meditating and doing a quick round of yoga, she'd listed three things she wanted to work on that day. Number one on the list should have involved her client, but with Neve working her nerves, she'd moved "Ignoring Neve's gibes" to the top, sliding "Patience with Chase" to spot number two. Three was "Self-awareness of her own fragility." Not that she was fragile. But she was somewhat vulnerable at this particular time, and she could own that about herself.

"Neve, I think inventorying the cabin is a solid idea, but shouldn't we focus on making the list of household items along with a repair list before we start selling off everything we come upon? You know, first things first."

Neve gave her a sharp look. "I didn't say we should sell the Fostoria. I said we *could*. You're hearing what you want to hear, as usual."

"I'm not." But maybe she was. Irritability had whittled out a place inside her and now scratched around, making her want to let the harridan she normally gagged and bound out to rampage. She took a deep breath and blew it out before glancing out the window for the twentieth time. She'd asked Chase to be home at four that afternoon. They were volunteering at the senior care center where her grandfather had spent his remaining years. Then they would attend a committee meeting for the Mount Larsen Fall Festival, which would be held in a few weeks. The organizers had agreed to let both her and Chase serve on a committee.

Neve rose from the floor, knocking the dust from the knees of her jeans. "This place needs a lot of attention. These bookcases need painting and the floor refinishing."

"Yeah," Olivia said, noting the tone shift in Neve. Her sister was overly interested in getting the cabin in order. "You want to do that?"

"Well, after last night, after I got over the amusement at your actress who knows zilch about anything, I started remembering why I liked this place. Same as you, I guess." Neve shrugged and closed the cabinet door beneath the built-in bookshelf. She glanced around, wincing at the ugly light fixture. "I mean, with some elbow grease and a little money, we could make this place nice again."

Olivia started to say that Neve had no money and then realized that was another bitchy thing to say. She wasn't sure why she was so angry at her sister—because Neve supported her father? Because she saw counselors and therapists as the enemy? Because Neve had stayed in a failing marriage until it had damaged her? Because she didn't seem to give a damn about much in life? Olivia didn't understand her sister. So she said, very neutrally, "Yeah, we could. It's something we need to discuss."

Neve looked at her. "Why don't you like me?"

Olivia flinched. "What?"

"You don't like me. You used to like me. Before Scott. Before Marley died. Before Dad screwed up. We used to be close. We're kind of opposite people, but we liked each other at least."

"I *love* you," Olivia said.

"No, I don't think you do. I think you don't love much of anyone anymore. You're successful with a program that probably works, but you're full of so much resentment, anger, and disgust for people who are weaker, I'm not sure how you're still in business, honestly."

A volley of stinging needles flung her way would have been gentler than her sister's words. "That's not true."

"Maybe not wholly, but it's at least half-right."

Olivia shook her head. "I'm successful because I dedicated myself to practices that work. I don't hate you. I am sometimes annoyed with you because . . . a lot of things."

"Because I can't keep a job? Because you have to give us money to make ends meet some months?"

Olivia hadn't expected Neve to be so blunt, but her sister seemed on a mission. "Okay, fine. Sometimes it bothers me. I send Mom a check each month to help both of you, and you always seem to need more."

"Maybe Mom can come live with you."

"What? No."

"Why not? She's your mother, too. You've been content to let me care for her while you do yoga in Beverly Hills. She's an inconvenience to you, but she's one to me, too. I get to care for her by default because I have no power. But if Mom was taken care of, I could start over somewhere new. I'm trapped where I am."

Olivia looked away, knowing Neve's words were true. "And where would you go?"

"I don't know. Maybe here. I could work as a stylist for someone. I'm still good at hair."

"I always wondered why you stopped."

"I'm probably an embarrassment to the great Olivia *Han*. A sister who can't even keep a job cutting hair. But you know, you can't pretend your past or the people who once lived in it away. You changed your name. There's so much wrong with what you've done, how you live. You help others deal with their pasts, but you don't deal with your own.

Instead you send us a check and pretend us away. Dad served his time and you won't even talk to him. Aren't you supposed to face the crap in life? You seem to think you shouldn't."

Those words weren't true. Yes, she sent her mother a check each month, but it wasn't merely to mollify her mother or soothe Olivia's conscience. It was because her mother had severe rheumatoid arthritis and could no longer work. It was because Neve couldn't seem to hold down a decent-paying job. It was because Olivia now had more than enough money and wanted to share it with her family—the only two she had left, not counting the father she'd written out of her life. Even if her mother and sister were . . .

Her thoughts had started down a horrible path.

Different.

Trouble.

A burden.

"I don't do that," she managed to say.

Neve turned away from her. "Then why don't you ever visit us? Why do you pretend we don't exist? Mom and I know. We *know*. We hear it in the words you say to us."

Her sister's words tore at her. She'd never thought they wanted her around. The rare times she visited, both her mother and sister seemed nonchalant about the expensive pastries she brought, the conversation she tried to make, the stories she told. Olivia no longer felt like a part of her family. Most of the time she felt cut loose. "I don't mean to make you feel that way, Neve. I'm sorry."

Her sister swallowed and glanced away, but Olivia didn't miss the sheen of tears in Neve's eyes. The sight made her feel sick. Neve walked toward the kitchen. "I have to call Mom and check on her."

Neve left Olivia standing in the foyer devoid of her normal composure.

She'd made her mother and sister feel small.

By her words. Her actions. Her charity.

She had never wished to do that.

The door opened and Chase appeared, looking very unlike the sullen, defensive actress she'd first encountered at the rehab center. The woman wore tight jeans, rubber boots, a flannel shirt five sizes too big for her, and a smile that made her blue eyes dance.

Olivia reined in her raw emotions and tried to plaster a neutral expression on her face.

"I did it," Chase said, setting the black purse Olivia had insisted she take on the small bench by the door, her face radiating with accomplishment. "I caught a trout."

Looking quite pleased himself, Zeke followed. "I'm a helluva guide, Olivia."

"He is. He taught me how to swirl the line and even tie on the jig. Do you know what a jig is?" Chase asked, tugging the shirt off, revealing the tight T-shirt beneath, and holding it out to Zeke. "Thanks for letting me borrow this."

Zeke took the flannel, his gaze remaining on Chase as she tugged her hair into a ponytail and grabbed the expensive athletic jacket hanging on the coatrack. "Sure."

"We need to go, Chase. We have to be at Rock Glen in twenty minutes," Olivia said in order to interrupt the intimate display of . . . affection going on right in front of her.

She'd worried about letting Chase go with Zeke on the outing. The only thing that made her relent was knowing what kind of guy Zeke was. Yeah, he was a dude, but she remembered how her grandfather had talked about his neighbor, praising his generosity and big heart. Zeke had left a high-stress job working as an attorney for a corporate raider to live a smaller life, one in which he volunteered with the Boys & Girls Club and helped at the Northern California food bank. Besides, he didn't seem remotely Chase's type, being that he was a good deal older and didn't look the type to date silly blonde actresses. Zeke seemed like a gentleman, the kind of guy Chase probably hadn't been around very often if Hollywood rumors were to be believed.

Still, a reminder that Square One required total focus on healing and reconstructing one's life without romantic attachments might be necessary for Chase. If a client was in a committed relationship, Olivia had a relationship counselor brought in to work with the couple, but if the client was unattached, romance was heavily discouraged. Compliance with this dictate was in the contract.

"You're going to Rock Glen?" Zeke asked, looking puzzled.

"Olivia volunteered us to run their games this afternoon. It's another part of adulting. Not sure what part, but I like games." Chase wriggled her shoulders in a playful manner.

Zeke raised an eyebrow.

"Okay, let's go," Olivia said, picking up her bag and grabbing a sweater. Perhaps she also needed to say something to Zeke about steering clear of Chase. Learning how to set boundaries with friends was important for Chase to learn, but this seemed to be tripping toward something more than friendship.

"Thanks for taking me fishing, Zeke. Who would have guessed how much I like catching disgusting fish?" Chase raised a hand to high-five the big guy.

He slapped her palm. "Watch out for Mr. Cavendish. He will cop a feel. I play piano there sometimes, and I've seen him in action."

"You play piano?" Chase asked.

"I'm a helluva piano player."

"You're a helluva lot of things," Chase teased.

Olivia turned and rolled her eyes. "Let's go."

She called up to her sister that they were leaving, her heart dinging a little at the hurtful words they'd just exchanged. Olivia was surprised by how much she disliked the discord between her and Neve. How many times had she parted from her sister with hard things between them and not given it more than a passing thought? More than she could count. Why did it matter this time?

Maybe she was the one who had changed?

And why was that?

She wasn't sure. Maybe it was this place? Maybe it was the timing? Maybe her life was coming full circle. She wanted to stop the static disruption but couldn't seem to do it. She'd have to deal with her emotions and put together a plan to manage them.

A plan was always a good . . . plan.

When she and Chase climbed into the car, Olivia turned to her client. "Stop whatever you're doing with Zeke."

Chase made a face. "We're not doing anything. We're just friends."

"Who are flirting with danger."

"Look, if I wanted to fuck Zeke, I could. So cool your jets." Chase buckled in before reaching over and turning on the radio.

"Remember the contract. No romantic relationships when you're completing the Square One program. Friendship is fine. But that is where it needs to stay."

Chase's response was to turn the radio up louder and slide on her sunglasses.

Olivia decided not to peck any more at Chase and instead drove to Rock Glen Retirement Center. She was pretty certain that her client understood her stance with Zeke.

Thirty minutes later, she and Chase sat at different tables playing dominoes. The older gentlemen at Chase's table were patiently teaching her how to play. Olivia could hear their teasing and laughter every few minutes. Chase was plying them with charm and her baby-blue eyes. Must be useful to be an actress and be able to play any parts one needed. At least the actress had stopped playing parts with her.

At least some of the time.

Olivia slid her domino to the end of the train. "Thank you for letting me come play with you ladies."

Erma, a wizened woman with blue hair and ill-fitting dentures, cackled. "We didn't have a choice."

"Okay," Olivia said, biting her lower lip. "Why didn't you have a choice?"

"We don't have choices here. They roll us down the hall and park us here. We have good manners, so we sit here with people like you who come to do 'volunteer' work with the 'elderly,'" another woman, this one with flaming red hair, said. Her name was Rita. Rita the Red.

"While I would agree with encouraging you to participate in things you enjoy, I would disagree that you are obligated to sit here with me and make nice in order to make me feel better about myself. Do any of you ladies wish to play dominoes?" Olivia asked, understanding now why her table had been so morose compared to Chase's. These ladies didn't want to play games and make forced conversation.

She glanced around at the five assembled, two in wheelchairs. They shrugged their shoulders and looked uncomfortable. Finally, Erma said, "We don't mean to be rude."

"You're not. What would you like to do? If anything?"

"I'd like someone to do my nails," one of the ladies said, holding up a hand threaded with blue veins and spotted with decades of living. "I used to have such pretty nails. My hands would look better if my nails were painted."

"And I want my hair to look good, like my daughter's. Patrice comes to wash and trim it in our beauty shop, but she can't style it. I always look like a sticker burr or like someone shaped my hair into a helmet, which is probably better than the burr look," another lady said. Her hair did, indeed, look burr-ish.

Chase had turned to look over at them, obviously having heard the comments about hair and nails. "What's going on over there?"

Olivia leaned back. "Chase, are you up for doing a spa day next week for these ladies?"

Chase pushed away from her table of attentive gentlemen and rose. There were groans from several of the men as Chase came to stand beside Olivia. "You wanna do a spa day? Like what? Skin care or beauty?"

"Nails, hair, maybe makeup?" Olivia said, shooting a questioning look at her group.

The older women had perked up like wilted daisies given water. Their former bored expressions had disappeared, replaced with contained excitement. They shifted looks back and forth to each other.

"Oh, that will be fun. I know so many tricks from all the makeup artists I worked with over the years," Chase said, snagging a nearby chair and dragging it over to the table, next to Rita the Red. "Olivia, I bet you're good at painting nails, all precise and whatnot, and I can totally do the makeup. If Neve's still here, she can do hair. Didn't you say she used to work in a salon?"

"Neve's leaving tomorrow."

"Oh, well, we'll find someone else. You think Zeke's good at hair?" Chase looked so delighted with herself.

"Zeke?" Erma said, wriggling her eyebrows, which seemed to have only a few hairs left in each. "He's a hottie."

Chase laughed. "You ladies know Zeke? He said he plays the piano here sometimes."

"We don't like Zeke. He's not welcome here," one of the older men at Chase's former table called out. The man sounded put out, which made Olivia's mouth twitch.

"They don't like him," Rita said with a giggle. "'Cause all of us don't have to be rolled down here when Zeke comes. We roll ourselves."

Chase looked delighted with this information. "Okay, so next week instead of playing games, we prepare for our own games, ladies."

Rita grinned, the silver on her bridge giving a little twinkle in the fluorescent lights buzzing overhead. "Bring Zeke with you. I'll let him do me. My hair, I mean."

The ladies around the table tittered like wrens.

Erma grinned. "Oh, I do love it when you misbehave, Rita."

"You ladies are bad," Chase said, her eyes dancing. "I think I'm going to fit right in."

⁓

Chase drew a snowman in the margin of the legal pad Olivia had given her for the meeting of the Mount Larsen Daughters of Gold Prospectors, which cohosted the Mount Larsen Fall Festival with the Redmond Civitans. She wasn't certain what she was supposed to take notes about since she'd essentially been relegated to selling tickets for the agriculture exhibit in the Cornucopia Hall on Friday evening. Olivia had been assigned to the food booths—something about a runner with money and food tickets. They'd given them both green aprons with pumpkins and Ferris wheels stitched to the pockets. Chase had never been on a committee and hadn't expected it to be so tedious, but it was.

Very.

"So now that we have brought you two up to speed and made sure all of our volunteer positions are covered, we need to talk about security and the carousing the people who run the carnival rides do in their mobile village. Dianne McFarren said she saw one of them smoking weed last year, and as you know, we cannot have that sort of activity in full view of children who may be passing by."

Several of the women launched into horror stories of all the things "carnies" did that could be construed as inappropriate and a safety risk.

Quickly the conversation moved to calling the police as soon as they saw the first signs of carousing, which seemed to be their term for getting loaded.

Chase raised her hand. "Um, excuse me."

The ladies—half of whom had treated her like an alien, trying not to stare at her too long through their sideways glances, and half of whom seemed to not care that she was a celebrity—looked at her.

168

Olivia's eyes widened as she opened her mouth as if she was about to stop Chase from speaking.

Chase held up her other hand in her life coach's direction. "Why don't you just ask that any such activity be done in private? Like, call the manager. You could also post a sign in the vicinity that says any inappropriate actions will be addressed. That way, people know. Most people who are blowing off steam after work aren't looking to offend other people."

One woman narrowed her eyes. "People define inappropriate behavior in different ways."

That was definitely true.

"I'm just saying calling the police shouldn't be the first response. A lot of people don't intend to cause a scene."

"Like you?" one woman said.

The prickles of shame came back with a vengeance. Why had she said anything? Now they were turning their intolerance and judgmental looks in her direction. Heat suffused her face. "Well, yeah. Like me."

A few of the ladies looked away, as if they were embarrassed, but no one said anything.

Chase swallowed. "I did some things I'm not proud of. Obviously. But I never intended to hurt anyone."

"Children watched you."

God, this was so uncomfortable. She should have kept her mouth shut and drawn more snowmen friends for her fat snowman staring at her from the margin of her notepad. "I wasn't thinking about that at the time."

A woman who didn't look much older than Olivia cleared her throat. Her green eyes reminded Chase of Zeke's. She wished Zeke were here right now. Why she felt that way, she wasn't sure. "So what *were* you thinking when you did those things?"

"I was thinking about forgetting all the bullshit in my life. Your kids never entered my mind. I just wanted to feel good. But I've learned that I can't escape my emotions or my feelings by numbing myself. I guess what I'm saying is that you never know what someone is going through, so why not give them the benefit of the doubt? Those people who are running the Tilt-A-Whirl might need someone to . . . I don't know . . . *not* call the cops on them? Sometimes asking people to stop what they're doing works."

A woman wearing a pantsuit and a lot of lipstick pressed her lips together before holding up a finger. "Listen, I get you're doing a bunch of touchy-feely therapy crap, but the fact is a lot of those people are dangerous. If they were normal people, they wouldn't be tramping around the country."

"Define *normal*." Olivia tilted her head and narrowed her eyes. She also used her therapy voice.

Lipstick lady glared at Olivia before finally saying, "You know what I'm saying is right. Those people are—"

"Val, listen to your words. 'Those' people?" another woman said, shaking her head. This woman wore a bohemian-style dress with a head wrap. "Look, ladies, we're getting off track. Our new committee members here are merely reminding us we are all human beings, and as such, we should extend grace whenever possible. Madam President Marsalea, I vote we send an email to the owner of Midway Attractions addressing our concerns regarding the appropriated space for the carnival operators and their required behaviors. We should also make a sign and post it in the area outlining our stance on illegal activities, noise, and other expectations and whatnot. The authorities can be contacted if those are violated. That seems fair and hospitable to our guests, who are doing an important service for us." She eyed Val as she delivered the last statement.

Several people nodded, others turned away, all withdrawing their attention from Chase and readdressing the president, who called for a motion. Fifteen minutes later, after the successful vote on the carnival workers, Chase and Olivia gathered up their notepads. Chase had written a few sentences about the sale of tickets so it looked like she'd actually done some thoughtful consideration of how to tear a ticket in half. As she stood, a few women came by to say hello and tell her they were happy she'd joined their group. A few looked starstruck, others warm and welcoming. Val gave her a frigid look and went to talk to the president, no doubt about her opposition to the motion and vote about the letter and sign.

An older lady named Carol, who had a tornado of silver hair surrounding her lined face, patted Chase on the back, drawing her attention away from the scowling Val. "Dear, I hope you might be able to help me since you're of that world. I'm Carol Steadman, the chairperson for our celebrity dunking booth. We're really struggling to find celebrities. The booth raises money for the Northern California Children's Hospital, and so it's an important part of our philanthropic goals for the year. So far we have Eddie Spaghetti, a children's author, and Sofia Rendon, an anchor at KTJL. Oh, and a rodeo clown. We had one of the actors from *Modern Problems*, but she had a schedule change. Since you're a celebrity, I thought you . . . you know."

"You want me to get inside a dunking booth?" Chase asked, with visions of her plummeting into icy water as people laughed and jeered. Sounded scary.

"Well, yes. It's for the children, after all, but I also thought you might recruit a few more celebrities. I'm sure you know a lot of them, right?" Carol clasped her hands together and used some trick to make her eyes look beseeching. Like Puss in Boots in *Shrek*. Chase felt her reservations melt.

"Uh, I might be able to ask a few friends." She didn't want to tell Carol her friends in the business were in short supply, but she could call her agent, Marshall, and ask if he might have a few ideas. Then Spencer popped into her head. The Hammer would be a huge coup, and since Olivia seemed, well, a little interested in Spence, which was weird, and he had called her therapist "cute," she might talk him into coming for the weekend if he had no other obligations. Still, Spencer wouldn't want to be advertised as a participant. "I tell you what, Carol. I'll volunteer to be dunked; then I'll make some calls and see who I can find."

Carol clapped her hands together and looked delighted.

Chase held up a hand. "But only if my appearance is not officially advertised. Let's make the celebrity dunking booth something exciting. Like, *you never know who you might be dunking*, especially since some of the people I ask may be last minute. Feel free to spread a few rumors. Get people excited."

"So I can't tell people who will be there?" Carol looked confused.

"It will work. Trust me. People know I'm in town, so chances are they will think it's me. But they won't *know*. And that makes it more fun."

Chase spent the next few minutes chitchatting (something she'd never really done) about Carol's poodle, Larry, and the salad selection at Panera Bread Company. Not that there was a Panera in Cotter's Creek—it was just Carol's preferred restaurant when she went into Redmond to see her podiatrist.

When Chase and Olivia finally pulled out of the parking lot of Mountain Perk, the only coffee shop in Cotter's Creek, Chase said, "Man, that was rough."

Olivia chuckled. "Have you ever served on a committee before?"

"No. I had no clue how hard it is. They talk about everything, don't they? Then they wanted to call the police because someone smokes? Jesus."

"There are all kinds of people with all kinds of opinions on a committee. Being on one teaches you the ability to compromise and sometimes overlook stupidity."

"Yeah, but some of them were cool. I guess. That hippie lady and Carol."

Olivia nodded. "Serving on committees and volunteering for charities can be rewarding. Look at you, helping Carol get celebrities for the dunking booth. Think of how much money you're helping to raise for sick children. That's a good feeling, right?"

Chase nodded, because it was a good feeling. "I like helping kids. I guess I should have been using my powers for good all along."

Olivia steered away from the small town and its cobbled main street lit with old-fashioned lantern light posts and toward the darkness that ensconced the rustic cabin, which was looking a little better with their cleaning efforts. "Helping kids is why I started doing what I do. There are a lot of children who can't change their circumstances, the same way you couldn't change yours."

Chase stilled at those words. "I could have done something to help myself if I hadn't wanted a part, like throw my audition or something, but back then, I liked pleasing my mother. And my dad."

"Everyone likes pleasing their parents when they're young. When you're a child, you trust that your parents are doing the right thing for you. Do you think your mother didn't do right by you?"

"I'm not sure. Before I started acting, I was normal, I guess. My mom took me to the park and played games with me. I remember her reading books to me. She was a regular mom. Then someone suggested that she take me to try out for a children's shampoo commercial. I mean, we didn't have much money. My mom had started doing billing for a medical office because she couldn't afford to put me in day care, and she couldn't get any acting jobs because, well, of me. What was she going to do with me? My dad worked on sets occasionally, so I couldn't stay with him. They fought a lot over me, over each of them being unfulfilled because they couldn't get work."

"You felt like if you weren't in the picture, they would be successful?"

Chase stared out at the dark trees swishing past. "My mother was a good actress. I've seen her in some of the sitcoms and made-for-TV movies she was in. She was never in a big role, but whatever she got cast in, she brought it. So, yeah, she might have been successful. My dad had too many issues. He was messed up. Died messed up."

Olivia made a sympathetic face. "That's hard to live with."

"Yeah, but then I got the commercial, and my mom realized she didn't have to work if I did. So I sold myself on every casting call. I could size up the casting director, almost know what they were looking for. After a while, my mom didn't have to worry about money. I brought in enough for us to get a nicer place."

"Did that make your mother a bad mother?"

Chase chewed on her lip and thought about that. "Sometimes. I think she got caught up in the life. It's easy to do. She's competitive, and she grew up kind of poor and bucked her parents to come out to LA to make it big. She was the Little Miss Georgia Peach Queen and could tap-dance, after all." Chase laughed at the thought that that was all one needed to make her own breaks. If only.

Olivia's mouth twitched.

"But I think she did what she could to survive, including sticking me in the business."

"Do you think she loves you?"

Chase pressed a hand to her stomach. Did her mother love her? She'd spent so much time being angry at her mother for pushing her, she'd never really thought much about Lorna as a person. If Chase were a mother, would she have pushed her daughter into fame, fortune, and eventually an appalling public unraveling that was displayed on *E!* and every gossip rag? Chase didn't think she would, because now she understood what that kind of life could do to an innocent. Lorna hadn't known. She'd just wanted to stop sweating rent every month or worrying about how to pay for Chase's braces. "I don't know."

The cabin appeared in the break, the shutter still hanging loose, the swing still drunk on its uneven chains, but the rocking chairs were new, and the screen door was repaired. The place looked how Chase felt—a little off, a little neglected, but better every day.

"What are you going to do about Neve?" Chase asked Olivia, noting how pretty Olivia looked in the glow of the moon.

Olivia issued a big sigh. "I guess I don't know, either."

CHAPTER FIFTEEN

A week later

Chase clicked the top of her pen and closed the workbook. She'd just finished the latest chapter and felt the need to talk to her mother for the first time in forever. Which was weird, but examining her thoughts, feelings, values, and boundaries with a sincere effort had allowed her to see her life from several different directions. Not to mention, Olivia's questions about her mother, about who her mother was and why and how she raised Chase the way she did, had made Chase realize she had never seen Lorna outside of the box she'd put her in.

Oh, Lorna had her faults. Her mother had made mistakes. But so had Chase.

A lot of them.

But Chase felt more ready to have some of the conversations she needed to have with her mother. Would they ever be super close? Maybe. But at this point Chase was willing to move in a direction she'd never traveled before in her relationship with her only remaining parent. She had talked to Olivia about telling her mother what had happened to her with Peter Rinduso, but she wasn't sure she was ready to actually say the words *I was raped, and Dad didn't do anything about it, and that screwed me up.* Chase wanted to get her relationship with Lorna on solid ground before telling her mother the grievous wrong her father had done her. Olivia believed Chase telling her mother about the rape could change their dynamics, but Chase didn't want her mother to see her as a victim. They'd agreed to shelve the conversation until Chase had come to terms with what had happened to her. She still waded through the hurt, the betrayal, even the irrational guilt she'd felt at talking to her dad's friends the weekend of the rape. Part of her had believed she was at fault, and she was trying like hell to reconcile the knowledge that she'd done nothing wrong.

Some shit was so woven into who she was, it was like pulling thread from bedsheets to remove the skewed beliefs.

Zeke's truck bumped up toward the cabin, and she made a mental note to ask Olivia about filling the potholes in the drive. Wending around the many dips in the driveway made one almost dizzy. Plus, it felt very adultlike pointing out something that needed attention.

Today Chase would be raking the front yard while Olivia met with a guy who was replacing the windows and someone who was measuring the cabin for new flooring. Olivia hadn't said anything about Chase recruiting help, so when Zeke had asked what her plans were for the day and if she was interested in taking a drive to scout a river, she'd been "adult" enough to tell him she had to get some things done around the cabin. Zeke had volunteered to help so they could get it done more quickly, and Chase wasn't saying no to an extra pair of hands.

Especially when they belonged to her temporary neighbor.

Olivia appeared in her doorway, looking much more relaxed since Neve had left. Which had been only five days ago. Olivia's sister was coming back to help them do a spa day with Rita and the girls the next night, much to Olivia's irritation. The therapist had spent Neve's last night at the cabin reading in her room while her sister and Chase reorganized the kitchen and hung the new curtains over the formerly busted window that had gotten a new pane of glass. Chase realized that Olivia practiced avoidance when it came to Neve. She understood. Neve wasn't the easiest of people. But even Olivia's sister seemed to mellow as the minutes ticked by. At the end of the evening, Chase and Neve had even shared some laughs.

"What's Zeke doing here?" Olivia asked, her hands braced on either side of the door.

Chase stood and roped her hair into a ponytail. Her roots had grown out so much that her hair looked ombré. Neve had said that when she came back, she'd bring some supplies to make Chase blonde again, but Chase wasn't sure she wanted to go back to platinum high-lights. Maybe embracing her light brown and layering in some caramel would give her a beachy honey look that would be less party girl. "Zeke volunteered to help me with the leaves."

Olivia arched an eyebrow. "We talked about Zeke."

"We did, but I decided that as an adult who is learning to navigate her own world, I can determine who my friends are. Full stop, Olivia."

"Friends? You sure about that?"

Chase grabbed a sweatshirt she'd found in a closet that must have been Olivia's grandfather's. She'd managed to wash it without the red bleeding onto her ugly underwear Lorna had purchased, which was a lesson she'd learned the last time she'd done laundry. Thus she had a few pink pairs of underwear. Pulling on the sweatshirt that said WORLD'S BEST DAD, she looked at Olivia and practiced being vulnerable.

"I don't have a lot of friends, Olivia. Not ones who want nothing from me. I know Zeke's a little into me. I'm not blind. And I'm kinda into him if you want to know the truth, but I like having him as a friend right now. He's not doing things to get me into bed. He's treating me with kindness and respect. I can't remember too many people in my life doing that for me. So, yeah, I'm going to rake leaves with my *friend*."

Olivia blinked a few times. "Well, that was honest."

Chase picked up the workbook. "I'm actually thinking about some things this time. I'm trying, Olivia. Just give me a little space and a little trust."

Her therapist's gaze worked its way from Chase's eyes to her defiant jaw, her crossed arms, her akimbo stance. Then she nodded. "Okay."

"Good. And then maybe you can think about doing the same with your sister. Neve respects you, and I'm nearly certain that she wants to get along with you. She doesn't seem to know how to say that, though."

Olivia had opened her mouth and then closed it, with the same expression the fish she'd caught had had—sorta stunned. "How would you know that?"

"I am very good at reading people, oh therapist of mine. That's why I'm a good actress. I also just completed an entire chapter on family and forgiveness. So I'm hopped up on thinking about making amends and crap like that."

Chase gave a salute and then went down the stairs to greet Zeke, who looked pretty adorable in his rugged mountain man khaki pants and buffalo plaid shirt that was open to a somewhat fitted T-shirt. He wore boots and may have trimmed his beard and sideburns. Chase had to admit that her "friend" was yummy. With a capital *Y*.

"I brought an extra rake because I wasn't sure what Olivia's grandfather might have in the outdoor shed. I see Olivia set some bags out here, but I have a better idea. I hitched my trailer up. Let's pull it around, pile the leaves on a tarp in it, then drag that out to the compost pile." Zeke gestured past the newly hung swing with its no-longer-rusted chain to the large wooden structure that she had to assume was a compost bin.

"That sounds easier."

He started down the step, turning to wait for her. "I'll unhitch the trailer. Meet you at the toolshed. Let's see what we're working with rake-wise."

Chase walked around the side of the house, noting the carpet company van pulling into the driveway, and made her way through the brittle piles of leaves to the corrugated tin lean-to that sat next to the carport. A rusted lock sat crooked in the door latch, which meant anyone could have gotten inside and taken whatever they wanted. Chase doubted there would be anything left, but she was surprised to find the musty shed still filled with aged shovels, rakes, and clippers. Various paint cans and bins of screws and nails sat on sagging wooden shelves. In the back corner, a pair of glowing eyes caught hers.

"Jesus," she said, stumbling back and colliding with Zeke.

He caught her waist and wrapped an arm around her. "Easy."

She didn't want to like the way he felt against her so much, but she did. Zeke didn't have to grow on her. He was already there.

The cat leaped to the hard-packed dirt floor and issued a plaintive meow.

"The beast," Chase said, watching the tomcat as it curled its still-matted tail around its feet.

"Your archnemesis," Zeke chuckled, leaving his arm around her waist for a second longer than he likely should have. He stepped away from her, sliding forward and extending a hand toward the cat. "He may have changed his ways, by the look of it."

The scary feline arched its back and glided beneath his hand, the hum of a purr filling the shed. Beast looked positively tame, a virtual pussycat.

"Is that cat purring?" Chase said with an unbelieving laugh.

"You ladies may have just gotten a new pet."

"Or you did." Chase knelt and extended her hand. The cat made its way to her, rubbing against her pant leg. Gone was the hissing monster who'd scared the crap out of her the first day she'd arrived at the cabin. In its place was lovable, ratty Beast, her new . . . pet?

Of course, she knew she couldn't keep a cat. The cat lived here outside Cotter's Creek, but maybe for another week or so she could pretend that the once-feral but somewhat friendly cat had a home here at the cabin. Beast needed some food, maybe a trip to the vet to make sure he was vaccinated and whatever else animals needed. Maybe she could even find him a home . . . if she could get the sad creature spiffed up a bit. A bath would likely do wonders. Did cats take baths?

"Should we feed him something?" she asked, glancing up at Zeke.

"He looks like he's been keeping himself fed on vermin."

"Ooh, gross," she said, drawing her hand back.

"Let's get to work. Beast can find a patch of sunshine on his own," Zeke said, turning and looking over the offerings leaning against the shed. He pulled out a sturdy, well-used rake and handed it to her. "This one ought to do the trick. It's better than the one I brought."

She followed him out of the shed, leaving a tail-twitching Beast behind, wondering how long it would take to rake the front yard.

Answer: a long time.

Even with the tarp and trailer, the afternoon slipped by as they raked up leaves and dumped them onto the compost pile. Chase had borrowed some gloves from Zeke, but since his hands were larger, they'd rubbed a blister on her palm. Finally, as the day faded to a lovely golden right before the sun found its bed over the mountain, Zeke swept the last of the leaves onto the tarp and made the last trip to the huge pile they'd made.

Chase leaned against her rake in relief. Her arms hurt from the constant sweeping motion, her knees and back ached from the constant bending and scooping of the leaves, and she felt absolutely gritty from the dusty endeavor, but she also felt a great sense of accomplishment as she looked over the smooth expanse of fading grass. She'd tied her sweatshirt around her waist, and her hair had fallen in clumps from her scrunchie, so she knew she looked a mess. Zeke had shed some clothes, too.

Thank you, sweet Indian summer, for the gift of forcing that man to take his shirt off. Amen.

"You know, it's kind of late to make the scouting drive. Instead we could grab some of the firewood stacked next to the shed and do a fire in the firepit." Zeke slid her a sideways glance.

"A fire? We can do that here?"

"We've had decent rain, and as long as we clear a ring of ground around the firepit, we should be legal. And I'm nearly certain I have some graham crackers and marshmallows. We could make s'mores. Well, that is if I can find those Godiva chocolate bars my sister sent me on my birthday."

Making s'mores. Another thing Chase had never done. Once her mother had taken her to the beach with some friends. At the end of the day, they'd gathered around a fire on the beach with hot dogs and big marshmallows, but her mother had gotten angry at one of the guys and dragged Chase back to their house before they lit the fire. Chase had been devastated to not sit around the fire eating delicious, sticky marshmallows while the adults played the guitar and drank adult beverages. She'd pitched such a fit that her mother had actually tossed her in her room and locked the door.

Chase smiled. "I would much rather do that. And if you can't find the Godiva, I think Olivia has some candy in her room. She went to Redmond the other day to pick out a rug and new windows while I learned to reconcile my bank statement, and I saw her sneak a bag of Halloween candy into her room. Math makes me hungry, so I totally noticed."

"Sweet. Let me ride back to my house, shower, and grab what I have. I'll be back in twenty minutes."

She wanted to go with him and see his place, but she also wanted to shower. She could suggest they shower together, but she wasn't quite ready to take that step. She might not ever be ready, because she didn't want to destroy what she had with Zeke. Sex felt like it could untie the closeness she felt with him as a friend.

"Well, if you have any issues starting the fire, just know that I know how to use kindling," she said, rubbing her upper arms. Now that the sun had slid farther down, the September air had grown cool.

"You're really getting this adulting thing down," he said with a wink. "I'll be back soon."

She walked toward the cabin as he jogged to his truck, mulling over his words. *Adulting.* Such a strange concept, but Chase was stunned at how much she had changed over the last week and a half. For one thing, she'd stopped resenting Olivia and had started being more open to talking about her past with her. They'd discussed her father, the devastation of the rape, the ways she could deal with the hurt and guilt. Then there were the practical things that didn't involve her emotions—the simple tasks of learning about credit and how it works, looking at her past taxes (something Lorna had been opposed to sharing but Olivia had managed to get from the accountant because they were Chase's tax forms), and making a budget had opened her eyes to how much money she wasted. Her mother had given her a sizable allowance that she usually depleted before midmonth. Chase hadn't known about some of the properties she owned, the amount in her rapidly dwindling savings, or that she had a retirement plan. Her mother had done everything without Chase's knowledge, and though Lorna had paid herself, her mother had been more than fair with her.

Olivia had made Chase write a will, keep a journal, and read a few self-help books, but none of those were better than the feeling of accomplishment Chase had when mastering things she'd avoided for too long.

"The yard looks great," Olivia said from the new rocking chair she'd ordered on Amazon. Olivia had put it together by herself, something Chase had marveled at. She'd never thought about putting furniture together, and now understood the difference between a Phillips- and a flat-head screwdriver.

"Thanks. Zeke's going back to his house to get stuff for s'mores. We thought instead of going to scout fishing spots, we'd build a fire in that firepit out back. I mean, if that's okay with you?"

Olivia held a book in her lap, but she hadn't been reading it. Instead she'd been engrossed in watching the trees drop leaves on the lawn Chase had just raked. Which was totally annoying, but Zeke had pointed out that such was life. You washed dishes only to fill the sink with more. You hung up clothes that would eventually grace the bedroom floor. You fell in love only to mourn a broken heart. That was the vicious, joyful circle of life. Zeke seemed to find beauty in all the processes.

"It's okay with me."

"Do you want to join us?" Chase asked. A part of her didn't want Olivia to say yes, because she wanted Zeke all to herself. Sitting beside him made Chase happy. She'd forgotten what that feeling was, and now she was a junkie for the warmth she felt when she was with Zeke. He was a deep breath at the end of the day.

But Olivia looked . . . surprised that Chase had invited her. "Do you really want me to?"

No.

"Sure."

The look of pleasure on Olivia's face made Chase feel guilty. Maybe Olivia needed a friend, too. Maybe she needed some s'mores. The shadows had deepened beneath Olivia's eyes, and Chase had become convinced that her therapist wrestled with demons. It was ironic, but not amusing. Chase still wrestled with her own demons, but Chase figured Olivia didn't take her own advice.

"Maybe I'll come out for a bit," Olivia said, rocking her chair with the tip of one foot.

"Cool." Chase went back inside, made short work of showering and blow-drying her hair, and even walked over to the bunk room to put the sheets Neve had used on the lower bunk. Olivia hadn't even asked her to wash them. Chase had just remembered that they needed to be laundered before Spencer arrived the next weekend. For some reason it felt like she, rather than Olivia, was hosting her friend. She'd done some fancy talking and had gotten Spencer to agree to come only after she promised to buy him tickets for all the rides and mentioned that it was for sick children. Spencer was a sucker for kids. Big softy.

Chase hadn't learned how to fold a fitted sheet. Apparently sorcery was involved, so she'd tossed the sheets in the dryer to get the wrinkles out. That was how sane people did it.

As she lifted the mattress to tuck the fitted sheet deeper between the box spring, noting that the April Fresh fabric softener was totally dope, she felt something hard beneath her hand.

"Huh," she said to no one, since she was totally alone. She lifted the mattress higher and felt around, noting that the hard lump seemed to be the size of a book. Her fingers encountered a tear in the mattress cover, and she pulled out what looked to be a sketchbook.

The front of the pad had the name *Marley* written across the top.

Chase opened the sketch pad to find childish doodles. Sunshine. A dog. Several pages of trees with cheerful faces. A few with people, the women delineated by triangle dresses and long hair. One looked to be a family, with each child labeled. Olivia had been drawn bigger than the other girls, her hair a helmet of brown. The woman had a necklace on, and the man smiled the biggest, his eyes large and blue. Looked to be a happy family. Olivia would probably enjoy flipping through her sister's memories.

The sound of Zeke's truck rambling up the drive launched Chase into action, quickly making up the bed with the sheet so tight a drill sergeant would be impressed.

Chase stashed the sketchbook in her room, making a mental note to give it to Olivia later, swiped on her best lip gloss, and fluffed her hair. She'd pulled on a tighter long-sleeve shirt in a blue that made her eyes pop and leggings that had cute ties at the ankle. She jammed her feet into wedge booties and told herself she was not trying to look cute . . . though she knew she was.

Pushing out the door, she found Zeke trudging across the yard carrying a bag and two camping chairs strapped over his shoulder. Behind him, the sky had darkened to a navy, a galaxy of stars hanging above the deeper contrast of the mountain. The air smelled of an unknown crisp freshness that might have come from the trees or clean water or some other outdoorsy thing. All Chase knew was that she loved every sight, smell, and feel of what spread before her.

She turned and grabbed one of the throws off the tweed couch and then dropped it on the back of the couch as she tugged her puffy jacket on. Then she picked it up and went to snuggle under the stars beside a fire with a guy who made her feel like she was a normal girl.

Olivia was nowhere in sight. Her therapist had been spending a lot of time working on her book that was due. Olivia kept talking about deadline this and deadline that. But that worked for Chase because sometimes she needed a break from the constant analysis of her words, discernment of her motivations, and perusal of her expressions.

Huh. Maybe her vocabulary had improved, too.

"Hey," she said, coming around the corner to Zeke raking around the firepit he'd dragged to an even patch of ground that was open to the skies. He'd set up the chairs. "Looks like you know what you're doing."

"This time of the year is usually too dangerous to do a fire, but the wetter-than-normal start to fall has brought us a little gift. Still, I like to be safe. Fire is a very real danger out here. All we need is a few dry logs and we're in business. Here, sit." He gestured to the camp chair he'd set on an even spot. Then he went over to the lean-to and brought back a few logs.

Zeke had changed into a pair of jeans and a soft Henley shirt that was the color of his eyes. He heaved the logs onto the rusted round pit, tossed a few leaves at the base, and used a lighter to ignite the leaves. The leaves caught fire, curling into themselves, their crackling carcasses launching up into the cooling air. Chase settled in the chair, mesmerized by the orange flames dancing against the bark. The pop and crackle of the logs catching brought satisfaction. Smoke wafted up to the canopy above them to dance with the brilliant stars.

This was the stuff of commercials and glossy photo ads. And for a moment, it belonged to Chase.

Zeke nodded at the fire's progress and settled into the chair next to her. He leaned over and pulled a bottle of wine from the depths of his basket.

"Zeke, I can't—"

"It's sparkling grape. I found it in the fridge from when my sister visited with her twin girls. She and I drink wine, and those two divas love to swill their own 'wine' in fancy glasses." Zeke pulled out two pink plastic wineglasses.

Chase smiled at the thought of Zeke buying fizzy grape juice and pink goblets. Again, this guy was too good for someone like her. "You thought of everything." She took the glasses while he opened the sparkling juice.

He poured them each half a glass and then pulled out a Bluetooth speaker. The plaintive sound of jazz music spilled out, somehow sounding exactly right for contemplating a fire and swigging sparkling grape juice with a rugged fisherman who made her sink into herself and like who she was when she was with him.

Exactly so.

For a few minutes, neither said a word. After a song or two, Zeke reached over and took her hand. His big thumbs rubbed over her blisters.

"I saw you got these earlier. Hands this pretty shouldn't have blisters," he said, staring down at where her hand was cradled in his.

"I'm kind of digging them. Like a badge of honor, like something that says I'm not completely worthless as a human being," she joked.

Zeke looked at her, his smile soft. He lifted her hand and brushed her palm with his lips. "You're so hard on yourself."

His beard was soft and his lips ever so gentle, but it was the disbelief in his words that turned her into a puddle of . . . something.

God, was she falling in love with Zeke?

She'd never been in love. Or at least if she had been in love, it had been booze-soaked toxicity built on shifting sands.

He dropped her hand from his lips but kept it cradled in his big warm one.

"You make me feel like a normal person, Zeke," she said.

Zeke squeezed her hand. "Chase, you know you're a real person, right? I know your world has done a number on you. I remember what it's like in that hustle. You're always donning a persona to work people to your advantage. It's an exhausting way to live. I jumped out before I got sucked in, but I started much later than you. You were born into chaos, growing up with all the wrong information about the world. You're still you. You still matter. You fucked up. But you still matter, honey."

Tears pricked at her eyes. She'd wanted to not feel so much tonight—only enjoy being with a guy on a sort of date. She'd been on dates before, or what seemed to be dates. She wasn't sure. Was hooking up with a guy at a club a date? Or going to a premiere with someone? She'd gone out to dinner with guys a few times, but it had never felt like a date. It had felt like eating with someone. A date seemed something more.

Sitting here with the man who had the right words, who wasn't trying to get her in bed or use her in any way, who gently kissed her hand like a courtier, felt like a date.

"You know all the right things to say," she said finally, after juggling the wineglass so she could swipe her finger at the moisture beneath her lower lashes. Because she didn't want to let go of his hand.

"No, I'm not saying the right things because they'll get me somewhere. I'm telling the truth, Chase. Stop tearing yourself apart. Everyone does dumb stuff, everyone screws up. That *is* being human." He released her hand, and she immediately missed his touch. Who would have thought that Chase London would have found holding hands so sexy, so comforting, so necessary in life?

Zeke leaned over and rummaged around in the basket. "Let's have some s'mores. Or hot dogs? I brought both."

"Um, hot dogs and then s'mores?" She clapped her hands at the thought. Roasting weenies and marshmallows to the sound of a clarinet was thrilling. That thought made her giggle.

"What?" he said, smiling up at her as he pulled out some metal prongs.

"This is so much fun."

"And you haven't even tasted the s'mores yet."

"I don't need to. This is the best night ever."

CHAPTER SIXTEEN

Olivia put a second coat on Martha Courtney's nails and maneuvered the fan so the "Some Like It Hot" nail polish could dry. Across from her with makeup palettes and brushes so specific that she couldn't fathom how to use them sat Chase sponging foundation on another patron of Rock Glen Retirement Center. Chase wore her hair swept back, and her bottom lip caught between her teeth as she critically eyed her workmanship.

Across the room in a makeshift salon chair borrowed from the Cutup Salon, Neve stood teasing Rita's red mane into a bouffant high enough to get her a role in *Hairspray*. Olivia had seen the community theatre advertisements for the musical at the Sak-N-Sav a few days ago and wondered if that was the influence for Rita.

Neve had arrived late last night, right after Olivia had left Zeke and Chase to the rest of the s'mores. She'd moseyed out to say hello to Zeke but immediately felt like a third wheel. Chase had been sitting close to him, snuggled beneath one of the throws Olivia had picked up in Redmond. They'd been laughing about Zeke's childhood escapades looking for Sasquatch. Chase had gotten marshmallow in her hair, and Zeke reached over at one point and wiped the chocolate from the corner of her mouth. He'd sucked his finger into his mouth, and the poignant intimacy elbowed Olivia back toward the porch.

Olivia wasn't in favor of Chase starting a relationship even at this point in her recovery, but she also couldn't deny that Zeke had been a good influence on the actress, a role model for what being an adult was. He was patient, kind, and said all the right things. He seemed to be far from the selfish, shallow men that had existed in Chase's life to date. Outside of Spencer, of course. So far Chase and Zeke had seemed to stay in the friend zone, but something was building between them. Olivia wasn't sure if she could or should stop it. Maybe Chase needed Zeke in her life.

She left them to finish off the s'mores, and as she was climbing the front porch steps, her sister pulled into the drive.

Neve drove an old Nissan that had a dent on the passenger side. No doubt her sister needed a new car. The headlights caught Olivia, so she lifted her hand in greeting, though she wished for the millionth time that her sister would have stayed home. But Neve never did what was easy or sensible. This inheritance had snagged her interest, and she now saw fixing up the cabin as a profitable endeavor. She'd been sending Olivia paint samples and cheap fix-ups for house flips. Suffice it to say, Olivia now had a Pinterest account to keep up with all the Pins Neve had sent her.

Olivia wasn't certain what they should do with the cabin, but she could agree with her sister that whatever it was, updates were needed. And she'd been thinking about Chase's comment about her sister. If she stepped back, she could see the issues between them—Marley's death had been hard on everyone, and their father's arrest and trial even more difficult in a different way. Pair that with Olivia's success and prickliness about her career, and Neve's lack of a profession and devastating divorce, and they were creating a recipe for dysfunction every time they met up. Maybe Olivia needed to let off the gas when it came to her sister and give her a little grace.

Neve climbed out, looking to be in a decent mood. "Hey, what's with the fire?"

Olivia glanced over to where Chase and Zeke sat, heads together. "Chase raked leaves today. Zeke helped her, and they decided to reward their hard work with hot dogs and s'mores."

Neve smiled at the couple in the distance, who'd started laughing again. "You gotta big problem if she's not supposed to be into a guy. 'Cause that looks like she's way into him."

Olivia sighed. "Yeah, but I can only control so much. I can coach her actions, but I can't control her heart."

"Did you just hear your own words?" her sister said, lifting two bags from the back of her car. Neve rose and leveled a look at Olivia over the hood.

Olivia gave her a flat look.

Neve just smiled. "Anyway, I brought stuff for doing hair tomorrow. Chase said I needed fancy doodads and lots of hair spray."

"Chase used the word *doodads*?" Olivia felt relieved Neve had tossed her an olive branch. Her words were a reminder to herself. Hearts couldn't be controlled. She knew that very, very well. Thing was, she wasn't sure she trusted her heart, or if her heart had been deceived by what she had erected long ago. Did she still love Conrad?

She wasn't sure.

Neve shook her head. "No. But I inferred it. Hey, I know big words, too."

Olivia took one of her sister's bags and opened the door for her. Her inclination was to scathingly return Neve's volley. But she was going to be kinder to her sister, starting now. "I know you're smart, Neve."

Her sister made a face. "Is there a trap ahead or something?"

"No." Olivia set her sister's bag at the foot of the stairs. "How long are you staying?"

Neve turned and closed the door. "I'm not sure. I actually wanted to talk to you about that."

Olivia didn't like the harbinger in her sister's voice. They needed to discuss the house, but agreeing to fix the place up wasn't the same as making a decision on what to do with the place. "Okay. Have you eaten?"

"I grabbed something on the way up, but I wouldn't mind a cup of tea or maybe a decaf coffee." Neve moved toward the kitchen. Olivia followed.

Neve filled the red teakettle with water and set it on the stove, striking a match to light the fire since the starter on the burner was toast. Olivia moved toward the bistro table set against the kitchen wall. She'd gotten only three chairs because there wasn't room for a fourth. She'd taken the old dinette table and chairs to a junk shop.

"I like the table. It's the perfect size," Neve said, pulling coffee mugs from the cabinet and setting them on the chipped Formica counter.

"Thanks. The power of Amazon."

Neve pulled out a chair across from Olivia and sank down. "So Mom is letting Dad move back in."

Olivia flinched. "What?"

"She says two incomes will be better. He got a job with another sanitation company near our house."

Olivia's stomach contracted, and for a moment the hot dog she'd eaten tried to make an encore appearance. "But they're divorced."

Neve looked down at her clasped hands. Her sister still chewed on her nails. "You know Mom believes Dad was totally innocent, those girls were coached in their testimonies, and that allegations were brought to destroy him because he had those drug dealers arrested."

Olivia frowned, not wanting to have the conversation they always seemed to have. "Then he shouldn't have taken the plea. But regardless, whatever happened between Dad and those girls was inappropriate. Even you know that, right?"

Neve shrugged. "I don't know, Liv. I think he probably shouldn't have let them in his office, let them sit in his lap, hugged them, and all that stuff, but I don't think Dad's a pedophile. I mean, guys are led with their dicks, but come on."

"That's a platitude people accept to give bad behavior a pass. It's a misogynist defense, like men have no control over their penises. Not true. Those girls were children, Neve. No one gets a pass on that."

"Dad made some mistakes, that's for sure. Maybe he missed Marley. Maybe he was sad that we had grown up and left the house. Maybe he wanted attention or something. I don't know. Middle-aged guys go whack-a-doodle when their hair starts thinning and their prostates get big or whatever. At any rate, Dad served his time. He not only paid for his bad choices by doing time, but he also lost his family and his career."

"Why is Mom doing this? They were done. She didn't speak to him for years. It's bad enough both you and she still have a relationship with him, but . . ." Olivia closed her eyes as if she could shut out the words her sister had spoken.

"They meet up occasionally. He's been wooing Mom. Last week he asked if he could come back home and be part of the family again." It seemed evident by the way Neve wouldn't meet her gaze and by the way she picked at a hangnail that she hadn't wanted to deliver this news. "Maybe it's time you just—"

"No." Olivia shook her head as the kettle started a low-pitched whine. "He ruined our family."

"Liv," Neve said, tapping the table. "You are a therapist who teaches people how to deal with family who—"

"Not this sort of thing. I don't have to forgive him. I don't have to acknowledge him in any way. You don't understand. You weren't there when he said I was the enemy, you . . ." Olivia trailed off because she couldn't tip over into that chasm in her soul. Too dangerous.

Walk away. Close the door. Distract.

"Can we not talk about that right now?"

Neve seemed relieved to set the topic of their family aside for the time being. "Sure. I respect your right to feel as you do."

"Thank you. Uh, so, Chase is having someone stay next weekend for the festival. I wasn't sure how long you were staying," Olivia said, pushing back and rising as the kettle reached train whistle stage.

Neve watched her. Olivia could feel her disappointment, but she didn't want to talk about her parents. Her mother had lost her damned mind, and her father was a black hole in Olivia's heart.

"I'm not sure. Maybe a week or two in order to oversee some of the repairs and remodeling we're doing. Uh, I wanted to broach something with you. I know you had suggested using the cabin occasionally for what you're doing with Chase, this adulting camp or whatever, but I . . . well, I thought maybe I could live here."

Olivia jerked around, spilling hot water on the burner. The hissing startled her, and she set the kettle down too hard, splashing some water onto her wrist. "Ow!"

Olivia lunged toward the sink, ran cold water, and stuck her seared flesh beneath the frigid stream.

Neve got up, pushed the spout away, and took Olivia's hand, turning it over. "You need to be careful. I wish we had some aloe vera to put on it. Granny used to keep some on the windowsill." Neve grabbed a paper towel and folded it, pressing it gently on the angry welts.

"Thanks," Olivia said, withdrawing her hand and shuffling back to the table.

Neve set about opening tea bags and filling their cups. She found honey in the pantry and then added a dollop of half-and-half to each cup. Finally, she brought the honey and the steaming cups to the table. "Dab a little honey on the welts. It actually helps to heal."

"You want to live *here*?" Olivia asked, nodding her thanks as her sister pushed one cup toward her.

"I want a fresh start," Neve said, sipping from her cup. The tea bag tag fluttered against the side of the chipped mug that had been given to participants of the Mount Larsen Art Festival. "If Dad is moving back in, I don't want to live with them. I don't have a job right now. I've been

194

filling in at Tonya Stillman's salon when they have events. I thought about opening my own place here or seeing if someone in town might have a stall for me to rent. I could pay you some rent? Or maybe you could finance the house for me and it could eventually become mine? Or not. But I wouldn't mind living here for a while. Maybe forever. I forgot how much I liked it here. There are good memories here, you know."

Olivia did.

But there were also memories that broke her heart. Memories she didn't want to talk about, didn't want to resurface like an old air bubble in a shipwreck, rising to the top long after it should have come up. Olivia still tried to press the bad down because she wasn't sure she could live with herself if she let it all come completely undone. "I . . . I don't know what to say."

Neve bit her lower lip, pausing to seemingly gather her thoughts. This was new for Neve. Usually she said exactly what she thought, feelings be damned. "It's a big decision. Maybe you could think about it?"

Olivia looked down at her sister's hands. Neve had turned forty last year. She'd been divorced for many years, stuck taking care of their mother, financially unstable because of the poor choices she'd made. Maybe her sister deserved a do-over, but Olivia wasn't sure she wanted to sell this cabin to her sister. Or if she even wanted Neve here. Her sister's track record wasn't the greatest. Right now, Neve thought she wanted to live in Cotter's Creek, but three months from now, she might decide the isolation was too much and head back to her old stomping grounds. Such was Neve. "I'll think about it."

Neve nodded. "I appreciate that, Liv."

Olivia couldn't remember a time when she and her sister had had such a lengthy conversation. Or a time when Neve had been so agreeable. Of course, her sister wanted something from her. So perhaps that was the reason behind her ministrations moments before. But Olivia hoped it wasn't.

Olivia looked at her scalded hand. How long had it been since someone had taken care of her?

She couldn't remember.

She hadn't dated in several years. Every now and then someone might hold a door for her or take her arm at a conference when there was ice on the steps. Other than that, she rarely received much consideration from anyone she wasn't paying. Having her sister tend to her, if only for a few seconds, had made her feel . . . cared for.

Olivia took a sip of her tea, not liking the vulnerability she felt. "Chase and I are working the Mount Larsen Fall Festival next weekend. You might want to volunteer to help there, too. I mean, if you want. But if you do, we'll have to shift some sleeping arrangements. Chase is helping one of the ladies get celebrities for the charity dunking booth, and at least one is staying here that weekend."

"Celebrities?" Neve perked up, her eyes lighting with interest. "Like who?"

"Spencer Rome, for one," Olivia said, ignoring the squiggles of . . . something in her stomach. So she'd had a crush on him when she was younger. Okay, and maybe a little bit in the present? Big deal. Everyone had celebrity crushes. He was just a guy . . . who looked amazingly gorgeous. But just a guy.

"Get out!" Neve's mouth dropped open. "He's staying *here*? With us?"

"Um." Olivia looked around the kitchen, envisioning the Hammer fixing a ham sandwich at the counter. Seemed absurd to let a guy like Spencer stay in a ramshackle cabin that needed new carpet and paint. And those were the easy things to fix. "Yeah. Chase actually likes this place. I think she thinks it's like summer camp. I told her we could put him up in Redmond, but she said he would love the vibe here."

"I need to lose ten pounds, color my hair, paint my toenails, and get a bikini wax," Neve said, looking a little freaked out.

"You think he's going to see that you haven't had a bikini wax?"

Neve grinned. "A girl should always be prepared. I mean, he could be into older gals who have, you know, experience. Yeah, I don't have a job or a waxed hoo-ha, but I have plenty of wisdom in certain arenas, arenas that a man appreciates. Who knows, I might rock the Hammer's world."

"Oh Lord." Olivia rolled her eyes, but she smiled.

This was the most intimacy she'd had in forever with her sister. Sure, back when they were teens, they had their issues, but it had been like this between them—jokes, teasing, something that felt like love. Olivia was almost scared to feel what she felt, but it was also addictive. A part of her had missed Neve, craved some closeness with her.

"So if you had a shot with a guy like him, would you take it?" Neve asked, her eyes still dancing.

Would she?

Olivia had framed in her mind the idea that there was a certain kind of man for her. That man was nothing like Spencer Rome. And if she were truly honest, the guy she envisioned sitting next to her in the rocking chair as she faded to gray was nothing like Conrad Santos, a man she'd yearned for—for far too long. Perhaps she'd idealized Conrad because she knew she no longer had a chance with him. They had closed the book after the first chapter of their awkward start, one that for her had been the culmination of all her hopes as a girl. Truth was, though she'd believed Conrad to be her ideal, she had no expectation of having him. So he'd been safe to desire. But Spencer Rome wasn't even in her neighborhood of expectation. He wasn't in her universe. So why even consider such a thing? "I don't think so. How could I ever fit with someone like him? Besides, why would he even want someone like me?"

Neve made a face. "What do you mean? You're pretty."

"No, I'm not. I have even features, nice skin and hair, and I guess I'm fit, but pretty? I've never been pretty."

Chase strolled in. "You're pretty. Why do you think you're not?"

"Because I'm not. I see my reflection in the mirror. I don't deceive myself. Acknowledging my positives is one thing, but lying to myself is another." Olivia picked up her mug and hid behind it.

"I asked her if she had a shot with someone like Spencer, would she take it? She thinks she's not pretty enough," Neve said, squinching her face as she studied Chase. "Do you have marshmallow in your hair?"

Chase actually blushed, lifting a hank of hair coated with gooey white. "Uh, yeah, I accidently got too close to one of the roasted marshmallows Zeke was trying to put on my graham cracker."

Neve gave her a sly look. "Is that what they call it these days?"

Chase gave Olivia's sister the flat stare she used when she was put out. "Zeke and I are friends, Neve."

"Mm-hmm," Neve said, taking a sip of her tea, her brown eyes dancing above the lip of the cup.

"We are," Chase insisted, turning toward the counter and snagging her own cup. She sifted through the box of teas Olivia had bought, withdrawing an herbal one. Yesterday, Chase had revealed she'd been sleeping better than she had in years. Working hard and examining emotions seemed to do that to a person. Of course, Olivia hadn't been sleeping as well. Her body was tired but her mind was alive, searching every night, discomfited by the ghosts of her past clinking their chains.

And now her father would be even more in her life, whether she acknowledged him or not.

"Well, I'm beat. I worked this morning, fought LA traffic, and that nine-hour drive is wearing on me. Tomorrow will be fun, but I'll be on my feet fixing hair. Off to get my beauty sleep." Neve rose and poured out her remaining tea. She rinsed her mug and set it aside, presumably for coffee the next morning.

"Did you bring some fun glitz for their hair?" Chase asked. She seemed relieved to quit the topic of Zeke.

Neve saluted. "As you wished, princess."

Chase frowned at the moniker.

Neve's gaze landed on Olivia. "Night, Liv. Night, princess."

Chase took Neve's chair. "Ugh. She's already on my nerves."

Olivia wondered if Neve and Chase might actually be cut from the same cloth. Mercurial, stubborn, smart, and talented, each woman had tripped out of the gate but also had great potential. They both took risks, which sometimes worked, sometimes didn't. "Try to give her space. She's come to help us, and that's something."

"She's got her own reasons." Chase dunked her tea bag into the hot water.

"True, but everyone needs a second or third or twentieth chance, right?"

"Maybe. So do you like Spencer?" Chase asked.

Olivia drew back. "What? No."

"I saw the way you looked at him in the car that day."

"So? He's very handsome."

"You've worked with lots of other handsome celebrities and athletes before. You shouldn't be starstruck." Chase dipped her marshmallowed hair into the hot tea and sucked it off.

"That's disgusting."

Chase blinked and shrugged a shoulder. "My hair is clean, and I can't go to bed with sticky gunk in my hair. And you're avoiding the question. If you have the hots for him, I can mention you're into him. Spencer's a giving guy, you know. Besides, he told me you were cute."

"No. Absolutely not. I don't have the hots for him. Wait, he said I was cute?"

"Yeah, he called you my cute therapist. Just so you know, Spence's type is not bimbo. He likes the librarian type. He digs nerds."

"I'm not a nerd."

Chase giggled and sipped her tea, glancing away.

"Okay, maybe a little, but Spencer doesn't even like me, remember? He essentially censured me for trying to take you back to Cedar Point. Trust me, Spencer Rome wants no part of me."

Chase smiled. "He might. He could have a fetish for hard-ass jailers or something."

"Well, thanks, Chase," Olivia said.

"I'm joking. Like seriously joking. Just wanted you to know I could put in a word is all. I think he would be all over it."

Olivia stood. "Do not. I'm not interested."

Much.

~❧~

Martha Courtney knocked her hand on the table. "You're daydreaming again, Miss Han."

"What?" Olivia blinked, having forgotten she was sitting in a senior citizens' home painting residents' nails. She'd been so wrapped up in the thoughts of her sister and of Spencer's impending arrival that she'd forgotten to live in the present.

Which was a good present to be in. The residents were having a fantastic time getting dolled up for a Saturday evening. The center had even gotten into the spirit of things and decorated the dining room with white cloths and flowers. Word on the hall was the gentlemen in the establishment had chipped in and hired a guitarist to accompany dinner with music. Romance and excitement hovered in the air.

"I'm sorry. Just woolgathering, I guess," Olivia said, running her thumbnail along the edge of Martha's nail to remove where the polish had bled into the crevice.

"You were thinking hard," Martha said with a smile. "I guess when you're young, there is much to think about. When you're my age, you sink into your memories because the future involves things you don't want to think about."

Olivia returned the brush to the polish bottle and twisted it closed. "I think I'm more lost in memories than I am thoughts. It's been a long time since I've been in Cotter's Creek. For some reason, memories that make me both sad and disturbed have awakened. I left them alone for too long, I suppose."

Martha patted her hand, careful not to touch anything with her nails. "I learned long ago that when you let the crow you need to eat sit too long, it's really hard to chew."

"It's not really something like that. It's something I pretended away and let get heavier and heavier. Now my past and all those emotions I refused to feel are like a piano hanging out the window on a fraying rope."

Martha gave her a tender smile. "I know about letting things build up. Take my brother, Floyd, and his wife, Alice. I spent a long time hating them, and you know what it was over? Missing my daughter's wedding. They had had plans to visit England, a vacation they'd been saving for years to go on. They went to England and I was furious. After that, I heaped every slight done to me onto a huge pile until it was so high I couldn't see over it. Then Floyd died. And I never got a chance to clear the air with him. That was hard." Martha stared off into space.

Olivia watched Martha, thinking about the things she'd left unsaid. She hadn't said those things because . . . because she had blame in everything that had happened. And most people do what they can to avoid blame. The human condition is thus—people avoid the things that make them bleed.

Martha looked at her expectantly, so Olivia finally said, "That must have been very difficult to not be able to say the things you needed to."

"It was, but I have to live with my failure. The lesson I learned has kept me from letting things fester until I erupt with all that nasty gunk. I say the things I need to say. I'm honest, and I don't let hardness build up. Case in point: I had to tell Merle Nathan that her dentures needed relining. Those things clacked around so much in her mouth, I thought I might throat-punch her every time we sat at the same table, bless her."

Olivia smiled. "Well, I daresay that's something you needed to have said. We couldn't have poor Merle with a collapsed windpipe."

Martha giggled. "She's my best friend. I would have restrained myself somehow."

"Who's telling tales about me over there?" asked a diminutive woman with a fascinator of feathers in her iron-gray hair.

"Just gossiping with Miss Han here," Martha said, blowing on her nails. "Merle, I'm up next for hair. What do you think I should ask for? I don't want a nest in my hair."

Merle removed her chin from Chase's grasp. "This isn't a nest, Marth. Feathers are all the rage this year."

Martha widened her eyes in disbelief. "Well, at least your makeup looks good."

"I had a professional do it," Merle said, giving Chase a wink.

Chase's own face was completely devoid of makeup. Her skin looked dewy, a natural rose flush graced her cheeks, and her brilliant eyes were no longer as haunted. "I'm not a professional, but I've worked with so many that I picked up some good tricks. You look splendid, Merle."

"And good timing, too. There's that handsome Zeke." Merle craned her head, looking over Chase's shoulder. Chase turned and caught Zeke's gaze. The look on the young actress's face reminded Olivia of some of the characters Chase had played in her teen romance movies. In those, she'd been acting besotted. She wasn't so sure the woman was acting at present.

Zeke stopped when he got to Merle and Chase's table. "Afternoon, ladies. I've been sent in here by the gentlemen to let you know the ladies in the kitchen are making chocolate lava cake. They said you'd want to know."

"Hot damn," Rita said, giving the woman next to her, awaiting Neve's ministrations, a fist bump. "That's almost as good as the messenger. Just saying."

Zeke had the grace to blush. "You ladies are good for a man's ego."

Martha rose and waved over the next victim for Olivia's manicures. "Sugar, you don't need us old hens to make you feel good about how nice you fill out those pants. I'm sure these younger ladies can vouch for our excellent taste."

"I certainly can," Chase said, giving Zeke a saucy grin. "And not only that, but he makes a great s'more."

"Really?" Rita drawled, sashaying by as she patted her red hair, which had been swept up on one side with a rhinestone clip. Neve had added some extensions that almost matched the fiery red and used the curling iron to make fat curls that almost brushed her shoulders. "I am not opposed to s'mores, Zeke."

"But you're getting lava cake. How can I compete?" Zeke teased. "Besides, I came by to ask Chase if she wanted to have dinner with me."

"Oooh, overlooked for a blonde again. You know that it's not true they have more fun. Why do you think I went red?" Rita lifted a shoulder and her painted-on eyebrows.

Chase may have pinked a little when Zeke essentially asked her out in front of the older ladies. "Maybe I should go red, then. I mean, you're looking pretty hot, Rita."

Rita preened as Neve walked over. "I brought some color for you, Chase."

"She's perfect the way she is," Zeke said.

Chase definitely colored at that remark, her gaze finding Zeke's before she looked over at Neve. "Thanks for bringing that for me. I want to ditch this platinum, which feels not so much like me anymore."

Neve nodded. "I think you're right. And maybe I can talk Olivia into some warm highlights, too. Maybe all us girls need a little pick-me-up."

"Ooh, yeah," Rita said, narrowing her eyes at Olivia. "That plain brown isn't doing her any favors."

"Hey," Olivia said, picking up a piece of her hair and looking at it. "I like plain brown."

"Well, honey, it shows," said Merle, patting her hand in a conciliatory manner.

"Says the woman with a bird's nest in her hair," Olivia quipped.

Martha hooted. "See? I told you, Merle."

Neve raised her eyebrows, her expression one of delight. "That might be the meanest thing I've ever heard Liv say."

"Well, it's obvious that you're not one of her clients. She doesn't hold back on me," Chase said.

The ladies tittered, and Zeke regarded Chase a bit too fondly. Friendships had a way of turning into other things. She and Conrad had tilted that way, burning hot and then sputtering when reality dumped an ocean on them. Would Zeke and Chase go the same way? And how would the actress handle the pain if that happened?

But Olivia didn't want to think about all the complications at present. She wanted to bask in the warmth surrounding her, savoring the gentle teasing, taking pleasure in the excitement of the older ladies patting their hair and fussing over their lip color as they recaptured a part of themselves they had forgotten—the part that relished the glamour and glitz. And honestly, Olivia wanted to relish the tenuous sisterhood she'd bridged with Neve. Though storms were on the horizon in regard to their father and the cabin's future, Olivia wanted to savor this moment, one in which she had a glimmer of hope that she and Neve could grow toward a better relationship.

How nice it would be to lean toward her sister instead of always going it alone. Olivia had chosen that direction too often, and though this new path with her sister might have potholes and thorns, she wouldn't be on it alone.

For now, that was enough.

CHAPTER SEVENTEEN

Chase attached an armband around the wrist of the kid wagging his hand inside the ticket booth and made change for the two twenty-dollar bills he'd given her. "Here you go. Have fun."

He gave her a gap-toothed grin and ran back to where his parents stood with a few other kids. Being stuck in a single-person ticket booth ensured that most people didn't know who she was, which is why the committee had moved her from the agricultural exhibit to carnival ride sales. The festival goers were too busy begrudgingly coughing up the thirty bucks for the all-you-can-ride band to search for the actress they'd heard was working the carnival as a volunteer.

Not to mention that Chase was no longer a platinum blonde. Neve had stripped off the color, returning her to a warm brown, trimming her hair into a shoulder-length bob. Then she'd added caramel-and-gold highlights that made her look like autumn personified. When she'd looked in the mirror the last few mornings, she'd seen a stranger. After the initial shock, Chase found she loved the new look. She looked more serious, like someone who knew herself better.

And she did.

Over the past week, she'd worked harder at self-reflection. She'd even called her mother and conducted a normal conversation with Lorna. Funny how something as simple as a conversation looked different when she wasn't angry. She could tell her mother had been surprised by how reasonable Chase had been, especially when it had come to a discussion of her career. Chase had been honest—she had misgivings about her current path. She was going to fulfill her obligation to Conrad, but she wanted space to figure out what else she wanted from life.

"What else would you do?" Lorna had asked.

"Go back to college? Maybe start my own production company specializing in acquiring female-focused films. That could be really cool. Or perhaps I would like to direct? Or maybe leave the business altogether? I guess what I'm saying is that I never really got to choose my path, and I want a chance to do that."

"You think I made you become an actress? Because I didn't. You wanted to be in commercials. You said so."

"I was four years old, Mom. I wanted to be a princess and have a pet dragon. Children can't choose what to do with their lives when they're . . . four years old."

Silence had reigned for a good ten seconds.

"Mom? Lorna?"

"You called me Mom," Lorna said, something sounding like a catch in her voice.

That revelation caused Chase to sit down a bit too hard on the bed. "Well, you are my mother."

"You just haven't called me that in years."

"Maybe because I was an asshole. Or maybe because sometimes you seemed more my manager than my parent. I have only you to protect me, to hold my best interests in your heart. I'm not blaming you for seeing me as more of a product than a person. I put those barriers up. I became less your daughter. If anything, therapy with Olivia has allowed me to see that. I have caused many of my own problems, but I'm also going to fix them myself . . . starting with managing my own affairs."

Her mother cleared her throat. "What does that mean? You don't want me to act as your manager?"

"No. It means I'm going to have a say-so in my life. If I stick with acting, I will weigh in on where I appear, what parts I read for, and who I work with. I want to see income and expense reports. That sort of thing. And it's not because I don't trust you. I just need autonomy over my own life. Letting you do everything for me takes away my agency, takes away the investment I need to have in myself. We need to set boundaries for each other, because you need to have your own life, too. It's crazy, but I realized as I worked through this recovery workbook that you don't have much of a life, Mom. You gave yourself up for me, and that's not really fair to you."

Lorna had sighed. "You've been doing a lot of thinking. Maybe too much."

"It's way overdue, Mom."

Another few seconds ticked by. Finally, Chase said, "I'm sorry for the way I've hurt you with my actions. I'm going to do better. Hopefully, we can find a way back to being some kind of family."

"Chase, I . . . I don't . . . have words. I'm overwhelmed."

"That's okay. I've had a lot of time to think about who I was and who I want to be. Maybe you need some time, too. The main thing is that things will be different. I'm done with being that old Chase. Forever."

Chase had hung up the phone, feeling a million pounds lighter. She walked downstairs and handed Olivia the phone. "Done."

"And?"

"Went very well. You can check communicating my feelings for my mother off the mental health checklist."

Olivia nodded. "How do you feel?"

"Like I'm a different person."

And Chase truly felt that way as she searched for Spencer in the sea of people at the festival. He should have arrived in Cotter's Creek thirty minutes ago. She'd left his bracelet, bought with the money Olivia had paid her for painting the shutters, at the front gate under the name Roman Suede. He'd said he would come incognito so no one would recognize him, and Chase was worried that his disguise might be a seventies porn star. How did one make a guy who looked like Spencer fly under the radar?

"What did you do to your hair?"

Chase yelped and spun toward the glass window to her left, where a guy in camo, wearing a bright-orange hat and sporting a grizzled beard, leaned against the pane.

"Wait," she breathed, her eyes widening. "No way. Spence?"

He turned, lowered his mirrored glasses, and grinned. "Whatcha think about the beard? I had makeup do it, and then they loaned some wardrobe to me."

"You look like a country boy," she said, not bothering to hide her amusement.

"Excellent," he breathed with a grin. "You know, I thought about getting a chaw, too, to complete the whole rural look."

"A what?"

At that moment, three teenage girls approached the booth. Spencer quickly shoved his glasses back on and walked away. The girls looked at him suspiciously, then at each other. One giggled and made a face.

Chase suppressed a smile. Obviously they thought Spencer was totally weird.

They weren't far off.

She took the money and secured the bracelets on the girls' wrists. Seemed it was important to do it for them so that they couldn't do it loosely to shrug off and pass on to someone else.

"So can you leave? It's been forever since I've ridden a Tilt-A-Whirl or the Ferris wheel," Spencer said, leaning back onto the ticket booth so she could hear him. "And your hair is different, but I like it. You look like I always thought you would look."

Chase made a face. "And what's that?"

"A cool chick."

"Thanks, Spence. I would like to think so. Oh, and I can't leave for another two hours. But, you know, Olivia is done in ten minutes. She can go with you." Chase had no idea if Olivia liked to go on carnival rides, but she might want to take a ride on Spencer, and if so, Chase could give her that shot. Even if she said she didn't want it.

She did.

"Nah. I can wait on you." Spencer crossed his arms and glanced around at the activity swirling around him.

The scent of popcorn and the greased axels of the carnival rides permeated the midway, along with the shrieks of kids whipping through the Blue Torpedo, a looping coaster. The sun had started its descent behind the large Cornucopia Hall, casting fingers of gold on the food trucks and exhibits lining the thruway that pointed patrons to the carnival games and rides. Chase had never been to a festival and itched to taste the stickiness of candy apples and feel the wind on her face as she whooshed by on the Scrambler. She only had to wait a few more hours before Zeke came to fetch her, and she didn't want Spencer tagging along, even if he was a great guy.

She glanced back at Spencer, who looked ridiculous. "I thought you liked smart girls."

Spencer grinned, his teeth a blinding flash beneath his fake beard. "True. But that one is prickly and buttoned up like a Victorian spinster."

"All the more fun to undo the buttons."

Spencer lifted his eyebrows. "Touché."

"And if you want to know a pinkie-swear secret," Chase continued, sticking her hand out the small window in Spencer's direction. He hooked his around hers, giving it a wag. "She has a crush on you."

"No," he said, his eyes widening. "The shrink?"

"She's not a shrink. And she's not so bad once you get to know her," Chase said with a shoulder shrug.

"Way to sell me on her." Spencer laughed, and, even looking like a psycho, he was pretty cute. "So where might this little cactus be? If she has a thing for me, maybe I can win her a stuffed animal or see if she'd be interested in taking a ride on the Tunnel of Love."

"There's no Tunnel of Love, weirdo. And she's over at the food trucks wearing a gorgeous green apron just like this one. Approach cautiously, since you look like something out of a 'Weird Al' Yankovic video."

"Exactly what I was going for," Spencer said as he sauntered away. He walked about ten paces, turned, and said, "You owe me more than this bracelet." He lifted his arm and showed the fluorescent band beneath his long-sleeve thermal camo.

Chase rolled her eyes and concentrated on the gaggle of teen boys heading her way, each holding money for bands. They were doing banner business. Tomorrow she'd sit in the dunking booth and hopefully raise some money for the children's hospital. A few Oakland A's baseball players and a Laker were also coming, thanks to Olivia's contacts. Chase had also netted both Spencer and Chelle Gomez. Chelle was one of the members of Clash of Culture, a girl band with a growing following. She'd done rehab with Chase once upon a time and had managed to stay sober and still create decent music. People at the festival were going to be jazzed by the celebrities. Something about being the person who helped make that possible gave Chase a warm glow.

An hour and a half later, Zeke walked her way. For some reason he wore a cowboy hat, which normally she would think was lame-o but surprisingly suited his broad forehead and short-clipped beard. He reminded her of Chris Pratt a little, with the warm eyes and at-the-ready smile.

"Hello, cowboy," she said with a smile.

"Hello, stranger. I was supposed to pick up a blonde at this ticket booth. Maybe you've seen her?" Zeke asked, peering around on either side of the single booth.

"You don't like it?" she asked, not necessarily caring, because she liked it and what she liked was more important. Still, some part of her wanted him to see she wasn't the girl who had admitted to doing not-so-smart things over the past few years. She wanted him to think she was . . . changed.

"Come out and let me see."

"I can't yet. I'm waiting to be relieved by"—she picked up the schedule she'd been given—"Annalisa Batton?"

Zeke's eyes widened.

"What?" Chase asked, sensing his emerging panic.

"Nothing. She's just a girl I dated last year."

Chase didn't like the weird reaction in her gut. She hated Annalisa. Abhorred her. Wouldn't pour water on her if she were on fire. But instead of showing this, she summoned her acting skills and placidly said, "Well, I'm sure you'll want to say hello."

"I'm sure I will not. She told people I was a jerk just because I said I wanted to take things slow. Not to mention, she booked the Eureka Hotel for a wedding reception."

"What does that—"

"*Our* wedding reception," he clarified.

"Oh." Chase gave her alarmed face . . . because that truly was scary. She never thought about marriage. Seemed so odd to think about being a bride. Being someone's *wife.* "So how about I hand off the money to her and meet you at the Dunkin' Dogs booth over there?" She pointed to a hot-dog stand that specialized in exotic dips for the fair-size hot dogs.

"Deal." Zeke gave her a two-finger salute and walked toward the hot-dog cart just as Chase saw a curvy brunette wearing a tight sweater and hoop earrings coming her way. She had a bead on the ticket booth, so Chase was nearly certain the attractive woman was Zeke's ex and her replacement.

Yep. Chase hated her.

"Hey," Annalisa said, giving Chase a smile. "You sure look different. I mean, I've seen your movies and stuff. I like your hair, though."

That was her greeting. Figures.

"Thanks. Do you want to step around back so I can tally up the money? Laverne somebody is supposed to come pick up the large bills in a few minutes."

"Sure." Annalisa gave her a wide smile. "I hear you're dating Zeke Kittridge."

"No, we're not dating, per se. We're friends."

"Oh, well, that's good, then. I mean, I can't see him with you. He's just not made that way."

"What does that mean?"

Annalisa blinked a few times and looked sheepish. "Well, you're a movie star, and he's . . . well, he's a bit rustic."

"I like rustic. And on second thought, yeah, we're dating."

Annalisa's face went from fake cheerful to thundercloud. Chase opened the back door of the ticket booth and stepped aside so Annalisa could squeeze inside. The woman wore too much perfume. Perfume that smelled like gardenia. Bluh.

Chase could tell that Annalisa didn't like her, either. Or maybe the woman felt weird around famous people. Not that Chase was famous anymore. Well, kind of. She was fodder for gossip rags and celebrity news programs. Wait, that was infamous, wasn't it?

Five minutes and two complete countings of the ten-dollar-bill stack later, Chase made her way to Zeke. People noticed her now that she was out from behind the etched and smudged glass. Even with her hair a different color, the festival goers seemed to know she was there. Carol had done her job of spreading the news about pop-up surprise celebrities.

"Ready?" she asked, just as Zeke dunked his hot dog into a container of cheese. "Gross."

"Have you tried it?" he asked, swiping a finger under his lip where the cheese dripped. She noted for the twenty-third time that he had really nice lips.

"No. I've never been to a small-town festival. And I'm saving room for candy apples."

He dunked the hot dog into the cheese dip and held it to her mouth.

Such an intimate act in front of so many people, but then again, it was just a hot dog in cheese. She opened her mouth and took a bite. Way better than those horrible pizza rolls with the nacho cheese. "Mmm. Not bad."

"Right?" he said, his green eyes dancing, reflecting the orange bulbs crisscrossing overhead. "Let's bounce and get that candy apple. Oh, and I saw Olivia heading to the midway with some weird-looking dude."

Chase tried to finish chewing the hot dog while not laughing. "What did he look like?"

"Like he belonged in a ZZ Top video. A little unsafe, to be honest."

"Who's ZZ Top?"

"Oh Lord," Zeke groaned, popping the last of the dog into his mouth. "You're too young for me."

"You're only six years old than me, but who says I want to date a thirtysomething dude anyway?"

"Date?"

"I told Annalisa we were. She made me mad when she said that we didn't go together," she said, hoping she hadn't misread Zeke. She couldn't have. He was her friend, but he wanted her.

And she wanted him.

"You told her that?" Zeke looked a bit shocked. "What did she say?"

"She said nothing, but I can tell it made her mad. Are you upset with me?" Chase hadn't felt this vulnerable in a while. She stood beneath the twinkling lights of a Northern California rural festival, asking a guy eating a hot dog he was dipping in cheese to date her.

Zeke grinned. "I'm not upset. I'm amused. And so you know, I've always wanted to date a girl who knew what to do when a guy yelled *Action!*"

"Are you making sexual innuendos?"

Zeke guffawed. "Hell, I hope so."

"Maybe I'll let you get to first base tonight."

Zeke waggled his eyebrows and crooked his elbow. "Let's play ball."

"Sure, but you gotta tell me something," she said, taking his elbow and looking up at him. "What exactly is first base?"

His laughter made her blush. Which she never did. But she didn't care. Lots of guys had hit a home run with Chase London, but not very many had ever stopped to savor first base. She was pretty sure Zeke knew exactly how to slide into first and do it in a way she would remember forever.

⁓

After having been nearly scared to death by a stranger who bent down to whisper "Wanna take a ride with me?" Olivia recovered sufficiently to discern that the man beneath the ridiculous *Duck Dynasty*–esque disguise was the handsome Spencer Rome.

"Why are you dressed like you're about to skin a raccoon in preparation to winter on the mountain?" she asked, untying the apron she'd been wearing for the last four hours. Her feet hurt, her stomach growled, and she still hadn't checked on Chase to make sure she was doing okay selling tickets. Neve had gone to a few local salons to put in applications and talk to the owners, so Olivia hadn't had anyone to relieve her. Finally, someone else arrived to work the evening shift. Chase planned to stay a few hours since she had to work the dunking booth the next day. Olivia should invest some time in enjoying the community festival, spending a little money, and being a good neighbor, but she truly longed for a hot cup of tea and some time working on the outline for her book, but that likely wasn't going to happen.

"I'm practicing in order to play the villain for a movie I'll be filming in a couple of weeks. Do I look like an outlaw meth dealer?" Spencer asked, his grin through that ridiculous beard dashing any hope of looking the least bit villainous.

"Well, you don't look quite as shiny as you normally do," Olivia conceded, passing the apron to one of the ladies running a fish-and-chips food truck called Great Scot.

"Excellent. And what do you mean by shiny?"

Walked into that one.

"Um, you know, pretty. You're a pretty boy with a shiny smile and other, um, attractive qualities." Jesus, she sounded like a fangirl.

His smile this time wasn't shiny. No, the way his lips curved was soft . . . and knowing . . . and she may have focused for way too long on his lips, which the man seemed to notice. "So you feel like squiring me around the festival since Chase is occupied? I don't know anyone else here, and if I walk around by myself dressed like this, someone is bound to call the police. Help a guy out."

Did she want to go with Spencer? Of course, her libido—that part of herself she ignored all too often—clamored for a little alone time with the übersexy superhero, but the common sense she stored front and center flashed out a warning that sounded like the old *Lost in Space* robot. *Danger, Danger!*

Of course, all these weird thoughts were moot because she didn't have a fighting chance of anything even slightly romantic happening between her and the Hammer himself. Still, if there was an itty-bitty chance of doing something more than merely wandering around with him, she could end up like a starving man standing in front of a steaming plate of prime rib. Something more with Spencer could satisfy her hunger, but it might also be mortifying and messy—two things she abhorred in life.

"You want *me* to escort you? To do what, exactly?"

"I don't know. Ride the Ferris wheel, eat foot-long corn dogs, and go into that fun-house thing with all the mirrors?" Spencer stroked the beard that upon closer inspection looked like it could be coming loose by the left sideburn.

"I don't do those sorts of things," she said, sounding quite priggish, which made her want to reach out and snatch the words back.

"Oh, you don't? Well, what shall we do? Pour a spot of tea? Or perhaps take in *The Portrait of a Lady*? Henry James proper enough for you?" He tempered his censure with a smile that warmed the cockles of her heart, whatever those were. "Come on. You know you like corn dogs. Everyone does. They're delicious. And when's the last time you rode a carnival ride?"

A vision of her and Marley riding something that looked like a spider, the carts on the legs whirling as the machine dipped and twisted, flashed in her mind. Marley had loved to ride, begging for one more time even if the line was too long. The memory of her golden hair whipping into her face, gummed up by cotton candy, the sheer joy shining in her eyes, made Olivia's stomach clench with tenderness and regret. The last time she'd ridden a carnival ride had been with her sister at the end of the Santa Monica Pier many years ago. "I guess I'm stuck with you."

"That's not the usual reaction ladies give when I ask them to take a ride with me." Spencer grinned and wiggled his eyebrows, which looked to be his own, as they were not as dark as the false beard.

He seemed amused by her response to his charm. Spencer likely didn't get told no much at all, and damned if she was going to buck that tradition by continuing the prudish protest when corn dogs and Spencer Rome were part of the deal. "I'm sure it's not. You seem to have them hopping after you. Okay, sure. Let's go, but first I need to buy some tickets."

"I'll get you a wristband. That way you can ride everything. Be right back." He jogged away before she could tell him she only wanted to go on a few rides. Maybe the Ferris wheel because, though it looked high, it moved slowly. No way she was getting on anything that spun. Vomiting on the Hammer wasn't going to be her most embarrassing story for the rest of her life.

Before she could blink, he was back. "I talked her into letting me put this on you, promising that I would put it on tight enough that you can't cheat and give it to someone else. Let me see your wrist. She could be watching."

Olivia held up her arm, trying to shove the Oxford button-down she'd worn beneath her apron to her elbow. She'd paired the large shirt with jean leggings and a pair of UGG boots that were comfortable to walk in. She doubted Spencer had ever gone out with a woman who dressed like a soccer mom. If she'd had some Starbucks in hand, she could have been a walking stereotype.

Spencer pushed her sleeve up, and she noted how nice his hands were as he looped the coated paper back around her wrist, pulled off the backing, and folded the sticky part. The slight brushes of his skin on hers didn't make her feel tingly like romance books said, but they did make her want to feel his hand in hers. His weren't workingman hands, but neither were they long, artistic ones. They looked like the hands of a man who modeled a watch . . . naked.

She swallowed down her nervousness when she thought about him sprawled on those white sheets. All that splendid golden flesh. Good heavens.

"Okay, let's roll." Spencer didn't wait for her. Just plowed through a few clumps of stragglers, heading toward the midway.

Olivia dutifully followed behind him.

Spencer stopped outside the barn. "What's in there?"

"My sense of smell says farm animals. I believe there is a show and then an auction tomorrow." Olivia wrinkled her nose at the pungent fragrances leaking out. She heard a few moos and maybe a squawk or two.

"I like animals," he said, looking like he would insist on wading through the barn.

Olivia gestured to the line in front of the Ferris wheel. "The line is short. Let's start here. I don't think I can eat your lauded foot-long corn dog after having toured a barn."

"Okay, cool." Spencer seemed a most agreeable sort, which was a nice change of pace considering she'd been dealing with Chase and Neve for the past few days. *Agreeable* wasn't a term to describe either of them.

They walked over and got in line behind two kids who were making bets on which color cart they would get. The bigger kid won with his choice of pink. The carnival worker secured the kids and brought the next blue car down for her and Spencer.

"Easy, now," the mustached man said, taking Olivia's elbow and helping her into the swinging cart. Olivia sat on the cracked vinyl bench, discovering it was much smaller than she would have thought. Her thigh snugged right next to Spencer's when he sank down and pulled the bar tight against them. The car released and started rocking, forcing her to slam her hand on the handle in front of her.

Spencer grinned with delight as the cart lifted. "Now you can't get away from me."

Her stomach flopped over. "Why would I want to get away from you? You're not going to be weird or anything?"

They rose even higher, and Olivia peered over the side at the shrinking ground beneath her. She hadn't been on a carnival ride in a long time and forgot how . . . somewhat scary it felt at first. No control when you're on a ride like this.

"Joking. I thought you wanted to be near me," Spencer said, stroking his beard. That thing was definitely coming off on one side.

Then she actually registered his words.

"What does that mean?"

"That you like me," he said as they rolled to the top and stopped with a jerk.

"Oh." She clutched the bar as if she could stop the rocking of the cart. He slid an arm around the back of the cart and tried to center his weight, slowing the rocking.

"You're not going to fall," he said.

"I know. I just don't like rocking like that. And why do you think I like you?"

"A little birdie told me."

"Oh, well, that little birdie had no business telling you anything about me. She's meddling where she shouldn't." Olivia felt a flash of anger at Chase. She'd asked her not to say anything, and here she sat, swinging thirty yards above the earth with a guy who thought she was into him. And maybe she was. A little. But now she had to wonder what, if anything, Spencer hoped to gain by noting her attraction. "Are you making fun of me?"

He drew back. "No. Of course not. I'm a little rusty on my flirting skills, so I'm sorry if they came across as too teasing."

"Flirting? Why would you flirt with me?" Olivia couldn't keep the shock out of her voice.

"Because you might be fun to unbutton." His teeth flashed against the darkening sky.

"What?"

"Philosophically speaking, of course. You are an enigma. Very in control and reserved in your emotions. I wanted to coax you out by flirting with you a little but . . ." He rubbed a hand over his face. "I'm, like, totally botching this. What I'm trying to say in an unintentionally weird and somewhat skeevy way is that I'm attracted to you, too. I mean, if you are attracted to me like Chase suggested."

Olivia knew her mouth had fallen open. He was attracted to her? Her?

Right as he was about to say something, the Ferris wheel cranked up, and they dropped.

Olivia screamed.

Spencer laughed.

It took two rotations before she could even breathe again. "Oh my God, I don't remember this thing going so fast."

Spencer grinned at her, placing his arm around her shoulders in what she assumed to be comfort but felt . . . well, it felt kind of good. For a few minutes of whooshing through the Northern California dusk, Olivia was able to actually enjoy her stomach separating from her insides every time they rose and fell. The car rocked, but she'd stopped being concerned about that since Spencer had his arm around her, holding her tight.

Finally, the wheel eased to a halt, making their cart swing a little. They were close to being let off the ride.

Spencer called down to the operator. "Hey, if you'll move us around and let us off last, I'll give you a twenty."

"Sorry, buddy, I have rules—"

"Make it a hundo?"

She didn't hear a protest. The cart dropped again, and the operator allowed them to go past the departure ramp. Obviously a hundred-dollar bill talked.

"Why did you do that?" she asked, loosening her grip on the bar in front of her.

"Because we couldn't finish our conversation when the ride was going, and you might take off and not talk to me once the ride is over," Spencer said matter-of-factly.

True.

"What do we need to say?" she asked, looking over at him.

He was so handsome framed against the night sky, even with the odd beard covering the expanse of granite jaw. Spencer stroked the beard again like he couldn't keep his hands off it. "That we're attracted to one another."

"Okay, so we're two adults who are single and are—wait, are you single?" she asked.

The cart climbed again as the operator let off another set of riders, once again putting Spencer and Olivia at the very top.

"I'm single."

"But why me? You have a lot of women who are . . . I mean, I'm pretty normal. Sort of passably attractive, but nothing like Chase or the other women you must work with in the industry. I can't be your type."

"How do you know my type?" he asked.

"I don't. I'm just saying that we don't go together in any conceivable way. This is such a strange conversation to be having. You're a hot movie star, and I'm a repressed—at least from the sound of it—therapist. Why would you want me?"

"I'm a guy. And let's try for inconceivable."

"What?"

"You said conceivable way. I said—"

"I get it, but, Spencer, this isn't a movie. This isn't *Notting Hill* where you say you're just a guy looking for a girl to love him."

Spencer made a face. "Who said anything about love? Dude."

Olivia opened her mouth a time or two, trying to think of something to say to that. "I mean, I know. But still."

"You look really pretty right now. You have intelligent eyes, nice skin, and I really dig your mouth. It's very kissable. It's like an invitation to a kiss."

She almost lifted her fingers and pressed them to her lips. Instead she blinked at him. He dug her mouth? Did that mean . . . would he . . .

"So can I kiss you?" he asked, staring intently at those lips he'd mentioned.

"You want to kiss me?"

"Well, I'm not a Viking pillager who takes what he wants. I always let the lady do the ravaging."

"Do what?"

"Pillage. Take what she wants."

The invisible switch that resided somewhere below her belly button and right above her pelvic floor switched on, and a low thrum of desire began to vibrate inside her as she thought about her fingers trailing over his six-pack. He had to have one. Had to. She would be happy to take what she wanted from him. Thrilled, even. "Okay. You can kiss me. Or we can kiss. Both of us together."

Way to sound weird, Liv.

"Yeah?" he said, sliding the hand that had been resting on the back of the car to the nape of her neck. Just as he leaned toward her, the car dropped again.

"Oh," Olivia said, grabbing the forearm he'd moved toward her, her mouth falling open as they stopped jerkily on the next level.

Spencer laughed, and then he totally took advantage, covering her mouth with his. And if Olivia thought her stomach had dropped when the ride had started, she couldn't have come close to imagining the pleasure of being kissed by a superhero on the Ferris wheel.

CHAPTER EIGHTEEN

Chase walked next to Zeke toward the front gate of the festival, holding a huge stuffed frog and occasionally pinching off the pink cotton candy in the bag she carried and popping it into her mouth. Spun sugar was so dope. "I can't believe you won this for me on the first try."

Zeke shrugged. "I was an all-district pitcher."

"That poor carnival guy. He had no clue he'd be coughing up this adorable froggy woggy," Chase said, addressing the silly, albeit cheap, prize Zeke had won her by knocking down milk cans. She'd had lots of guys give her expensive gifts, but she wasn't sure she'd ever liked anything as much as she liked this stuffed frog.

"Baby talking to an amphibian? Now I've seen everything." Zeke slid her an amused look.

Chase laughed because she'd had the most fun tonight. They had traipsed through the barns, admiring heifers and pigs, holding their noses because farm animals apparently were odorous. Very odorous. But the young cows were cute with their thick eyelashes and big chocolate eyes. Several of the children who had raised them were there to provide information, their eyes gleaming with pride in their accomplishments. Several of them asked for her autograph or a quick selfie. No one was too weird about a celebrity being in their midst, which was a relief. Cotter's Creek had been really good about not making her feel stalked, but she had worried about being out in the crowds where some might make her feel too under the microscope.

After touring the barns, she and Zeke had ridden a lot of carnival rides, ramming into each other on the bumper cars, holding tight as they spun around above the ground on swings. She'd totally taken advantage of holding his hand beneath the sight lines of the cars as they plunged, rolled, and spun their way into laughter and breathlessness. Occasionally, when they were away from prying eyes, she had let her head fall against his shoulder, eliciting a smile from him. She really wanted to kiss him but had decided to let him make the first move.

So why hadn't he tried yet?

She glanced over at him as if she could decipher why he played it so cool. Didn't he want to kiss her? She thought he did. Maybe he was being respectful? Waiting on her?

"What?" he asked.

"Nothing. I had a good time."

Zeke smiled, setting his cowboy hat on her head. "Me too, cowgirl."

"I had no clue candy apples were that good. If I had tried them before I shotgunned my first beer, I probably wouldn't have had to go to rehab four times," she said, making a face.

"Damn, why didn't someone let you eat candy apples?" Zeke said, giving her a smile. It felt good not to have to pretend with him. Her warts were fairly obvious, but they hadn't scared Zeke away. Well, not yet.

"Probably because I was always on a diet."

"Well, that sucks." Zeke waved at a few overly curious people as they departed the entry gate. Some people had snapped pictures of them as they passed by, but she'd seen no paparazzi, so that was a good thing. Still, chances were Zeke would find himself in a magazine or two. She hadn't asked him if that would bother him. "People are taking pictures of us."

Zeke nodded, kicking a rock on the gravel road that led to the parking lot. "How do you feel about that?"

"Me? I'm used to it. I was more concerned about you. How do you feel being my new 'love interest'? That's what they're going to probably say. Although since Spencer is here, they could assume we've 'made up.'" She crooked her fingers as she muttered "made up" after shoving one more piece of cotton candy into her mouth.

"Could that be true? You and Spencer Rome?" Zeke shoved his hands into his jean pockets and looked up at the autumn moon hanging on the horizon like a giant stage prop. He seemed to be trying to hide his emotions, but they were there for her to see anyway. Zeke wanted the idea of her and Spencer to be very much untrue. Something about his expression tilted her toward him more than the Scrambler had earlier.

"No. Spencer and I have never been anything but friends. That doesn't mean those meatheads who chase celebrities and spin conjecture about their lives know that. Chances are, you and I will be made to look like we're together. Like you're my new guy."

"You said we were dating, but I wasn't sure if you were joking or not. So if I'm your 'new guy,' what does that mean?"

Chase shrugged. "I don't know. I mean, we're friends. We said we'd be friends until I got my shit together. If I've learned anything through this whole process—outside of reconciling a bank statement to the penny—it's that being vulnerable means being courageous, means taking a chance. Still, I'm afraid to mess things up with you by starting something that could hurt both of us. I'm not sure I'm strong enough, and how would this work logistically? It's a bit like I'm in a bubble here. What will happen when I go back to the world I live in?"

Zeke slowed his walk, eventually stopping. "That's a lot to unpack. I guess first I have to say that I understand being afraid of messing things up. I've really enjoyed being your friend. You're a good friend, Chase."

"Really?" The word escaped her before she could think much about it. She'd never felt like much of a friend before, not really. Some of the people who hung with her did so because of who she was on the outside, not who she was on the inside. Of course, she'd never really thought about being an intentional friend before. Maybe she felt so isolated because she'd never cared enough to find out what kind of friend she could be.

"Yeah. You listen and offer encouraging solutions. You're willing to take advice. You try new things, like dipping hot dogs in cheese, and you practice respect and consideration. I would say that's a great job at friendship. As to the other, well, I understand feeling insulated here, though I think Olivia's whole adulting thing was supposed to resemble the real, not-so-safe world. The world, whether here or back in LA, always has the potential to smack a person upside their head. You're not necessarily safer one place over the other."

Chase thought about that. "Well, in some ways coming here has felt, well, maybe not like a smack upside my head, but it's felt real. And let's face it, I failed at a lot of things."

"But you didn't stop trying. You learned."

She had indeed learned some useful things that would help her be a better person. Something about his noticing made her feel so . . . so proud. When was the last time she'd been proud of herself? She couldn't remember. "I did. If I'm honest, I thought Olivia's whole Square One was stupid, but I have learned things that have made me a better person while at the same time coming to terms with things I avoided too long. I'm not there yet in regard to emotional healing. Maybe that's why I'm afraid. I . . . I . . . ." She couldn't say what she wanted to say. Chase couldn't be that vulnerable yet. The words *I'm falling for you* were on the tip of her tongue, but she wasn't going to let them escape. That would make her more vulnerable than she'd been waking up naked next to a stranger two months ago.

Two months? Hard to believe she was the same person who'd snorted coke and slept with that random guy. She felt so different. So . . . absolutely changed.

Zeke took her sticky hand in both of his. "It's okay. I think I know, because I feel the same way. I'm worried that you will make me fall in love with you and then decide that a regular guy like me isn't worth the while."

If he'd punched her in the stomach, she wouldn't have felt it less. "I wouldn't."

"You could."

His words weren't wrong. How would Zeke fit into her world? He belonged here in the woods, stomping through the streams, paddling the creeks, being that Grizzly Adams mountain man. She couldn't picture him walking down Rodeo Drive in the midst of all that excess, all that glittery slickness. It would be like tossing an emerald into a bin of rhinestones. You couldn't take someone as authentic as Zeke and expect him to exist with people like her, people who had gone so long pretending, they believed their own bullshit.

But what if she had truly changed?

A group of teenagers whooped and hollered as they pulled their big truck into the parking lot. A row over, a family was folding a stroller into a minivan. Behind them another couple, this one older by several decades, made their way to a dark sedan. All around, people were peopling, but standing there next to Zeke felt more. Just more.

She always felt that way when she was with him. Like she could be enough. Like she was a person who had weight and substance. When she was with Zeke, Chase London felt changed. But soon she would go back to who she was. Would that world remold her into what she used to be, the way a stream carved a path through the land? Was she strong enough to resist, to be unmoved?

"Let's not worry about the future. Let's do the present. Come on," he said, tugging her toward his truck.

She let him lead her, open the door for her, and help her into the truck. For the next few minutes, they drove back to the cabin, the fluffy frog between them, her half-eaten cotton candy carefully wrapped up because she could need it at some point. She was nearly certain cotton candy could be a not-healthy-but-better-than-cocaine coping strategy. Zeke tuned the radio to a station that played love songs. Lionel Richie and Diana Ross teamed up for one about love lasting, like, forever, and it seemed to be sending a message to them.

Or not.

She wasn't sure what to do with Zeke.

But she wasn't ready to walk inside the cabin without trying to figure it out, so when they pulled into the driveway, she pointed toward the edge of the woods that hid the stream. "You want to take a walk?"

Zeke raised his eyebrows. "A walk?"

"The moon is pretty, and I don't want to go inside and make small talk with Neve." *I'd rather spend more time with you.*

He glanced over at her. "Sure."

She didn't wait. Just bailed out, leaving her frog and new coping food in the seat. He met her halfway across the yard, catching her hand in his. They crunched through the traitorous leaves that had the audacity to fall and repopulate the front yard. The warmth of his hand was little respite against the coolness of the evening. October had arrived to deliver the first kiss of winter.

They walked toward the stream, led by its gurgle. Somewhere in the distance, an owl hooted and flapped. They picked their way around several rocks that gleamed almost phosphorous in the moonlight and found one large enough to sit on. The hardness of the rock was cold on her bottom and thighs, so she eased her knees up and clasped them.

"Are you cold?" Zeke asked.

"A little."

He wrapped an arm around her, and she fell against him as natural as a dog curling into its bed. She stayed still, listening to his heartbeat, wanting more, wanting his kiss, his everything, but too afraid that she didn't deserve him. She'd done too many things that shamed her, and he was a man who spent his free time playing the piano for senior citizens and brought meals to his neighbors.

But she wanted him.

As if cementing that conclusion, his lips brushed her hairline. So tender.

"Zeke?" she whispered.

"Yeah?"

"When are you going to kiss me?"

The chuff of his laugh echoed in his chest. "I've been waiting until you were ready."

"I think I'm ready. I've been ready since the moment you brought me chili and—"

He silenced her in the most obvious of ways, and those lips delivered everything she could ever want in a kiss. He tasted of laughter, of candy apples, of the wind whipping through her hair, of desire, of all things she'd never known.

Then it was over almost as soon as it began.

She pressed her fingers to her lips, frightened at the way her heart tripped against her ribs. "Did I do something wrong?"

Zeke pressed his lips to her forehead. "No way, baby. It's just if I keep kissing you, I won't stop, and I promised myself that I would let our friendship stand no matter what. But if we tip over to where I really want to go, friendship may not be possible."

"It may not be possible anyway. What if we're too late?"

He lifted her hand and kissed her knuckles, but he didn't respond to her question. Rising, he helped her up. "I don't know. Maybe. You have no idea how much I want you, but I don't think the timing is right. You're not really ready, Chase."

She swallowed hard, unwilling to surrender the hum of desire he'd stirred in her but also touched by his self-control. He'd put her welfare above his desires. She'd never, ever been with a man who did that.

So she followed him from the hidden spot back to the reality of the cabin.

They emerged into the clearing just as Olivia's car pulled into the driveway. Following closely behind was Spencer's odd Bronco. She'd nearly forgotten about Spencer. She'd not even thought about how he would get to the cabin. Some kind of friend she was.

The engines were shut down, and both Olivia and Spencer climbed from their respective vehicles.

Chase opened her mouth to alert them of her and Zeke's presence so they wouldn't scare the daylights out of them, but just as she started to call out, Olivia and Spencer met on the broken concrete path to the cabin and . . .

"What the hell?" Zeke whispered.

"They're kissing. They're . . . oh!" Chase turned to Zeke, her eyes wide as that big harvest moon over his shoulder.

"That's more than kissing. Damn."

Chase threw a hand over her mouth and tried not to giggle so she wouldn't alert the couple that was truly stumbling toward the door like two teenagers who couldn't stop touching each other. That was Olivia totally grabbing Spencer's ass. Olivia. Her therapist. She managed stifling her laughter and whispered, "I'm the best matchmaker in the whole world."

Zeke started laughing softly. "Suddenly I feel better about meeting the Hammer."

"I think it's going to be tomorrow, though," she said as Olivia started untucking Spencer's shirt.

"I think you're exactly right."

When Olivia made her way to the kitchen for coffee, she said a prayer that both Chase and Neve had slept in. She'd slipped from her bed, careful not to make noise. Spencer had been snoring lightly, one muscled arm flung above his head, the mouth that had done wicked, wicked things to her slightly open. The sheet caught at his waist, and that beautiful torso framed against her white sheets made her swallow hard.

She'd just done that.

Oh God.

Grabbing a robe, she went in search of coffee and a moment to gather herself, her thoughts tripping over the shame, the censure, and, okay, the delight that she'd finally had really good sex.

But when she'd entered the kitchen, Neve and Chase were sitting at the bistro table, eating Cheerios and jointly staring at her iPad. Dang it.

They both looked up . . . and at that moment, Olivia knew they knew she'd slept with Spencer last night. Her mission to try like hell to stop touching him while climbing the stairs had failed. Oh, and she'd tried not to make too much noise once they'd reached her bed, but he was really good at the bedroom stuff, so she may have allowed an exclamatory orgasmic moan to escape a time or two.

Double dang it.

"Well," Chase said, a twinkle in her eyes. "How did you *sleep* last night?"

Yeah, glee tinged those words.

Olivia tried to fight the full-body flush but knew that was impossible. So she went to the coffeepot, grabbed a mug from the mug holder, and poured a cup. As she lifted the coffee to her lips, the sacred aroma gave her temporary respite. Then she turned around to those two women watching her like cats about to play with a poor mouse. They both looked delighted.

Olivia leaned against the cabinet. "I slept good. You?"

"I slept fine," Neve said, grinning as she took another sip of her own coffee.

"Well, I didn't. I kept hearing noises all night. Noises that sounded very real and not fake," Chase said, setting her spoon in her empty bowl.

"Oh, for heaven's sake," Olivia said, wishing she could press her hands against her flaming cheeks.

Chase laughed.

Olivia schlepped over to the table, pulled out a chair, and sank down. She put the coffee down and pressed her hands over her face. "What in the hell have I done?"

"Um, you did the finest man I've ever seen," Neve said, pulling Olivia's hands from her face. "I mean, seriously, Liv. Score."

Olivia looked at both of them. They looked happy for her. She hadn't seen Neve happy in a long time. And Chase didn't look like the haunted actress running from her problems. She looked like someone Olivia had known longer than two months. "I'm so embarrassed. I can't believe I did that."

"Why are you embarrassed? Sex is natural. Sex is fun," Chase said.

"You're quoting George Michael?" Neve said, still smiling.

"Who?" Chase asked, looking momentarily confused. Neve made a face like she couldn't believe the actress didn't know who sang "I Want Your Sex."

"I shouldn't have done that. I don't do things like that," Olivia said, shaking her head.

"Was it good?" Neve asked, tilting her head in a quizzical way. Like their old boxer Tim-Tim.

Olivia didn't have words for how good it had been. Maybe it was because it had been a long time since she'd shucked her drawers for any man, or maybe it had been that she'd fantasized about Spencer. Or maybe it had been the right time, right guy, right place. No matter, what she'd done with him in her grandparents' mountain cabin (dear Lord) had been about the best sex she'd ever had. Ever.

"Uh, yeah, it was."

"I bet. They don't call him the Hammer for nothing," Chase teased.

Olivia let herself smile at that one. "Okay, enough."

Chase shook her head. "Oh, no. I got berated for just hanging out with Zeke. You got dirty with a superhero. You have to take what we dish."

A creak at the doorway had them all turning their heads. Spencer came in, his hair ruffled adorably, clad only in pajama pants. He looked . . . hotter than anything she'd ever seen. Good heavens. "Morning, ladies. Hope you saved me coffee."

He padded over toward the coffeepot in his bare feet. Seriously, even his feet were pretty.

Neve looked at her and mouthed, "Holy shit."

Olivia got it. This man was a fantasy guy with his tanned, toned torso, strong, jutting jaw, and baby-blue eyes that warmly took them all in when he turned back toward them. "As you know, I would prefer tea, but I can drink coffee. Not picky."

He smiled and looked at them like he expected them to say something, but all three of them didn't seem to have words.

"What?" he asked.

"Nothing," Chase said. But Olivia saw her wink at Spencer.

He didn't even turn red. Instead he lifted an eyebrow as his gaze met Olivia's.

She knew she was the color of the red kettle sitting on the stove next to him, but she also felt pleasure at the warmth and maybe slight possessiveness in his eyes.

Spencer's mouth turned up as he held her gaze. "I don't have to be back until Wednesday. Thought I would stay an extra day. It's been fun."

"Obviously," Neve drawled.

Spencer lifted his cup in acknowledgment and said, "I'm going to grab a shower. You coming, Olivia?"

Neve and Chase turned to her, their eyes dancing. She blinked a few times, ripping her gaze from Spencer's back to her half-full coffee cup.

Spencer stepped back and turned his head, arching that devastating brow.

"Yeah, are you coming, Olivia?" Neve repeated, grinning like a fool.

Chase actually tittered.

"Yeah, I think so," Olivia said, scooting her chair back, leaving her coffee and following Spencer out the kitchen door. Chase's and Neve's laughter followed her, but for some reason she didn't care. She couldn't remember a time, outside of college, when she'd felt such a part of something natural, something family-like, and that it was with her sister and Chase was about as odd as anything.

Spencer reached back a hand, and she took it.

And that felt good, too.

CHAPTER NINETEEN

The water was cold.

Chase sprang back to the surface, sputtering and shooting daggers at Zeke, who stood several yards away, grinning like a naughty boy. He juggled the two balls he had left to throw from behind the red line.

All-district pitchers should not be allowed to participate in the dunking booth. And stupid celebrities should know better than to wear a white T-shirt to sit in said dunking booth. Of course, as soon as she took her first dunking and ended up chilled, she'd known that was a bad decision. Really bad.

But it had been good business for the dunking booth.

People clapped as she climbed the steps that would seat her back on the lever. She tried to calm her chattering teeth and not look so blue. The earlier warmth that had spurred the T-shirt had disappeared with a cold front blowing in. "Good shot, but I bet you miss the next two times."

For one thing, Zeke had taken notice of the way her T-shirt clung when wet. For another, it was a white T-shirt. But the most telling predictor that she would not go back into the water was that Zeke had seen her shivering. Zeke was her last customer before she traded out with Spencer, and she was willing to bet after proving he still "had it" when it came to pitching, Zeke wouldn't send her back into that freezing water. Just to be certain, she unwound her arms from her breasts and arched her back a little.

Zeke totally noticed. He may have even swallowed hard.

The booth had been a big success. Starting with the second baseman for the A's, they'd worked their way through the pop singer, the spaghetti author, and a weatherman who was subbing for the news anchor. Chase had talked Carol into having her nephew build a covered area from which the celebrity appeared, eliciting gasps and applause. Well, except for the weatherman. Carol had revealed that he'd slept with his coworker and she'd been married. No one really liked him, but he was the only one who could come from the news station. At any rate, this grand reveal had drawn quite a crowd and kept the line for the dunking booth long. They'd already tripled their donations from last year, and the Hammer hadn't even made his appearance.

Sure enough, Zeke missed on the next throw.

She hammed it up, sticking out her tongue, stretching her arms back, allowing her breasts, with nipples that were likely hard enough to cut glass, to be showcased. Part of her was embarrassed, and part of her liked the way Zeke couldn't seem to focus on the bull's-eye.

He threw.

Missed again.

The crowd booed. Zeke grinned, giving her a wink, and she knew he'd missed on purpose. Thank goodness, because she couldn't take another plunge into that cold water.

Chase waved at everyone before carefully climbing toward the curtained platform where she could see Spencer holding a towel.

"Good work, Ladybug," Spencer said, holding out the towel and then wrapping her shoulders with it.

"It's so cold," she managed through chattering teeth.

"Good thing you got a lumberjack to warm you up," Spencer joked, briskly rubbing her arms.

Chase wiped her face and pulled away, keeping the big towel. "What are you wearing?"

"My surf suit."

"You know the ladies are going to want to see that chest."

"Unlike you, I'm not selling sex here." Spencer looked down at her pebbled nipples.

"Hey, stop looking." She wrapped the towel around her and made a face.

Spencer just laughed and unzipped his skintight surfer wet suit so that part of his chest was revealed. "Don't worry. You're like my sister. So cover the hell up. Anyway, I guess I should have a sense of humor about being a sex object."

"And so humble about it," she said sarcastically.

"Hey, I know who I am."

Those words were like an ice cube down her shirt. Which she totally didn't need. But that didn't make the impact any less. Spencer knew exactly who he was. Always had. Being an actor for him had always been so easy. For a long time, he'd looked so much like a child that he hadn't had to deal with being sexualized the way she had. Because it had taken him a while to go through puberty, he'd played geeky characters, the way Anthony Michael Hall had back in the 1980s. It wasn't until he'd turned twenty-two, put on forty pounds of lean muscle, and done the ad for the watch company that he'd achieved sex symbol status. Spencer knew how to navigate Hollywood. Maybe it was easier because he was a white male whose father was a music executive. Or maybe it was just who he was. Spencer hadn't fallen into the ditch the way Chase had.

"What about Olivia?" Chase asked.

"What about her?" he asked, cocking his head.

"She's . . . not like us. She doesn't . . . I guess I'm regretting telling you that she was into you."

Spencer made a face. "Why?"

"Because I don't want her to get hurt."

"We're two grown people. No one forced anyone to do anything. It's not like I pressured her or talked her into it. Totally not that guy, and you know that."

"I know you didn't do anything like that. I guess I just feel responsible because I could see you were both into each other. Thing is, I didn't think beyond last night. I just don't want Olivia to be another conquest. So I wish I hadn't tried to play matchmaker."

Spencer's face went from his normally charming, devil-may-care to something that could be deemed offended. "Look, Chase. You didn't force anything. I'm not stupid. I could see the way she looked at me, and you knew she was my type. I like Olivia. She's wound up pretty tight, but underneath, she's interesting, smart, and someone who doesn't treat me like a side of beef. I know she likes the goods, but I like her goods, too. You have nothing to do with that."

"I guess that's true. I merely felt a little responsible and don't want her to be surprised by—"

The microphone Carol used to announce the next celebrity squelched.

Spencer set his hand on her shoulder. "Hey, I'm not using her. If I want sex, I can get that. I didn't feel obligated, and it wasn't a charity fuck."

Chase nodded.

"Ladies and gentlemen, do we have a treat for you," Carol said into the microphone. A buzz of excitement swept through the crowd just as Zeke stuck his head into the curtained area, looking concerned. He took in the sight of her standing with Spencer, and she didn't miss the flash of jealousy in those pretty green eyes.

"Looks like I'm on," Spencer said, giving her a wink. "Don't worry, Ladybug. It's all good. I promise."

Chase nodded.

Carol continued her introduction. "He normally fights crime, taking out the bad guys with just one punch. His strength is only measured by his need for justice. Mount Larsen festival goers, put your hands together for the righter of wrongs, the enemy of evildoers, a hero for the ages. Let's welcome . . . the . . . Hammer!" Carol sounded like one of those guys who announced boxers in an arena. The former real estate agent had really missed her calling.

A huge gasp and resounding applause broke out as Spencer threw back the curtain and stepped on the platform, waving at the crowd.

Chase turned back to Zeke and rolled her eyes. "They could probably take off the *m-e-r.*"

Zeke looked momentarily confused and then smiled. "Oh, a ham? Yeah, he's that."

"But a really nice guy."

"You're freezing. Let's get you into something dry," Zeke said, holding up the bag she'd packed with her change of clothes. He stepped inside, ensuring the curtains were secure all around. "I'll wait outside so no one tries to peep."

"Look at you. Trying to get me dressed. So opposite from most guys, who try to get me out of my clothes."

Zeke gave her a look. "I'm good at that, too."

"Are you now?" she flirted, batting her eyes.

"But you said you wanted a funnel cake. You're going to have to choose. Sex with me standing up in essentially a changing room with thousands of people right outside or delicious, hot funnel cake," he teased.

"Can I do both? At the same time?"

"Like George Costanza?"

"Who?"

Zeke shook his head. "I've got a lot to introduce you to."

239

"Is that an innuendo?" she asked, taking the duffel bag and dropping the towel. His gaze went right to her girls, but to his credit he yanked his eyes back to her face in under a second.

"Do you want it to be?" he asked. His eyes slid down again to where her hands gripped the sopping hem of her T-shirt.

Chase pulled the shirt over her head, dropping it with a splat onto the wood floor. She knew what she was doing. She liked the feeling teasing Zeke gave her. Which was probably wrong, but maybe a girl had to have that sometimes. She unbuttoned the cutoff jeans and wriggled them down her hips. Beneath, she wore a pink thong that matched her lacy bra. She wrung out her ponytail, turned away from him, and then started to unhook her bra.

"Chase." Zeke's voice sounded strangled. "I should go outside."

She turned her head, peeking over her shoulder at him as she unhooked the front clasp and let the straps fall down her shoulder. "Do you really want to?"

Zeke blinked and shook his head.

"Okay, then. Can you dig that sports bra from my bag?" Chase wasn't super modest. She'd acted and modeled enough to learn that her body was just a body. But she also knew what her body could do to a man. She loved doing exactly that to Zeke. She let the bra fall to the floor and cupped her hands over her breasts. "Zeke?"

"What?"

"The sports bra. Oh, and grab the undies, too. I can't walk around with those wet." She gave him her Lolita smile.

Zeke managed to paw through her bag and find the flimsy scrap of lacy Lycra and her lavender sports bra. He held them out to her, his eyes finally rising to her face. She smiled. "You *are* good at helping a girl get dressed."

She took the sports bra, allowing him just a peek before turning back around and wriggling quite ungracefully into it. The soft warmth against her chilled flesh paired with the sexual tension in the small space made her happy. Then she hooked her thumbs in her thong and tugged it down her legs, stepping out, smiling when she heard Zeke's soft gasp. She may have taken sliding the dry panties into place a bit slower than she needed, but she figured Zeke appreciated the show.

Outside the dressing tent/holding area, she heard a splash and applause.

"The Hammer just went down," she said with a grin, turning around and taking the bag from Zeke, who seemed to care less about making money for charity and more about the impromptu peep show she'd just given him. His eyes were no longer on her face, and his breath had hitched up a few notches.

She pulled out a T-shirt that she tugged on quickly, slid into some leggings, and covered them both with a large hoodie that fell to midthigh. The peep show had been fun, but she was still very cold. The warm clothing felt like heaven. As soon as she tugged on her UGGs, Zeke swept her up against him and buried his face in her neck.

"What?" she said with a laugh.

"You nearly killed me with that," he muttered against her skin, dropping a hot kiss against her throat.

"I wanted you to know the lay of the land."

"Hmm?" he murmured, sliding his lips up her neck, dropping a peck on her jaw as he lowered her to the floor.

"You know, in case we get to try out those taking-the-clothes-off skills you have. Now you have a map."

He looked down at her, and she'd never seen a man want her quite so much. Oh sure, she had been with a lot of guys who were caught up in lust, but in Zeke's beautiful eyes, she saw something more. There was tenderness, regard, affection, and something she was too afraid to hope for.

Smiling, she rose on tiptoe and kissed the cheek just above the line of his beard. The soft hairs tickled her chin, and he smelled like Zeke— like woodsmoke, mint, outdoors, home. "I think we just tipped over."

"Yeah, you made sure of that, but I can't say I'm protesting too much."

"Funnel cake?"

"You really like foreplay, don't you?" he asked.

"I wouldn't know," she said, finding truth in that. She'd never taken this long in a romance. Hell, some of her relationships started with a glass of wine and ended the next morning with her hungover and naked in a random guy's bed. So far, she and Zeke had shared one kiss.

One wonderful, soul-stirring, gentle kiss.

Her world was rocked.

But as sweet as all this was, the shadow of reality hovered close by. She was Chase London, about to go on location in England for a new film. He was Zeke Kittridge, a fishing guide in Cotter's Creek. Their lives were apples and oranges. Oil and water. Movie star and regular Joe.

Zeke stooped down and picked up her discarded, wet clothing and pulled out the plastic grocery bag she'd found to store her wet things. He carefully folded her clothes, placed them in the bag, and tossed them into the duffel. Then he stood and extended his hand.

Chase took it, feeling that taking his hand meant something more than going for a funnel cake. More like accepting that they could no longer turn back.

Zeke parted the curtains, and they went down the steps, the hoots and squeals from the crowd revealing that Spencer was giving them the show they wanted. Waiting at the bottom was that shadow of reality in the form of Conrad Santos. Olivia stood next to him.

Chase let go of Zeke's hand. "What?"

"We need to talk," Conrad said.

⁓

Olivia had stayed home from the carnival that day because she had needed to process what she'd done. Or rather, who she'd done.

Thankfully, Neve had followed Spencer and Chase out the door, going to the Cutup Salon to fill in for one of the stylists. Her sister seemed happy to have the work and had thankfully made no more jokes about Olivia's temporary insanity.

Because that's what it had been. She'd lost her head . . . and then her panties.

She had no clue how to handle having slept with someone like Spencer. In some ways it was surreal because Spencer was, well, a movie star, but on another level, he was like a normal guy. They'd kissed, he'd bought her ice cream, they'd painstakingly tried to tape his beard back on his face to keep him under cover, laughing when it sagged on one side. They kissed again, this time sealing the beard's fate, and then Spencer had asked her if she wanted to go back to the cabin and continue where they'd left off.

And she'd said yes before she could talk herself out of it. Of course, on the way home, she'd talked herself into and out of sleeping with him several times. The whole idea was crazy . . . but also exciting. She wanted him with the same kind of intensity as when she got a craving for a certain food or to watch a certain series. The urge wouldn't go away until she indulged. If she refused herself, that need would be all she thought about. But she had self-control. Or at least she always had. Craving ice cream and indulging in rocky road was far different from craving and indulging in Spencer Rome.

So when she killed the engine in the driveway and climbed out, she'd been determined to tell him it was a ridiculous idea and that she would be going to bed alone.

But then he kissed her again, and she lost all reason.

Yep, her head and her panties.

Olivia padded into the living room, taking in the new curtains along with the rug that had arrived that morning. Everyone had left for the festival, and so she'd had to remove the old one by herself. The braided rug hadn't been moved in ages and left a ring in the center of the room. The floors needed to be refinished, but until that could happen, the new rug would freshen up the space. She lit a candle, poured another cup of tea, and stared at the blank computer screen. Chapter Fourteen was on financial independence, but she couldn't summon the energy to write the introduction.

The cat Chase had been feeding tuna hopped onto the windowsill, looked through the screen, and issued a plaintive meow.

"Jeez," Olivia said to the empty room, setting aside her tea and rising. She went to the door and stepped onto the porch. The cat leaped gracefully onto the freshly painted porch and sauntered over to curl about her ankles. She shut the new screen door and sank onto the front porch step. The cat purred as it wended around her waist. She reluctantly held out a hand for the thing to pet itself. "I'm not getting another cat, so don't try to win your way into my heart."

Beast, as Chase named it, didn't seem to care.

"Obviously I'm having trouble saying no to pushy males. Or at least pushy males who are really cute."

The cat commenced purring as if agreeing with her.

At the end of the drive, a flashy red convertible neared the crooked mailbox, slowing as if looking for an address. Dark hair and sunglasses told her exactly who it was as he maneuvered the low-slung sports car into the driveway.

Conrad.

Her heart dropped into her stomach while at the same time aggravation reared its head.

He hadn't bothered to call or wait for her to find time in her schedule. Of course, she'd been putting him off because she hadn't wanted to deal with the excavated feelings of the past. For the past week and a half, she'd focused on therapy with Chase, fixing up the cabin, and working on her book. Ignoring the emotions dredged up by Conrad hiring her, coming to this cabin, and her sister's presence in her life was a coping strategy she was all too familiar with. Olivia knew how to shut down her emotions and focus on the task at hand. Problem was, she could hold off emotions, but some people had a way of shoving past her resolutions to ignore what would be uncomfortable.

Case in point, her past hurtled up the bumpy drive toward her.

She gave Beast a final pat and stood on the top step as Conrad stopped the car and climbed out. Shielding her eyes against the afternoon glare, she wished away the acid churning in her gut, but it refused to take a hike. "Con, what are you doing here?"

Conrad's loping walk took him to the bottom of the steps in seconds. He smiled up at her, familiar and handsome as ever in his khaki jeans and denim shirt rolled to midforearm. "Well, Livy, darling, I got tired of waiting for you to decide when I could come. Plus, I needed that drive up. Things have been stressful lately."

Olivia nodded. "It's a good drive, but don't you think you should have called first?"

"And have you give me the runaround?"

She made a face. "I'm not. I'm doing what you hired me to do."

"And I'm here to check on that. And give you a little nudge."

A nudge?

Her feelings for Conrad were all over the place. She'd spent so much of her adult life wishing they could be together, knowing they couldn't, regretting so much of what they'd done—there was too much to unload. Better to leave what they were inside the dump truck parked in her heart.

Conrad climbed the steps to stand beside her, looking down with those pretty brown eyes that had always seen inside her. So familiar, but so far away, because that's what time did. Time made strangers of even the oldest friends. "Why can't you let me be close to you again?"

"You know why, Con."

He reached out and brushed her hair back. "God, Livy, I just want to press rewind and change what happened. That night—"

"Con, I don't want to talk—"

He pressed a finger over her lips. "No, let me say it. That night was one of the best nights I've ever had. I know you don't believe that, but for the first time in a relationship, I felt like I fit in my skin. All the upheaval with Marley, all the trying to control my life and what she was doing, all that darkness seemed to melt away that night. I couldn't believe how right you felt in my arms, and the way you looked at me, I saw what my future could be. My best friend had been there all along, and I had been blinded to who I was supposed to be with."

Her heart thudded hard against her ribs, because that's exactly the way she'd felt. She'd waited so long for him to see her, to really see her. Once he had, she'd finally felt whole. Finally, he had discovered what she'd known for a long time—they were meant to be.

Of course, she hadn't known that when he'd phoned her that Saturday evening.

Conrad had said he wanted to talk to her about Marley and what he should do with her sister. Olivia had been so tired of discussing that situation, her first inclination was to tell Conrad she was busy with her thesis. Marley was so many wonderful things, but Olivia's sister was also a master manipulator, puppeteering her family, her friends, and definitely Conrad, who she pulled to and fro so often the man likely had permanent whiplash. So Olivia had led with "I don't think—"

"Please, Livy. I just want to be with someone I can talk to tonight. We don't have to talk about your sister, but I need you."

Magic words.

She'd just completed a jog on the beach, so she told him to come on over, hopped in the shower, and then put some salmon in to bake. She scrounged around in the fridge and found the bottle of white she'd hidden from her roommate, Alicia, under a bag of salad greens. Alicia didn't eat healthy, so if Olivia needed to hide something, the green and leafy veggies provided camouflage.

By the time Conrad arrived, she had a tossed salad, medium-rare salmon, and glasses chilling in the fridge.

Conrad wore jeans, a button-down, and hiking boots. His hair was shaggy around his lean face, and he sported a goatee that somehow suited him. Mirrored sunglasses perched on his head. The man didn't look as devastated as he'd sounded on the phone.

She'd elected to wear linen shorts, a cute floaty top she'd found at Anthropologie, and leather flip-flops. She'd told herself it wasn't a big deal, but she'd french braided her hair and dabbed on some makeup anyway. Oh, and some perfume her mother had bought her for Christmas.

Conrad had swooped in and wrapped her in a big hug, lifting her off her feet. "It's so good to see you, Livy girl."

When he set her down, she swept a hand toward the inside of her condo. "Come on in. Alicia and her boyfriend went to Cabo for the weekend, so we won't be disturbed. I fixed some dinner if you're hungry."

He stepped inside, taking in the Pottery Barn knockoff canvas couch, Indonesian-inspired print throw, and Moroccan rug, all courtesy of Pier 1. "Nice place. And I'm starving."

They'd sat on the couch, eating dinner, sipping wine, and catching up. Conrad had been working as a production assistant, Olivia working on her master's in social work. Both were on track with their careers, lived frugally, and loved being in Southern California.

And both were miserable about Marley.

"I told her we were done over two months ago. I just couldn't be with her anymore, Livy. She would be fine for weeks, and then I wouldn't hear from her for days. When I finally did, she was messed up." The anguish in his voice made her gut clench.

"I know. She refuses to go to Sunday dinners with our family, and when Dad got that big civic award, she no-showed. She hasn't looked healthy in a long time, but I talked to her a few days ago, and she actually sounded better. She said she was going to try rehab. That's the first time she's broached it on her own. That's a good sign."

Conrad sank back on the couch. "I'm so glad to hear that. The last time she called me was a few weeks ago. She didn't know where she was, crying, begging me to come get her. I've done that too many times to count. I told her no, but I felt so guilty. We haven't been together in a long time. We're so over, but she still calls me, and it still hurts. Did I do the right thing? Because I keep thinking that maybe I should have picked her up."

Olivia had read study after study on addiction, on enabling addicts, and still didn't know what to do about her sister. Marley had always been like sunshine breaking through on a stormy spring day. Though she could be a pill, her sister made people smile, laugh, believe in fairies and Santa Claus. Inquisitive, whimsical, and prone to making up lots of stories, Marley had always been more vulnerable to pain, hurt, and injustice than the rest of their family. Marley was more than an empathizer—she seemed to eat others' pain, taking it in and maybe holding on to it too long. "At some point we have to practice self-care."

Even as she said those words, something niggled in her conscience. Marley had told Olivia about doing better, feeling hopeful, and then she'd asked if Olivia would loan her enough money to pay rent. Olivia had gone from feeling buoyant that her sister wanted to change to annoyed. She'd gone down the "just until I get my next gig" path too many times before, so she told her that she couldn't loan her money this time. Marley would have to figure out how to deal with her life on her own.

Marley hadn't gotten mad. She said that she understood and would figure it out. Olivia had hung up feeling guilty but resolved. Still, she understood how Conrad felt.

"So you think she's okay?" Conrad looked worried, and something in that expression irritated Olivia. He'd spent years pining for Marley, and then once she was old enough to take notice of him, he'd taken her around to parties with filmmakers and directors, launching her into acting, introducing her to the lifestyle that brought her to where she was.

He'd made Marley his girlfriend, and even when she hadn't wanted him anymore, he'd still been there for her, waiting for the dregs of Marley's affection like a loyal spaniel.

"I do. Marley is going to have to take some responsibility for herself. You, along with everyone else, don't deserve to worry more about her bad choices than she does. Look, if it makes you feel any better, I'll call her and you'll see she's fine." Olivia flipped open her phone and dialed her sister's number. After four rings, it went to voice mail. "Hey, Mar, it's Liv. I met up with Con for dinner, and we were thinking about you. Call me when you get this."

She snapped the phone closed. "There."

Conrad actually looked a little more relieved. "I'm sorry. You're right. It's just she sounded . . . not good."

"But that was weeks ago. She's better. She said she's going to rehab." Too many times, Olivia had seen her sister looking worn down, just done with trying to shake her addiction. One time she'd seen track marks on Marley's arms, and her sister had that haunting look of heroin addiction. That discovery had both squeezed her heart and made her angry. Why was Marley doing this to herself? Why wouldn't she let Olivia help her? And then she'd called and sounded like her old self. Olivia wanted to hope that it was true—that her sister was finally ready to get help. "She'll call. More wine?"

Conrad nodded, and they'd sat drinking not only that bottle but a few beers she'd hidden behind the diet cranberry juice. Eventually, they'd turned on *Saturday Night Live*, and their mood shifted with the antics of Fred Armisen and Amy Poehler. She'd eventually laid her head on Conrad's shoulder, and he'd wrapped an arm around her. They'd both been well into a second beer when they'd kissed.

For her, it had been absolute magic.

By some unspoken agreement, they'd kissed again. And again. Eventually they'd shed clothes until there was no going back. Afterward, as the television flickered over them and the empty wine bottle had been knocked to the floor, Conrad whispered, "I never knew."

The incredulity in his voice had made her smile because she'd always known they'd be so good together. They were soul mates. To her, their being together had been quite obvious.

Retreating to her bedroom, they'd raided the pantry for OREOs and shared the iPod earbuds, listening to the music they used to dance to as kids. They made love again, this time savoring each other, exploring the smooth span of a back, the silky softness of an inner arm, and when they were exhausted, giddy with something newfound and wonderful, they'd curled into each other and slept until the sun rose high in the California sky.

Olivia made him breakfast—an omelet with fresh avocado and mozzarella—and they'd sat sipping coffee, both of them marveling, smiling like fools, ignoring the fact that Marley would be between them. That this bubble of happiness would be pierced. It was inevitable.

Early that afternoon, Conrad left, giving her a kiss and a promise to come back that night.

Then she'd found her phone wedged into the cushion of the couch. Marley had called three times, each message more and more mumbled, more and more alarming. Conrad had been correct—Marley wasn't okay—and that made Olivia feel both guilty and angry. She was finally happy, finally with the person she'd always loved, and, of course, Marley was going to take that away from her. And really, Olivia should have known better than to think Marley was turning a corner, no matter how determined her sister had sounded last time.

Marley's last message ended with "I'm sorry, Liv. I wanted to forget, and it doesn't work. Don't hate me. Please don't."

Olivia had thrown her hair into a ponytail, tugged on some sneakers, and driven to the apartment Marley shared with two other actresses. When she knocked, dragging both of Marley's roommates out of bed, she'd discovered that Marley hadn't been there in four days. One of the roommates mentioned a motel down by the beach, and Olivia recalled how much Marley had loved the bungalow they'd rented for a week one summer when their house had to be fumigated.

The drive to Venice Beach had taken longer than she'd expected, and by the time she arrived at the Beachcomber Inn, the sun had started to sink into the Pacific. The early spring day had tugged on its finest golden robe over the sapphire sea edged in lacy sea-foam. The seagulls dipped and swooped, their cries urging her toward the run-down motel rather than the beauty of the water crashing onto the hard sand.

After threatening the motel clerk with a made-up law regarding endangerment of a guest, Olivia procured a key to Bungalow 8. She'd stared at that silent door, knowing that what was on the other side would not be good. Pressing a hand against it, she let her forehead fall beside it, a silent prayer released to the heavens above, one that would not be heard.

When she'd entered the room, she'd found her sister lying beside the bed in a pool of vomit, clutching the matching linked hearts necklace their mother had given each daughter one Christmas, calling them the treasures of her heart. Olivia had sunk onto her knees with a wail, knowing that her sister had been dead since the night before. While Olivia had been screwing Conrad and making plans for a life she'd never have, she'd missed her sister's calls.

"Marley, no. No, no, no," Olivia said, clutching her stomach and rocking. "Why . . . God, why?"

No answer.

Only the birds crying outside, an echo to the pain inside her, and silence from her beautiful twenty-one-year-old sister, golden hair plastered to her head, blue eyes sightless.

Trembling, Olivia rose and went into the bathroom, snagging a cheap hand towel before going back to her sister's body.

Carefully, she rolled Marley onto her back, wiping the vomit from her face and closing her eyes. She smoothed the hair from her face, tucking the strands behind her ears, brushing her cheek with the back of her hand. Her mind tripped over itself on what to do—call the police, how to tell her parents, how to get Marley's car back to her apartment. She stood, and that's when she saw a page from the motel notepad lying on the bed.

Marley's handwriting scrawled across the page.

I couldn't do it anymore. I'm sorry. Forgive me.

Olivia lifted the note, closing her eyes. Marley had done this on purpose. She'd no longer wanted to live.

The paper shook in her hands, and her knees gave way. Olivia thunked onto the unmade bed, her gaze never leaving Marley's words on that paper.

She'd done this on purpose.

Anger flooded Olivia, intermingling with the shock and sorrow. Crushing the note in her hand, Olivia closed her eyes, squeezing them hard, trying not to scream with primeval rage.

Her sister had killed herself.

"You're so stupid, Marley. Stupid. What about us, huh? We have to live with the thought we weren't worth you trying to live. We loved you, you asshole. Why did you do this?" she asked her silent sister. She wanted to punch a hole in the wall in anger, frustration, absolute grief.

But maybe no one had to know. Not if there had been no note. Her parents wouldn't have to live with the knowledge that their child had chosen death over life. Everyone knew Marley had a drug problem. One of her roommates had shared her alarm one night when she couldn't get Marley to wake up. If the note was never seen, no one would know that it was intentional and not an accident.

Olivia shoved the crumpled note into her pocket and walked outside to her car. She'd left it unlocked in her panic, and thankfully her purse was still sitting in the passenger seat. She pulled out her phone and dialed 911, knowing that her life would never be the same again.

No more OREOs in bed with Conrad. She knew that deep in her bones. Because Conrad still loved Marley, and she knew him well enough to know that this would break him. This would take what they had last night and shred it into nothingness.

She and Conrad were over.

Done.

Gone was the life she could have had with him.

So now, standing on the porch of her grandparents' cabin over thirteen years later, she couldn't imagine how they could make a fire from cold ash. "That was too many years ago, Con. That grief would have sat between us unmoved. We made the right decision."

Conrad's eyes narrowed. He never liked to be challenged. Affable most of the time, the man was also stubborn to his core. "But what if we'd been wrong?"

"Con, why are you doing this? Because I can't do this again with you. I can't. It hurt enough the first time. I don't know if this is about Chase or about rectifying what happened to Marley . . . but I don't want to go back in time. We can't change anything about what happened."

He rubbed a hand over his face and blew out a breath. "I don't know. When I see a girl like Chase, I have this inclination to do something. To stop her from ending the way Marley did. Because I didn't help Marley when she asked for it."

"I didn't either."

"But she called me before she overdosed. That night when we were together, she'd been calling me the whole time. Jesus." He pressed his finger into his eyes, a man tortured.

"She called me, too, Conrad. Probably called Neve. Maybe Mom. I didn't ask, but she could have. Everyone who loved her wished they'd done something different. I actually counseled one of her roommates a few years after Marley's death. She carried the same burden, but ultimately, I'm not sure we could have stopped Marley. I truly believe that." Probably more than anyone else, since Olivia was the only person who knew that Marley had intentionally killed herself. Would that change the guilt for Conrad? For her mother? For even Neve? Olivia had never thought how telling the truth about the day she found Marley might lessen the hurt inside others.

Would good come from admitting that Marley had taken her life?

Olivia needed to think about that before she admitted the truth.

"I know," he said, dropping his hand and looking at her. He gave her a ghost smile. "I know this is out of left field. I've been assessing my life lately. I'm not getting any younger, and when I thought about the times I was happiest, it was with you in my life. I couldn't get that thought from my head. I needed to, at the very least, see you and see if . . . I know I'm making a mess of things. I guess the memories wouldn't turn me loose."

What to say to that? Back then, she'd spent too many nights crying over the loss of Conrad, so she'd decided to stop dragging around the damaged part of herself, amputating it by ignoring his calls, his birthday cards, the occasional invitation to a Hollywood screening or party. Instead she'd thrown herself into her career and tried to forget. "I don't know what to say."

Conrad gathered her to him and pressed a kiss to her forehead. "You don't have to say anything. Just think about it."

Olivia nodded even though she had no clue how to feel. Last night she'd slept with Spencer, who she liked. A lot. The man was easy to be with and made her feel worthy of his attention. And now the man she'd always wanted had shoved his way back into her life. Two men to balance on top of Chase, her family, and the truth about Marley's death. How had her life gotten so complicated?

Conrad looked at the cabin. "So this is it? Where's Chase?"

"Everyone's at the Mount Larsen Fall Festival. Are you staying the night or . . . ?"

"I thought I would if you have room."

"We'll have to switch up sleeping arrangements because Neve and Spencer Rome are staying here, too."

"Spencer Rome is here?"

"Chase talked him and a few other friends into volunteering for the celebrity dunking booth. Most of the hotels and motels are full because of the festival, so staying here is likely your only option. Hope you don't mind rustic."

"I guess I should have called."

He should have, but too late for that. "We can make do. Come on in."

"I also have a legit reason to drive up. I need to talk to Chase about the role."

"Yeah?"

"The production company is insisting she read for the part."

"I thought it was an established offer and this whole thing was part of getting her insured."

Conrad shrugged a shoulder. "If it were strictly up to me, yeah. But I have others I have to answer to, investors who are fronting money for production, and they have a problem with her history. A few of them want assurances, and they want to open it to other actresses. She'll understand. It's part of the business. Until there is ink on a contract, there are no guarantees."

Olivia held open the door, trepidation awakening at his words. Chase expected to go to work as soon as she was released from Square One. The actress had transformed in the past weeks, and Olivia had planned for them to return to LA in a few days. Time for Chase to spread those wings and leap from the nest into the great wilderness of Tinseltown. Yet here was her first true test. "I understand; still, she's going to be upset. She thinks she's going to work in a few weeks. You sent her the schedule."

"I realize I may have been hasty. But let's not put the cart before the horse on worrying. I brought a revised script so she can start creating her vision for Cecile. I have faith in Chase. She's a very talented actress, and she has a lot riding on this role. Even if it doesn't work out, we've given her the opportunity to resurrect her career and mend her reputation. How is she, by the way?"

"Put your things inside, and we'll go down to the festival and you can see for yourself."

Conrad smiled. "That sounds promising."

"I think you'll be pleased by how much Chase has changed."

CHAPTER TWENTY

When Chase had climbed down the steps of the dunking-booth changing room, she'd been turned on, elated at the success of the booth, ready to extend her foreplay session with Zeke, but Conrad standing at the bottom had put a squealing stop to her happiness.

Well, in a way.

She wasn't necessarily unhappy about having to read for the part, just on notice that her career depended on more than her sobriety. Her talent would have to determine her path, too.

Chase hadn't had to read for a part since she first started out in the business. At the height of her popularity as an A-list actress, she was offer only, and then when her stock slid toward B-list, the producers of the movies that she acted in were happy to have someone with some notoriety to give the films a PR boost. She wasn't necessarily surprised to have to read for the part of the damaged ballerina, but she'd allowed Conrad's assurances to give her security for her future. So, yeah, it stung a little that she wasn't guaranteed the role.

And then to further the upheaval inside her, Olivia told her that it was time to return to LA.

Chase's initial reaction was to scream *no* and run like a spoiled child down the midway. Because she wasn't ready to leave. Here in Cotter's Creek, she'd felt like she finally belonged somewhere. Over the past few weeks, she'd not only completed her therapy and adulting boot camp, but she'd contributed to the community, surprisingly found a sort of friendship with Neve and Olivia, and fallen half in love with Zeke. How could she give that up to go back to what she'd been? Her new normal didn't sound as good as her present not so normal.

After both Conrad and Olivia finished giving her the lay of the land, Chase lost her craving for funnel cake and happy flirting with Zeke. Spencer had driven her to the festival, but Zeke tuned into her emotions and volunteered to take her home.

Their ride back to the cabin had been silent.

She hadn't known what to say and needed time to process what to do when it came to Zeke and her emerging feelings for him. They'd both agreed that they would be friends, but earlier with the striptease, she'd tossed that label aside for something more. And now, she would be leaving. Something more probably wasn't a good decision, even if her heart urged her toward Zeke. *Tangled* wasn't even the word for what she felt as they moved toward the cabin and her uncertain future.

On some level she understood that she'd relied on Zeke to help move to a better place, to be a better person. Did that mean her feelings were magnified because she'd needed someone like him to make her feel better about herself? Or were her feelings true? Analyzing her motives for actions in her past had given her insight into how people filled the holes in themselves, how they rationalized feelings . . . and addictions. What if she had conjured up feelings for her rugged neighbor in order to cope with her rehabilitation?

She didn't think she'd done that, but did she truly know?

Yeah, she liked him and liked herself when she was with him.

But was that enough to build a future on?

As she had climbed from Zeke's truck, she'd looked back into the interior, where he sat looking uncertain himself. "I guess we need to talk, but I think I need time to process some things. I don't want to screw things up between us."

Zeke drew in a deep breath and let it loose slowly. He looked so sad that her heart clutched in her chest. "You know, Chase, I'm not sure there's much to say. You're leaving Cotter's Creek, right?"

"Yeah, but . . ." She stopped, sucking her lower lip between her teeth, trying to read him, trying to say the right thing. "You'll still want to see me, right?"

He directed his gaze over the steering wheel, not looking at her. Classic self-protection. "What do you want me to say? That I don't want you to go? I don't. That I don't want things to change? I don't. But thing is, Chase, you aren't some girl who lives next door. This isn't your home. You live in a world that's far from all this. You're a girl who hangs with Spencer Rome and reads for parts in a film that could snag an Oscar. You've sipped cocktails in Paris, hung out with guys whose records I own, and have a place in Malibu. That's a whole 'nother life from this one."

"Yeah, but I'm still who I am."

This time he looked at her. "I think you believe that now. But it's easier to believe that here. It took me a long time to figure out my life. To know who I am. I came back here and built a life I'm proud of. I'm mostly content here, and I'm not leaving to go back to a place that wasn't good for me. I did New York and hated myself. I'm not up for LA."

Chase gripped the door handle, white-knuckling against the hurt. She wasn't worth him giving an inch? Obviously, she wasn't worth risking his comfort for. Emotions she hadn't felt in a long time flooded her—that prickling shame, that feeling of not being enough. "So when I go back to LA, whatever this thing we had between us is—it's over? It's that cut-and-dry?"

Zeke studied her, his pretty green eyes an enigma. He was protecting himself. She understood that inclination. Still, his words were an ultimatum that didn't sit well with her. Why must everything be on his terms?

"Chase, thing is, I don't have the right to ask anything of you. You have your life, and I have mine. I let myself get sucked into believing in something that can't work because, damn, you're hard to resist. I tried so hard to just be friends, but . . . I want more."

"So why can't we . . . try? It's not that far away."

He swallowed hard and shifted his gaze away. "Because you're an actress, and you're going back to pick up your career and dust it off. That's your right, maybe your destiny, but I can't see how you're going to truly want to keep me around. I'm not the kind of guy who does red carpets. I'm sorry. But I think at this point we have to just stop everything right here."

His words felt like an arrow through her chest.

You're not worth it.

Chase slammed the truck door and turned toward the house. What was the use in talking to him any further? They were done before they'd really started. A kiss? Some hand-holding? That wasn't a relationship anyway. Why had she even deceived herself into believing that she could have something as real as Zeke?

Chase had been stupid.

She could feel him watching her as she walked up the drive, carrying the bag with her wet clothes. What had been campy, flirty fun half an hour ago had been doused with water colder than that of the dunking booth. Conrad was here, the script would be waiting, and she had to pull her shit together in order to get this role.

Her fledgling career sat on a high cliff, and one misstep would send her plunging to the rocks of doom beneath. There would be no recovery if she failed this time. And who would she be if she wasn't Chase London the actress?

She'd talked a big game to her mother, things about finding her own path and going to school, but she knew those were stupid slippery straws that she could never grasp.

Chase had functioned in this "real" world of Cotter's Creek pretty well, but she hadn't needed to get an actual job, handle a not-so-big paycheck, stick to a budget, or worry about how to advance a career. No, this was a safe simulation, a mere taste of what true adulting was.

Behind her, Zeke shifted his truck into reverse and started rolling away from her. Part of her wanted to turn around and gesture him back, but the other part of her knew his words were true. She didn't know who she was, and she couldn't ask Zeke for anything more when she had no clue what her tomorrow looked like.

Chase fetched the key from the hidey-hole beneath the arm of the swing. Zeke had come up with that idea when they were repairing and hanging it. Clever man.

Her heart seized in her chest, but she ignored it because she had to. Zeke wasn't coming back, telling her he would change his life for her . . . even though she had no clue what her life would look like. He wasn't going to risk his heart for someone like her. He knew her track record, knew the life she'd led, probably even knew more about who she was than she did.

Who was she?

Or maybe a better question was, *Who did she want to be?*

Chase turned around and sat on the swing, kicking it into motion as Zeke's headlights swept over her. She raised her hand, but she doubted he saw it. All of this felt so final. So wrong.

Still, she couldn't stop it. This life she'd been leading here in Cotter's Creek was temporary. It had always been a "just for now."

Chase sat in the quiet coolness of the fading afternoon, mulling over what was to come, and at the heart of every journey her mind took toward her possible future was the question, *Is this really what you want, Chase?*

Spencer's truck rolled up and shut off. Her favorite superhero climbed out, hair still damp from the dunking booth. He looked subdued. "Hey, where's your lumberjack? I expected him to be here warming you up."

He slammed the door and strolled her way.

"Zeke's not my lumberjack," she said.

"You okay?" he asked, climbing the porch steps and kicking at the glider of one of the rocking chairs. It creaked as it rocked.

When she didn't answer, he shrugged and sat down in the rocking chair. "You're sure sour for a gal who had Conrad Santos hand-deliver her a script. I'd be jacked to have a shot at one of his films."

Why didn't Chase feel that way? Instead she felt obligated. "He's paying for all this, you know."

"Conrad Santos? He's paying for your therapy? That's pretty generous." Spencer's pretty eyes widened.

"So generous. He wanted me for the junkie part in his next feature but needed me cleaned up enough to get insured. That's what I'm good for—playing the junkie."

"Come on, Ladybug, you know that's not true. You're a hell of an actress. Only one with a Golden Globe on this porch." Spencer had lost the surfer boy shtick and replaced it with the insightful, intelligent person she knew lurked beneath the charming, give-no-shits veneer he donned.

"Big deal. That was fourteen years ago when I was a kid. *What have you done for me lately?* is the Hollywood mantra. I think my answer to that question is a rap sheet and multiple rehab stints. Not too many directors looking for someone like me."

"Conrad Santos is."

Chase shrugged her shoulders. "Maybe. He hooked me up with Olivia because they're friends from back in the day, but he may have had other motives and used me to get close to her."

"You think he's into her?" Spencer's brows drew together, and he looked . . . upset. Hmm. She'd known Spence for a long time, and she'd never seen him serious over a woman. Then again, she hadn't been around him much. Still, she noted his irritation, that slight worry. Maybe Spencer needed a little competition. Wouldn't be bad for the guy who always got the girl.

"Maybe. He looks at her kinda weird, but they go way back. Olivia's sister died from an overdose, and Neve said Conrad dated her sister or something. Anyway, maybe that's why they both feel obligated to help lost actresses get their shit together. That role Conrad promised me now requires I read for it."

Her words sounded bitter. She wished that she didn't feel that way, because she was truly grateful for Conrad caring enough to get her help, and she was thankful for Olivia, even if she'd hated the woman for the first couple of weeks. Olivia had grown on her. Even her shit-stirring sister had begun to feel like family.

But that was all made-up crap in her head, because they weren't a family. This wasn't their home. Zeke wasn't her guy. This playacting was over.

Spencer nodded, staring out into the distance at the overgrown hedges by the mailbox. "So read for the part. If that's what you want."

Chase remained silent, studying the way the late-afternoon sun fell on the slick new paint beneath her sneakers. Her hair lay damp on her collar, making her chilled, but she couldn't seem to want to take a shower and pretend like things were normal when inside twisted a tornado of doubt, confusion, and fear.

What. You. Want.

Those three words haunted her. She'd never thought of any alternative for her life . . . other than running away and assuming the identity of regular ol' Katie. She'd half-heartedly taken some college courses when she'd gotten her high school equivalency diploma, thinking she could handle acting, snorting coke, and English 102, but when she had to go on location, she'd fallen behind in her classes and figured she could always get her degree later. Her major had been English with a minor in theology, and her heart hadn't really been into pursuing a degree. So she stuck with what she'd always done—secure a role, complete the film, get a check, and move to the next opportunity.

"No one has really ever asked me until recently what I wanted. Weird, huh?" she said finally, looking over at Spencer, who seemed to expect an answer to his directive.

"Not really. I went through that a few years back. Even thought about climbing behind the camera and directing, but ultimately I decided I love my craft. I get to put on a cool costume, film fight scenes, get the girl, and become a hero to millions. But maybe you don't love that. It's okay to stop, Chase. Some people might think you're crazy to give up on fame and fortune, but you have to decide your life for yourself. You have that right. Your life belongs to you. Not your mom. Not Conrad Santos. Not even Olivia. *You* get to decide."

Chase pulled both legs up and wrapped her arms around them, resting her head on her knees. "I guess I do."

Olivia's car appeared at the end of the drive. Spencer watched its progression, his blue eyes intent on the forthcoming interaction. Strange to see her friend twisted up over Olivia. When Chase had engaged in her matchmaking, she'd expected a little flirting, but those two had jumped into that puddle with both feet, not even thinking about how they'd get muddy. And now Conrad had arrived with fists full of mud.

Politics and Square One made strange bedfellows, it seemed.

"I'm going inside to start gathering my things," she said, rising as Olivia parked behind a red sports car she assumed to be Conrad's and killed the engine. Conrad said he'd left the script on her bed, and she wanted some time to read through it, getting a feel for the part she'd be reading for. Plus, she had a load of delicates in the dryer that needed folding. Yep, still adulting.

Later that evening, Chase opened the door to Olivia's room and set Marley's sketchbook on the neatly made bed. She'd been packing her things and had rediscovered the art tablet under her completed recovery workbooks. She'd intended to give it to Olivia a week ago when she'd found it but had forgotten about it when Zeke had arrived that night to make s'mores.

Zeke had distracted her that day just as he distracted her now.

She clutched her chest as if she could stop the pain and looked around at the room, noting Olivia's toiletries set out with serial killer precision. The room was bare of anything personal, sort of like the way Chase had kept her own room back in rehab, as if she refused to be claimed by a place. Olivia was the queen of erecting barriers, it seemed.

Earlier as they'd prepared supper for the odd assembly under the roof—an Oscar-nominated director, a washed-up actress, the Hammer, a therapist, and an out-of-work hair stylist—she'd felt like Olivia teetered on the same cliff on which she herself was standing. Olivia had been forced in her conversation, mostly quiet as she listened to Neve's rambling and Conrad's tales designed to regale them with his privileged explorations of the world that seemed to lie at his feet. Spencer had been oddly quiet, his gaze weighing and measuring Olivia as she fake smiled through the overfamiliar touches of the handsome director. One could cut the tension with a hacksaw. Screw that. More like a chain saw.

"What are you doing?" Olivia asked from the doorway, looking perturbed that Chase had invaded her personal space.

Chase tapped the sketchbook. "I found this over a week ago when I was putting sheets on the bunk beds. It was hidden in the liner of the mattress, oddly enough. I meant to give it to you earlier, but it got buried under some of my stuff and I forgot."

Olivia's gaze slid to the bound tablet. "What is it?"

"I think it's your sister's drawing tablet. There are kids' drawings in it."

"Neve's?"

"No, your other one. Marley?"

Her therapist's eyes softened as she looked back at the sketchbook. "Oh, okay. Thanks."

"Sure. I'm going to finish packing. I guess everyone else will leave when we do?"

"Except Neve. I think she's going to stay here for a while."

Chase widened her eyes. "Really? She's moving here or something?"

Olivia looked slightly annoyed, but her gaze kept finding that sketchbook as if it were a flower delivery and she hadn't read the card. "Maybe. We're not sure, but she's asked to stay and oversee the renovations we're doing. She got a job today, so she's committed to staying in Cotter's Creek for a while."

Strange how Neve and Olivia's relationship had changed during their time at the cabin. Hell, funny how hers with her life coach had changed, too. Maybe there was a truth here that wasn't as easy to find in their normal lives. Mountain air, gurgling creeks, and simple living seemed to provide answers to questions she didn't know she had. "That's cool. You two seem to be getting along better. Well, I probably need to let Spencer know we're heading out tomorrow . . . unless you want to tell him?" Chase wasn't sure how Olivia was handling the whole Spencer/Conrad thing. The director had made sheep's eyes at Olivia while Spencer brooded.

"Uh, you know, you might want to tell him. I need to gather my things together myself."

"Chicken," Chase said.

"Maybe so." Olivia turned from her, effectively dismissing the conversation.

Normally, Chase might have teased her, but her own heart felt tender, and it didn't seem wise to poke at a hornet's nest. So instead she backed out of the room. "I'll go pack."

"Great."

Chase stopped when she reached the door. "Are you sure I'm ready?"

Olivia turned back around. "You're ready. We have a few more issues to clear up and can address that on the drive. Just some self-evaluation, nothing you can't handle. I'm proud of you, Chase. I really didn't think you would do as well as you did. I mean, you literally ran away, but once you set your mind to get better, you did. And that tells me so much about you."

"What do you mean?"

"That when you want something, you get it."

Chase nodded. "That's true, but my issue is sometimes I don't know what I want."

Olivia smiled. "Kid, that's living life. Most everyone doesn't know what is right or wrong. We have to live life to find out."

CHAPTER
TWENTY-ONE

Olivia had spent most of the evening trying to figure out what to do about her life. And like Chase, she had no clue.

About anything.

She'd ended the past summer a competent, capable professional. Currently, she was a boozy, emotional wreck thanks to two glasses of crisp sauvignon blanc with dinner and two truly handsome men drawing lines and staring each other down with classic pissing match posturing. Oh, and toss in the very confusing issue of her sister actually playing nice and treating her, well, like a sister rather than Nurse Ratched, and she was more than off-kilter. After dinner, when she'd agreed with Neve staying at the cabin and overseeing some of the renovations, her sister had hugged her. Actually hugged her!

Olivia couldn't remember the last time the two of them had touched willingly.

And tonight they would be sharing a bed the way they had long ago when they were girls. Back then they'd snugged into the bunk beds wearing matching floral nighties their grandmother had sewn for them.

They'd read old Berenstain Bears and Holly Hobbie books gleaned from swap meets, trading them back and forth as they took comfort in the sound of their mother reading stories to Marley in the next room. Olivia wasn't sure she was prepared for the intimacy of having her sister sleeping beside her again. She felt like an exposed nerve, trying to avoid any discomfort.

And if truth be told, she hadn't been prepared for the intimacy of a man lying beside her, either, arm thrown across her stomach. Still, Spencer's hardness, solid and warm against her curves, had restored something inside her. His delicious heaviness pressed her toward the best sleep she'd had since she'd come to the cabin.

Of course, unless she'd changed her sleeping habits in the last twenty years, Neve was going to kick her like a mule and snore in her ear all night.

Olivia shook her head and set about gathering her things to pack. She picked up the sketchbook Chase had left and set it on the nightstand and then started folding the shirts and pants she'd tucked into the chest of drawers. She'd just tugged on her nightgown and grabbed her toothbrush when the bedroom door opened.

"Hey, you're already packed?" Neve asked, slipping into the room, carrying a chevron-patterned duffel bag. She shut the bedroom door softly, taking in the rolling suitcase at the end of the bed. "I got the guys some blankets. Getting colder for sure."

"That was nice of you."

"Spencer looked a little upset that I'm the one sharing the bed with you tonight. I can sleep on one of the bunks if you want a little more alone time with the stud muffin."

Olivia shook her head. "No . . . um, no. I think it's better we proceed as we are."

"Proceed as we are?" Neve echoed with a small grin. "I've never seen someone who counsels others toward a healthier mindset run so fast from her own issues."

"I'm not running. I'm merely giving myself some time to think about . . . those two. I don't know what to do with either of them." Olivia didn't want to be irritated at her sister. Not after they'd gotten along so well for the past few days, but she tired of Neve needling her about facing things. But perhaps Neve could help her pick. Isn't that what sisters were for—helping you figure crap out?

Neve must have assumed as much when she said, "No-brainer to me. Spencer is the cat's meow, and Conrad is so . . . Conrad."

"What does that mean?"

Neve shrugged. "Con's so much all the time. The focus always has to be on him. I'm surprised he's content to be behind the camera."

"He's not like that. He's a good person. Does a lot of things for other people." She was nearly certain about this, though she didn't actually know since they hadn't been around each other much.

"I didn't say he was a bad person. Just the kind that demands a lot from a person. I recognize it because that's how Scott was."

Olivia bristled. "Con is nothing like Scott. He's successful, brilliant, and generous. He's paying for Chase to do the program."

"Out of guilt over Marley, and now he's messing with you. Why's he doing that? It's because he has an empty place and he figures you can fill it because you always did that for him. Even as a kid, you propped him up and made him feel better about himself."

Truth edged her sister's words, but Olivia wasn't ready to hear them about Conrad. She knew Conrad, had always known him. Neve didn't know what had happened between the two of them the night before their sister had died. Neve couldn't understand the bonds they'd always shared with one another. Instead of arguing with her sister, Olivia leaned over and turned on one of the matching bedside lamps and slipped toward the door. "I don't want to argue about Con. Let's drop it. I'm going to brush my teeth and clean my face. That should give you enough time to get ready for bed yourself."

"Chicken." Neve's mouth curved down, and her eyes glinted.

"Bock, bock," Olivia said, disappearing out the door, closing it behind her.

She turned and crashed into Spencer. "Oh!"

"Hey," he said, softly, catching her elbow and steadying her.

"Sorry, I didn't know you were there. I mean, I was going to brush my teeth." She gestured weakly toward the closed bathroom door and tried to still her racing heart. She wasn't sure if it was tripping over itself because she'd been startled or because Spencer was once again wearing only pajama pants that snagged sexily on his hips, revealing that delicious little V in his lower abs. She swallowed and tried to redirect her gaze.

But, damn, the man was too beautiful.

Still, she couldn't choose Spencer over Conrad merely because he did weird things to her body.

Wait.

Why was picking between them even a thought? She and Spencer had slept together, and that was it. He hadn't indicated he wanted anything more than the one night . . . and, okay, morning. Besides, she didn't really know Spencer at all. Like what if Spencer wasn't even his real name? What was his birthday? His favorite color? Did he like cats? He could be allergic to cats for all she knew. That was a deal breaker. Humphrey and Bing were her babies. She couldn't—

"Are you okay?" he asked, stepping back and looking alarmed. "Cause you look super stressed."

"I—I—I wanted to know if you like cats," she stammered. And then felt stupid. How had that just come out of her mouth?

"Cats?" He looked confused.

"Uh, because there's a cat that Chase dubbed Beast who's been hanging around. I wanted you to know in case you're, um, allergic or something."

Spencer grinned, and she felt that in her girl parts. Good Lord, how could anyone ever be angry at this guy?

"I like cats. Not allergic. But I'm thinking you're feeling awkward about things between us, but there's no need to be. We're cool, all right?"

"Cool?" she repeated, wondering what in the hell that meant. Was he done with her like some schmoozy Cary Grant, plying her with charm, never intending to call her again?

He grabbed her elbows, sliding his hand up her arms and drawing her closer to him. Lifting a hand, he smoothed back her hair and pressed her against him. "I'm saying that it's cool if you need time to know what you want. We don't have to hurry anything."

"Hurry anything?" she murmured, sinking into him, trying not to inhale him like she was a crazy person. But he smelled so good—a sort of spicy warmth mixed with fresh from the shower. She had no clue how he made the fresh-and-spicy combo work, but, Lord, he so did.

"For something to happen between us. What I'm saying is that I'd love to spend more time with you, but I don't want you to feel pressured. Last night was—" He stopped talking and glanced over to his left, and she pulled back to see Conrad halting on the top step of the staircase. Conrad's eyes swept from Spencer's face to Olivia's, then down to the way Spencer cradled her in his arms.

Olivia stepped back, and Spencer dropped his arms, and she knew they looked as if they'd been busted. A giant ball of awkwardness cleared the net and splatted at their feet.

Damn it.

Conrad glanced away and then brought his attention back to her. "I turned off the lights downstairs and checked the locks."

Olivia pulled her gaze away. "Thanks. I was just . . ." She inched around Spencer, retreating toward the bathroom as quickly as she could. The therapist inside her said to calmly address the situation. The very evident chicken inside her screamed, *Abort! Abort!*

Both Neve and Chase had established that she was, in fact, a chicken, so she rolled with it, shouting a hasty "Good night" before closing the bathroom door.

She sagged against the cool wood and caught her reflection in the mirror. She looked like she felt—unraveled.

Her life unspooled, slipping from the roll so quickly she wasn't sure if she could catch up. Pressing her hands to her face, she sucked in a deep breath and then released it before running some water and taking care of her nightly bathroom ritual. After she'd flossed her teeth twice and dabbed on a second layer of eye cream, she cautiously opened the door and peeked out.

All clear.

Sighing with relief, she hopped like a silent bunny to the room she shared with her sister and jetted inside. Maybe Neve could set aside her view of Conrad and help her figure out what she should do.

Neve sat cross-legged in the center of the bed and flinched as Olivia exploded into the room. When Olivia closed the door a bit too hard, her sister glanced up. In her lap was the sketchbook. "What the fuck is this?"

Olivia pressed both hands onto the back of the door. "Chase found that under the mattresses in the bunk room a week ago. She'd forgotten about it and handed it to me a few minutes ago."

A feeling of foreboding rose inside Olivia because Neve looked similar to someone who'd seen a horrible accident. Her mouth hung open slightly, her eyes unblinking, her hands useless beside her. "Have you looked at it?"

"Not yet. Chase said she thought it belonged to Marley." Olivia lifted herself from her slumped position and moved toward the bed. "What's wrong?"

Neve slid the book off her lap and angled it toward Olivia.

The open pages toward the back of the book were ones similar to what Olivia had seen all too often in the therapy world. Childish depictions of familial figures—girls evident by pigtails and dresses, a mother with dark holes for her eyes, a man . . . a father with jagged teeth and a grossly oversize penis. The colors were dark—purple, black, and red.

A telltale sign of abuse.

Olivia leafed to the next page, the images breaking her into two pieces—rational therapist, horrified sister.

Penises. Blood. Dark clouds. Tears. Pictures that told a story of a child in pain.

Marley.

"What *is* this, Liv?" Neve said, tears in her eyes. "Marley drew these. Is this supposed to be Dad?"

Neve pointed to another rendering of an angry man, large penis jutting from between his legs. The girl in the picture had tears coming from her eyes. In a conversation bubble she'd printed in capital letters: STOP.

Olivia's hands trembled as she turned yet another page. Inside, the earlier trepidation about Spencer and Conrad had disappeared, replaced with utter devastation. She couldn't answer Neve because she wasn't sure if it was their father.

But then again, she was.

Her mind flipped back to things Marley had said as a child, things that an older sister might dismiss, as Marley always applied theatrics to every situation. Things she said, like, "Daddy likes me the best," or "Daddy says I'm special." Once Marley had declared that if Mommy died, Daddy would marry her because she was his special girl. Things that Olivia had resented because she'd been a bit jealous of Marley. Being the plump middle child between two svelte beauties wasn't easy, especially as she'd always felt like the odd sister out. So she'd not wanted to hear her younger sister brag about how she was their handsome, accomplished father's favorite.

In hindsight, though, Marley's words were ones sexually abused children often uttered because the abuser applied such tactics to justify and reassure the child he was abusing that she was special. Master manipulation.

"Liv," Neve demanded.

"I don't know. I mean, it looks like—"

"I'm going to fucking kill him." Neve sprang from the bed, pacing back in forth in her striped pajamas, her hands pointed and stabbing into the air. "He did this. He did that. He's a fucking liar. He lied to all of us. He's dead. Dead to me. I—I . . ."

Olivia shut the book and sank back into the pillows. "Oh my God. That's why she killed herself. She tried to tell me, and I . . . Jesus, I tried to be a therapist to her and not a sister."

Neve stopped in her tracks. *"Killed herself?"*

Olivia felt herself fall down the deep hole she'd covered so carefully for too many years. Nothing to stop her now as she plunged into the past. She covered her face with her hands and tried to make it go away. She didn't want to talk about Marley. She didn't want to remember that horrible afternoon, her sister's empty eyes, the letter saying Marley couldn't do life anymore.

Now she knew the real reason Marley had checked out of her life. It wasn't merely addiction. It was something more horrible, something her sister had carried, internalized into destruction, and then ultimately couldn't deal with any longer.

Marley had been sexually abused by their father.

How had Olivia not known? She'd been a social worker and therapist. She'd seen more of this sort of thing than she'd ever wanted to see. And when Marley had asked if Olivia would help her, Olivia had refused, pulling the tough-love card. So Marley had overdosed, killing herself.

Jesus.

Neve pulled Olivia's hands away from her face. "Liv. What are you saying? Tell me."

"I—I—" She fell back onto her elbows and closed her eyes, not wanting to say the things she had to say. Tears slid down her cheek, and a sob welled in her gut. "Oh God, Neve."

Neve poked her. Angrily. "Tell me. Now."

Olivia opened her eyes and sat up, trying to swallow her grief. Her sister still stood over her, a furious harpy ready to shred anyone in her path to bits. "Just sit down, okay?"

"I can't."

"Please, Neve. Please just don't stand over me. Sit."

"Fine." Her sister sank down next to her, shoving her leg over. She looked like a bull being penned. Olivia felt a trickle of fear snake inside her because Neve looked out of control. "You said she killed herself. You *know* this?"

"Okay, okay." Olivia sucked in a deep breath and tried to find the words. "So you know how I found Marley, right? I was the one who went to the beach motel."

Her sister nodded.

"When I got there, well, I knew there was no need to try to resuscitate her. I tried to clean her up." Olivia could hardly say the words. Her voice trembled, but she tried to focus on the facts and not her feelings. "I closed her eyes and used one of the towels to wipe her face. I glanced over on the bed and saw a note. She'd written it on the notepad from the motel."

Neve rubbed her eyes and looked away. "She committed suicide? That's what you're telling me? That you essentially lied to your family and let us think it was accidental?" Her sister's voice rose with each question.

"I was trying to protect Mom and Dad. I thought it would be easier for them to think it was an accident. For you to think it was an accident. I'm sorry, but I thought it would make it easier." Her words sounded pleading to her own ears. She'd thought she'd done the right thing, but now it seemed . . . wrong.

"What gave you the right to keep that from us? Marley *killed* herself, and now we know why she was so messed up. She was abused, and you, you . . . you kept that a secret."

"I didn't know *this*. I had no clue about that." Olivia gestured to the heartbreaking sketch pad. "But I knew she OD'd on purpose. It wasn't an accident."

"Jesus, Liv." Neve's voice was filled with such anguish.

"I tried to protect our family."

"From what? The embarrassment? Where's the note she left? I want to see it." Neve's face had fashioned into a mask of outrage.

"I tore it up and threw it into the ocean. I was waiting for the police, and after they came and took my statement and the coroner came, I walked down the beach. You remember the one we went to that time when the house was getting fumigated? We had so much fun there, and that's where she went to . . ." She couldn't say the words that her sister had chosen a place full of good memories to die. After they'd taken her sister away, Olivia had stood on the hard-packed sand facing the drowning sun. The cool spring wind tore at her hair, whipping it into her eyes and mouth as she dug the crumpled note from her jean pocket. Olivia remembered the way the pieces had fluttered around her—swirling, scattering, eventually sticking to the sea-foam as it sucked the horrible words into the sea. Those bits ebbed and flowed as her tears dripped down her face.

"Fuck." Neve sprang off the bed. "And Dad did this. Oh my God, he *did* this, and he did that to those girls, too. I believed him when he said that they'd been coached to say those things. When he said that he'd only been affectionate. But he lied, because he did this to our sister. Oh my God, he did that to Marley, and she bore that. She *bore* that."

Olivia watched helplessly as Neve covered her face with her hands and then sank onto her knees, sobbing.

"Neve," Olivia said, sliding off the bed. "We didn't know. She never told us."

She reached for her sister, but Neve slapped her hands away. "Stop. Don't touch me. Oh God, don't."

Olivia sank onto the wooden floor beside the bed her grandparents had slept in, beside the quilt her granny had hand stitched, and cried the tears she'd been holding inside her forever. Drawing up her knees, she let go of the pain, the guilt, the secret. Eventually, Neve crawled over to her and wrapped her in her arms, rocking her. Olivia held on to Neve, clutching her as her body emptied itself of all she'd held inside for far too long.

For many minutes they sat sobbing their grief. For their sister. For the situation they had been raised in. For not knowing. For the things they might have said, the false beliefs they'd held, the mistakes they'd made.

Eventually, Neve went into big sister mode, patting Olivia's back. "Shh, it's okay, Liv. You didn't know."

Olivia clutched her sister harder. She couldn't seem to stop the pain from spilling out. She'd held tight to it, shouldering alone the knowledge that Marley had killed herself.

"Liv, Liv, come on," Neve murmured into her damp temple. "You aren't responsible. It's okay, it's okay."

"You don't understand. That night . . . that night that it happened, Conrad came over to my house. He wanted to talk about Marley, and it was the same old song and dance. I told him she was better—I thought she was—and then we drank a bunch of wine . . . and—" Olivia swallowed and squeezed her eyes closed, shaking her head.

"You slept with him," Neve finished for her.

Olivia nodded. "I loved him so much, and he never saw me. He only saw her. I thought . . . I was stupid. I wanted him, and finally he seemed to want me. All that time that we were together that night, she was alone." The last word came out as a wail. The sob rose again, and Olivia stuffed her fist into her mouth, shaking her head. She couldn't take the onslaught of pain, the horror of her own words.

Neve grabbed her by her forearms. "Stop. You're not responsible, Olivia. You may have made a mistake, but her death isn't on you. You aren't responsible, Liv."

But maybe that's what she'd thought all along—that she was responsible. Marley had called her three times while Olivia was screwing her ex-boyfriend. How many times had she wondered if things might have changed if she'd only answered? How many times had she imagined her sister all alone in that ratty motel room wishing for someone to answer the phone, wishing someone would help her, wishing their father hadn't . . .

"I shouldn't have done that. It was a selfish and weak thing to do."

Neve shook her head. "It was human. I shouldn't have married Scott. We all screw up, Liv. You're no different. You make mistakes. That's the only truth in life—we all fuck up, sugar. You're not exempt from it."

Those words did something to her. Neve gave her something more generous than anything she'd ever been given—her sister who at times she'd hated gave her a pardon.

Olivia sat up, swiping at her undoubtedly ravaged face. Then she opened her eyes, seeing that understanding in her sister's eyes. "But I should have realized there was abuse. That was my field, and I never suspected, not really. She said things like she was special to Daddy or Daddy loved her more. Once she told me that Dad wanted to marry her. But I thought that was Marley being Marley. She never said Dad touched her, but I can't discount those drawings or the fact that she always wanted to spend the night with friends, come up here every summer, stuff like that."

Neve's face was puffy and her eyes red rimmed and glassy. "None of us suspected. Dad never acted that way with me. You?"

Olivia shook her head. "No. He always seemed bothered by me."

"I can't believe he did that to her . . . to those girls. It's fucking up my mind." Neve pressed her hands against her eyes. "What do we do?

Can he be arrested? Do we tell Mom? He's moving his stuff in with her in a few weeks. This is an effing nightmare."

"We'll file a report. Talk to Mom. Drop him off a cliff." Olivia sniffed, swiping at the tears still eking out.

A sound at the door alarmed them.

Chase stuck her head in, looking concerned. Their raging and sobbing had no doubt alarmed the rest of the house. "Are you two okay? Oh God. Did someone die?"

Olivia looked at her sister. Neve reached over and clasped Olivia's hand as she looked up and said, "Yeah, someone did."

CHAPTER TWENTY-TWO

A week later

Chase kicked at the surf and tilted her face up to the sun. She had spent the past week at the Malibu beach house finishing up the Square One program. As of that morning, she was officially done with the intensive sobriety, adulting, and therapy program. Cue "The Graduation March."

Both she and Olivia had been driven from the depths of the serene house in order for an appraiser hired by the potential buyer to do a full assessment. Olivia sat on the hard-packed sand, hair whipping behind her, as she stared out into the depths of the waves.

Chase looked down at her. "I'm sad that the house is selling, but I also realize that I pretty much had to sell it. It's been nice living out here, though."

"It has," Olivia said, looking up at her. "I never thought I wanted to live on the ocean, but there's something restorative about it. I'm sorry you'll miss being here."

"Since I rarely spent time here, it feels odd to miss it, but I don't want to go back to my apartment. It's just alien to me now. I don't think I belong there anymore. Honestly, I'm not sure where I belong. I'll have to make a decision on where to live soon since I don't want to live with Lorna, but I'm not sure I want to live alone again. Crazy as it sounds, it was nice living with you and Neve . . . even though your sister sort of drove me crazy at times."

Olivia smiled. "She'll do that to you."

"Why did you let her stay at the cabin?"

Olivia leaned over and struggled to her feet. "I don't know. No, I do. She needed a fresh start. I needed to find benevolence when it came to her. I've pretty much denied her true kindness for too many years."

Chase glanced over at Olivia's face. "Because of whatever happened that night? In the bedroom?"

Olivia's face shuttered. "No. Maybe."

"You said someone died. That sketchbook was on the bed. It had to do with your sister."

Olivia sucked in a breath and released it, closing her eyes. Pain had flashed through them, and Chase immediately felt as if she shouldn't have asked.

The night she'd found Olivia and Neve on the floor, tear soaked and devastated, Chase had waited for Olivia to tell her she was okay before retreating back to her bedroom. Spencer had stood framed in the bunk room door, rubbing at his eyes. He'd arched a questioning brow, and Chase had responded by shrugging and saying, "She's okay. They had some kind of come-to-Jesus meeting or something. Go on back to bed."

Concern etched his face, but Spencer had glanced at the closed door to Olivia's room and then stepped back and shut his own door.

Chase had gone back to her room and tossed around the entire night, plagued by Zeke's face and the way Olivia had looked when she'd opened her bedroom door to check on her.

So utterly destroyed.

That image had shaken her, but when she emerged the next morning, she'd found Neve in the kitchen making pancakes and Olivia sitting at the table sipping coffee. Both looked . . . settled.

Spencer had already returned to the city, sending her a text telling her he had forgotten he had a meeting for late afternoon, which was code for not sticking around to watch Conrad Santos steal his bacon. Not literal bacon, of course. Conrad emerged looking well rested and ate his pancakes in silence. When Olivia rose to retrieve her phone, he followed her out of the kitchen and cornered her in the dining room within earshot of Chase and Neve.

"Are you sleeping with Spencer Rome?" he'd demanded.

Neve lifted her head, sat the fork containing a bite of pancakes aside, and widened her eyes at Chase.

Chase dropped her mouth open, mimicking Neve's wide eyes. They both stilled and listened . . . because how could they not?

"That's not any of your business, Con," Olivia said.

"I told you about my feelings yesterday, Livy. I think it's a little bit my business if you're seeing someone else You should have given me a heads-up so I didn't look like a fool," Conrad said.

"OMG," Neve mouthed.

Chase held up a shushing finger.

"I'm not seeing him, necessarily, and I wasn't trying to make you feel foolish," Olivia said in a careful manner.

"What does 'necessarily' imply?"

"Look, Conrad, I am not in the right place for this conversation at present. I appreciate everything you've done for Chase, and I value our friendship and our past, but I'm not sure I can give you what you want."

"Why? All I'm asking for is to spend some time together and see if what we had all that time ago is still there. We were good together. You remember that." Conrad's voice sounded . . . hurt and sort of patronizing at the same time. Like he was irritated Olivia didn't see things his way.

"Con, I'm not saying I don't want to spend time with you, but this is all very . . . confusing. I need some time to think about . . ." Olivia paused for a few seconds.

"What? About how you've always felt about me? Livy, we have a second chance," Conrad insisted.

"Con, I don't think this is the time for this conversation. Let's get back to LA, and we can talk later in the week, okay?"

No doubt Olivia had figured out that she and Neve could hear their conversation. And really, it was kind of shitty of Conrad not to realize that. She and Neve were in the next room with only an open doorway to separate them. Of course they could hear him demanding an answer from Olivia and putting her in an embarrassing situation. Douche move, but Conrad was accustomed to getting his way—a side dish to having Hollywood power.

Neve's expression reflected the same feeling.

Now Chase knew Conrad and Olivia had some sort of past. But Olivia hadn't addressed it even on the ride home when they talked about her progress in learning how to adult. Olivia also hadn't mentioned anything about the night before, about how Chase had found her and Neve crying on the floor of their bedroom.

Chase had decided to wait and bring it up at a later time, but the week had passed with no opportunity. Olivia had fallen back into her usual demeanor, not quite distant but definitely more professional, as if she were trying to resurrect her old self.

Still, the week had been decent, even as Chase missed the cabin, the community, and, of course, the guy she'd found in Cotter's Creek. She and Olivia had done some exit interview stuff, expanding the adulting lessons to include her normal world in LA, which meant acclimating to the beach house kitchen, applying to reinstate her driver's license, going to court-ordered community service at a senior-living community where she called out bingo, and completing the Square One self-evaluation. She had a few final counseling sessions with Olivia, wrote a self-actualization plan, and worked on her audition, which would be in about four hours.

The beach was fairly empty since it was a weekday toward the middle of October. The weather was California perfect, but instead of looking bolstered by the fair day, Olivia wore whatever troubled her on her face.

She turned to Chase. "When you were raped, and you said your father didn't care . . . that he—"

"Gave me to Peter Fucking Rinduso?"

Olivia flinched. "Yeah. Peter Fucking Rinduso."

Chase wasn't sure where this was going. They'd talked about her rape several times, and finally Chase had been able to cry, lay down her feelings, and internalize Olivia's words about the situation not being Chase's fault. Finally, Chase had felt the anger those memories dredged up and used that force as she cleaned the kitchen. That freaking kitchen sparkled after she scrubbed the baseboards with the fiery rage of a thousand suns. "We already talked about this. I mean, what more is there to say? I was betrayed. And shamed. And made to feel worthless. My father treated me as if I were nothing, and then to make it worse, he introduced me to vodka."

Olivia had turned back to stare at the horizon, her face portraying sympathy, but then she got a more pointed look. "You asked about why Neve and I were crying that night. About the sketchbook. Did you look at it?"

Chase shrugged. "Yeah, I flipped through. It was pictures of flowers and little girl stuff, but I only looked at a few pages. Zeke arrived and I had to hurry."

"If you flipped toward the middle or back, you would have seen not-so-happy pictures. You would have seen evidence of a child who had been sexually abused." Olivia's voice quivered slightly, and she cleared her throat as if she'd betrayed herself. Her gaze stayed on the waves rolling over.

Chase felt her stomach lurch. "You're saying Marley was abused?"

Olivia nodded. "I'm sure you noticed that Neve goes by Neve Hancock and I go by Han. That's because my father was arrested for sexually molesting several of his students. He was an elementary school principal."

"Oh God," Chase said, wanting to reach out and comfort Olivia in some way but knowing that her touch might not be welcome. Olivia stood stalwart against emotion and even now looked like an island, as if what she was saying were about someone she didn't know, like a case study, instead of about her own life. "I'm so sorry."

"I had my doubts about his innocence, but before his trial, my father and I had a falling-out. He was angry at therapists, who he thought misconstrued his affectionate nature, and so he accused me of supporting my career over my family. But Neve and my mom believed him when he said that it was politically motivated by a group of parents and that the children had been coached. He was found guilty and served time. But we never knew if it was true, and now we do."

Chase swallowed hard and closed her eyes tight. She didn't know much about Marley but had seen her name scrawled in a few books and found some old pictures of her as a child. She'd been blonde and beautiful. Chase didn't fail to note her own resemblance to Olivia's youngest sister. "That's horrible, Olivia."

"But not any more so than what happened to you."

"I don't know. I think it could be. I didn't love Peter. He was a random guy who . . . who took what he wanted. My father didn't hurt me."

"But he did. He let it happen."

"But he didn't *do* it. He was messed up, using drugs and drinking all the time. I'm not even sure if he understood what happened to me, or maybe he couldn't remember that I was a child. I'm not making excuses for him, because that whole deal was a horrible thing to let happen to your daughter, stoned out of your mind or not, but your dad knew what he was doing."

Olivia bent down, grabbed a handful of sand, and flung it into the crashing waves. She did it again and again until she was breathing hard. Then she stood with her head bowed and covered her face with her sandy hands.

Chase stood beside her, never trying to stop her, because she understood.

"I'm sorry," Olivia said, sucking in a deep breath and releasing it. She brushed her hands against her thighs and then swiped at her tear-soaked face. "I shouldn't have lost control like that. I've spent a lot of this week trying to decide what to do about what we discovered, how to tell my mom the truth, how not to take a crowbar to my father's head, and how to deal with how Marley died and what happened to her."

"Why would you apologize to me? You're doing what you've always told me to do—you're owning your feelings, working through them, expending energy in a positive way. Okay, well, I'm not sure if throwing sand is positive." Chase shrugged with a soft smile.

Olivia looked at her, sniffling a little. Her brown eyes didn't look so distant. Instead they reflected tenderness. "You really have learned some things, haven't you?"

Chase looked at her watch. "And we're about to see if they pay off in a few hours."

"Oh God, that's right." Olivia slapped a hand over her mouth and then sputtered against the grains of sand on her lips. "Yuck. But the audition is today, and I laid all this on you. I'm sorry, Chase. You need to be distraction-free."

"It's cool. I feel really good about this read. I think I've nailed the character, so I'm planning on rocking this bitch." Chase smiled, trying to believe her own words.

"You know Conrad is on your side. He wants you, and that's a powerful ally."

"We'll see." Chase looked out at the ocean at the seagulls dancing in the air, a boat skipping along the horizon, and to her left, surfers skidding along the curling waves. She embraced the feeling of control she'd nurtured in herself, that calm centeredness she needed to take with her to the casting director's office. "I'm going to head out in thirty minutes. Lorna's picking me up. I mean, *Mom* is picking me up. She's going to take me by my apartment to get some clothes and drive me to the audition. She's practicing being supportive, and I'm practicing letting her be supportive. It's part of our agreed-upon boundaries."

Olivia's mouth curved a little. "That's great, Chase."

"But if you're feeling down and want me to stay, I can get my mother to go by and get my clothes without me. I want to make sure you're okay." Chase reached out and brushed Olivia's back, the first time she'd voluntarily touched her therapist.

It was at that moment she realized Olivia had become more than a therapist. Chase felt like they'd gone through some life-altering event together, like a plane crash or some kind of odd journey through a dangerous jungle. On second thought, they both kind of had done just that—each wading through the unknown. Chase had started out a total wreck and had gotten her shit together—well, somewhat together. Olivia had been about as collected as a person can be, but this woman standing beside her on the California beach today was struggling.

So yeah, Chase felt like perhaps she needed to be there for Olivia.

"Go, Chase. I'm fine. I'm grappling with a lot of things, but Neve is actually helping me this time. Oddly enough, I think I gained a sister." Olivia pressed her lips together and gave a laugh of disbelief. "Life is weird sometimes."

"Well, that's for dang sure," Chase said, giving Olivia a smile. "Okay, I'll be back later."

Olivia lifted a hand as Chase jogged toward the house.

Thirty minutes later, Chase walked to her mother's Mercedes humming in the driveway and climbed inside.

Lorna's eyes widened. "Oh my. What did you do to your hair?"

"Said adieu to the party girl," Chase said, pulling the seat belt across her and clicking it into place.

"Well, you look totally different. Not only the hair, but you're also heavier and—"

"That's called healthy. I'm free of drugs and alcohol. I've been eating, okay, not totally healthy but much better. I'm the weight I'm supposed to be." Chase tried to keep the impatience from her voice. She wasn't a product. She was a person.

"Oh, of course," Lorna said, pushing her sunglasses back into place and shifting the car into reverse with spidery-thin hands tipped in vermillion. Perfume wafted toward Chase, so she cracked the window a bit.

A few minutes ticked by as her mother navigated Pacific Coast Highway, the sunlight flashing in between the beach houses and businesses. Finally, Lorna glanced over at her. "So what are you planning to wear?"

"I have a Victorian tuxedo blouse I'm going to pair with jean leggings and heeled ballet slippers that tie into a bow. My hair gathered into a low ponytail, minimal makeup, small earrings."

"Mmm."

"What?"

"Don't you think that's what every actress is wearing when she reads? You need to stand out."

Chase trampled the irritation. God, she was trying here. "We'll look at what I have when we get to my place."

Lorna smiled as if she'd won. But Chase wasn't letting her mother run roughshod over her. She would choose what she wore.

"And what's your take on the character? Conrad sent me the script, and I think most of the other actresses will go for vulnerable, maybe even confused. What if you make your character certain? Like whatever drug you're doing gives you power but also makes you inscrutable. Like an enigma with a strong personality. What do you think?" Lorna glanced over at her.

"Maybe."

"What's wrong?"

"I merely think you should let me decide how I handle my read. You're not an acting coach. I talked this over with Marshall and then called Peggy just to run it by her. I appreciate your input, but I've been prepping a certain way, and I feel comfortable with what I have." Chase tried to sound confident, polite, and firm.

Lorna made a face. "Whatever you want."

"Thank you."

An hour and a half later, she and her mother emerged from her three-bedroom apartment in the South Park district of downtown with Chase wearing the Victorian shirt, a short black skirt, and simple wedges—a pseudocompromise with her mother. Her hair was pulled into a low knot with soft wisps around her face. Lorna had been adamant that she show off her long legs and not fall into shtick. Wasn't a bad suggestion.

As they drove to the casting director's office, Chase tried to gather herself, find that centeredness she'd captured standing on the beach with Olivia, but her mother and all the back-and-forth they'd done had her rattled. She practiced inhaling through her nose and exhaling softly through slightly parted lips, drawing on her affective memory of the times when she'd been blasted out of her mind.

"Are you nervous?"

"Of course not." Chase looked out the window, realized that she wasn't being honest. "Actually, a little. It's been a while since I read for a part. Feels weird."

"You shouldn't have to read. Conrad essentially promised you the part, and don't think I didn't let him know that."

"Nothing was guaranteed. You know this business."

Lorna looked grumpy as a toad. "I do, and I know you don't thrust a person into rehab and tell her you're doing it so she can be insured, only to backpedal. Very unprofessional."

"He has people to answer to, and my track record hasn't been so hot. It's not his fault."

They pulled into the parking lot, and Lorna put the car into park, turning off the engine.

"What are you doing?" Chase asked.

"Going with you."

"No. I don't need my mother to go with me. That's bizarre. Go shop or something. I'll call you when I'm done." Chase didn't wait for her mother to answer. Instead she grabbed her bag and climbed out of the car. She looked down at the plain manila folder in her bag and almost smiled. When she'd looked at the casting director's email about headshots, she'd found a copy of *Tinseltown Tattler* with her picture from some awards show plastered across the front and had been tempted to submit it. She'd been wearing a light-pink, fluffy gown and looked to be impersonating a junkie ballerina. Seemed appropriate. But she'd not done it and found some dated headshots instead.

She pushed into the office door and checked in with the receptionist, then settled onto an uncomfortable chair with about five other women, none of whom she recognized.

But they recognized her.

And that made her super embarrassed.

Because they knew she'd screwed up her life so badly that she couldn't be trusted based on her name and past work alone. These actors were still striving to make it to where she'd been, and they probably resented like hell that she'd squandered away her good fortune. Perhaps they even resented the fact that they had to compete with someone who was such a train wreck.

But not anymore, Chase. You've changed, and you have to accept your past and the scrutiny it brings. Actions bring reactions.

"Miss London?" a harried-looking assistant said from the open doorway.

Chase stood and offered a genuine smile while batting away the giant flamingos flitting around her stomach. Wait. Flamingos didn't flit. But those wings thrashing around were bigger than butterfly wings, that was for damn sure.

"Thank you," she said, sliding past the woman who held the door ajar.

In the audition room she found the casting director, who she recognized from the picture on the email she'd sent with the directions and call time, a camera guy, and a woman who looked sour. The assistant holding the door handed the manila folder with her headshot and résumé to the sourpuss while Chase set her purse on the floor beside her, grabbed her sides, and gave those assembled a nod of greeting. "Hello, everyone."

The casting director looked up and smiled. "Hello, Miss London, it's nice to see you. Thank you for taking the time to come in today."

"I was under the impression it was pretty much required." Chase gave a self-deprecating laugh, showing that she wasn't being whiny, just acknowledging that she hadn't had an option.

The casting director smiled back, and the sour-looking woman made an irritated face, which immediately caused a niggle of alarm inside Chase. The casting director picked up a piece of paper. "So, Chase, I believe you know who I am. This is Jim. He'll be filming. Mary, who met you at the door, is my assistant, and this is Maggie Stiles, who works with the production team. Normally, I would ask you to tell us about yourself, but since we all know who you are, that won't be necessary."

"I'm willing to answer if you want. I feel pretty much like a new person today, and I'm excited to read for you." Chase gave them a winning smile and then held the paper with her lines up. "Who am I doing the sides with?"

The casting director lifted a finger. "I'll do the honors. When you're ready."

Chase tried to center herself, but her gaze kept straying to Maggie, who no longer looked sour. Instead she radiated dislike. How could she not like Chase without really knowing her? Unless she knew her. Maybe Chase had done something to her? Dissed her? Kissed her boyfriend? Something horrible in the past?

No. Clear your mind, Chase. Find your calm. You are a professional. You have starred in twelve movies. This is not even a leading role. Conrad wants you. This is a formality.

The casting director cleared her throat and arched a brow as if she were growing impatient and wasn't exactly waiting until Chase was ready.

What was the first line?

Crap.

Chase glanced down at the sides, looking at the arrow she'd drawn. God, she looked so unprofessional. She couldn't even remember her first damn line.

Chase looked up at the casting director. "I know what I saw, Detective Murdoch."

"I think you believe what you *think* you saw, Miss Cavendish. However, the lanterns had been extinguished on your street." The casting director read with little emotion.

"Are you calling me a liar, sir? I know very well what I saw in the darkness. Inspector Ashwood carried a large bundle to a wagon parked—" Chase shifted her gaze from the casting director and caught Maggie's expression. Unmitigated anger poured from her eyes.

Chase stopped.

The casting director looked confused. "What's wrong?"

"She's looking at me as if she wants to kill me," Chase said, nodding toward Maggie.

The production assistant blinked. "What?"

"I'm sorry, but you're staring daggers at me. Is something wrong?" Chase asked.

"Oh. I'm sorry. I just got a call from the seafood market about the fish I'd ordered for my mother's sixtieth birthday celebration, and I'm irritated because it was placed . . . you know, not important." Maggie waved her hands and shook her head. "I didn't mean to project my irritation toward you."

The mention of fish brought Zeke to mind, making her heart ache a little. She missed him, and over the past week had thought of so many things she wanted to tell him, to show him, to experience with him beside her—like the sun sinking into the Pacific, the abandoned bird's nest she'd discovered in the rocks, or the delicious fish tacos she'd made on her own, even zesting lime and roasting ancho chilies. Even now, in the midst of one of the most important auditions of her life, she wished that she were with him, standing in rushing waters, lassoing the line about her head so she could land the fly perfectly in the current.

"Miss London?" the casting director interrupted her wandering thoughts. "Would you like to start again?"

"No."

That word came out before she even comprehended she'd said it, but when she did realize what she'd just uttered, she knew that she meant it. She didn't want to start again. She didn't even want the role.

"What?" Maggie asked, blinking. "I'm sorry. I didn't mean to distract you. Conrad will—"

"No, it's not you." Chase held up her hand. "It's merely that I just figured out that I don't want to do this."

The casting director looked at both the assistants, and the cameraman turned off the tape and leaned back in his chair, looking as if he couldn't care less about her stopping the read.

Chase released the sides, the pages wafting toward the floor. She shouldn't be so inconsiderate, but letting that script go was symbolic. She didn't have to do this. Didn't have to be an actress. This life wasn't the one she wanted . . . maybe hadn't ever been the life she'd wanted. At any rate, she'd decided then and there what her life would not be.

"Sorry to have wasted your time. Maggie, please tell Conrad I will be in touch. Fact is, I don't think I'm right for this role after all."

"But . . . but . . ." Maggie looked alarmed, like she couldn't believe Chase didn't want a role in a Conrad Santos film.

Chase grabbed her purse and tugged it on her shoulder. "It's fine. I have to go. Thanks." She gave them a wave and hurried toward the door that led to the holding area.

She startled a few people when she burst into the room, but she didn't stop to explain. Sunshine met her when she pushed out the door, and she paused, took a deep breath, and pulled on her sunglasses.

Her mother sat in the car and waved at her.

Okay, Lorna was about to flip her lid. Then again, Chase didn't have to say anything to her mother about ducking out of the audition. In fact, she didn't have to tell anyone anything. If Chase had learned anything over the course of the last few months, it was that she was in charge of herself, her decisions, her body, her mind, her gifts, her time, her every-freaking-thing.

She walked over to her mother's car and climbed inside. "I'm done."

"So how did it go?"

Chase shrugged. "Different than I thought, but I feel good about it. I feel really good."

Lorna looked over and smiled at her. "Well, that's great news, Chase. I honestly think this was merely a formality and you already have the part. Conrad had to toss the investors a bone and say he was looking at other actresses, but remember, he wanted you from the beginning. I mean, he paid Olivia to get you straight. So this is very good news on top of selling the Malibu house. That's going to put us into the black."

Chase resented the fact that Lorna's main concern was what this would bring her . . . but then again, it wasn't going to bring her diddly-squat. Still, her mother didn't know that. "What if I don't get the part?"

"Oh, honey, don't worry. You will, but just in case, I'll talk to Marshall, and we'll see what he can find. For the first time in a long time, I feel good about your future."

Chase smiled. "Yeah, so do I."

Lorna's pleased expression reminded her of Sylvester in the Looney Tunes series when he tied on a napkin and sharpened his knife over poor little Tweety. Lorna thought she was about to eat. "Are you going back to the Malibu house?"

"Just drop me at my apartment so I can grab some things I want to take with me. I'm essentially done with Square One and will see Olivia only once a week at her office for the next few months."

"Until you go on location."

"Yeah." Chase shrugged and averted her gaze so her mother wouldn't see that she knew she wasn't going to the UK to shoot the Santos film.

Lorna turned on the radio and opened the sunroof. California sunshine poured in as the wind blew their hair. Chase savored the calm before the storm, and, of course, she had to figure out her entire life. Just a little thing.

That thought made her laugh.

But oddly enough, she wasn't upset about it. The skills she'd learned over the past month had given her confidence in her ability to handle failures and figure things out. As long as the beach house sale went through, she could afford to take a few months to figure her life out. And she could start a repayment plan to Conrad. No way was she allowing him to pay for her rehab and adulting boot camp when she wasn't going to pay off in dividends for him.

"You're smiling a lot," Lorna said, glancing over at her.

"I am, aren't I?" Chase said, smiling even bigger.

CHAPTER
TWENTY-THREE

Olivia had just finished cooking dinner—a nice shrimp scampi recipe handed down from her aunt Toni—when she got the call from Lorna.

"Chase is missing," Lorna said, not bothering to respond to Olivia's greeting.

"Wait. What?" Olivia looked around for an oven mitt with which to pull the crusty french baguette from the oven. She'd enjoyed cooking on the Malibu house's Viking range, something she rarely had time to do, as her business took so much of her energy. Allocating over an entire month to work with Chase had a silver lining in that she'd cooked more during the past few weeks than she had in the entire year. Since she and Chase had concluded the Square One program earlier that day and Olivia would be moving back to her place the next morning, she'd texted her mother for the recipe to her favorite meal in order to celebrate the milestone. Besides, she was fairly certain after having caught Chase practicing her scene that the actress would be successful in nailing the audition. A double celebration! She'd realized that Chase was, indeed, quite talented, morphing into a paranoid, trembling ingenue with the flick of an internal switch.

Totally freaky how good she was at becoming someone else.

"I got a call from Marshall, who received an unexpected phone communication from Con Santos."

"Chase didn't get the role?"

"No, she didn't. Because she quit in the middle of the audition. She told them she didn't want the part!" Lorna sounded as if she were a lawn mower trying like hell to remain chugging but sputtering in spite of the effort. "And now she's missing. I can't find her. She won't answer—"

"How can that be?" Olivia interrupted, locating the oven mitt and pulling the nearly too-brown bread from the oven. She switched the oven off and set the baking sheet on the stove.

"Is she there with you?" Lorna asked.

"No. I thought she was with you." Olivia hadn't worried when Lorna and Chase hadn't returned to the beach house. She assumed that they might have other business to handle, and technically Chase was no longer committed to the program. Her time was her own. Still, this situation didn't sit right with her. She wasn't shocked that Chase had halted her audition, but it seemed odd that Lorna hadn't known how the audition had gone down. "So Chase left the audition without you knowing?"

"No. She came out and acted pleased with herself. Said that it went fine, good, even. But Marshall said that the whole audition was a colossal failure. That Chase forgot her lines, struggled to remain focused, and imagined ill will coming from a production assistant. Chase tossed her script on the floor, grabbed her purse, and took off."

Olivia frowned at the sauce starting to congeal in the pan. "But she acted like everything was fine?"

"Yes. And that's the way she behaves when things are spinning out of control. She projects positive confidence, and then the next thing you know she has a belly full of pills and booze. I'm frightened because she seemed so changed. I thought you had fixed her." Lorna's words were accusatorial and angry, but she heard the fear lacing them.

"I'm not sure—"

"Acting is Chase's life. It's all she knows how to do. She had plans to climb back on top with this role. Oh God. What if she hurts herself? Would she do that? I read once that when people make up their minds to commit suicide that their family always thinks they're better, and then . . ." Lorna had tears in her voice now.

Chase's mother's words felt like an arrow thunking through Olivia's chest.

"Okay, you're making really large, irrational assumptions, Lorna. Chase likely went to talk over what happened with a friend." Olivia pressed a hand against her stomach. Lorna's words had wriggled into her own head and gut. But Chase was fine. She probably needed some time to herself and would be waltzing through the door in a few minutes. "Let's go over what happened when she came out of the audition."

"She got in the car, acted happy, and started talking about going on location and stuff. I took her to her apartment because she said she had to get a few things. I waited outside for her because she said it wouldn't take long, but I sat there for forty-five minutes and she still hadn't come out. Which irritated me because I had an appointment to get my nails done at four. I texted and got no answer. Called, no answer. Went up to her place, knocked and knocked, and she didn't come to the door. I got scared and went and found the building manager. She begrudgingly let me in only because I was the emergency contact, but Chase wasn't in the apartment."

Olivia turned off the sauce. The worry inside her had burgeoned into something with teeth. Surely Chase wasn't about to throw away everything they'd done because she'd flubbed an audition. The actress had been down about Zeke, but she'd seemed so confident and focused on a new life. She wouldn't use. And surely she wouldn't do something like . . .

Like Marley.

No. Chase wasn't like Marley. Not really. They were a little bit alike, but Chase was in a good place.

Don't worry, big sis. I'm in a good place. I'm cool.

"Okay, so did you try to track her with the phone app?" Olivia asked, pressing down the panic.

Lorna sighed. "Of course I did, but you told me to turn it off, and Chase fixed it so I couldn't locate her."

Olivia licked her lips and thought. "Let me call her. She'll likely answer me. Maybe."

"Call me back."

Olivia hung up the phone and paced the floor. Outside, daylight retired, the orange globe sinking into the darkened Pacific Ocean. A family walked down the beach, laughing as the wind caught their beach ball and their small child scampered after it. She took a deep breath and tried to calm herself.

Then she dialed Chase's number, tapping her fingers against the marble of the counter while she awaited the rings. Four full rings passed before the phone went to voice mail.

"Chase, this is Olivia. I made shrimp scampi for dinner and hope you're planning on joining me to celebrate the conclusion of Square One. Please call me back."

Sounded not so threatening or panicked. And no mention of the audition. But just to be certain Chase knew Olivia was trying to reach her, she texted the same thing to Chase's number. For a few seconds, little bubbles appeared after her text.

"Oh, thank God," Olivia breathed.

But then the bubbles went away.

She scowled at the phone before texting. **Call me. I'm worried.**

No bubbles. No nothing.

Chase? Is everything okay? Please respond.

Who would Chase call? Where would she go? Spencer? He seemed to be her go-to person, but Olivia wasn't ready to talk to him. She'd been avoiding him the same way she'd been avoiding Neve's texts and messages. She'd needed time to sort through so much, but during the week she'd found she could make no headway on deciphering her path when it came to Conrad, Spencer, and her love life. Heap on the fact that she and Neve planned on having a meeting with their mother and then researching what they could do regarding their father's probable sexual abuse of their sister, and she had shoved it all to the back of her emotional closet to address on another day.

Instead of figuring out how to handle the world spinning beyond her control, Olivia had thrown herself into writing the book, which was horribly behind schedule. Then she worked on notes for an upcoming lecture she'd be giving to a cybersecurity company on strategies to handle interns and trainees. So yeah, she didn't want to talk to Spencer. Had even thought about pretending that she hadn't slept with him, uh, four times, and was just trying to erase it from her memory, even though she knew that would be impossible because it had been four *incredible* times.

Still, adults did things they didn't want to do. Olivia was fairly certain she'd uttered those exact words to her clients a bajillion times.

She scrolled down her contact list and located Spencer's number. She'd entered THE HAMMER under his company name, and they'd giggled about the sexy innuendos he'd muttered in her ear before diving back under the covers.

Maybe she should text?

No, that was the coward's way out.

She dialed the number, but it, too, went to voice mail. She elected not to leave a weird, rambling message and instead hung up.

She was about to text him when the phone rang in her hand.

Spencer.

"Hello?"

"Hey, Olivia. Did you just call?"

"Uh, yeah, I, um, wondered if you had talked to Chase lately?"

"No. I texted her this morning. She was reading for the role today. She texted back the thumbs-up and that was it." In the background she could hear the clink of glasses and the low hum of conversation. He sounded like he was at dinner. Oh God, what if he was on a date?

Her heart trembled at the thought.

Which was stupid because she'd blown him off, and Chase's safety was paramount over her insecurities. "Oh."

"So what's up?"

"Um, I just . . . well, to be honest, Chase didn't have a great audition, and I can't seem to find her. She disappeared and isn't answering her phone. She seems to call you when she's looking for a friend, so I thought she may have reached out over the past few hours."

"Let me check my messages."

She waited while he did, listening to feminine laughter and the tinkle of forks hitting plates. "Am I interrupting you?"

"No. I'm . . . at a . . . thing," he said, sounding distracted as he no doubt checked all forms of communication. "I just texted her. I'll try Snapchat, too."

"Thank you. Let me know if you hear from her."

"Will do. Oh, and I'm sorry we didn't get the chance to say goodbye last week. I had some things I needed to get back to, and you seemed to have your hands full with . . . lots of people. You obviously have my number and know how to dial it. Give me a shout when things settle down for you."

Olivia was super worried about Chase, but that didn't stop the pleasure at the thought of Spencer keeping his door open a crack for her. The whole question was—should she step inside? "Oh, sure. I will . . . or might do that. Um . . . yeah."

Damn it. She sounded like a teenage girl.

"Ciao."

"Bye."

Olivia clicked off the phone and looked at the screen with the hope that Chase had responded to her text. Nope. So Olivia called her again. This time the phone went straight to voice mail. Chase had turned the phone off.

Crap.

Olivia dumped the sauce with the perfectly pinked shrimp into a plastic storage container and set the angel-hair pasta into the fridge next to the Caesar salad she'd fixed with the homemade Parmesan croutons and salty Parmesan curls. She ripped off a piece of the bread, hoping it would still her nerves, but it tasted like paper. Besides, it wasn't as if she could eat with the boulder of worry pinning down her stomach.

She slipped on her sandals and trotted up the floating staircase to Chase's room.

Nothing looked out of place or different. Chase had made her bed, as she'd done most days. The bathroom was tidy, clothes still in the dresser, nothing to suggest anything amiss. A chick-lit book lay on the bedside table, bookmark in the middle, and a few hair bands scattered the glass top. Chase's journal sat on the pillow. Her client had been utilizing journaling as a way of relaying her feelings, thoughts, intentions. She'd shared a few of her entries with Olivia during their counseling sessions, but only because it was her choice. Olivia respected Chase's privacy, but perhaps with the woman disappearing and not answering her phone, Olivia needed to check the last few entries?

She lifted the journal and turned to where the pen marked the place.

I'm nervous about this audition because it's been so long since I've done one. My mother seems to think it's a courtesy and that I have the part, but I'm not so sure. I feel I need to do a lot to overcome the reputation I've established. I was an effing disaster on Tarantula Girls, *and those rumors were leaked and . . . ugh! But as Olivia says, "I can't undo my past. I can only live with it, accept it, and move forward intent on not making those poor choices again."*

God, I miss Zeke. I know this has been a constant theme, but I do. I think it could have been love, or still is. When I think about him, my heart aches, and I want to tell him so many things. Like about that bird's nest. He'd probably know what kind of bird built it. He's so smart. And sexy. And sweet to me. God, I needed him. And I still want him.

But maybe I need to respect how he feels. This life I lead—or will lead—isn't what he wants. I get it. I do. I don't know if I want it myself. But it's who I am. Olivia said that I don't have to do it. I can do something else, but what do I have if I don't have this? Nothing. I have no skills. I have no other purpose. My mother would kill me! At any rate, I guess I owe Conrad that much. He did all this for me, and I can't not follow through. Olivia is shouting about dinner. Funny how I used to hate being around her but now can't imagine her not shooting me that look she gives or making "suggestions." That's what she calls her bitching. Suggestions. LOL. Off I go . . .

Olivia bit her lip at that last line. She had always thought the word *suggestions* was a more agreeable way to point out others' failures to make the correct choices.

She thumbed through a few more pages but saw nothing alarming. Some grumping about her, little hearts drawn around Zeke's name, a few inspirational quotations. The only thing that pushed her alarm button was Chase's emphatic position that she owed it to Conrad and her mother to land this part and that she was nothing without acting.

But would that drive her to do something drastic?

She tapped Zeke's name, drawn in bubble letters on the last page, and then pulled her phone from her back pocket. Zeke answered on the second ring.

"Hey, Zeke, this is Olivia."

"Hey." He sounded surprised, which seemed natural.

"Have you happened to hear from Chase?"

"No. We haven't spoken since the night before you guys left. Why?" His voice had grown more concerned with each syllable uttered.

"No big deal. I just wondered."

"Something's wrong." A statement, not a question.

"Not necessarily. She's officially done with my program, and I couldn't get in touch with her. I thought maybe she'd talked to you recently."

"Something's wrong."

"No, no. I didn't mean to alarm you. I'm, uh, getting another call, so I have to go. Hope you're well. Take care." She punched the button, switching over to Lorna.

"Did you find her?" Lorna demanded.

"Not yet."

"Call the police. We need to report this."

"Lorna, she's only been gone for four hours. You can't report her missing. Let's give her some space," Olivia said, even though she felt very much like Lorna. She didn't like the way Chase had disappeared. And deep down inside, she felt much the way she had when it came to Marley—unable to control the situation.

She was scared for Chase.

"So what do you want me to do?" Lorna asked.

"Wait. I think we have to wait and trust Chase."

"Oh God."

Exactly.

Olivia hung up after reassuring Lorna several times that there was nothing more that could be done, and she ignored Zeke's calls, texting him that everything was okay. Even though it wasn't. But she didn't need two people blowing up her phone all night long.

She went downstairs to wait for Chase's situation to be resolved. As she sat, sipping some hot tea, she discovered what it felt like to be a parent waiting up for a teen, wondering if she were okay, hoping and praying that she would come through the door, but as the hours ticked by too slowly, her prayers were not answered.

Eventually she nodded off, so when her phone buzzed with a text, she yipped. Lifting the phone to read the text, she made a confused face.

Neve.

Guess who just showed up on my front porch.

CHAPTER
TWENTY-FOUR

The first thing that registered with Chase as she padded down the stairs of the cabin at Cotter's Creek was that Olivia looked terrible.

The second thing was . . . Olivia was *here.*

"What are you doing here?" she asked the woman sitting in the old green tweed chair sipping coffee from a chipped mug. Olivia's hair was half-up, half-down, her face pale, her shirt buttoned wrong. Total mess.

"I should be the one asking that question. What the hell, Chase?"

Chase took the last two steps, trying to figure out how to say what she'd planned to say. The rational conversation she'd played over and over in her head as she'd sunk against the window of the Greyhound bus heading north (utilizing a sanitizing wipe on the window, of course) had sounded well thought out. But now, after waking up and seeing all the frantic texts from her mother, Olivia, Spencer, and even Zeke, Chase had nothing.

Well, she had something, because she'd pretty much figured her life out, by golly.

But she needed some coffee before she attempted to fix her mistake. So she held up a hand. "But first, coffee."

"Don't you use some T-shirt slogan on me," Olivia said, slamming down her mug with rapid velocity. Coffee sloshed over onto the side table, but Olivia didn't seem to care. The look on her face suggested the possibility of attempted murder in the very near future. "You scared the hell out of me! Don't you remember what I told you about Marley? How could you?"

"Oh God, Olivia! You thought . . . you thought . . . I would never."

Honest-to-God tears appeared in Olivia's eyes. One slid down her cheek, and she dashed it away with impatience. "That's what she said. Those exact words. But I found her lying in a pool of her own vomit, her eyes open, and a fucking letter beside her telling me she couldn't do life anymore. Why did you turn off your phone? Why did you run away?"

Neve came into the living room, shot Chase a look of rebuke, and walked over to her sister. She perched on the arm of the chair and laid a comforting hand on Olivia's shoulder. Two sisters as a stalwart front. "Shh. Let's all take a deep breath."

Olivia jabbed her finger in Chase's direction. "And see what else you've done? You've made Neve the voice of reason!"

Neve may have smiled before schooling her face into one of general calmness. "Go get some coffee, Chase. Think hard as you traverse the dining room about what you need to say."

Chase wasn't stupid. She did as she was bid, acknowledging the low hum of Neve's murmured "Calm down" and "She's okay."

As horrible as she felt about turning off her phone and not telling anyone where she was going, a small part of her found comfort in the thought blip that the three of them sounded like sisters.

Yesterday when she'd arrived at her apartment, she hadn't planned on giving Lorna the slip. But when she'd gone inside, tidied up, and hopped into the shower, thinking she'd get some clarity beneath the pulsating blast about how to tell her mother she had chucked the role, she'd found the Xanax she'd hidden in a baggie in her shampoo bottle. Her hands had shaken so hard she'd dropped the bottle, mostly because her first thought had been to thank God no one had found them. She could take them if she needed to.

And then she'd remembered that she'd changed her entire life. That she was an adult. That she had worth. That she didn't have to numb herself, because her life wasn't bad and she wasn't a loser who couldn't deal with the hard things life brought her.

She'd climbed out of the shower, opened the baggie, and flushed the pills.

Then she sat on her toilet, naked and shaken by her thoughts. Sifting through all the therapy speak she'd heard over her life, she'd landed upon the fact that she'd found something that in the past would have chained her to her old life, and she'd broken that chain. She had flushed the Xanax and thus flushed any remnants of her old life away.

Taking her phone, she started deleting her contacts. She no longer needed her dealers—time to backspace over all the so-called friends who had merrily led her down the path of temptation and heartbreak, and then she got to Kittridge.

Zeke.

He'd been one of the best things in her life. They'd talked extensively about everything, and he'd been like a North Star, pulling her in the right direction. So why had she let him push her away? Why had she let go so easily if he gave her so much?

North Star.

North.

Cotter's Creek. The cabin. Beast. Neve. The way the leaves crunched under her boots. S'mores, candy apples, old people who loved her for her and not because she'd won a Golden Globe. All those things twisted around themselves to deliver something she desperately wanted to call her own but was afraid to change her world for.

But what if she wasn't afraid to change her world?

She'd already started the process when she let those lines slip from her fingers and flutter to the floor. Why not do it all the way?

So she'd climbed back in the shower, washed the soap from her hair, and let the hot water wash away the last of her junkie thoughts. Then she braided her wet hair, dressed, packed a bag, and pulled on a ball cap and sunglasses. She'd gone down to the workout area where there was a second entry to the building and called for an Uber, turning off her location services so Lorna couldn't track her. She would deal with her mother eventually, but she wanted to make a plan first. If she figured out her life without any interference from Lorna, Olivia, Conrad, or anyone, Chase could stand firm on her choices. She controlled her life, and she alone would decide what her tomorrow would look like.

She got dropped off at a bus station and bought a ticket for Redmond, which was as close as she could get to Cotter's Creek and still get an Uber. Then she'd turned her phone off, climbed onto the bus, and headed back where her life had been much clearer. She wasn't going to rely on other people to rescue her. She was an adult, and she was in charge of her decisions and those repercussions.

Unfortunately, in her determination to operate autonomously and therefore close herself off to focus on her great plan for her life, she'd forgotten that doing so could scare the willies out of those who cared for her. Not a great move, so she would have to deal with that oversight by apologizing.

She poured a cup of coffee, wincing at the acidity but embracing the jolt, and went back to the living room. Olivia's face still looked tear streaked, which made her feel like the present Beast had left on the front porch last night. Which was totally gross.

Both Neve and Olivia looked up.

"I'm really sorry, Olivia. It was irresponsible of me to turn off my phone and not let anyone know my plans. Thinking about other people is new to me, so that's the only excuse I have, which is pretty flimsy. I didn't think about Marley or . . . how you might construe my actions."

Olivia swallowed hard and opened her mouth. Nothing came out. She closed it and looked away. For ten full seconds. Neve shot her a look that said, *Go with it.*

Finally, after several more seconds: "Truly, Olivia. I'm very, very sorry to have worried you."

Olivia nodded. "I just don't understand why you would do that—turn off your phone and not answer."

"I did text. I typed 'All good,' but I discovered this morning that it didn't send."

Olivia didn't look convinced.

"I promise. It never sent. Look, my mom had been calling me, then you texted, and I felt overwhelmed, like I needed some distance. I came here because I think my future is here. Not here here, but part of it is here. And I wanted to make the decisions about my life by myself. It was a little spontaneous, but when you figure out what you really want in your life, you want to get there as soon as possible." Chase walked over and sank onto the sagging couch. Funny how she liked that damn couch.

"You're talking about Zeke?"

"Yeah, that's part of it. I want to see where we can go, and he's here. Thing is, I like it here. I like this place because it's cozy, if not a little rough around the edges. I like the woods and the creek, the senior center, and going fishing. I never got to do those things, and they make me feel more real."

Olivia sucked in a breath and then exhaled with an "Okay."

But she still sounded confused.

"Look, I know it may seem impulsive, but it's not. I didn't want the part in the film. I . . . I just didn't. I don't want to be an actress right now. I'm not saying never, but I want to try a new path."

"And that is . . . ?" Neve asked, finally joining in on the conversation.

"I'm going to apply for an online university and take some writing classes."

"Writing?" Olivia said, cocking her head.

"Yeah," Chase said, clasping her hands and looking down at them, feeling vulnerable. "I've enjoyed keeping my journal, and I thought perhaps if I wrote about my journey, my life the way it unfolded, the mistakes I made, all that stuff, that I might be able to help someone else who is going through or might have gone through what I went through . . . what Marley went through."

Olivia blinked at her a few times, the befuddlement clearing. "You want to write a book?"

"I sent Marshall—you know, my agent—a long text last night about taking a break from working. I told him I planned to write my story, and this morning he gave me the name of someone at a publishing house. He's going to talk to a literary agent he knows and maybe even option it for film. I also mentioned my mother to him. Lorna was a fine actress back in the day, but she gave everything up for my career. Lorna needs to focus on herself, too. Not me. Marshall said he would check around. See? I'm being responsible. And I was going to call you and my mom right after I had coffee. I just needed that coffee first. Maybe two cups even." Chase unclasped her hands and leaned back.

Neve raised her eyebrows. "That's quite a change."

Chase nodded. It was, indeed, but she felt more certain about this new direction than she had about anything other than Zeke. Of course, she still had to talk to him and see if he felt the way she did. She suspected he did. He, too, had called her last night when her phone was off, leaving a message that he was worried about her. She'd texted him before she'd come downstairs, asking if she could see him today.

There was only one other thing to do.

"So, Olivia and Neve, I have a favor to ask," Chase said with a hopeful smile. "Can I stay here to write the book? Stay in my old room? I can pay rent and help Neve with some of the renovations. I'm great at raking. Okay, so-so, but if Zeke gives me a second chance, I can probably borrow his tarp."

Olivia straightened in her chair and did the blinky-blink thing again. "You want to live here? In the cabin? This is all so . . ."

"Bizarre? I know. But it's right for me."

Neve shrugged. "I don't mind. I could use a little company. I've been talking to that blasted cat like it's a person. At least you can talk back."

Olivia stared hard at Chase for a few seconds, and then she glanced at her sister. "Um, sure."

Chase felt relief flood her. "Thank you. For everything."

Tears filled Olivia's eyes again. "You're welcome."

"Oh, and one more thing. Um, this might make you not so okay with me, but I'm going to say it anyway because you taught me some things," Chase said, taking a big breath. "But I think you need me to teach you some things."

Olivia cocked her head again. "What?"

"There's this Garth Brooks song—yes, I know who Garth Brooks is, thank you very much. Anyway, it's about standing outside the fire and how that's, like, super safe. I mean, I know I have been standing inside the fire, burning like a fool for way too long. But you're not even close enough to be warm, Olivia."

Neve's mouth formed a little O of alarm. "Maybe I better step—"

"You don't have to," Olivia said.

"What I'm saying is that you won't let anyone inside because you don't want to get hurt. Your family hurt you, maybe Conrad, I don't know, but you live so cautiously that it's hardly living sometimes. That morning when you came down after partaking of the Hammer, you looked happy."

"Well, she'd had a lot of orgasms," Neve said.

Olivia jabbed her with her elbow.

"Ouch," Neve said, shoving her sister's arm. "Hey, I have ears. I heard everything that night."

Olivia colored, but still she didn't speak. Her expression remained an enigma.

"Spencer's a good guy, and he likes you. That's pretty great," Chase said.

"I never said he wasn't a good guy. I just don't know him. I did that without thinking and—"

"And maybe that's what you need more of in your life. You can't always live in a bubble. Life is messy. For me, it was too messy, and the lack of boundaries in my life kept me from moving in any direction. But you have too many boundaries, and you're stuck. You can't plan things like falling in love. I know. I fell in love with a bearded giant in the forest. On the surface, he's all kinds of wrong for me, but deep down he's my perfect soul mate."

"Soul mate?" Olivia repeated, her expression clouding. "I thought Conrad was my soul mate. Things with him were always so complicated, but I believed that we truly belonged together. I pined for him, knowing that our past prevented any kind of future. But then he showed up with you, saying things about missing me, how he wanted to try again, and I—I—"

"Had moved on? Like me?" Chase said softly.

Olivia seemed to think about those words; then slowly she began to nod. "Yeah, I think I did."

Neve leaned over and kissed her sister on top of the head. "Look at you. Just growing up before my very eyes."

Chase started laughing, and eventually Olivia joined in, looking at her sister. "Who *are* you?"

Neve held out her hands and shrugged. "Someone who got tired of her own bullshit. I'm really glad both of you caught up. I was still mad at you when I came here all those weeks ago, Liv, but after being here for a while, I don't know. I just got tired of who I was, who we were. Maybe this cabin, as homely as it is, has some kind of magic in it?"

They all three looked around as if Neve's words might be true. The place still looked stuck in 1983, but there was something to the clunky furniture and nubby couches. The new rug and curtains complemented the homey charm, and the smell of lemon furniture polish and burning bread—

"Is that bread burning?" Chase asked.

"Shit!" Neve leaped up and ran to the kitchen, leaving Chase and Olivia smiling at each other.

"So you really are that good?" Olivia asked, her voice holding a bit of awe.

"I really am."

"I'm so happy about that, Chase. I truly am."

Chase smiled. "And I hope you can reach that place. I know you've got a lot weighing on you, and I appreciate you sharing that with me when we were at the beach yesterday. Like I was your friend and not your client."

Olivia stood up and walked over to Chase, sinking down beside her. She extended her hand.

Chase slid her hand into Olivia's.

"I think we've hit that level. Clients have never given me advice. Well, other than the infamous 'Go fuck yourself,' which is immensely popular."

That made Chase giggle. "I think I used that one."

"You did. More than once." Olivia squeezed her hand and released it. "So Spencer . . . you really think he's interested?"

"Yeah. You know he is. Do something about it. I mean, it may not work out, but it could be a fun few months, right?"

Olivia smiled. "Yeah. I think it could."

EPILOGUE

Seven months later

"I can't believe we just did that. We are so bad," Olivia said, hooking her bra and pulling down the mirror in Spencer's new convertible and checking her makeup. "We're going to be late."

"We won't be late," Spencer said, cranking the car and pulling away from the scenic overlook. "Have you seen the way I drive this car?"

Olivia grinned at him. "You are so humble."

"I know. It's one of my best qualities, along with my lovemaking skills, rock-hard abs, and ability to hug these curves—all curves, for that matter."

She rolled her eyes and adjusted her skirt. She glanced down at her watch and frowned. "We're so going to be late."

"But I wanted to make sure you look your best for the wedding. And you know you look absolutely amazing right after you come," Spencer said, putting the pedal to the metal on the BMW.

The wind tore at her hair, but she didn't mind. She'd stopped flat ironing it and let it go wavy. Neve had added some honey highlights and taught her about products that would give her tousled beach waves. Spencer seemed to like it. He touched her hair constantly. No, he touched *her* constantly, and she loved it.

They were on their way to Cotter's Creek for Zeke and Chase's wedding. The ceremony was to be held outside Zeke's house, near the gurgling creek. Chase was almost four months pregnant, and the last time Olivia had seen her, she'd been glowing and nearly done with her book. Oddly enough, Olivia's publisher had bought the book in an auction, so not only were they friends, but they were both writing for the same house.

Spencer reached over and brushed her cheek. "You look happy. Are you happy?"

"Ecstatic," she said, catching his hand and giving it a squeeze.

Olivia had done exactly what Chase had suggested and stopped avoiding the fire. When she'd gotten back to LA the next day, she'd called Spencer and invited him to dinner.

He said yes.

She discovered very quickly that the fire Chase spoke of could be quite warm and exactly what she needed in her life. Shortly after she and Spencer began officially dating, she and Neve had confronted their father about Marley. He had eventually admitted to abusing Marley, breaking down, begging them to understand that he was a changed man. Their mother had severed ties, and all the Hancock women were attending therapy together, working on their wounds, trying to be a better family to one another. They weren't perfect, and there was lots of muck to wade through, but coming home to Spencer made her day lighter.

They weren't technically living together, but they stayed at her place during the week and his on the weekend, mostly because it was high in the canyon and farther from her office. Spencer had left for two months to go on location in Louisiana for a movie. She'd missed him madly and worried about all those gorgeous actresses. He'd assured her that he was too damn tired to screw around. Besides, he dreamed of her every night.

She was pretty sure that wasn't true—the dream part—but appreciated the little white lie, nonetheless. He was about to go back to work on *The Hammer*. Things would change again, but they'd both agreed that what they had was worth making it work.

Conrad had stopped calling after she told him that she was with Spencer. She hoped they would remain friends, but she couldn't control it if they didn't. Friendship wasn't conditional based on what one person wanted. Only Conrad could decide if he would meet her halfway.

Two hours later, Spencer pulled into the driveway of the cabin she and Neve owned. The place looked totally different, with a new front porch, an expanded kitchen, and fresh paint. Landscaping had been put in, and four healthy ferns swung in the late-May breeze. Above the door, a rustic sign proclaimed the cabin MOUNTAIN MAGIC.

Neve came out wearing a maxi dress and waved.

"Where have y'all been? Chase has been freaking out," Neve called, not even bothering to greet them when they climbed from the car.

Lorna opened the cabin door, and out came Chase wearing a lovely white-lace dress with wildflowers woven in her hair. Lorna was already swiping at her eyes. "Doesn't she look gorgeous?"

She did. Chase looked like a new woman, and Olivia's heart swelled when she saw her. "Wow, Chase."

The former actress pirouetted. "Being pregnant suits me as long as . . . oh God, is someone wearing cologne?"

Spencer took three steps back. "I, uh, may have put some on."

Chase thrust out a finger. "Stay away from me. I will puke."

"How am I going to walk you down the aisle?" Spencer asked, adjusting his collar beneath the sport jacket he'd shrugged on and taking a few additional steps back.

Chase held a hand over her mouth and tried to take some deep breaths. Finally, she looked at her mother. "Mom, will you walk me down the aisle?"

Lorna's eyes grew big. "You want me? I'm the MOB."

"Technically, a parent should give you away. Not that you're giving me away. I belong to myself." Chase patted her cheeks, color restored.

That made Olivia smile. "You do belong to yourself."

"So maybe I should walk myself down the aisle," Chase said.

Lorna nodded. "I don't think you need anyone to make a decision for you. You have your own agency."

"Damn straight she does," Neve said, glancing over at Olivia. "We all do, and isn't that pretty damn cool?"

Lorna looked up at the dark clouds hovering above them and frowned. Then she looked down at her watch. "Oh, we have to go. Only ten minutes until the ceremony starts. I hope this rain holds off long enough. Spencer, you drive me since I need to be seated beforehand."

Neve jogged down the steps. "I'll come, too. I want to see the inside of the car. Here's the bouquet." She handed Chase a bouquet of mixed wildflowers and picked up her umbrella.

Seconds later, with much bustle and exclamation, Spencer managed to get Lorna and Neve in the small car. He gave Olivia a salute and a sweet, sweet smile.

"Well, now," Chase said, her voice light with laughter.

"Yeah, I'm liking this taking chances thing." Olivia lifted an eyebrow. "Guess you're stuck with me driving you to your wedding."

Chase smiled. "I'm not sad about that. You're the person who gave me all this."

"No, you're the person who gave yourself all this. I just showed you the way. You did the hard work."

Chase smiled and walked down the steps, taking Olivia's hand and swinging it as they walked to the very practical Toyota Chase had bought once the Malibu house sold. "You probably weren't thinking that when I put the liquid soap into the dishwasher."

Olivia nodded. "Well, that's true. But the rest was all you."

"Or when I washed your whites with that red sweater?"

"Now you're making me wonder how I ever made it through boot camp with you," Olivia said.

Chase looked up at the gray clouds and frowned. "I didn't expect the rain today, but maybe we never do."

Then she slid a hand down to her still-flat stomach. "I'm thinking about naming her Marley. Would you mind?"

Olivia swallowed the catch in her throat. "No. I wouldn't mind at all."

And just then, the clouds parted and the sun came through.

Chase looked over at Olivia. "That was freaky."

"No, I think that just means she approves. Ready to get married?"

Chase's smile was as bright as Marley's sun. "Only because I was born for this role."

ACKNOWLEDGMENTS

No book is ever written without the help of others. From the hive mind of social media friends, who weigh in on locations, situations, and plausibility, to my family, who patiently waits for dinner . . . and often must eat cereal. Hey, Lucky Charms are a legit dinner when Mama is on deadline. This book was written during the COVID-19 crisis, a time of uncertainty and great stress for many people. Our family was no different, with my husband home, my children home, and my writing friends so far away. I thank my family for giving me some space, understanding that I couldn't watch a Harry Potter marathon when there were words to write.

I would like to thank my writing friends who helped me brainstorm the plot, specifically my friend Phylis, who is great at plot twists, and my friend Jenn, who always tries to throw a dead body into the story somewhere. Special thanks to my online writing communities—Fiction From the Heart and My Book Tribe—for always bringing me inspiration and straight talk when I need it most. And I can't leave out Deacon and Tilly, who snooze beside me and are sometimes patient when I am in the middle of a scene, the garbage trucks have arrived, and there is a pressing need to guard the perimeter. Delayed gratification is so rewarding.

Behind the scenes is my fantastic cheerleader, aka agent, Michelle Grajkowski, who pushes and pulls (and consoles) all with a smile on her face, and my steadfast, smart editor Alison Dasho, who says things like "I'm not worried. I have absolute confidence in this book," which is the best thing an editor can say to her author. And I can't leave out Selina McLemore, whose insightful guidance provided the bumpers for the story and kept me focused on what really matters. The entire Montlake team is fairly amazing at choosing just the right cover, getting the book to reviewers, promoting, shipping, placing, and positioning, all with an eye toward giving readers a good read. I couldn't feel more blessed by a publishing house.

And lastly, thanks to my mama and daddy, who taught me how to adult, but more importantly, gave me love, support, and encouragement so that when I fell down, I had a good reason to get back up and fight. I love you both more than you'll ever know.

ABOUT THE AUTHOR

Photo © 2017 Courtney Hartness

Liz Talley is the *USA Today* bestselling author of *The Wedding War*, *Room to Breathe*, and *Come Home to Me*, as well as the Morning Glory series, the Home in Magnolia Bend series, and many more novels, novellas, and short fiction. A finalist for the Romance Writers of America's prestigious Golden Heart and RITA Awards, Liz has found a home writing heartwarming contemporary romance. Her stories are set in the South, where the tea is sweet, the summers are hot, and the porches are wide. Liz lives in North Louisiana with her childhood sweetheart, two handsome children, three dogs, and a naughty kitty. To learn more about the author and her upcoming novels, readers can visit www.liztalleybooks.com.